Just Between Us

Adelaide Vaughn

Published by Adelaide Vaughn, 2024.

JUST BETWEEN US

First edition. October 7, 2024.

Copyright © 2024 Adelaide Vaughn.

ISBN: 979-8227956880

Written by Adelaide Vaughn.

Chapter 1: Fractured Reflections

The sun sets over the city, casting long shadows that stretch across my small living room, where the walls are adorned with fading posters from films I once believed would define my career. The smell of burnt coffee lingers in the air, a bitter reminder of my last failed attempt to fuel my creativity. I can almost hear the distant sounds of a saxophone playing a sultry tune, a nod to the jazz clubs I used to frequent, where dreams mingled with smoke and laughter. Now, the only melodies that grace my ears are the monotonous beeps of editing software and the incessant hum of the bustling streets below.

I run my fingers over the rough edges of my work desk, cluttered with half-eaten takeout containers and stacks of notes for projects that seem to blend together in a haze of frustration. It's a far cry from the vision I had when I first stepped into this city, wide-eyed and full of hope. Back then, the neon signs of Times Square felt like beacons guiding me toward my destiny. I could already hear the applause of audiences in my imagination, resonating in the dark theaters of my dreams. But now, that applause feels like an echo from a life I've long abandoned.

I turn away from the mirror, my heart heavy with nostalgia, and head to my small kitchen to pour myself another cup of coffee. The sound of the kettle boiling fills the silence, punctuated by the rhythmic tick-tock of the clock that hangs crookedly on the wall, a constant reminder of how time slips away. I wonder if Evan thinks of me at all. Does he remember the lazy afternoons we spent in Central Park, our laughter mingling with the rustling leaves? Or the way he would look at me, his eyes twinkling with mischief, as we dreamed up our future? Those memories swirl in my mind like the steam rising from my mug, but they are quickly overshadowed by the weight of unfulfilled potential.

As the steam dissipates, so does my resolve. I take a tentative sip, the bitterness stinging my throat, mirroring the pang of regret lodged in my chest. I sit on the edge of my unmade bed, my mind racing through the countless decisions that have led me here. I remember the night we both decided to pursue our dreams, hand in hand, vowing never to let anything or anyone stand in our way. It feels like a lifetime ago, yet the ache of that promise lingers, a haunting reminder of the paths we didn't take together.

I scroll through my phone, searching for any hint of connection to my past. Perhaps I could reach out to him, rekindle a friendship, or even something more. But the fear of rejection grips me tightly, a vice that squeezes the breath from my lungs. What if he has moved on? What if he has found happiness without me? My fingers hover over his name, a ghost of a conversation hanging in the air. I sigh and set the phone down, the temptation of reconnecting fading as quickly as it appeared.

Dusk falls softly, wrapping the city in a velvety blanket of indigo. The streetlights flicker on, illuminating the rain-slicked sidewalks. I pull my coat tighter around me, an attempt to ward off the chill that seeps into my bones. Maybe a walk would help clear my head. The streets of New York have always had a peculiar way of inspiring me, reminding me that life continues to move, whether I am ready or not.

I step outside, the rush of the city enveloping me like a warm embrace. The sounds of chatter and laughter float through the air, mixing with the distant echo of a subway train rumbling beneath the ground. The scent of street food wafts past, a delicious distraction that pulls at my stomach. I find myself gravitating toward a corner vendor, drawn by the allure of a steaming pretzel. The vendor, an older man with a wide grin, hands me the warm treat, and I relish the comforting taste of salty dough as I bite into it, momentarily forgetting my worries.

As I wander the streets, I pass by a group of aspiring actors rehearsing their lines on a street corner, their passion infectious. I stop, leaning against a lamppost, captivated by their energy. For a fleeting moment, I remember my own aspirations, the joy of creativity that once flowed freely through my veins. I smile, allowing myself to be swept away by their fervor, the echoes of their dreams intertwining with my own. The city is alive with ambition, and I find myself longing for a taste of that passion once more.

Lost in thought, I meander toward a small gallery tucked between towering skyscrapers. The warm glow of the lights spills onto the sidewalk, inviting me in like a moth to a flame. Inside, the walls are lined with stunning photographs, each image telling a story that resonates with my soul. I wander, entranced, studying the faces and places captured in time, each frame pulling at the strings of my heart. The artist's vision is raw and unfiltered, a stark contrast to the polished films I edit daily.

I pause in front of a striking portrait of a woman, her gaze fierce and unapologetic. There's a strength in her expression that makes me feel seen, as though she is challenging me to reclaim my own narrative. The photograph whispers to me, urging me to step out of the shadows of self-doubt and into the light of possibility. I take a deep breath, letting the artist's vision inspire me, a spark igniting within—a desire to break free, to take risks, to live fiercely and unapologetically.

With renewed determination, I step back onto the bustling streets, the sounds of the city echoing in my ears, each footfall a step toward reclaiming my dreams. The night is alive, and I am alive with it.

The city seems to breathe with me as I wander through the streets, each step resonating with the thrum of life pulsing all around. The chill of the evening air brushes against my skin, a sharp reminder that I am a part of this urban symphony, even if my notes have fallen a little flat lately. I pause at a street musician's corner, captivated by the soulful strumming of a guitar. His fingers dance effortlessly over the strings, creating a melody that intertwines with the laughter of passersby and the distant rumble of the subway. I toss a few coins into his open case, appreciating the simple exchange—a moment of joy for both of us in a city that sometimes feels too vast to navigate alone.

As I stroll further down the avenue, the allure of the local art gallery beckons me again. The outside walls are painted with vibrant murals, breathing life into the otherwise gray urban landscape. Stepping inside, I'm immediately enveloped in a cocoon of creativity. The scent of oil paint and varnish clings to the air, thick with inspiration. Here, I can momentarily escape the rigid confines of my editing bay and immerse myself in a world where art speaks louder than words.

I move from one piece to another, each canvas a portal to an artist's mind. A massive abstract painting explodes with color, splashes of crimson and cerulean colliding with chaotic energy. I find myself captivated by the intensity of it, as if the artist poured their heart into every brushstroke, unleashing their emotions in a vibrant cascade. Nearby, a delicate watercolor of a sun-drenched field captures the stillness of nature, invoking a sense of peace that resonates deep within me. In this sanctuary of creativity, I begin to see my own dreams flicker like fireflies in the dusk—fleeting yet radiant.

My gaze falls on a smaller piece tucked away in the corner, a striking portrait of a woman with piercing green eyes that seem to follow me. The artist has captured not just her likeness, but something ineffable—an aura of strength and vulnerability that speaks to my own heart. I feel a pull towards this painting, as if it holds a mirror to my soul. Who was she? What stories lingered behind her gaze? I can't help but wonder if she too felt lost in the chaos of the world, grappling with her own fractured reflections.

Just then, the door chimes, and a figure walks in—a tall man with tousled hair and an air of quiet confidence. His presence commands attention, and as he approaches the counter, our eyes meet. There's a spark of recognition in his gaze, a fleeting moment that sends my heart racing. It's Evan. My breath hitches, and for a split second, time stands still. The years tumble away like leaves in the autumn wind, and suddenly, we are no longer two strangers lost in a city of millions.

"What are the odds?" he says, his voice warm and familiar. I can't help but smile, the corners of my mouth curving upward in disbelief. We exchange pleasantries, and he gestures to the painting I had been admiring. "It's stunning, isn't it? I always thought art had a way of reaching into the depths of our emotions."

"It really is," I reply, my voice barely above a whisper. "It feels... alive."

He nods, his gaze lingering on the portrait. "I've been trying to reconnect with that feeling myself. Life got complicated after high school, didn't it?"

The weight of unspoken words hangs between us, the years stretching out like a chasm, but somehow, they seem less daunting now. Our conversation flows effortlessly, weaving through shared memories and the challenges we've faced since our paths diverged. I tell him about my work as an editor, about the projects that have pushed me to the brink of exhaustion, and how the city once felt like a canvas waiting to be painted with my dreams.

As he listens, I catch glimpses of the boy I once knew—the one who would stay up late dreaming of becoming a filmmaker alongside me. He shares his own journey, the detours life has taken him on, the struggles and triumphs that have shaped him. It's in his eyes, the flicker of passion igniting as he speaks about his recent venture into photography, capturing fleeting moments in a world that often rushes by too quickly.

We leave the gallery together, the chill of the night air wrapping around us like a familiar blanket. It feels strangely natural, walking beside him again, our shoulders brushing ever so slightly. The city glows beneath the streetlights, casting long shadows that dance playfully across the pavement. Each step feels lighter, as if the burdens we've carried are finally beginning to lift.

He suggests grabbing a bite at a cozy diner nearby, the kind where the neon sign flickers promising warmth and comfort. As we sit in a booth, the aroma of grilled cheese and fries wafts through the air, and we reminisce about our high school days. Laughter erupts between us, filling the small space with a contagious joy that feels foreign yet exhilarating. It's in moments like this that I realize how much I've missed him, how the years apart have only heightened the appreciation for what we once had.

With each shared story, we slowly peel back the layers of our lives, exposing the vulnerabilities we've kept hidden for so long. He shares tales of his travels, the people he's met, and the photographs that captured the essence of those experiences. I tell him about the struggle of finding my voice in a city that often feels like a cacophony of competing dreams. It's a bittersweet exchange, each revelation bringing us closer, yet reminding us of the paths we never took together.

As we finish our meal, a sense of urgency fills the air. The night is still young, and the city feels like a playground, ready to reveal its secrets. Evan suggests a walk through Central Park, and I find myself nodding eagerly, the thrill of possibility coursing through me. As we step outside, the chill has turned into a crisp, invigorating breeze, the stars twinkling above like scattered diamonds.

With every step, I feel a new energy surging within me, a reminder that I am not just a film editor lost in the chaos of deadlines, but a woman who dares to dream again. The laughter of children echoes through the trees, mingling with the rustling leaves, as we walk side by side, hearts entwined in a rhythm as old as time itself.

I glance at him, his profile illuminated by the soft glow of the streetlights, and realize that this moment—this beautiful, imperfect moment—is exactly what I've been searching for. The city, with all its hustle and bustle, has a way of reminding us that dreams can be rekindled, and connections can be rediscovered. And as I walk beside Evan, I feel the weight of the past begin to lift, replaced by the promise of new beginnings.

The moon hangs high above the skyline, a silver sentinel observing our every step as Evan and I stroll through Central Park. The path is illuminated by the soft glow of vintage streetlamps, casting gentle halos on the cobblestones beneath our feet. Each stride feels like a gentle pulse, syncing our heartbeats as the night wraps around us like a familiar shawl, heavy with possibility. The sounds of the city fade into the background, replaced by the gentle rustling of leaves and the distant laughter of couples sharing whispered secrets on park benches.

As we walk, I steal glances at him, the way the moonlight dances in his dark hair, how his laughter spills from his lips like a forgotten melody rediscovered. It feels surreal to have him by my side, like we are two stars pulled from our separate orbits, colliding for a brief moment in time. The air is alive with a sense of nostalgia, memories swirling around us like the crisp autumn leaves that crunch underfoot.

"What were you like in high school?" he asks, his voice low and teasing, inviting me to share pieces of myself I thought I had buried.

I chuckle, recalling my younger self—the girl who wore oversized flannel shirts and chronicled her life in notebooks filled with sketches and dreams. "Oh, you know, just your average geek. I had big glasses, a love for indie films, and a penchant for trying to impress you with my homemade horror flicks."

His eyes sparkle with mischief. "I still remember that zombie movie you made. I was genuinely terrified. And the ending? Classic!"

I laugh, warmth flooding my cheeks. "You were just being nice!"

"Maybe," he concedes, "but you had a vision. I admired that about you, even then."

The sincerity in his words strikes a chord deep within me, awakening a dormant yearning I thought long forgotten. We continue to walk, and I find myself sharing more than I anticipated—the dreams I'd stifled, the fears that had kept me up at night, and the struggle to find my place in a world that often felt hostile.

With every revelation, it's as if we are peeling away layers of years spent apart, revealing the raw and tender connections that still bind us. I tell him of the sleepless nights spent in the editing room, the anxiety of waiting for my work to be validated, for the world to acknowledge the filmmaker I always dreamed I could be. The city, once a playground of dreams, has transformed into a labyrinth of deadlines and unfulfilled ambitions, each corner leading me deeper into doubt.

"I can relate," he says thoughtfully, his gaze distant as if recalling his own battles. "After high school, I thought I had it all figured out. But life has a funny way of redirecting your path. I got lost for a while, wandering through odd jobs, chasing shadows of what I thought I wanted. It wasn't until I picked up a camera that I finally felt a spark again."

His passion radiates off him, an energy that warms the chilly night air. The way he talks about photography—the thrill of capturing moments, the storytelling through images—stirs something within me. There's a poetic rhythm in his words, a cadence that feels like an echo of the dreams we once shared.

"What do you see when you look through your lens?" I ask, genuinely curious.

He pauses, considering his response. "I see stories—fragile, fleeting moments that deserve to be immortalized. It's like holding a piece of the universe in your hands, capturing emotion before it slips away."

His eyes shine with fervor, igniting a fire in me that I thought had extinguished. Perhaps it's time to reclaim my own narrative, to redefine what success means for me.

As we wander deeper into the park, we come across the iconic Bethesda Terrace, its fountain shimmering under the moonlight. I pause, feeling the allure of the place seep into my bones. "I used to dream of shooting a film here," I admit, my voice tinged with yearning. "There's something magical about this spot—the echoes of stories waiting to be told."

"Why not? You have a camera, don't you?"

I laugh, the sound echoing against the marble columns, and suddenly it feels like anything is possible. "I do, but I haven't used it in ages."

"Let's make a pact. You pick a date, and we'll come back here. You can shoot whatever you want, and I'll be your reluctant actor."

The idea is both terrifying and exhilarating. "You might regret that offer," I warn, half-joking.

"Maybe, but I'm in." His grin is infectious, igniting a spark of courage I hadn't felt in years.

The laughter and lightness between us serve as a balm for the scars time has etched upon my heart. With Evan beside me, I feel as if I'm brushing away the dust that had settled over my dreams. As we sit on a bench overlooking the fountain, I take a deep breath, inhaling the crisp air scented with autumn and nostalgia.

The conversation shifts, and we discuss our lives since high school, the dreams that faded and those that transformed. I reveal the intricacies of my editing job, the unyielding pressure that suffocates creativity, while he shares tales of his travels, how he captured life in all its raw beauty—from bustling markets in Marrakech to serene sunrises in Bali.

The world feels expansive in his stories, and I find myself yearning to break free from my self-imposed constraints. The more he speaks, the more I feel the walls I've built around my heart begin to crumble. Here, in this moment, I'm reminded of the limitless possibilities that exist just beyond my fears.

As midnight approaches, the park begins to quiet, the sounds of the city mingling with the gentle lapping of water from the fountain. A sense of serenity washes over me, the chaos of my daily life momentarily forgotten. In this shared cocoon of vulnerability, it feels as though the universe is urging me to take a leap of faith.

"Evan," I say softly, the weight of my unspoken thoughts hanging in the air, "do you ever regret the paths we chose?"

He turns to me, his expression earnest. "Sometimes, but I believe every choice shapes who we are. The moments we didn't share taught us valuable lessons. They prepared us for this."

"This?" I echo, my heart racing.

"Whatever this is. The magic of reconnecting, the chance to rewrite our stories."

A silence envelops us, pregnant with the weight of his words. I look into his eyes, the flicker of understanding passing between us, igniting a yearning I can no longer ignore. Perhaps the past is not just a series of regrets, but a tapestry woven with moments of joy, pain, and growth.

With a newfound sense of courage, I make a decision. "Let's meet again. Soon. I want to capture those stories, both yours and mine. I want to remember what it feels like to create again."

His face lights up with a mixture of surprise and delight. "Absolutely. Let's turn this into something beautiful, together."

As we rise from the bench, the cool air invigorates me, and the stars above seem to shimmer in agreement. The world stretches before us, wide and full of potential. The city feels less daunting now, transformed into a canvas waiting for our brushstrokes. With every step, I feel lighter, as if I'm shedding the weight of my past, leaving behind the shadows that have held me captive for too long.

Evan and I walk side by side, no longer just fragments of what we once were but vibrant pieces of a story still being written. The future sparkles like the city lights, a promise of adventures waiting to unfold, and as I glance at him, I know that this moment is only the beginning.

Chapter 2: The Unexpected Reunion

The warm glow of the setting sun spills over the Manhattan skyline, draping the rooftop bar in a golden hue that mingles with the vibrant chatter and laughter surrounding me. It's a lavish affair, brimming with a crowd of ambitious dreamers, each clinking glasses filled with artisanal cocktails that catch the light like jewels. Yet, the atmosphere feels heavy on my shoulders, the weight of anticipation wrapped tightly around my chest. I can't help but feel out of place, a solitary figure in a sea of confident faces.

The bar, adorned with twinkling fairy lights and lush greenery, offers a stunning view of Central Park, where the distant sounds of children playing and dogs barking filter through the air. I sip my drink, the tang of citrus mingling with the gentle bitterness of gin, hoping it will soothe the jittering anxiety lurking within me. The crisp evening air carries the scent of freshly cut grass from the park below, mingling with the musky aroma of cocktails and the faint hint of a nearby food truck serving gourmet bites. I take a deep breath, trying to steady my racing heart, but it only seems to quicken.

Amidst the laughter, the hum of conversation grows louder, and I scan the crowd, my eyes flitting over groups animatedly discussing their latest projects. And then, across the room, I see him. Evan. My breath catches in my throat, and for a moment, the world around me blurs into a hazy backdrop. He stands in a group of filmmakers, his dark hair slightly tousled, giving him that effortlessly charming look I remember all too well. The way he leans against the bar, his smile bright and engaging, instantly draws me in. It's as if the years dissolve, and I'm transported back to a time when we shared laughter and dreams, exploring our ambitions under the bright lights of the city that never sleeps.

I hadn't expected to see him here, not after all this time. Memories flood my mind—late-night coffee runs, his infectious laughter that could fill a room, the way his eyes sparkled with creativity and passion. But those memories are bittersweet, tinged with the ache of what we lost. Could I really face him after everything that happened? The silence between us grew like a chasm, and now, here we are, two souls once intertwined, standing worlds apart. I can feel my heart thudding like a drum, each beat echoing my indecision.

As if sensing my hesitation, Evan's gaze locks onto mine, and a smile spreads across his face, genuine and warm. The noise around me fades, replaced by the sound of my own heartbeat, pounding wildly against the backdrop of the city's symphony. He looks different, more mature, but that familiar spark is undeniably present. He gestures to me, his eyes inviting me to step into the warm glow of his presence. It's a magnetic pull, a force drawing me closer despite the reservations fluttering in my stomach.

I take a step forward, the crowd parting as if it were choreographed, my movements feeling surreal as I navigate through the mingling guests. The closer I get, the more overwhelming the memories become—fragments of laughter shared over coffee, the way he would lean in closer during serious discussions, the electric energy that crackled between us. My heart races, battling the urge to retreat with the urge to embrace the moment.

"Evan," I breathe, surprised at the steadiness in my voice, despite the whirlwind inside me.

He turns fully to face me, his expression shifting from surprise to pure delight. "I can't believe it's you!" His voice wraps around me like a familiar melody, igniting a warmth that spreads through my chest.

The crowd around us fades into a blur, our reunion encapsulated in a moment that feels suspended in time. "What are you doing here?" I ask, my curiosity bubbling to the surface, mingling with the joy of seeing him again.

"Networking, of course," he replies, his smile teasing. "But honestly, I was hoping to run into you. I've missed our talks."

Those words strike a chord deep within me. My heart flutters at the thought that I hadn't been the only one reflecting on our shared past. The connection we had, the long discussions filled with dreams and aspirations, suddenly feels like it's alive again, crackling with possibility.

As the conversation flows, I can't help but steal glances at his face, trying to decipher the changes in him—there's a maturity in his features, a confidence that makes him even more attractive. The laughter in his eyes reminds me of our late-night discussions, the way we used to dive deep into our hopes, fears, and every nuance in between. It's all there, the chemistry that had once sparked so brightly.

"Are you still working on those short films?" I ask, genuinely curious.

"Yeah, I just wrapped one up," he replies, his enthusiasm infectious. "It's a quirky little piece about a bartender who accidentally becomes a matchmaker. It's got heart, humor, and a bit of chaos—just like real life, right?"

I laugh, picturing Evan orchestrating such delightful chaos, his creative mind always drawn to the unexpected twists of life. "That sounds amazing. You always had a knack for finding the humor in the mundane."

"Thanks," he says, his eyes shining with appreciation. "What about you? Still writing those articles for that magazine?"

"Yeah, I am," I say, feeling a mix of pride and humility. "It's been a journey, but I'm finding my voice in it, slowly."

He nods, his expression encouraging. "You always had a way with words. I remember how you could make even the most boring topics sound intriguing. You were my secret weapon during those brainstorming sessions."

The compliment warms me, and I can't help but smile, recalling those late-night brainstorming sessions filled with laughter and caffeine-fueled creativity. "You made it easy. We were a good team."

"Maybe we should team up again," he suggests playfully, a glimmer of something unspoken dancing in his gaze.

My heart stutters, a rush of hope mingling with the thrill of the unexpected. Perhaps this reunion was more than just a chance encounter. The air thickens with uncharted territory, and I can feel the remnants of our past flickering to life, igniting a fire I thought had long since extinguished.

Evan's laughter rings through the air, rich and melodic, weaving through the chatter of the crowd like an intoxicating song. The way his eyes glimmer with a hint of mischief transports me to a time when everything felt uncomplicated, and our lives were a tapestry of shared ambitions and spontaneous adventures. My heart dances a little as we slip into an easy rhythm, the kind of conversation that flows naturally, weaving in and out of nostalgia and present aspirations. He leans in slightly, and the warmth of his presence ignites a spark of hope within me, transforming the rooftop bar into our private universe.

"I remember the time you tried to convince me that an old diner on the corner was a hidden gem," he says, a playful smirk tugging at the corners of his mouth. "And we ended up with that awful meatloaf."

I chuckle, a bubble of laughter escaping my lips as the memory floods back. "Hey, I still stand by that! It had character," I protest, shaking my head with mock indignation. "And I might have been right if they hadn't run out of gravy that day."

"Gravy makes everything better," he quips, and for a moment, it feels like no time has passed at all. The laughter hangs between us like an invisible thread, binding us together, and the joy I thought I had buried deep within me begins to unfurl.

As we reminisce about old times, I catch glimpses of the man he's become—a blend of the familiar and the new. There's a depth in his voice, a richness that suggests he's experienced life in ways I've only begun to explore. My curiosity bubbles over, and I find myself leaning in, eager to uncover the layers of his journey since we last crossed paths.

"What's been the biggest challenge for you since we last talked?" I ask, genuinely interested. The question hangs in the air, charged with the electricity of our connection.

He hesitates, his gaze drifting to the shimmering skyline as if searching for an answer in the vast expanse of New York City. "Honestly, figuring out how to balance passion and practicality," he admits, a hint of vulnerability breaking through his confident façade. "I've had to navigate a lot of rejection and doubt, but it's all part of the journey, right? I'm learning to embrace the chaos."

His honesty strikes a chord, resonating with my own struggles. "I get that. It feels like every step forward is shadowed by uncertainty, doesn't it?"

"Exactly! But sometimes those moments of doubt lead to the most rewarding opportunities," he says, his voice imbued with conviction. "I've had the chance to work with some amazing people who challenge me creatively."

A spark of admiration flickers within me, igniting a sense of pride. "That's incredible, Evan. I always knew you'd find your way."

Our conversation continues, punctuated by laughter and shared anecdotes that span the years. Each story reveals a layer of who we are now, intertwined with the memories of who we once were. The rooftop bar fades into the background, and it feels as though we're suspended in time, cloaked in the warmth of our shared history.

But just as I begin to revel in this moment, a shadow of doubt creeps in. What if this connection is fleeting, an echo of the past that will dissolve once the night ends? I glance around, noting the vibrant atmosphere—the clinking of glasses, the distant sounds of laughter, and the soft music that fills the air. Everything feels electric, and yet a part of me tugs at the corners of my mind, questioning whether this reunion can lead to something more profound.

Evan catches my gaze, his eyes searching mine, and the intensity of that moment sends a shiver down my spine. "What about you? What's been your biggest challenge?"

I hesitate, the question hanging in the air like a whisper. "I think...finding my voice," I finally admit, feeling the weight of my truth settle around us. "For so long, I felt like I was just following a script that others wrote for me. Now, I'm trying to break free, to carve out a path that feels authentic to who I am."

His expression softens, a knowing smile playing on his lips. "That's brave. It takes courage to step off the well-trodden path. I admire that."

His words warm me from the inside, wrapping around my heart like a comforting blanket. It feels good to be seen, to have someone recognize the struggles I've faced in chasing my dreams. In this city filled with ambition and relentless drive, it's easy to lose sight of oneself, and I've often felt like a ghost flitting through the shadows, unseen and unheard.

Just then, the sun dips below the horizon, casting a warm orange glow across the sky. The ambiance shifts as the lights of the city flicker to life, twinkling like stars awakening in the twilight. The moment feels monumental, as if the universe is conspiring to remind us of the beauty of second chances.

"Do you ever think about what could have been?" I ask, curiosity mingling with nostalgia.

"Sometimes," he replies, his tone contemplative. "But I believe every choice leads us to where we're meant to be. Life has a funny way of bringing us back to the people who matter."

As he speaks, I can feel the gravity of his words settling between us, creating an invisible tether that pulls us closer. The conversation shifts, flowing seamlessly from past to present, and I find myself sharing parts of my life I've kept tucked away—the victories, the failures, the moments that shaped me.

Each revelation feels like a thread weaving us together, the fabric of our connection growing richer and more intricate. I talk about my attempts at finding balance between work and life, the endless hustle that sometimes feels suffocating. Evan listens intently, his eyes never wavering, and I can see the empathy reflected there, a shared understanding of the struggles we both face.

The evening deepens, the air growing cooler, but the warmth between us remains, a beacon of hope that fuels my spirit. My heart dances as we exchange stories, laughter bubbling up like champagne, effervescent and light. Each moment feels charged with possibility, as if the universe is encouraging us to explore the uncharted territory of what this reconnection could mean.

And just as I allow myself to dream of what might come next, the moment shifts once more. A couple nearby bursts into a joyous celebration, toasting to some unnamed success, the exuberance of their laughter echoing through the night. The sound pulls me back to the present, and I glance at Evan, a question lingering in the air between us.

"Where do we go from here?" I ask, my voice barely above a whisper, my heart racing with anticipation.

Evan meets my gaze, a flicker of something unspoken passing between us, and I can't help but wonder if this reunion is merely the prologue to a story we are meant to write together—a narrative bursting with laughter, challenges, and the sweet thrill of new beginnings.

The warmth of Evan's gaze envelops me, a comforting balm against the chill of uncertainty that had gripped me since I arrived.

His laughter, infectious and genuine, weaves through the air like music, and I feel a strange exhilaration coursing through my veins as we settle into the rhythm of conversation. The vibrant chatter of the mixer fades into a distant murmur, and we exist in a world crafted solely from the fragments of our shared past.

"Do you remember that time we got lost in Brooklyn trying to find that one film screening?" he asks, a playful glint in his eyes that sends a delightful shiver down my spine.

"Lost is an understatement! I thought we were going to end up on some reality show about clueless tourists," I reply, laughing at the memory. "But at least we discovered that amazing pizza place."

"True, true. Who knew the universe had pizza and the perfect blend of chaos waiting for us?" His grin is disarming, and I can't help but smile back, feeling a warmth spread through me that is reminiscent of our late-night escapades filled with dreams and aspirations.

As the evening unfolds, the vibrant energy of the mixer remains, but it feels secondary to our burgeoning connection. The bar is alive with creativity, but here, within our bubble, there's a different kind of magic swirling around us, lifting the mundane into the extraordinary.

"Tell me more about your latest work," Evan prompts, leaning in closer as if the distance between us could be measured in inches rather than years.

I launch into an enthusiastic recounting of my recent articles and the challenges I faced, my passion spilling forth like the champagne in the glasses around us. I talk about my attempts to distill complex ideas into digestible pieces, to engage readers with stories that resonate. His interest is palpable, and the way he nods and interjects with thoughtful questions makes me feel seen, not just as a writer but as a person.

"The way you talk about your work is infectious," he says, genuine admiration sparkling in his eyes. "You have this ability to bring people into your world, to help them see things through your lens."

His compliment wraps around me like a warm embrace, igniting a flicker of pride within my chest. "Thank you. It's been a journey, but I'm finally starting to feel like I'm finding my voice."

"That's what it's all about, isn't it? Finding our voice and using it to shape our reality," he reflects, and the weight of his words resonates deeply within me.

As the evening stretches on, we dive deeper into conversation, the topics ranging from the whimsical to the profound. We reminisce about our shared dreams, the wild ambitions that once seemed so achievable, and the disappointments that accompanied them. I reveal my fears—about the industry, about my place in it—and Evan listens intently, his presence steady and grounding.

"Every setback is just a setup for something greater," he assures me, his tone imbued with a sincerity that fills me with hope. "You're on the brink of something amazing, I can feel it."

Just then, a nearby group erupts in laughter, their clinking glasses drawing our attention for a moment. It's a reminder that life continues to buzz around us, each person enveloped in their own stories, their own battles. But here, together, Evan and I are cocooned in our shared narrative, weaving threads of hope and ambition into a fabric that feels surprisingly sturdy.

"Shall we take a walk?" he suggests, his eyes bright with mischief. "I know a perfect spot where we can overlook the park without the crowds."

Intrigued, I nod, and he leads me toward the staircase that winds down to a lower terrace, where the sounds of the mixer grow faint. The night air greets us like an old friend, crisp and invigorating, filled with the distant sounds of the city that never sleeps. The lights of New York sparkle like stars, and the view stretches before us—a vast tapestry of humanity, ambition, and dreams colliding under the night sky.

"This is one of my favorite places," Evan says, his voice low, almost reverent. "There's something about standing here that makes me feel alive."

I stand beside him, leaning against the railing as the cool breeze dances through my hair. "It's beautiful," I agree, captivated not just by the view but by the warmth radiating from him.

As we share the moment, the connection deepens, stretching back to the shared dreams of our youth. I turn to him, the moonlight casting a silvery glow on his face, revealing the contours of his expression—the intensity of his gaze, the slight curve of his lips. "Do you ever think about what we could have built together?"

Evan's eyes narrow slightly, the question lingering between us like an unbroken promise. "All the time," he admits, his voice thick with honesty. "But the past is just a stepping stone. It shaped us, yes, but it doesn't have to define us."

A flutter of excitement dances in my chest, igniting a spark of courage. "So, what if we wrote a new story?" I venture, the words spilling from my lips before I can second-guess myself.

He meets my gaze, the surprise melting into a grin that lights up his entire face. "Are you suggesting we collaborate?"

"Why not? We both have stories to tell, experiences to share. We could create something beautiful."

The idea hangs in the air, suspended in the magic of the moment, and I can't help but imagine the possibilities. The thrill of writing together, of intertwining our narratives into something vibrant and meaningful, feels like a promise—a whisper of what could be.

"I'd love that," he says softly, and his sincerity sends a shiver of excitement down my spine.

The night air feels electric, filled with unspoken possibilities and the intoxicating thrill of potential. Standing there, overlooking the shimmering expanse of Central Park, I realize that this moment—this unexpected reunion—might be the turning point I had been searching for.

As we begin to discuss ideas, my mind races with excitement, the creative juices flowing as freely as the laughter that spills from our lips. We talk about characters, plots, and settings, our imaginations intertwining seamlessly like the paths of the park below. The city pulses around us, each sound a testament to the lives being lived, the stories being written.

And in that moment, beneath the vast New York sky, I feel something shift inside me. The fear and uncertainty that had held me back begin to dissipate, replaced by a newfound sense of purpose and possibility. The connection between Evan and me is more than a mere echo of the past; it's the spark of a new beginning, a chance to forge something beautiful from the ashes of what once was.

With every word exchanged, every idea shared, the foundations of a new narrative take shape—one that intertwines our lives, aspirations, and passions. And as I stand beside Evan, the city twinkling around us, I can't help but feel that this is where I was meant to be all along.

Chapter 3: Unpacking Old Wounds

The café was tucked away between two dilapidated buildings on a street that was mostly forgotten. Weathered wooden signs swung lazily in the gentle breeze, each creak whispering secrets of the past. I pushed open the door, its brass handle cold against my palm, and was enveloped in the rich aroma of dark roast and freshly baked pastries. The barista, a young woman with ink-stained fingers and a crooked smile, greeted me with a nod, and I found solace in the familiar ambiance, a blend of hushed conversations and the soft clinking of cups. It felt like stepping into a sanctuary where time slowed, allowing me a moment to breathe amid the chaos swirling in my mind.

As I slid into a booth in the back corner, I looked around, taking in the mismatched furniture and walls adorned with local art. The café had a character of its own—an eclectic collection of memories stored in chipped mugs and worn-out chairs. Sunlight streamed through the tall windows, illuminating the dust motes dancing in the air, and I let out a sigh, hoping this would be the place where I could unpack the years that had piled up between us like forgotten luggage.

Evan arrived moments later, a vision of warmth against the gray backdrop of my life. His entrance drew a few glances; he carried an air of confidence, as if the world was an open script waiting for him to write his next line. When our eyes met, a flicker of recognition passed between us, the same spark that had ignited our friendship all those years ago. His laughter bubbled up like champagne, effervescent and intoxicating, and I felt a part of me thaw in his presence.

As we exchanged pleasantries, my heart raced at the thought of reconnecting with someone who had once meant so much to me. Yet, a nagging doubt loomed in the shadows, whispering insidious thoughts that made me question my worth. Evan was a successful screenwriter now, and I couldn't help but contrast his triumphs with my own perceived stagnation. He spoke animatedly about his latest project, gesturing enthusiastically as if the very idea could leap off the page. Each word he spoke wrapped around me, drawing me closer, yet it also reminded me of the distance I felt—a chasm carved by years of silence and self-doubt.

"Are you still working at that little bookstore?" he asked, tilting his head slightly, a teasing glimmer in his eyes. The question hit harder than I anticipated.

"Yeah, I'm still there," I replied, forcing a smile that felt more like a grimace. The bookstore was a refuge, a cocoon where I could lose myself in tales of adventure and romance, yet it also served as a constant reminder of my unfulfilled aspirations. I swallowed hard, trying to suppress the rising tide of insecurity.

"What about you? Hollywood treating you well?" I ventured, desperate to keep the conversation afloat. His laughter was like music, and I wanted to revel in it, to allow it to drown out the chorus of doubts echoing in my mind.

"Oh, you know how it is," he replied with a nonchalant wave, his eyes twinkling with mischief. "It's a rollercoaster. Some days you're on top of the world, and others... well, let's just say the writing process isn't for the faint-hearted." He chuckled, but beneath the humor, I sensed the weight of struggles he faced—an unspoken language shared between us, built on years of friendship and unfulfilled potential.

The conversation ebbed and flowed, drifting into murky waters. We navigated through the shared memories of our youth, recalling laughter-filled nights and whispered secrets. Yet, as we spoke, a strange tension filled the air, an invisible barrier that both drew us together and kept us apart. The laughter that had once flowed freely now felt stilted, punctuated by pauses where words hung heavy, like raindrops clinging to the edge of a leaf.

I caught him glancing at me, his gaze searching, probing. "You're still the same girl, you know," he said, and there was a sincerity in his voice that made my heart flutter. "You've always had that spark, that light." The compliment wrapped around me like a warm blanket, but it also stirred up a storm within. I wanted to believe him, to embrace the idea that I was still worthy of admiration, yet the shadows of my insecurities lurked close, ready to pounce.

"You know, I've been meaning to write," I said, the words tumbling out before I could reel them back in. "But... I don't know. I guess I've lost my confidence along the way." The admission felt like a pebble tossed into a still pond, sending ripples across the surface of my heart.

Evan leaned in, his expression shifting to one of earnest concern. "What's stopping you? You've always had a way with words. Remember those stories you used to write?"

The memory hung between us, bittersweet. I had once been a girl with dreams as expansive as the ocean, crafting tales that swept me away to far-off lands. But somewhere along the way, life had tossed those dreams aside, leaving me sifting through the wreckage.

The conversation flowed like a river, meandering through laughter and nostalgia, yet it was punctuated by silences that spoke volumes. In those pauses, I could feel the weight of unhealed wounds—both mine and his. We were two people caught in the throes of our own stories, struggling to bridge the gap between who we had been and who we had become. The lingering glances, the hesitations in our laughter—they were echoes of unspoken words, reminders that despite the distance, our past was not so easily shed.

As we parted ways, a mix of hope and trepidation swirled within me. I felt like I was standing on the precipice of something new and beautiful, yet the echoes of disappointment from the past lingered like shadows, urging caution. Would this be a new beginning, or just another chapter in the ongoing saga of my life?

The sun dipped lower in the sky, casting a warm golden hue that bathed the café in a soft, inviting light. As I made my way to the door, the sounds of clinking cups and murmured conversations faded behind me, replaced by the gentle rustle of leaves in the late afternoon breeze. My heart raced with an odd blend of excitement and trepidation, the weight of our conversation still hanging in the air like the scent of roasted coffee lingering on my clothes. Each step felt charged with possibilities, as if the world had shifted just enough to reveal paths previously hidden.

The streets outside were alive with the vibrant pulse of the city. People bustled past, laughter ringing out and mingling with the distant sound of street performers serenading the late afternoon crowd. I could feel the remnants of our conversation echoing in my mind, Evan's laughter a counterpoint to the insecurities that threatened to overwhelm me. With every face I passed, I saw a reflection of my own uncertainties, but also an ember of hope igniting within.

The park wasn't far, and I found solace in its expanse, a green oasis amid the urban chaos. As I wandered along the winding paths, I marveled at the beauty surrounding me. Trees stood tall, their leaves a patchwork of colors as autumn approached, whispering secrets in the gentle wind. A couple nearby tossed breadcrumbs to a gaggle of geese, their carefree joy a stark contrast to the heaviness that had accompanied my earlier thoughts. I smiled despite myself, feeling a warmth seep into my bones as I took a seat on a weathered bench beneath the arching branches.

Evan's words replayed in my mind like a favorite song, the notes both comforting and haunting. He saw something in me that I struggled to recognize—a spark I had extinguished long ago. The realization settled within me, filling the cracks of my self-doubt with something akin to determination. Could I really step back into the world of words? Could I reclaim the passion that had once fueled my dreams?

As I sat there, watching the leaves dance in the wind, I felt a rush of nostalgia for the girl I used to be—the one who scribbled stories on napkins during lunch breaks and dreamed of publication. There was a time when I believed in my voice, when the words flowed from my fingertips like a river of inspiration. But life had a way of washing away those dreams, layer by layer, until I was left clutching at the remnants, unsure how to stitch them back together.

My phone buzzed in my pocket, jarring me from my reverie. It was a message from Evan, a simple invitation to meet again, to talk more about the stories we once shared. A flutter of excitement coursed through me, mingled with apprehension. Could this be the catalyst I needed? I hesitated for only a moment before replying with an enthusiastic yes. Perhaps it was time to breathe life into the old wounds, to allow the healing process to begin.

The days leading up to our next meeting passed in a blur of anticipation. I spent hours in the bookstore, surrounded by the smell of paper and ink, enveloped by stories waiting to be discovered. Each title on the shelf seemed to whisper to me, urging me to dive back into the world of creativity. I found myself picking up pens and notebooks, sketching out ideas that had long lain dormant. It was like rekindling a friendship with an old lover—awkward at first, but then bursting with potential.

On the day of our meeting, I dressed with care, a modest but bright dress that made me feel both comfortable and confident. I let my hair fall in soft waves, hoping it would frame my face in a way that reminded me of those carefree days of youth. As I stepped outside, the air was crisp, tinged with the earthy scent of fallen leaves and the promise of change. I felt lighter, buoyed by the prospect of embracing the creative spark Evan believed still flickered within me.

This time, we chose a quaint bistro, its outdoor seating nestled among the trees that dotted the sidewalk. The ambiance was vibrant, filled with the chatter of diners and the clinking of forks against plates. Evan arrived shortly after I did, his eyes lighting up when he spotted me. He approached with an easy smile, the kind that seemed to illuminate everything around him.

"Hey there, ready for another round of catching up?" he asked, his voice warm and inviting. The way he spoke made me feel seen, as if the years apart had merely been a prelude to this moment.

"I'm more than ready," I replied, my heart racing with the thrill of possibility. We settled into our seats, the sun casting a golden glow on our table, and I felt a newfound energy coursing through me.

Our conversation flowed effortlessly, a lively exchange of dreams and aspirations. Evan shared his latest screenplay, his eyes sparkling with excitement as he described the characters and their struggles. I found myself hanging on his every word, captivated by the way he painted vivid pictures with his storytelling. The more he spoke, the more my own stories clamored to be told, eager to break free from the chains I had placed upon them.

"I've been thinking about writing again," I confessed, the words tumbling out before I could second-guess myself. "I just... I don't know where to start."

Evan leaned in, a knowing smile on his lips. "Start by telling the truth. Write what you know, what you feel. It doesn't have to be perfect; it just has to be real."

His encouragement was like a breath of fresh air, igniting the dormant embers of my creativity. We spent hours lost in conversation, laughter punctuating our exchange as we navigated through the intricacies of our lives and the dreams that had shaped us. It felt exhilarating to share my hopes and fears with someone who genuinely understood the struggle of finding one's voice amid the noise of the world.

As the sun began to dip below the horizon, painting the sky in hues of pink and gold, I felt an overwhelming sense of gratitude wash over me. This wasn't just a reunion; it was a renaissance—a rebirth of the dreams I had let slip away. In Evan's presence, I could finally begin to see the possibility of reclaiming my narrative, of weaving together the threads of my past with the aspirations of my future.

With the evening wrapping around us like a comforting blanket, I realized that perhaps it wasn't about leaving the past behind but embracing it, learning from it, and allowing it to inform my journey forward. As we parted once more, the air crackling with unspoken promises, I felt a sense of hope blossom within me—a quiet confidence that whispered of beginnings, urging me to take the leap I had long feared. The world was vast, filled with stories waiting to be told, and maybe, just maybe, mine was ready to be written anew.

The week that followed our second meeting unfolded like a patchwork quilt, each day stitched together with fragments of inspiration and hesitation. I found myself waking up early, the golden light of dawn spilling through my window, a soft invitation to embrace the day. The stillness of the morning provided a sanctuary where I could drown out the chaos of my thoughts and allow my imagination to roam freely. I would pour a cup of coffee, the rich aroma curling around me like a familiar embrace, and settle at my kitchen table, staring at the blank pages before me. They felt like a canvas, the stark white glaring back, urging me to paint my fears and desires into words.

With every scribbled sentence, I felt the heaviness of my insecurities begin to lift, replaced by a gentle swell of possibility. The memories of childhood dreams began to resurface, vivid and unyielding. I recalled how I used to spend hours at the library, my fingers grazing the spines of novels that transported me to far-off worlds. I could feel the whispers of those stories tickling the edges of my consciousness, nudging me to pay attention, to weave my own narrative into the tapestry of life. Yet, the specter of doubt lingered, lurking in the shadows like an unwanted guest, reminding me of the years I had let slip away, the times I had chosen silence over expression.

Evan's words echoed in my mind, a steady refrain. "Start by telling the truth." So I began to write. I poured my heart onto the pages, detailing the quiet moments of my life, the intricate dance of emotions that had shaped me. The stories flowed with ease, unearthing memories that were both sweet and sorrowful. I explored the feelings of loneliness that had crept in during my darkest days, the flickers of joy that had illuminated my path, and the relentless pursuit of a sense of belonging that seemed to elude me.

Each evening, I would look forward to our chats over coffee or dinner, the anticipation building with every exchange. Our conversations unfolded like a delicate flower, blossoming in unexpected ways. Evan was not only a storyteller; he was a listener, a safe harbor in a tumultuous sea of emotions. He would lean back, an inviting smile on his face, encouraging me to delve deeper into the stories I hesitated to share. The moments we spent together became a catalyst for my creativity, pushing me to confront the parts of myself I had long buried.

One rainy afternoon, as the clouds hung heavy and gray over the city, I found myself in my favorite corner of the bookstore, enveloped in the comforting scent of aged paper and binding glue. I had taken refuge there, hoping the rain would wash away some of the uncertainties clinging to my heart. The quiet ambiance was a balm, and I nestled into a plush chair, surrounded by the stories of others. I picked up a well-worn novel, its pages creased and yellowed, and began to read.

But my mind was elsewhere, caught in a whirlpool of thoughts about Evan and the profound connection we had rekindled. Each glance we exchanged during our meetings felt charged with unspoken words, layers of history wrapped tightly around us. The laughter we shared ignited something deep within, a longing that stirred at the edges of my consciousness, beckoning me to explore it. What had once been a platonic friendship now tinged with a sense of possibility, each moment between us a precarious dance of vulnerability and hope.

The rain poured down outside, creating a rhythmic symphony against the windows, but inside, I felt suspended in time, caught between the past and the future. As the droplets cascaded down the glass, I wondered if I had the courage to confront my feelings. Would I be able to voice the emotions that swirled within me, or would fear silence me once more?

In the days that followed, I found myself yearning for deeper conversations, a chance to delve into the intricacies of our lives with Evan. I decided to invite him to a local art exhibition, something I hoped would spark new dialogue and perhaps reveal hidden layers of our relationship. The gallery, housed in a charming brownstone, featured local artists whose vibrant works echoed the beauty of the city. The thought of exploring this colorful world together filled me with excitement and trepidation.

As I stepped into the gallery that evening, the soft lighting cast a warm glow over the eclectic array of paintings. The walls were adorned with bold splashes of color and intricate designs, each piece telling its own story. I felt a rush of inspiration wash over me, the atmosphere buzzing with creativity and potential. Evan arrived shortly after, his eyes brightening as he took in the artwork.

"Wow, this place is incredible," he said, his voice brimming with enthusiasm. I couldn't help but smile at the wonder in his eyes, mirroring my own feelings of excitement. We wandered through the exhibition, our discussions flowing easily, interspersed with laughter and thoughtful observations. As we stood in front of a striking piece that captured a sunset over the city, I felt the weight of unspoken words tugging at my heart, urging me to share my truth.

"What do you see?" I asked, turning to him, my pulse quickening.

Evan studied the painting intently, his brow furrowing slightly. "I see a world full of potential, a vibrant tapestry of life. It's beautiful and chaotic at the same time." His answer resonated deeply with me, mirroring the complexities of our own lives.

As I opened my mouth to speak, to share my thoughts on the piece and perhaps, to reveal more of myself, I was interrupted by a flurry of laughter from a nearby group. Their exuberance punctured the moment, scattering my resolve like leaves in the wind. I hesitated, the vulnerability that had begun to blossom feeling suddenly fragile and exposed.

"Isn't it funny how art can evoke such strong feelings?" I managed, diverting the conversation back to safer territory. Evan nodded, his gaze still focused on the painting, and I caught a glimpse of something deeper in his expression—a flicker of understanding that suggested he sensed my struggle, even if I wasn't ready to confront it.

The evening unfolded like a kaleidoscope, each moment a fragment of color, laughter, and silence woven together. As we moved from piece to piece, I felt the connection between us deepening, intertwining like the brushstrokes on the canvas. It was in those moments of shared appreciation and contemplation that I realized how much I craved authenticity, not just in my art but in my relationship with Evan.

Finally, we settled into a cozy corner café after the exhibition, seeking refuge from the evening chill. The warmth of the space enveloped us as we sipped steaming cups of tea, the fragrant steam curling upwards like wisps of forgotten dreams. I glanced at Evan, the soft glow of the café lights dancing in his eyes, and I felt a surge of courage swell within me.

"Can I be honest with you?" I ventured, my heart racing. The words felt like a leap into the unknown, but they were long overdue.

He looked at me, his expression open and encouraging. "Always."

"I've been thinking a lot about us... about this," I began, my voice trembling slightly. "I don't want to just drift along as friends anymore. I want to explore this connection we have."

The words hung in the air, heavy with significance. Evan's gaze sharpened, an intense focus shifting into his features, as if he were carefully considering the weight of my confession. "You mean...?"

"Yes. I mean it. I don't want to hold back anymore." My heart raced as the words spilled forth, releasing the pent-up emotions I had carried for too long.

Evan's smile spread slowly, a soft light illuminating his features. "I feel the same way. I've been hesitant, unsure of how you'd react. I'm glad you said something."

Relief washed over me, mingling with the thrill of revelation. In that moment, everything shifted—the air felt lighter, the weight of uncertainty dissipating like fog under the morning sun. We spent the rest of the evening lost in conversation, our laughter intertwining with our hopes and fears, mapping out a new territory together.

As we parted that night, the world outside felt imbued with a sense of magic. The streetlights flickered like stars, illuminating our path forward. In the depths of my heart, I knew we were on the precipice of something profound. Together, we could craft a narrative that embraced our shared past while allowing us to dream of a vibrant future. With a newfound sense of purpose, I stepped into the night, ready to reclaim my story—one where love, creativity, and friendship intertwined to create something uniquely beautiful.

Chapter 4: Chasing Shadows

The glow of the computer screen casts a pale light across the dimly lit room, illuminating scattered notes and half-empty coffee mugs that have long since surrendered their warmth. Each flicker of the cursor feels like a heartbeat, resonating with my own as I sift through the footage, capturing the delicate dance between joy and sorrow. The film unfolds before me like a tapestry woven from the threads of lives lived, each frame a brushstroke in an emotional portrait that feels both alien and intimately familiar. The characters I've created, lost in their own spirals of love and loss, seem to beckon me closer, their whispers a haunting echo of my own tangled heartstrings.

I lean back, running a hand through my tousled hair, the weight of exhaustion pressing down on me like a thick fog. Outside, the vibrant city of New Orleans hums softly, alive with its own rhythm. The faint sounds of jazz drift through the open window, mingling with the distant laughter of revelers spilling out from a nearby bar. The air is thick with the scent of spices and the remnants of a summer rain, and I can almost taste the bittersweet tang of nostalgia lingering in my mouth. This city, with its rich tapestry of cultures and stories, has become a sanctuary for my creative spirit, even as I grapple with the turmoil within.

As the clock inches toward midnight, my mind begins to drift, wandering down paths lined with memories. The night Evan and I had shared, punctuated by the clinking of glasses and stolen glances, plays on repeat in my mind, more vivid than any scene I've captured on film. His laughter, infectious and warm, reverberates through the quiet room, pulling me into the depths of what could be. Yet, just as swiftly, self-doubt creeps in, a shadow lurking at the edges of my thoughts. What if the connection we shared was a mere flicker, easily extinguished by the winds of reality?

Just as I'm about to drown in a sea of uncertainty, a notification flashes on the screen, slicing through my contemplative haze like a beacon in the night. Evan wants to meet again. The words sit there, pulsing with an energy that makes my heart race and my breath hitch in my throat. A torrent of emotions crashes over me—hope, excitement, fear—all blending into an intoxicating elixir that leaves me reeling. I stare at the message, my fingers hovering over the keyboard, hesitating as the reality of it settles in. A chance to see him again. A chance to explore what lingers beneath the surface.

But then the waves of doubt rise again, threatening to pull me under. What if this spark I felt was just a flicker of my imagination? What if I'm holding on to a moment that never truly existed? I close my eyes, envisioning his smile, the way it lit up his entire face, how it made the world around us fade into a blur. The possibility of revisiting that moment sends a shiver down my spine, an electrifying thrill mixed with the gnawing fear of disappointment. Turning him down, though? That feels like slicing through my own heart, a betrayal of the hopes I've nurtured in the quiet corners of my mind.

With a deep breath, I pull myself back into the present, feeling the coolness of the desk beneath my palms, the rhythm of my heartbeat echoing in the silence. There's a boldness in vulnerability, a strength in allowing oneself to be open to possibility. I open the message again, letting the words wash over me, and begin to type, my fingers dancing across the keyboard with a newfound resolve.

"Yes, I'd love to meet. When and where?"

I hit send, my heart racing, the anticipation swelling within me like a tidal wave. What had begun as a simple exchange of text had transformed into a promise—a promise of rekindled connection and the chance to explore the uncharted territories of our past. As I lean back in my chair, a sense of liberation sweeps over me, mingling with the anxiety coiling in my stomach. The air is thick with the scent of possibility, and I feel as though I've stepped onto a precipice, the world sprawling out beneath me, full of potential and risk.

The next day unfurls like the petals of a blooming flower, vibrant and full of life. The city thrums with energy as I make my way to our meeting spot, a quaint café nestled in the heart of the French Quarter. The streets are alive, painted in shades of gold and green, the sun casting a warm glow over the historic buildings that line the sidewalks. The aroma of freshly brewed coffee mingles with the sweetness of beignets dusted with powdered sugar, beckoning me closer as I approach the café's wrought-iron doors.

Inside, the atmosphere buzzes with conversation, laughter punctuating the air like a melodic symphony. I find a table by the window, the view offering a glimpse of the bustling street outside, where street performers sway to the rhythm of their own making. As I wait, I run my fingers over the smooth surface of the wooden table, tracing the grain with a mix of nervous anticipation and excitement. My thoughts flit back to Evan, wondering if he feels the same heady mix of emotions. Would he remember our shared laughter and fleeting glances, or had it faded into the background of his busy life?

Moments stretch into eternity as I sip my coffee, its warmth soothing my fluttering nerves. Just as doubt begins to creep back in, the café door swings open, and there he is. Evan stands in the doorway, the sunlight framing him like a halo, casting him in an ethereal light. The sight of him sends a rush of warmth through me, igniting the embers of hope that I had carefully stoked. His smile breaks across his face, genuine and bright, and in that instant, the world outside fades away.

I rise to greet him, my heart racing, each step toward him feeling like a leap of faith. The air around us crackles with unspoken words, the weight of our history hanging in the space between us, both thrilling and terrifying. As he approaches, I catch a glimpse of the man I remember—confident yet somehow disarming, his presence a blend of strength and vulnerability that tugs at my heart. In that moment, I realize that whatever comes next, I'm ready to embrace it, shadows and all.

The café is alive with energy, a perfect backdrop for the gentle storm of emotions swirling within me. Evan strides towards me, his confidence radiating like sunlight breaking through a cloudy sky. I catch a whiff of his cologne, an intoxicating mix of cedar and citrus, that pulls me deeper into memories of shared laughter and whispered secrets. It feels as though the bustling noise of the café fades into a distant hum, leaving just the two of us suspended in time.

"Hey," he says, his voice warm and inviting, carrying the familiar timbre that has long echoed in my dreams. There's a spark of mischief in his eyes, a hint of the boy I once knew, but there's also a depth that speaks to the man he's become. It sends a thrill coursing through me, igniting that flutter in my stomach that I thought had been extinguished by time and distance.

"Hey," I manage to reply, my heart racing as we both settle into our seats. The waiter arrives, and after exchanging the customary pleasantries, I find myself watching Evan as he scans the menu, a playful smile tugging at his lips. He looks up, catching me in the act, and the moment feels electric, a palpable tension dancing in the air.

"What are you having?" he asks, his eyebrows arched in mock seriousness, as if our breakfast choices hold the weight of the world.

I chuckle softly, my nervousness dissipating slightly, and share my thoughts on the coffee and beignets that have earned their reputation here. As I talk, I see his eyes light up with interest, his attention fully on me, and for a moment, it feels as though we're the only two people in the room.

When our orders arrive, the plates are a work of art, piled high with fluffy, golden beignets that shimmer under a dusting of powdered sugar. I can't help but smile as I take a bite, the sweetness melting on my tongue, paired with the rich bitterness of the coffee.

It's indulgent, just like this moment, and I feel my walls crumbling a little more with every bite we share.

We reminisce about our time together, weaving in and out of old memories, each story sparking new laughter. Evan recounts a mishap from our high school days—an ill-fated attempt at a school talent show where he forgot half his lines while I nervously fumbled with my guitar, the moment so awkward yet hilarious that it now feels like a cherished relic from our shared past. As I laugh, I can't help but notice the way his eyes crinkle at the corners, the warmth radiating from him almost tangible. The world around us fades, and the air thickens with unspoken words that hang like the steam from our cups.

"Do you ever think about that time?" he asks, a hint of vulnerability creeping into his voice, his gaze piercing mine with an intensity that takes my breath away. "About us?"

Every fiber of my being wants to lean into this moment, to dive deep into the pool of nostalgia and desire that we're both skirting around. "All the time," I admit, my voice barely above a whisper, thick with the weight of my honesty. "It's like a song that plays in my mind, never quite fading away."

He leans closer, the scent of his cologne intoxicating, and I can feel the electric charge in the air as he confides, "I've missed you, you know? More than I thought I would."

My heart stutters at the revelation, a rush of warmth flooding my cheeks. "I missed you too," I reply, the words tumbling out with a clarity that surprises me. "Life got so busy, and I thought maybe those memories would just become... memories."

Evan nods, the understanding in his eyes a balm for the ache of distance that had formed between us over the years. "I always wondered if we could've been something more. If I had told you how I felt back then, would things have been different?"

The question hangs heavy in the air, and I feel a mixture of exhilaration and fear surging through me. What would it mean to explore that possibility now, in this moment, when the stakes feel so much higher? My heart races, the allure of what could have been tantalizing yet daunting.

As the conversation flows, we share details about our lives—what we've been doing, who we've become. Evan talks about his recent move back to New Orleans, his passion for photography ignited during his travels. I watch as he animatedly describes the landscapes he's captured, the way the light dances across the bayou, and I can't help but be captivated by his enthusiasm. There's a hunger in his words that reflects a depth of experience I had only glimpsed before, and I find myself leaning in, eager to learn more about the man he's grown into.

When I share my journey through filmmaking, I see pride flicker across his face. "You always had such a vivid imagination," he says, his gaze steady. "I'm not surprised you turned that into something so beautiful." The compliment envelops me like a warm embrace, nudging my insecurities aside.

Our connection deepens, tethered by shared dreams and unfulfilled possibilities. As the morning light pours through the café windows, illuminating our faces, I realize I'm drawn to him in ways I hadn't fully acknowledged until now. Every laugh feels like a thread binding us closer, every shared glance a reminder of the chemistry that once ignited between us.

The weight of the world outside feels distant, the chaos of city life muted by the sanctuary we've carved out in this corner café. Yet, beneath the surface, the inevitable question lingers: where do we go from here? As Evan leans back, contemplating his next words, I can see the flicker of uncertainty mirrored in his expression.

"What if we just... take it slow?" he suggests, his voice low, careful. "I'd like to get to know you again, see if there's still something here."

The proposal washes over me like a wave, stirring both excitement and fear within me. Taking it slow sounds almost too good to be true, a chance to navigate the complexities of our shared past without the weight of expectation.

I smile, feeling hope swell within me, tentative yet insistent. "I'd like that. A chance to rediscover what we lost... or perhaps, to build something new."

Evan's face lights up, relief flooding his features as he nods, the spark of possibility igniting in his eyes. "Great. Let's see where this leads us."

As we leave the café, the sun casts a golden hue over the streets of New Orleans, a vibrant tapestry of life and color. I step out beside Evan, feeling a sense of purpose stir within me, the world feeling full of potential. There's a lightness in my chest, a belief that we're not just chasing shadows of the past but forging a new path together, each step echoing with the promise of what could be.

In that moment, amidst the rich aromas of the city and the music that seeps into the very fabric of the air, I am ready to embrace this new chapter, hand in hand with the boy who had once stolen my heart and now offers a chance at rediscovery. With every step, the weight of my doubts lifts, replaced by the intoxicating thrill of possibility that hangs in the air, waiting for us to seize it.

Days melt into each other, the once-clear boundaries of my life blurring with the excitement of reconnecting with Evan. As I navigate the labyrinth of my thoughts, I find solace in the sanctuary of my work. Each frame I edit, each cut I make, pulls me deeper into the world of storytelling, where I can manipulate reality as I please. It's a welcome distraction, allowing me to explore the tangled web of emotions without fully confronting my own.

The office is dim, save for the bright glow of the screen, where my latest project comes to life. Shadows flicker across the walls like ghosts of the past, and in those moments of solitude, the weight of my memories feels almost tangible. I cut together scenes that dance between elation and despair, watching characters experience the kinds of love I have tasted but never fully savored. The sound of a piano weaves through my thoughts, a haunting melody that feels oddly familiar, as if it were the score to my own story.

Just as I'm about to lose myself in the cinematic rhythm, the familiar ping of my phone jolts me back into reality. Evan's message is a breath of fresh air amidst the suffocating clouds of uncertainty. He suggests meeting at a local art gallery, a space filled with vibrant colors and whispers of creativity. My heart skips, the flutter echoing through my veins. This feels different, electric in a way that promises more than our last encounter—a chance to explore not just the shadows of our past but the brilliance of our present.

Dressed in a flowy sundress adorned with a pattern of blooming jasmine, I catch a glimpse of myself in the mirror before heading out. The fabric flutters gently against my skin, reminding me that warmth and brightness are possible, that vulnerability can lead to growth. The streets of New Orleans are alive with the sounds of the city, the sultry air thick with the aroma of street food and the distant strumming of a guitar. As I walk, my thoughts whirl like leaves caught in a brisk autumn breeze, the possibilities ahead expanding and contracting with every step.

The gallery is tucked away on a side street, its exterior unassuming, a humble facade that belies the treasures held within. The moment I step through the door, I'm enveloped in a world of color and creativity. Bright canvases hang like windows into other lives, each stroke of paint a glimpse into the artist's soul. The atmosphere buzzes with excitement, conversations mingling with the soft strains of jazz wafting through the air, lending an air of intimacy to the scene.

My eyes scan the room until they land on Evan, his presence commanding yet relaxed. He stands near a vibrant piece that bursts with color, an abstract interpretation of a sunset. He seems to lose himself in its swirls of orange and pink, an unguarded look on his face that draws me in like a moth to a flame. As I approach, I can't help but admire how the colors reflect in his eyes, turning the deep blue into a stormy ocean, brimming with possibility.

"Hey," he says, turning to me with that same disarming smile that makes the world tilt slightly on its axis. "What do you think?"

"It's beautiful," I reply, gesturing toward the artwork. "It captures a sense of longing, don't you think? Like the sun is reaching for something just out of reach."

He nods, eyes brightening as he engages in conversation about art and its capacity to evoke emotion. I find myself entranced, his passion palpable, flowing from him in waves. We stroll through the gallery, pausing to appreciate the intricate details of various pieces. There's a painting that depicts a couple dancing under a starlit sky, their forms blurred as if caught in a moment of intimacy and vulnerability. It resonates deeply with me, and I share my thoughts with Evan, who listens intently, nodding in agreement.

"This," he says, gesturing to the canvas, "reminds me of that feeling of being alive, doesn't it? When everything feels possible?"

"Exactly," I reply, my heart racing at the truth of his words. "It's like being swept away by the beauty of the moment."

As we continue to explore, the tension between us shifts, settling into a comfortable rhythm. The air is charged with an undercurrent of unspoken words and shared memories, intertwining our lives like the vibrant threads in the artwork around us. I can feel the gap between us closing, the uncharted territory of our past beginning to map itself onto the canvas of our present.

Evan leads me to a quieter corner of the gallery, where a large window offers a panoramic view of the bustling street outside. We stand in silence, the world flowing by in a blur, while we remain anchored in our shared space. "What's been the most surprising part of your journey since we last saw each other?" he asks, breaking the stillness.

The question hangs in the air, and I consider it for a moment, feeling the weight of my experiences wash over me. "Honestly? Learning to embrace the unknown. I used to plan everything meticulously, afraid of what might happen if I stepped off the path I had created. But now?" I let out a soft laugh. "Now, I think I'm learning to dance in the chaos."

He smiles, and in that moment, it feels like a veil lifts between us. "I get that. I used to be so focused on the destination that I forgot to enjoy the journey. Traveling helped me realize how fleeting everything is. You have to savor every moment."

As we speak, our connection deepens, the air between us thick with the potential of what could be. I can't shake the feeling that we're both at a crossroads, poised on the brink of something beautiful yet terrifying. The thought sends a thrill through me, igniting a flame of possibility that dances just beneath the surface.

Evan's gaze drops to the floor for a moment, an unusual seriousness settling over him. "You know," he begins, hesitating as if weighing his words carefully, "I've thought a lot about us. About what we could have been if we'd just been brave enough to speak up back then."

The vulnerability in his voice resonates deeply within me, echoing my own feelings of longing and regret. "I've thought about it too," I admit, my voice barely above a whisper. "What if we hadn't let fear dictate our choices? What if we had taken the leap?"

He takes a step closer, the air between us crackling with tension. "What if we still can?"

His question hangs in the air, laden with promise and uncertainty. In that moment, I feel as though we're on the edge of a precipice, the abyss below filled with potential. I can almost hear the distant melody of our shared history playing in the background, urging me to take the leap alongside him.

"Let's not let fear dictate us this time," I reply, my voice steady despite the flutter in my chest. "Let's explore this. Whatever 'this' is."

Evan's eyes light up, the weight of the world slipping from his shoulders as a smile spreads across his face. "Yes. I'd like that."

As we step away from the gallery, the sun hangs low in the sky, casting golden rays that dance across the cobblestone streets. The world outside feels alive, vibrant, bursting with possibility. Hand in hand, we navigate the bustling thoroughfare, laughter and conversation flowing easily between us like a well-rehearsed duet.

In that moment, as the sun sinks toward the horizon, I realize that the shadows we once chased are fading, replaced by a light that feels almost tangible. The journey ahead is still uncertain, but I'm ready to embrace it, to walk alongside Evan as we explore not just the streets of this enchanting city but the uncharted territories of our hearts. Each step feels like a promise, a commitment to discovery, and I find myself grinning at the thought of all that lies ahead. The world may be chaotic and unpredictable, but within it, I sense the stirring of something beautiful, waiting for us to seize it.

Chapter 5: The Script of Our Lives

The café nestled on the corner of a sun-dappled street in Brooklyn exudes an undeniable charm. Its weathered brick exterior, adorned with creeping ivy, invites both locals and wanderers alike. As I step inside, the comforting embrace of freshly brewed coffee envelops me, mingling with the sweet scent of pastries just out of the oven. The wooden tables, each with their unique imperfections, tell stories of whispered conversations and laughter shared over steaming cups. Sunlight streams through the large windows, casting playful shadows that dance across the floor, creating an ambiance where time seems to slow.

I scan the room, my heart fluttering with anticipation. Evan, my oldest friend, sits at a corner table, his tousled hair catching the light, his forehead creased in concentration. He looks up as I approach, his eyes lighting up with a mixture of warmth and something more elusive. There's a familiar spark between us, one that has flickered and faded over the years but now flares anew. As I slip into the chair opposite him, I can't help but notice the slight tremor in his hands as he slides the screenplay across the table.

"Hey," he says, his voice low and tinged with excitement. "I've been working on this. I'd love to get your thoughts."

I nod, my fingers brushing the paper as I pick it up. The scent of ink and paper greets me, grounding me in this moment. I can feel the weight of his words, the emotional resonance behind each line. As I delve into the story, the world around us fades. The characters leap off the page, embodying the complexities of love and the bittersweet ache of longing. With each sentence, I'm reminded of our shared history, the laughter we once shared, and the pain that lingered in the aftermath of our separation. It's as if he's reached into my heart and transcribed the very essence of my experiences onto the page.

Evan's writing has always had a way of capturing the nuances of life—the small, almost mundane moments that weave the fabric of our existence. In this screenplay, I see reflections of our past: the lazy afternoons spent wandering through Prospect Park, the long nights filled with secrets whispered under the stars, and the heart-wrenching silence that followed our split. He crafts scenes of vulnerability and raw emotion, stirring a familiar ache within me that I thought had dulled over time.

As I read, I find myself lost in the rhythm of his words, my heart racing at the beauty of his prose. There's a tenderness in his portrayal of love that resonates deeply, pulling me back to those days when everything felt possible, when we were two souls intertwined, dreaming of a future painted in broad strokes of hope. The dialogue crackles with authenticity, evoking memories of conversations we once had, filled with laughter and unguarded honesty.

"Do you think it works?" he asks, leaning forward, his gaze intense and searching. I can see the flicker of doubt in his eyes, the way he clings to my opinion as if it holds the key to unlocking his aspirations. I can't help but smile, both at his passion and the vulnerability he lays bare before me.

"It's beautiful, Evan," I reply, the words flowing easily from my lips. "You've captured something special here. It feels real, you know? Like you've taken pieces of our lives and stitched them together into something profound."

His expression softens, and I can see the relief wash over him, mingling with a trace of gratitude. We dive deeper into the intricacies of the plot, the characters evolving in our discussions, shaped by our memories and hopes. Our hands brush as we reach for the script, and an electric jolt courses through me, igniting a warmth that radiates from my fingertips to my core. I'm acutely aware of the lingering tension between us, an unspoken bond that stretches across the years, threatening to pull us together once more.

As we talk, I can't shake the feeling that we are standing at a precipice, on the brink of something transformative. The fear of reopening old wounds dances in the back of my mind, yet the thrill of possibility beckons me forward. What if this was the moment we had been waiting for, a chance to rewrite our own story, to reclaim the laughter and joy we once shared?

Our conversation shifts seamlessly, moving from the script to personal anecdotes, and I'm struck by the ease of our connection. It's as if no time has passed since we last spoke, the years melting away like snow under the warm glow of spring sunshine. I recount a memory of a rainy day spent in a cozy apartment, where we huddled together beneath a pile of blankets, watching our favorite movies and sharing dreams for the future. He laughs, the sound rich and genuine, and I can feel the weight of our shared history binding us closer together.

Yet beneath the laughter lies an undercurrent of tension, a reminder of the fractures that once divided us. I can't ignore the shadows of our past, the moments that left us bruised and hesitant. As much as I want to dive headfirst into the depths of this renewed connection, I find myself teetering on the edge, fearful of what might surface if we go too deep. But then, just as quickly, I remind myself of the screenplay, the characters striving for love despite their scars.

"Do you think it's possible?" I ask, my voice barely above a whisper, the question hanging between us like a fragile thread. "To find our way back to each other after everything?"

Evan's gaze pierces through the layers I've built, and for a moment, the world around us fades into a soft blur. He leans closer, his voice low and steady. "I believe it is. Maybe we just need to be brave enough to try."

With those words, I feel the walls I've erected begin to crumble, each brick falling away as the possibility of a second chance unfurls before us. The café, with its warm hues and aromatic delights, transforms into a backdrop for our potential. The clinking of cups, the laughter of strangers, and the soft jazz playing in the background all become part of the tapestry of our shared moment.

In that small corner of Brooklyn, surrounded by the echo of our past and the promise of what could be, I take a leap of faith, letting myself believe that perhaps this was the beginning of a new chapter—one filled with the kind of love that can withstand the tests of time, heartache, and hope.

The atmosphere in the café seems to shift subtly as our conversation unfolds, an almost tangible current weaving through the air. The clatter of cups and the soft murmur of patrons become a distant hum, a backdrop to the intimacy we're rediscovering. I glance at Evan, his eyes alight with passion as he leans forward, eager to share more of his vision. Each word he speaks draws me closer, inviting me to step beyond the boundaries of the past and into the realm of possibility.

"Have you ever thought about what makes a story truly resonate?" he muses, his voice a mix of curiosity and intensity. "It's not just the plot—it's the emotion behind it, the little details that make it real."

I nod, contemplating his words. It strikes me how he's not just talking about his screenplay but also about us. The tender moments we've shared, the awkward silences, and the profound love that once intertwined our lives—they're all pieces of a narrative we've yet to fully explore.

With a playful smirk, I interject, "So, you're saying we need more character development? Maybe throw in a plot twist or two?" The playful banter hangs in the air, tinged with an undercurrent of tension that neither of us can quite name.

He chuckles, and the sound resonates in the small space between us, filling the cracks of our shared history with warmth. "Absolutely. Every good story needs a twist, right? Something to keep the audience guessing." His gaze lingers on mine, the implications of his words swirling like the steam rising from our cups.

As I return to the script, I find myself immersed not just in Evan's world of fictional characters but in our own unresolved story. The words leap off the page, alive with emotion, yet it's the pauses between them that speak to me the loudest. I can see our past etched in the narrative—the moments when we stood on the precipice of love, teetering between desire and fear, caught in the push and pull of circumstances.

"Do you remember that summer?" I ask, my voice dipping into a softer tone. "The one we spent at the lakehouse with everyone?"

Evan's expression shifts, the corner of his mouth lifting into a nostalgic smile. "How could I forget? We thought we were so grown-up, but really, we were just kids playing house."

A wave of warmth washes over me as I recall the long days spent splashing in the water, the campfire nights filled with laughter and secrets shared under a blanket of stars. "And you dared me to jump off the dock," I continue, laughter bubbling up inside me, "only to land in the lake and come up gasping for air."

"That was hilarious!" he exclaims, shaking his head as if reliving the moment. "You were so dramatic!"

The sound of his laughter washes over me like a soothing balm, and I can feel the distance between us begin to dissolve. "You were the one who was supposed to catch me, you know," I tease, playful yet earnest.

"True, but I never expected you to jump like that!" he replies, his eyes sparkling with mischief. The memory lingers in the air, a delicate thread connecting our past to this moment, reminding us of the joy that once filled our lives.

As the conversation dances between memories and laughter, I can't help but marvel at how effortlessly we fall back into this rhythm. The old comforts blend seamlessly with the new, each moment steeped in the possibility of what could be. I'm reminded of the screenplay's central theme—finding joy amidst the chaos of life—and I wonder if perhaps we, too, are standing at a crossroads, ready to rewrite our own narrative.

"Do you ever think about us?" I ask, the question slipping out before I can filter it, raw and unguarded. The café around us fades into a quiet hum as I search his eyes for an answer, the weight of my inquiry hanging in the air like the steam rising from our mugs.

Evan's expression shifts, the lightheartedness replaced with a thoughtful seriousness. "I do," he admits slowly, his voice steady yet vulnerable. "Sometimes it feels like we're two characters in a story, waiting for the next chapter to unfold."

I nod, my heart racing as his words echo in my mind. The prospect of exploring those uncharted territories of our relationship sends shivers down my spine. "What if we wrote that chapter together?" I suggest, my voice barely above a whisper.

A flicker of something passes between us—surprise, hope, perhaps even fear. "You mean..." he trails off, searching my face for clarity.

"Yeah," I affirm, feeling a surge of courage. "What if we stopped tiptoeing around the past and allowed ourselves to be vulnerable? To really see where this could go?"

He leans back, considering my words, and I can see the wheels turning in his mind. The café around us buzzes with life, yet in this moment, it feels like we exist in a world of our own making. A tension hangs in the air, thick and palpable, as if the very universe is holding its breath, waiting for us to take that leap.

"Okay," he finally says, his voice steady but edged with emotion. "Let's do it. Let's see where this leads."

A rush of exhilaration courses through me, igniting something deep within. In that instant, the script becomes more than just a collection of words; it transforms into a living testament to our journey—a journey we're both willing to navigate, no matter how rocky the path may be.

We settle back into our conversation, a newfound understanding illuminating the space between us. The café transforms into a haven of possibility, the aroma of coffee mingling with the sweet scent of pastries. We become storytellers, weaving a tale that intertwines our past with the present, stitching together the fragmented pieces of our lives into a tapestry vibrant with hope.

With every exchanged glance and shared laugh, I feel the barriers between us crumbling, replaced by a sense of belonging that feels both exhilarating and terrifying. It's the kind of risk that could lead to both bliss and heartbreak, but in this moment, I choose to embrace the unknown.

As the sun begins to dip below the horizon, casting a warm glow through the café windows, I realize that we're standing at the threshold of something profound. A story waiting to be written, a new chapter just beginning, filled with the promise of love and the hope that we can navigate the complexities of our intertwined lives.

And as we delve deeper into our shared memories and dreams, I can't help but feel that perhaps, just perhaps, we're on the cusp of creating the kind of narrative that resonates not only with us but with the world—one that speaks of lost loves, second chances, and the beautiful unpredictability of life itself.

The lingering scent of freshly ground coffee fills the air as our conversation deepens, wrapping around us like a comforting embrace. I take a sip from my cup, the warmth seeping into my palms, and I can't help but marvel at how the simplest of moments can hold such weight. The sun filters through the café windows, casting a golden hue over Evan's face, highlighting the subtle contours of his expression as he passionately discusses his screenplay. It's a stark reminder of the creativity that flows from him, a river of ideas and emotions that never seems to run dry.

As he talks, I let my eyes wander to the walls adorned with eclectic art—paintings that speak of the city's soul, images bursting with color and life. The café feels alive, each patron a character in a story that is uniquely theirs. I can't shake the feeling that we, too, are characters in a narrative, one that intertwines laughter with moments of silence, where the past and present collide in a dance of vulnerability.

Evan's laughter breaks through my reverie, and I refocus, captivated by the glimmer in his eyes. "You know, I almost didn't bring this," he admits, a hint of embarrassment creeping into his voice. "I thought, what if it's too personal? What if it's just a bunch of words strung together?"

"Personal is good," I reply, leaning in, my curiosity piqued. "That's what makes a story resonate. It has to come from a place of honesty."

He nods, his expression shifting to one of contemplation. "That's what I'm aiming for. I want it to feel real, to touch people in a way that makes them reflect on their own lives."

A comfortable silence envelops us, charged with unspoken thoughts and feelings, as if the very air vibrates with possibilities. I glance down at the script again, tracing the handwritten lines with my finger. Each stroke reveals more than just words; it unveils pieces of Evan's soul, fragments of his heart laid bare on paper. It makes me wonder about the stories we've yet to tell, the moments we've yet to live.

As the afternoon sun shifts, casting elongated shadows across the café floor, a question arises within me. "What if your characters don't end up together?" I ask, my voice barely above a whisper. "What if they find their way to happiness, but it looks different than expected?"

Evan's brow furrows, and I can see the wheels turning in his mind. "That's a twist I hadn't considered. But life isn't always about happy endings, is it?"

"No," I agree, feeling a sense of melancholy wash over me. "Sometimes it's about learning to be happy on your own, finding peace in the uncertainty."

He watches me, the weight of our shared history hanging in the air, as if we're both grappling with our own truths. I can sense the hesitation that lingers between us, the fear of revisiting old wounds, yet there's also a glimmer of hope, the promise of new beginnings woven into our conversation.

"Maybe that's what this screenplay is really about," he says thoughtfully, his gaze steady. "The journey toward understanding oneself, the beauty of self-discovery amidst the chaos."

I nod, feeling the resonance of his words. It reflects not just his story but ours as well. The ups and downs, the moments that once felt insurmountable, now unfolding before us like pages in a book we've yet to write.

"What about your characters' flaws?" I prompt, eager to push the boundaries of our discussion. "Flaws make them relatable. They can be messy and imperfect, just like us."

Evan grins, a twinkle in his eye. "Right! They should stumble, learn, and grow. That's the essence of being human, isn't it?"

A warmth spreads through me at the realization that we're not just talking about fiction; we're delving into the intricacies of our own lives, the flawed beauty that binds us together. The café transforms into a sanctuary of shared dreams and fears, a cocoon where we can safely explore the tangled web of our emotions.

In that moment, I decide to share a secret, a piece of myself I've tucked away for far too long. "I've often felt lost since we... well, since everything happened," I confess, my heart racing. "Like I was wandering without a map, unsure of where I belonged."

His expression softens, a mix of empathy and understanding illuminating his features. "I can relate. It's like we were two ships passing in the night, trying to find our way back to each other but drifting apart instead."

With those words, I feel a swell of emotion rise within me, and I'm grateful for the vulnerability that has blossomed between us. The connection we once shared, so vibrant and raw, now rekindled in the warmth of this intimate space.

"I think we both needed time," I say softly, the truth ringing clear in my heart. "Time to grow, to understand who we are apart from each other."

He nods, and a comfortable silence envelops us once more, filled with the weight of everything left unsaid. I wonder if he feels it too—the shifting energy, the magnetic pull that seems to draw us closer.

Just then, the door swings open, ushering in a gust of cool air. A couple enters, laughter spilling into the café, a stark contrast to our quiet introspection. I watch them for a moment, their easy camaraderie reminding me of the joy we once shared. Yet, as I turn back to Evan, the world around us fades into the background once again, leaving just the two of us suspended in this moment of rekindled connection.

"Do you believe in second chances?" I ask suddenly, curiosity pushing me to voice the question that has lingered in my mind.

His gaze locks onto mine, unwavering. "I do. I think they're essential, like breath to our souls. Life is too short not to explore the possibilities that come with them."

The air is thick with unsaid promises and whispered hopes as I process his response. I feel my heart quicken, excitement mingling with trepidation. "Then what do you think our second chance looks like?"

Evan leans forward, his expression earnest. "I think it looks like us being honest with ourselves, being brave enough to explore what's next. A story that isn't afraid of the hard truths but also embraces the beauty in the messiness."

"Together?" I whisper, the word hanging between us like a fragile thread, as if acknowledging it could tip the balance of everything we've built so far.

"Together," he confirms, and the simplicity of that word sends a thrill through me, igniting a spark that feels both terrifying and exhilarating.

I can almost see the plot unfolding before us, the twists and turns waiting to be explored. The screenplay becomes a metaphor for our lives—a canvas of uncharted territory waiting for us to make bold strokes, to create something uniquely ours.

As the afternoon sun begins to dip lower in the sky, casting long shadows across the café, I realize that I'm not just reading Evan's script; I'm beginning to write our own. With every shared glance, every laugh, every confession, we are crafting a narrative that is rich with the promise of redemption, laughter, and love.

The world outside buzzes with life, but inside this small haven, we are cocooned in possibility. The warmth of our connection envelops me, a safe harbor amidst the uncertainties that lie ahead. I feel ready to embark on this journey, knowing that no matter what obstacles we face, we have the strength to navigate them together.

And as I look into Evan's eyes, I see not just a friend but a partner in this grand adventure, one who dares to explore the depths of love, heartache, and everything in between. The script of our lives is still being written, and with each passing moment, it feels more like a beautiful work of art—messy, intricate, and undeniably ours.

Chapter 6: The Fractured Heart

The city skyline shimmered like a mirage under the golden hue of the setting sun, each building standing tall as if it were an unwavering sentinel of dreams and aspirations. I perched on the edge of my vintage armchair, the leather worn and familiar, enveloped in a cocoon of shadows and whispered memories. The air in my apartment was thick with the scent of chamomile and the faint aroma of the lavender-scented candle flickering on my coffee table, a small solace amidst the swirling tempest of thoughts and feelings. It was a Wednesday evening, but the pulse of the city outside made it feel like a moment suspended in time—a moment that I feared would drift away like smoke from the candle wick.

Evan's laughter echoed in my mind, a sweet reminder of our shared past that felt both comforting and threatening. It danced in the corners of my memory, teasing me with its warmth while reminding me of the walls I had carefully built around my heart. What if he saw me only as a reflection of who I used to be? The awkward girl with frizzy hair and uncertain dreams had transformed into someone more vibrant, but did that version of me resonate with him? My fingers itched to reach for my phone, to call him, but fear clamped down on my resolve like a vise, squeezing out any boldness that might have dared to take flight.

My journal lay open on my lap, a silent witness to the conflict raging within me. The pages were filled with the scrawls of my innermost thoughts, each word a thread in the tapestry of my evolving self. I took a deep breath, inhaling the calming scent of lavender, letting it wash over me as I dipped my pen into the ink of my heart. The words flowed, transforming my anxieties into a tangible release. "I'm terrified," I wrote, the pen scratching against the page, "of being vulnerable again. The world outside is bustling with life, yet inside, I feel like a fragile shell, ready to crack at the slightest touch."

As I continued to write, my emotions spilled onto the paper like vibrant paint on a blank canvas. I captured the ache of my insecurities, the haunting specter of doubt that hovered over every interaction. Memories of my first crush on Evan flooded my mind—his boyish charm, the way his eyes sparkled with mischief as we chased fireflies on warm summer nights. We were young and reckless, a pair of dreamers in a world that promised infinite possibilities. But now, standing on the precipice of rediscovery, I felt like a puzzle piece that had been flipped over, unsure of where I fit.

With each stroke of the pen, I unearthed the roots of my fear: it wasn't just about Evan. It was the haunting echoes of past failures, the weight of expectations that felt heavier than a mountain on my chest. I was afraid of being seen, truly seen, as the woman I had fought to become. The fear of rejection loomed larger than the skyscrapers that painted the skyline, casting shadows over my heart. What if he looked at me and saw only a ghost of the girl I once was?

In a desperate attempt to escape the spiraling thoughts, I leaned back in my chair, staring at the ceiling, searching for answers in the cracks that spidered across the paint. The flickering candlelight played tricks, morphing shadows into familiar shapes, as if my past were creeping back to remind me of what I had tried so hard to forget. The ghost of my younger self lingered there, begging for acceptance, for a chance to step into the light of understanding. I closed my eyes, willing the memories to fade, but they only intensified, a cacophony of laughter and unspoken words filling the silence.

I imagined Evan walking through my door, his tall frame silhouetted against the glow of the city. He would smile that lopsided grin that had always made my heart flutter. Would he embrace me as if no time had passed? Would he notice the way I had changed, the woman I had become, the battles I had fought to stand here, vulnerable yet hopeful? The fantasy was intoxicating, but I felt the pull of reality, a firm reminder that dreams rarely aligned with truth.

As the city buzzed outside, I found myself lost in thoughts of possibility. Maybe, just maybe, I could redefine my narrative. The heart that felt fractured could find a way to mend. It would require courage—a leap of faith into the unknown where Evan existed, a space where my fears clashed with the potential for joy. The possibilities shimmered like stars against a velvet sky, and for the first time in days, a flicker of hope ignited within me.

I set my pen down, the ink drying on the page, and allowed myself a moment of stillness. Outside, the streets were alive with the rhythm of city life, laughter, and chatter weaving a tapestry of connection. It was a reminder that amidst the chaos, beauty thrived. I took a deep breath, the weight of my insecurities momentarily lifting, and gazed out the window. The skyline stood like a canvas of dreams, each light a heartbeat echoing the stories of those who lived below.

In that moment of clarity, I realized that vulnerability was not a weakness but rather a courageous embrace of what it meant to be human. Perhaps it was time to take a step forward, to meet Evan not just as the girl he once knew but as the woman I had grown to be. The city pulsed with promise, and my heart began to beat in rhythm with it, daring to hope, daring to believe.

Each morning, the sun peeked through my sheer curtains, casting a soft glow across the room, illuminating the remnants of my late-night musings. The journal, filled with my confessions, sat nearby, its pages fluttering slightly as if echoing my unsettled thoughts. I would often wake to the rhythm of the city—a chorus of honking cars, distant laughter, and the soft thud of footsteps on pavement—an ever-present reminder that life marched on, relentless and undeterred. Yet within the confines of my mind, time felt like a molasses river, thick and slow, trapping me in a web of uncertainty.

Work had become a sanctuary, a place where I could lose myself in deadlines and projects, but even there, Evan lingered in the corners of my focus. His presence morphed into an ethereal phantom, hovering just outside my reach, tempting me to unlock memories that had long since settled in the past. Every time my phone chimed, a part of me leapt in anticipation, only to be met with the mundane—emails, meeting reminders, updates from clients—nothing that matched the electric thrill of what I felt when Evan was near. I could almost hear his voice whispering through the air, teasing me with echoes of our shared laughter.

One particularly overcast afternoon, I found myself seated at my desk, a cup of herbal tea steaming beside me, the faint scent of chamomile mingling with the fragrant air of my workspace. The muted glow of my computer screen flickered before me, illuminating the task list that felt more like a chain than a roadmap. As I clicked through my emails, I caught a glimpse of my reflection in the window, the muted cityscape behind me. My hair, tied up in a messy bun, a few rebellious strands falling out of place, framed my face with a certain disheveled charm. I smiled at the thought; if only charm could conquer insecurities.

The more I tried to focus, the more my thoughts slipped into daydreams—daydreams of laughter and late-night conversations with Evan, where words flowed as effortlessly as the wine we had shared, and each glance ignited a spark. There was a magnetic quality about him that had always drawn me in, like gravity pulling on my heartstrings. But that allure came wrapped in a heavy layer of fear, a weight that kept me anchored in the safety of the familiar, too terrified to take the leap into the uncharted waters of vulnerability.

As the afternoon light began to wane, casting long shadows across my desk, I decided to step outside, hoping that fresh air might cleanse my mind of the swirling doubts. The streets hummed with life, a tapestry of sounds and colors, each face reflecting a story of its own. I wandered aimlessly, letting the rhythm of the city guide me, the pavement warm beneath my feet as I traversed familiar paths that somehow felt different today. It was as if every corner held the potential for revelation, waiting for me to unlock the doors of my heart.

I found myself at a small café, the kind that nestled into the corner of a bustling street, where the scent of freshly brewed coffee wafted through the air, beckoning me inside. The walls were adorned with eclectic art, each piece telling a different tale. I settled into a cozy nook by the window, ordering a cup of rich dark roast, allowing the warmth to seep into my bones. As I sipped, I pulled out my journal once more, the blank pages inviting me to pour my heart into them like a painter with a canvas.

The café buzzed around me—laughter bubbling up from a table of friends, the clinking of cups, the barista calling out orders with an easy smile. Yet, even amidst the vibrant tapestry of humanity, I felt a distinct solitude, a sense of being both part of the world and an observer in it. I began to write, each word a step toward untangling the emotions that knotted my insides. "What if I'm not enough?" I scribbled, my heart racing with each line. "What if he sees the cracks and decides to walk away?"

Suddenly, a familiar figure caught my eye through the window, his tall silhouette cutting through the crowd like a lighthouse beam in a storm. Evan strolled by, his hair tousled by the wind, a warm smile spreading across his face as he caught sight of something—or someone—beyond the glass. My heart raced, a wild drumbeat echoing in my chest, as I fought the urge to bolt toward the door. Instead, I remained frozen, a statue in a moment that felt both exhilarating and terrifying. He paused, glancing around, and for a fleeting second, our eyes locked. In that instant, time suspended, the chaos of the café fading into a distant hum.

But the moment shattered as quickly as it had crystallized. He turned and walked away, swallowed by the throng of people, and the weight of missed connection settled heavily in my chest. I felt an overwhelming urge to chase after him, to reach out, to say something—anything—but the fear held me back like chains forged in doubt. I buried my face in my journal, the tears pooling in my eyes blurring the ink. Each droplet felt like a release, a small victory in acknowledging the vulnerability I had fought so hard to keep at bay.

I closed the journal, the blank pages now echoing with the emotions I had spilled. What if I could embrace that vulnerability? What if I allowed myself to be seen by Evan, flaws and all? The thought was both terrifying and liberating, a tightrope walk over a chasm of self-doubt. As I took another sip of my coffee, the rich flavor grounding me in the present, I realized that perhaps the journey was not about crafting a perfect narrative but about navigating the messy, beautiful chaos of being human.

With renewed resolve, I set my cup down and pulled out my phone, fingers hovering over the screen. My heart raced as I drafted a message, the uncertainty still nagging at me but tempered by the flickering hope that maybe, just maybe, this was the moment to reach out. Each word felt like a step into the unknown, but isn't that where the magic of life often thrived? I hit send, my breath catching as I watched the message disappear into the digital ether, a tiny ember of possibility igniting within me.

The days unfurled like petals, each one offering its own hue of uncertainty and hope. I found myself at a crossroads, where the weight of nostalgia danced alongside the exhilarating prospect of new beginnings. My message had been sent into the ether, and with each passing hour, my heart oscillated between thrill and terror. Was it brave or foolish to reach out? The café had become my refuge, a small sanctuary where I could blend into the background and observe life's intricate tapestry without drawing attention to my own inner turmoil.

I returned there the following afternoon, the sun spilling through the windows, casting a warm glow on the worn wooden tables. The barista, a quirky woman with vibrant pink hair and an infectious laugh, recognized me immediately. "Back for more?" she asked, her smile genuine, as she expertly prepared my usual—a creamy cappuccino topped with a dusting of cocoa powder.

As I settled into my corner table, I allowed the hum of conversation to wrap around me like a soft blanket, the familiar cadence comforting. I watched as people moved about, each absorbed in their lives, and I felt a sense of connection to their stories, each moment a note in the symphony of urban existence. It was an invitation to lose myself in the rhythm of the world, if only for a little while.

Just as I began to immerse myself in a novel I had been meaning to read, the door swung open, and a familiar silhouette stepped inside. Evan stood there, momentarily silhouetted against the golden light, as if he had emerged from a painting—a figure of both past and possibility. My breath hitched, the book slipping from my fingers as I tried to gauge his expression. Would he smile when he saw me? Would he wave, acknowledging our shared history? The air felt electric, crackling with unspoken words.

As he crossed the threshold, a rush of emotions cascaded through me—joy, fear, and an overwhelming desire to leap from my seat and embrace the very essence of our connection. But as his gaze scanned the room, I ducked my head, pretending to be engrossed in my book. The moment felt surreal, a delicate balance between wanting to be noticed and the safety of invisibility.

He approached the counter, ordering with that easy confidence that had always drawn me in. I watched him interact with the barista, his laughter ringing like music in the air, a melody that felt achingly familiar yet strangely distant. Just when I thought he might glance my way, he turned, heading toward the back of the café, oblivious to my presence. The disappointment settled over me like a dense fog, heavy and damp.

But then, like fate intervening, he paused, caught the eye of someone seated nearby, and then—miraculously—turned toward my corner. Our eyes met, and in that moment, the chaos of the café faded into a silent void. His smile bloomed like a sunflower reaching for the sun, bright and warm, igniting something within me. I returned the smile, a timid yet genuine gesture, the barriers I had built around my heart beginning to crack.

He walked over, his approach deliberate and confident, and suddenly, I was drowning in the depth of his gaze. "Hey," he said, his voice low and inviting, as if it were the most natural thing in the world for him to be standing in front of me after all this time. "Mind if I join you?"

My heart raced, and the world around us faded, leaving only the warmth of his presence. "Not at all," I replied, my voice barely above a whisper, the walls of self-doubt crumbling with every word spoken.

As he settled into the chair across from me, the comforting aroma of coffee enveloped us, and a thousand questions swirled in my mind, each one battling for dominance. We exchanged pleasantries, reminiscing about old times with a lightness that felt both exhilarating and foreign. The ease of our conversation came as a surprise, like slipping into a favorite old sweater—familiar yet somehow different.

"I saw your message," he said casually, stirring his coffee, the steam curling up like whispers of a secret. My heart stumbled at the admission. Had he really received it? Did it linger in his mind as it did in mine? "I've been meaning to reply. It's just... life has been a whirlwind."

"I understand," I replied, the weight of his words settling over us. "It feels like we're all racing against time sometimes."

He nodded, his expression thoughtful. "Yeah, it's like we're caught up in this current, trying to stay afloat, and sometimes you forget to reach out."

The vulnerability of the moment hung between us, raw and palpable. I felt a shift in the air, the subtle tension that spoke of uncharted territories and hidden truths. I could sense the potential crackling like static electricity, teasing me with the promise of something more.

"I've missed talking to you," he admitted, his voice steady yet soft, threading through the noise of the café. "You always had this way of making everything feel lighter."

My heart soared at his words, a blend of pride and longing intertwining. "I've missed you too," I confessed, the honesty spilling out before I could second-guess myself. "It's been... different, without you around."

A brief silence enveloped us, pregnant with possibility. The connection we had once shared felt like a fine thread, woven tightly yet frayed at the edges, waiting for the right moment to be pulled taut again. We exchanged stories, laughter spilling from our lips like the rain outside, each revelation peeling back layers of time that had distanced us.

But as the conversation deepened, the specter of my insecurities returned, lurking at the edges of my thoughts. What if this was a fleeting moment? What if I was just a passing thought in his life, a nostalgic remnant of a bygone era? I glanced at him, the sunlight catching the warmth in his eyes, and felt a pang of fear wash over me.

He seemed to sense the shift in my demeanor. "What's on your mind?" he asked, his voice low and soothing, like a gentle wave lapping against the shore.

I hesitated, the vulnerability rising within me like a tide. "I guess I'm just... trying to figure out what this all means. Us, I mean. There's so much history between us, but things have changed."

Evan leaned back in his chair, his expression contemplative. "Life has a way of changing us, doesn't it? But that doesn't mean we can't rediscover what we had. It's just a matter of being willing to embrace it."

His words hung in the air, a challenge and an invitation all at once. The café buzzed around us, yet I felt cocooned in this moment, an island amidst a sea of voices. Maybe I was ready to let go of the past, to open my heart to the uncertainty of a future with him.

As the afternoon light began to fade, casting a warm golden glow across the café, I made a decision. I would lean into this connection, allow it to breathe, and discover what it meant to us now. The fear would always be there, lurking in the shadows, but perhaps it was time to step into the light and embrace the adventure that lay ahead, together.

Chapter 7: Hidden Vulnerabilities

The dim lights of the indie theater wrapped around us like a warm embrace, the aroma of popcorn mingling with the rich scent of old wood and upholstery, drawing me into a world both familiar and exciting. The screen flickered to life, illuminating Evan's features in ethereal hues, his laughter mingling with the crackle of celluloid. As the opening credits rolled, I stole glances at him, each subtle shift of his face revealing the delight and intensity he brought to every moment. It was as if the film was merely a backdrop to the story unfolding beside me, a tale of two souls navigating their intertwined paths amid the chaos of life.

The first few scenes, laden with a blend of humor and poignant heartbreak, cast a spell over the audience, drawing us deeper into the narrative. I found myself leaning closer to Evan, our shoulders brushing against each other. It felt natural, an unspoken invitation to share more than just this cinematic experience. With every subtle movement, he became my anchor, tethering me to this moment, a moment that felt suspended in time. I had always known he was someone special, but sitting here, enveloped by the dim light and the gentle sound of the audience's collective breaths, I could feel the barriers I had built around my heart begin to crumble.

As the plot thickened, so did our conversation. During a particularly quiet moment in the film, I felt an urge rising within me, one that had been dormant for far too long. "Do you ever feel like you're just stuck?" I asked, the words tumbling out before I could fully comprehend their weight. "Like you're going through the motions, but not really moving anywhere?"

His gaze shifted from the screen to me, deep pools of understanding reflecting back. "All the time," he replied, his voice low, almost a whisper that demanded attention. "It's like trying to swim in quicksand. You exert all this energy, but you're just sinking deeper."

My heart raced, and I found myself drawn into his honesty, his raw vulnerability resonating with my own struggles. The movie continued to play in the background, but it felt as though the real story was unfolding between us, punctuated by moments of laughter and silence that spoke volumes. I could feel the warmth of his body beside mine, a constant reminder that I was not alone in this labyrinth of self-doubt and ambition.

"Sometimes I think I should be doing more," I confessed, a hint of vulnerability creeping into my voice. "I worked so hard to get where I am, but now it feels like I'm on a treadmill, running but not getting anywhere. I worry I'm not living up to the expectations everyone has for me."

Evan nodded, his expression a mixture of sympathy and solidarity. "I get that. It's exhausting, trying to keep up appearances. Sometimes I wonder if anyone really knows how lost I feel, how heavy this weight is." The flickering screen cast shadows across his face, revealing a depth that I hadn't seen before. His honesty was disarming, and I could see the remnants of pressure etched around his eyes, the lines of expectation and fear mingling with the flicker of hope.

With each revelation, I felt the walls I had so meticulously constructed around my heart begin to crumble. This was not just a night out; it was a chance to connect, to be seen and understood in a world that often felt isolating. As the film ebbed and flowed, punctuated by moments of laughter and tears, I felt a shift within me—a realization that we were not alone in our struggles.

We began to share fragments of our pasts, weaving a tapestry of experiences that painted a picture of two imperfect souls trying to navigate life. I spoke of my early ambitions, the dreams that felt so tangible in my youth but had since morphed into shadows of doubt.

Evan listened with rapt attention, his expression revealing a depth of understanding that was both comforting and empowering.

"Back in college, I thought I had it all figured out," I continued, my voice steady but filled with emotion. "I was so sure of my path. But as the years went on, it all seemed to slip through my fingers. I thought I would be in a different place by now, doing something meaningful."

"I get that," he replied softly. "It's like we set these timelines for ourselves, but life doesn't always play by the rules we create." His eyes sparkled in the darkness, a quiet acknowledgment of the shared chaos we faced. "I've had moments where I thought I'd found my passion, only to have it morph into something else entirely. It's scary."

Scary indeed, the realization that we were both grappling with the same fears, feeling lost in a world that demanded clarity and purpose. I could feel the energy shift, a warmth blossoming between us as we delved deeper into our vulnerabilities, uncovering hidden truths we had kept locked away.

As the film reached its climax, a scene of heart-wrenching choices and the bittersweet nature of love played out before us. I glanced at Evan, his face illuminated by the screen, and I saw not just a friend but a kindred spirit, someone who understood the labyrinth of uncertainty I had been navigating.

In that moment, something shifted within me—a spark of determination ignited by our shared fears and dreams. The connection we forged amidst the flickering images felt like a promise, an unspoken agreement that we would not only face our vulnerabilities but also rise together, hand in hand. The film may have been a mere backdrop, but it served as a catalyst for a deeper understanding, a reminder that we are all searching for connection in a world that often feels disconnected.

The credits began to roll, but I could hardly pull my gaze away from him. The laughter and chatter of the departing crowd faded into the background as we lingered in the afterglow of our conversation. I wanted to hold onto this moment, to wrap it around me like a favorite blanket. With every word exchanged, I felt the armor I had worn for so long start to slip away, leaving me open and vulnerable, but also incredibly alive.

The theater began to empty around us, the murmur of voices and the rustle of jackets creating a tapestry of sound that faded into the background. I was lost in the moment, still wrapped in the warmth of our shared confessions. As the last of the audience filtered out, I could feel the soft weight of Evan's gaze on me, a gentle nudge encouraging me to dig deeper into the recesses of my heart.

"Do you want to grab a coffee?" he asked, his voice laced with an eagerness that matched the spark igniting within me. The thought of lingering in his presence, perhaps prolonging this evening of vulnerability, sent a thrill down my spine. I nodded, unable to muster the words as a smile crept across my lips, an unspoken agreement dancing between us.

The cool evening air enveloped us as we stepped outside, a sharp contrast to the cozy confines of the theater. Streetlamps cast pools of soft light onto the sidewalk, and I felt the world outside awakening with possibilities. The vibrant energy of the city pulsed around us, as couples strolled hand in hand and groups of friends laughed boisterously, their joy intertwining with the delicate notes of a nearby busker strumming a guitar.

Evan led the way to a small café tucked between two larger buildings, its inviting glow spilling out onto the street. A bell jingled as we entered, the scent of freshly brewed coffee wrapping around us like a warm blanket. We settled into a corner booth, the rich wood contrasting with the eclectic decor of vintage photographs and art adorning the walls. I loved the cozy intimacy of the space, as if it held secrets waiting to be discovered.

We ordered our drinks, and I could hardly contain the flutter of anticipation that raced through me as I observed him, how he animatedly discussed the film, his hands painting pictures in the air. His passion was intoxicating, a balm soothing the uncertainties that had plagued me for far too long. As we waited for our drinks, I found myself increasingly drawn to him, every glance lingering a moment longer than necessary.

"So, what's the dream?" he asked, his eyes sparkling with genuine curiosity. "What do you really want to do?"

I paused, the weight of the question settling around us. It felt as if I were standing at the edge of a cliff, peering into the depths of my own aspirations. "I've always wanted to tell stories," I admitted, my voice barely above a whisper. "To create worlds where people can escape and feel something—anything. But I haven't quite figured out how to do that yet."

Evan leaned in closer, his intensity urging me to continue. "That sounds incredible. You're a storyteller at heart. What's holding you back?"

With a deep breath, I gathered my thoughts, the walls around my heart crumbling further. "Fear, I suppose. Fear of failure, of not being good enough. It feels like every time I try to carve out a path, there's this nagging voice telling me it's a waste of time. But talking to you tonight... it's given me a glimmer of hope."

A flicker of recognition danced across his face, and he nodded slowly. "I get that. I feel like I'm always trying to keep up with what everyone expects of me. Sometimes, I forget what I want for myself. It's like I've been living someone else's script."

I took a sip of my coffee, its warmth spreading through me, igniting a spark of courage. "Maybe we can write our own scripts," I suggested, my voice steady, laced with a newfound determination. "We can help each other find our paths. You with your dreams, me with mine. What do you think?"

The smile that broke across his face was radiant, a light illuminating the shadows that had lingered just moments before. "I'd like that," he replied, his tone earnest. "There's something about being vulnerable together that makes me feel alive."

We continued to share our thoughts, weaving between dreams and fears, as our coffees cooled on the table, forgotten in the haze of our conversation. Time slipped away unnoticed, as if we were suspended in a bubble, the outside world fading into a distant echo. I felt an undeniable connection forming, a thread binding our aspirations together in a tapestry of shared experience.

Evan's laughter punctuated the air, infectious and warm, wrapping around me like a favorite song. I discovered that his humor was as captivating as his sincerity, and I reveled in the way he effortlessly transitioned from serious discussions to playful banter. It felt as though every moment we spent together was a puzzle piece falling into place, crafting a picture I had longed to see.

As the night deepened, the café began to empty, but we remained, savoring each other's company like the last sip of a cherished drink. Evan leaned back in his seat, his eyes glimmering with mischief. "You know, I think we should have a storytelling challenge. We'll each write a short story and share it with each other. No pressure, just for fun."

I laughed, the idea lighting a fire within me. "That sounds like a blast! But just so you know, I'm not going easy on you. I've got some wild ideas up my sleeve."

"Bring it on," he replied, his confidence infectious. "I'm ready for anything."

We left the café, the night still alive around us, laughter mingling with the cool breeze. The world felt lighter, brighter, and somehow full of promise. I could feel the energy of the city thrumming through my veins, urging me to step beyond my self-imposed boundaries.

As we walked side by side, the streetlights casting halos around us, I could see the glimmer of potential in Evan's eyes. It was a light I had often sought in myself, and for the first time in a long while, I felt it reflected back at me.

"Do you ever think about how much our stories could overlap?" he asked, a thoughtful expression crossing his face. "It's wild to consider how two people can have such different experiences yet find common ground."

"It's comforting," I said, my voice softening. "It reminds me that we're all part of something bigger, even when we feel isolated. It's like we're all writing our own narratives, but sometimes those narratives intertwine in the most unexpected ways."

His smile deepened, and I felt a warmth bloom in my chest, a sensation that made the cold air seem less biting. We were venturing into the realm of possibilities together, a journey of exploration that transcended the fear of the unknown.

As we approached my apartment building, a mix of reluctance and excitement washed over me. I didn't want this evening to end, not when I felt so seen and understood. "Thank you for tonight, Evan. It's been... well, it's been everything," I murmured, the sincerity behind my words filling the air with an electric energy.

He stepped closer, the space between us charged with something unspoken. "No, thank you. I needed this, more than you know." His gaze lingered, and I could feel the tension between us crackle like static electricity, pulling me in, urging me to lean closer, to embrace this newfound connection fully.

In that moment, I realized that we were both searching for something—an anchor in a turbulent sea, a light in the darkness. And maybe, just maybe, we had found it in each other. As I turned to head inside, I glanced back one last time, the warmth of his smile wrapping around me like a comforting embrace, promising that this was only the beginning of our intertwined journeys.

The chill of the night air licked at my skin as I stepped into the warmth of my apartment, the door clicking shut behind me like a breath held too long finally released. The soft glow of my living room lamp painted the walls with a golden hue, casting long shadows that danced to the rhythm of my racing heart. I paused for a moment, allowing the remnants of our conversation to linger, echoing in the corners of my mind. It was astonishing how a single evening could unravel so many threads, revealing a tapestry rich with emotion and uncharted territory.

As I sank onto my well-loved couch, a sigh escaped my lips, the kind that carries the weight of both relief and exhilaration. I could still feel the warmth of Evan's presence, the way he leaned in to listen, his undivided attention a comfort I had craved without fully realizing it. The city outside my window hummed with life, the distant sound of laughter and chatter intertwining with the soft rustle of leaves stirred by the breeze. I allowed myself to revel in the afterglow of our connection, the exhilarating promise that we were exploring something deeper than mere friendship.

The prospect of writing our stories, of sharing dreams and fears, ignited a spark within me, a sense of purpose I hadn't felt in ages. I glanced around my cozy apartment, filled with the remnants of countless projects—sketchbooks piled high, half-finished stories whispering from the pages, and an array of art supplies that had long since collected dust. It was as if I had been waiting for this moment, the push I needed to breathe life back into my creative spirit.

With a newfound resolve, I grabbed a sketchbook and a pencil, settling into the nook of my favorite chair, the soft fabric embracing me like an old friend. I felt the weight of the blank page before me, a canvas awaiting my thoughts, a blank slate for the stories I had kept tucked away. I began to write, the words flowing like a river unleashed from a dam. My fingers danced across the paper, capturing the essence of my fears, dreams, and the exhilarating prospect of the unknown.

The following days unfolded with a vibrant energy. My interactions with Evan began to shape not only my creativity but my entire perspective on life. We exchanged texts, playful banter woven into messages that echoed throughout my day. Each reply was like a secret promise, a note tucked into my pocket, reminding me of the connection we were forging. He suggested we meet at our favorite café for a "storytelling showdown," a challenge I welcomed with eager anticipation.

When the day arrived, the sun bathed the city in warm light, illuminating the world in shades of gold. I arrived early, the familiar aroma of coffee and pastries swirling around me, invigorating my senses. I claimed a table by the window, allowing the sunlight to spill over the pages of my sketchbook as I prepared for our meeting.

Evan entered a few moments later, the sunlight haloing him as he crossed the threshold. His smile was like a burst of sunlight, brightening the room and igniting a spark of excitement in my chest. He slid into the seat across from me, his eyes alight with mischief. "Ready for a battle of words?" he teased, gesturing dramatically with his hands as if he were about to reveal a grand performance.

"Absolutely," I shot back, unable to suppress my grin. "Just don't cry when I win."

We exchanged stories, each more absurd and heartfelt than the last, our laughter bubbling over like the froth of our coffees. He told a tale of a cat that believed it was a lion, recounting its grand adventures in the neighborhood, while I responded with a whimsical story about a lost sock searching for its partner in a world where laundry was a magical realm.

But amid the laughter, the undertones of our vulnerabilities remained. Each story revealed snippets of who we were beneath the surface, bits of our souls woven into the fabric of our words. As we delved deeper into our storytelling challenge, I could see the masks we wore start to fade, revealing the raw, unvarnished truth of our dreams and insecurities.

"Sometimes I feel like I'm just a spectator in my own life," Evan confessed during a lull in our playful exchange, his voice tinged with an unexpected heaviness. "Like I'm watching everything unfold around me, but I'm not really a part of it. You know?"

The words hung between us, resonating in the silence that followed. I nodded, my heart aching for the boy who had shown me so much of his soul. "I know exactly what you mean. It's like we're on a merry-go-round, moving fast but never really getting anywhere. I want to jump off and run free."

Evan leaned forward, his eyes intense and earnest. "Then let's do it. Let's not just talk about our dreams. Let's chase them together."

The weight of his declaration settled over me, a palpable energy igniting within the depths of my heart. I felt an overwhelming urge to say yes, to leap into this unknown territory alongside him. "Okay," I replied, a smile breaking across my face. "Let's be brave, together."

After that day, everything shifted. We began to carve out time for our dreams, a ritual forming in our shared space of creativity. We met often, sometimes for coffee, other times for long walks through the vibrant streets of our city, where the sights and sounds inspired our stories. The world became a living canvas, and our imaginations ran wild.

One evening, while wandering through a quaint bookstore nestled between two bustling cafés, we stumbled upon a small poetry section. The delicate pages whispered secrets of love, longing, and life's intricate tapestry. As I flipped through the books, a particular collection caught my eye—a compilation of poems that spoke to the very essence of vulnerability we had been exploring together.

"Let's write our own," Evan suggested, his voice infused with excitement. "A collection of stories and poems reflecting our journey.

We can share our vulnerabilities, our triumphs. We can inspire each other and others."

The idea took root, blossoming into something beautiful. We spent countless hours brainstorming, each line an exploration of our hearts, each verse a testament to our growth. We sought inspiration from our surroundings—the lively street art, the soft glow of twilight settling over the skyline, the rhythm of city life that pulsed around us.

One fateful afternoon, while sitting in a park beneath the sprawling branches of an ancient oak tree, I caught a glimpse of something extraordinary. Evan had his head tilted back, laughter spilling from his lips as he recounted a particularly hilarious moment from his past. The sun caught his hair, turning it into a golden halo, and in that instant, I realized how far we had come.

It was no longer just about escaping our insecurities or sharing fears; it had become a journey of empowerment. We were unearthing hidden strengths, embracing the beauty of our imperfections. The words we penned transformed into a shared mission, a beacon guiding us through the uncertainty that had once felt insurmountable.

As the seasons changed, so did we. Each story brought us closer, weaving our lives together like a tapestry that could withstand the trials of time. I found myself looking forward to every moment we spent together, the thrill of creation becoming a language of its own—a dialect only we understood.

On the cusp of something magnificent, I knew our connection had blossomed into a bond far more profound than I had ever anticipated. The path ahead felt bright, illuminated by the flickering flame of hope we had ignited together. Whatever lay ahead, I was ready to embrace it, side by side with Evan, two storytellers crafting our own narratives in a world waiting to be discovered.

Chapter 8: A Torn Heart

The phone buzzes with an urgency that shatters the fragile peace I've tried to cultivate. My heart sinks as I see my boss's name flashing on the screen, a reminder of the world that waits just outside this tender bubble I've shared with Evan. I answer, my voice strained yet composed, an echo of the calm facade I've worn since the day I stepped into the demanding life of a book editor. The moment I hear the crisp sound of his voice, the weight of expectation presses against my chest.

"Hey, I know it's last minute," he begins, and I brace myself, the sting of dread curling like smoke in my gut. "But we have a pivotal editing deadline coming up. Can you dive in on this project right away?"

It feels like a boulder rolling downhill, gaining speed, and there's nothing I can do to stop it. I nod, even though he can't see me. "Of course, I'll get right on it."

Once I hang up, the world outside my window blurs into a wash of colors—green leaves shimmer under the afternoon sun, the distant sounds of laughter from the park below me intertwine with the faint hum of traffic. The very things that once filled me with joy now seem like distant memories, mere whispers of a life that feels just out of reach. I can't help but think of Evan's smile, the way his eyes light up when he talks about his latest project, and the warmth of his hand brushing against mine.

Regret creeps in like a shadow. I can't shake the feeling that I'm sabotaging something good, something delicate. Just as I begin to open my heart to him, allowing the walls I've built so carefully to crack, I find myself retreating, clinging to the familiar chaos of my job. With a sigh, I gather the scattered pages of the manuscript strewn across my desk, each one a reminder of my commitment to a career that, while fulfilling, often feels like a relentless treadmill of expectations and deadlines.

The days blur into a rhythm of late nights spent at my desk, illuminated by the glow of my computer screen, the clack of keys my only companion. I pour myself into the work, finding solace in the familiar dance of words and edits, but the truth is a constant ache within me. I miss Evan. I miss the way he looked at me as though I was the only person in the room, the way he made me laugh so easily, as if the weight of the world fell away whenever he was near.

Even in my darkest moments, I can't help but recall the sweetness of our last date—the warmth of his laughter as we shared stories over candlelight, the way the flickering flames seemed to reflect in his eyes, dancing with unspoken promise. It feels almost cruel that I must sever that connection, if only for a while, as deadlines loom like storm clouds overhead, threatening to rain on my newfound happiness.

My phone vibrates again, this time with a message from Evan. The simple text sends a thrill through me, and I hesitate for a moment before opening it.

"Hey, hope you're doing well. Just wanted to check in. Miss you."

A pang of longing strikes my heart, a bittersweet reminder of what I'm missing. My fingers hover over the screen, the temptation to respond fighting against the reality of my workload. I want to pour out my heart, to tell him how much I miss him, how desperately I wish I could let him in. But I can't. I can't let him see the chaos that comes with my responsibilities, the disappointment that accompanies my career.

I settle for a quick reply, a half-hearted smiley face punctuating my lack of real engagement. I worry my words sound hollow, like a fragile shell that could break under pressure. Each moment spent on my phone is a moment stolen from the work that looms like an insatiable beast, waiting to devour me whole.

As the week drags on, I lose myself in the labyrinth of revisions, immersing myself in the written word as though it might somehow fill the gaping void that Evan's absence has left behind. The sound of my coffee maker brews like a metronome, marking the passage of time as it becomes a ritual: rise, work, drink, repeat. The familiar aroma fills my tiny apartment, wrapping around me like a comforting blanket, but even that fails to dispel the coldness creeping into my bones.

In the evenings, I find myself staring out the window, watching the city light up like a constellation of dreams. I think of Evan wandering those same streets, the soft glow of the streetlamps casting shadows over his strong features. I picture him reaching for his phone, glancing at the screen, perhaps hoping to see my name light up, only to be met with silence. Guilt gnaws at me, a relentless reminder of my choices, my priorities.

I can't escape the sensation that I'm losing him, that this is the beginning of the end. It's a thought that sends chills racing down my spine, a haunting refrain I can't shake. Each day feels like a step backward, and I'm afraid I'll wake up one morning to find that the magic we shared has dissipated, replaced by a painful reminder of what could have been.

My heart is torn, suspended between the responsibilities I've built my life around and the delicate threads of connection I'm learning to weave with Evan. In the midst of deadlines and edits, the chaos that is my career pulls at me like a heavy tide, but I can still feel the flicker of hope, a small flame that refuses to be extinguished. All I need to do is find a way to balance both worlds without losing sight of the beauty blossoming in the space between us.

The glow of my laptop screen has become my constant companion, illuminating the late-night hours as I work through the layers of someone else's story. The characters leap off the page, each with their hopes, dreams, and heartbreaks—yet here I am, a spectator to their fictional lives, my own narrative lying dormant and unraveled in the silence of my apartment. I press my fingers against the keys, the rhythmic clicking echoing through the stillness, a soundtrack to my mounting anxiety. I glance at the clock, its hands mocking me as they inch closer to the deadline.

Each keystroke feels like a betrayal, a diversion from the warmth of what could have been with Evan. I picture him, leaning against the kitchen counter, his laughter spilling like sunlight into the dimness of my thoughts. The memory dances tantalizingly close, teasing me with the reminder of intimacy that seems so far away now. I can almost hear the echo of his voice, how it lilted when he spoke my name, a sound that had once felt like a melody crafted just for me.

Coffee cups stack up like tombstones on my desk, remnants of late nights and early mornings, each one a marker of the time slipping through my fingers. I take a deep breath, filling my lungs with the bitter scent, a jolt of caffeine that does little to dispel the fog settling in my mind. With every sip, I wonder if I'm running on borrowed energy, my spirit drained from the weight of responsibilities pressing down like an anchor, pulling me deeper into a sea of edits and revisions.

The door to my apartment creaks open, and I'm startled from my reverie. My roommate, Sara, steps inside, her presence a gust of fresh air that momentarily lifts the haze enveloping me. She tosses her bag onto the sofa with a dramatic flourish, her energy spilling into the room. "You're still at it?" she teases, peering over my shoulder at the glowing screen. "You're going to turn into a book yourself if you keep this up."

I manage a weak smile, the corners of my mouth barely lifting. "It's just a little deadline stress."

Sara raises an eyebrow, an expert at reading the unspoken layers beneath my words. "A little? I've seen you in a much better mood. What's going on?"

I hesitate, the urge to confide battling with my instinct to protect the fragile hope blossoming in my heart. But as she leans against the kitchen island, arms crossed, a look of genuine concern etched across her features, the dam within me begins to crack. "It's Evan. I'm pushing him away, and I don't want to, but this job..." My voice trails off, laden with unspoken fear.

"Have you talked to him?" Sara prompts, her tone softening as she studies me.

I shake my head, unable to find the words that would convey the turmoil inside. "I don't know how. I feel like I'm caught between two worlds, and I'm failing at both."

She steps closer, her expression shifting from playful to serious. "You're not failing. You're just busy. But you need to be honest with him. If he cares about you, he'll understand."

The truth of her words resonates, yet a fear of vulnerability holds me back. What if I admit to Evan how much I need him, only to push him further away? I turn back to my screen, hoping to lose myself in the text, but the words blur as I grapple with the overwhelming emotions swirling within me.

After Sara heads to her room, the quiet returns, but it's a different kind of stillness—one that feels charged with potential. I take a moment, the flickering light from my laptop casting a glow across the room, and I close my eyes. I think of Evan, of the way he brushed his thumb over my hand, the soft promises woven into our conversations. He's not just a distraction; he's a possibility, a chance to rebuild something beautiful from the ruins of our past.

Determined, I pull my phone from my pocket and open our chat. The cursor blinks at me, tauntingly waiting for me to take the plunge. My heart races as I type, pouring my uncertainty and longing into a message that feels both thrilling and terrifying.

"Hey, I know I've been distant. I've just been swamped with work. Can we talk?"

I hit send and feel a wave of relief wash over me, followed by a rush of anxiety. I want him to understand, to see beyond the surface of my chaotic life. The seconds stretch into eternity as I wait for his response, my fingers tapping nervously against the desk.

Moments later, my phone buzzes, and my heart leaps. "Of course! When?"

The simplicity of his reply is like a balm to my frayed nerves. "How about tonight? I'm free after seven."

His response is immediate. "Perfect. Can't wait to see you."

A smile blooms on my face, warmth flooding my chest. It feels like a new beginning, a chance to reclaim what I've almost lost. As I prepare for our meeting, I change into my favorite dress, a deep emerald that compliments my eyes. I run my fingers through my hair, letting the strands cascade over my shoulders, hoping to capture a bit of the magic I once felt when I was with him.

I glance in the mirror, noting the way the dress hugs my curves, how it makes me feel—confident, hopeful, ready to face the evening with a heart wide open. I grab my keys and step out into the cool night air, the city alive around me, buzzing with energy.

The walk to our usual spot feels electric, each step resonating with the anticipation of what's to come. The streetlights flicker like stars fallen to Earth, illuminating my path and igniting a spark of optimism within me. I can't shake the feeling that this conversation might be pivotal, a turning point in a story that's been yearning for resolution.

As I approach the café where we first shared our hopes and dreams, the warmth of the lights spills onto the sidewalk, inviting me in. I spot Evan seated at our usual table, his presence a beacon of comfort amidst the chatter and clinking of cups. When our eyes meet, a smile spreads across his face, and my heart skips a beat.

He rises to greet me, enveloping me in a hug that feels like home, the familiar scent of his cologne washing over me, grounding me in this moment. As we sit across from each other, the world around us fades, leaving just the two of us and the unspoken connection weaving between us.

"Thanks for coming," I say, my voice barely above a whisper, laced with the vulnerability I've carried for far too long.

He nods, his gaze steady and warm, encouraging me to dive deeper into the heart of what we both know must be addressed. The moment hangs between us, pregnant with possibility, as I prepare to unravel the tangled threads of my heart.

The café hums with a gentle buzz of conversation, the soft clinking of ceramic cups punctuating the air like a soothing melody. I sit across from Evan, the familiar warmth radiating from his presence grounding me in the moment. He leans forward, his eyes sparkling with a mix of concern and curiosity. The rich aroma of freshly brewed coffee surrounds us, weaving into the fabric of our conversation, offering a comforting backdrop to the emotional landscape we're about to navigate.

"I've missed you," he says, his voice low and sincere. The honesty in his gaze sends a shiver of warmth through me, igniting a flicker of hope amidst the chaos swirling in my mind.

"I've missed you too," I confess, my heart racing at the simplicity of the words. "I've just been overwhelmed with work lately."

"Tell me about it," he encourages, a gentle smile playing at the corners of his lips.

I take a deep breath, allowing the bustling café to fade into the background as I share my struggle—the relentless deadlines, the pressure to perform, and the guilt that clings to me like a heavy fog. As I speak, I feel the weight of my worries lift, the act of voicing my fears a small step towards freeing myself from their suffocating grip. Evan listens intently, his eyes never wavering from mine, a quiet assurance that I'm not alone in this.

"I don't want to push you away," I admit, my voice barely above a whisper. "It's just... I feel like I'm juggling too many things, and I'm terrified of dropping the ball on you."

He leans back slightly, a thoughtful expression crossing his face. "You don't have to do it all alone, you know. I'm here, willing to help however I can."

The sincerity in his voice sends a rush of emotion through me, and I can feel the tears prick at the corners of my eyes. This is what I've yearned for, a connection that transcends the chaos, a bond strong enough to withstand the storms of life.

"I know," I reply, my voice trembling slightly. "I guess I'm just learning how to let someone in after... everything."

Evan reaches across the table, his hand covering mine. The warmth of his skin against mine sends a thrill coursing through me, igniting a spark of comfort amidst the tension. "You don't have to rush it. We can take our time. I want to be here for you."

In that moment, I feel a shift within myself, a subtle transformation that whispers of possibilities. It's as if the air around us thickens with unspoken promises, a bridge forming between our past and the future we might create together. The café around us continues its lively hum, yet we're cocooned in a bubble of intimacy, where words flow like silk and every glance feels heavy with meaning.

"I'd like that," I reply, squeezing his hand lightly, anchoring myself to this moment. "I really would."

The evening unfolds like a tapestry, each thread woven with laughter and stories shared over coffee and pastries. I find myself lost in the rhythm of our conversation, forgetting the weight of the world outside these four walls. Evan shares anecdotes about his recent adventures, the excitement evident in his voice as he recounts the triumphs and mishaps of his art projects. Each tale draws me closer, the sound of his laughter a balm for the wounds I've been nursing in silence.

As the night deepens, I can't help but marvel at how effortlessly we've slipped back into this connection. The distance that had once stretched between us feels like a faint echo now, replaced by the magnetic pull of shared moments. I share my own stories, my passions for editing, and the joy I find in shaping narratives, feeling more alive with each word that escapes my lips.

But beneath the laughter, the truth still lingers—a quiet acknowledgment of the uncertainty that lies ahead. I can feel it, a thread of apprehension weaving itself into the fabric of our connection. What if I falter again? What if the weight of my responsibilities pulls me under before I can truly embrace this second chance?

Evan seems to sense the shift in my mood. "You okay?" he asks softly, his thumb brushing against my knuckles, grounding me in the moment.

I hesitate, the vulnerability of the moment wrapping around me like a shroud. "I just... I want to make this work. But I worry about the demands of my job. I'm afraid I won't be able to give you the time you deserve."

He leans in closer, his expression earnest. "I don't need you to be perfect. I just want you to be you. We'll figure it out together."

His words settle over me like a warm embrace, and I nod, allowing the tension in my shoulders to ease. For the first time in a long while, I feel the flicker of hope begin to take root within me, nourished by his steadfast presence.

As we finish our drinks, the café begins to empty, the clamor of voices receding into the night. I can hardly believe how much ground we've covered in such a short span of time. It feels like we're piecing together the fragments of a puzzle that had long been forgotten, rediscovering the joy of each other's company amidst the uncertainties that linger in the air.

When we finally stand to leave, I catch a glimpse of my reflection in the window. My eyes sparkle with a newfound determination, a glimmer of resilience emerging from the shadows of self-doubt. Evan steps closer, his warmth radiating like a shield against the chill of the night, and together we step out into the city that pulses with life around us.

The streets glow under the pale light of the streetlamps, casting soft halos around us as we walk side by side. Each step feels significant, an assertion of our choice to navigate this journey together. The vibrant sounds of the city envelop us—the distant laughter, the music spilling from nearby bars, the soft hum of conversations merging into a chorus of life.

As we stroll, I feel Evan's presence beside me, his energy intertwining with my own, creating an atmosphere of hope that fills the air. "What's next for you?" he asks, curiosity lacing his tone as we weave through the bustling streets.

I ponder for a moment, the possibilities unfolding like a colorful tapestry in my mind. "I think I want to explore more of my creativity," I say finally, a smile creeping across my face. "Maybe write something of my own one day."

He grins, a spark of enthusiasm lighting up his eyes. "I would love to read that. You have a unique perspective, and your words deserve to be shared."

His encouragement feels like a lifeline, a reminder that I don't have to navigate this path alone. The flicker of possibility ignites something deep within me, a yearning to embrace the stories waiting to be told, the worlds waiting to be explored.

As we reach a quiet corner of the street, Evan pauses, turning to face me. "You're going to be amazing. Just keep believing in yourself."

In that moment, as the city lights shimmer around us, I realize that maybe this is what it feels like to bloom after a long winter. The fears that had once stifled my heart begin to melt away, replaced by the warmth of connection and the exhilarating prospect of new beginnings.

I take a step closer, the space between us narrowing as I feel the magnetic pull of his gaze. "Thank you for being here," I whisper, my voice filled with emotion.

Evan leans in, brushing his lips against mine, a soft, tender kiss that sends a shiver down my spine. It's a kiss filled with promise and understanding, a silent vow that we're willing to weather the storms together. And in that moment, beneath the stars that twinkle like distant dreams, I realize that my heart is no longer torn; it is piecing itself together, stronger and more resilient than before, ready to embrace the beautiful chaos that life has to offer.

Chapter 9: The Breaking Point

As I sat hunched over my laptop, the dim light of my apartment barely illuminating the chaos of scattered notes and coffee-stained papers, a cacophony of thoughts invaded my mind. The clock on the wall ticked incessantly, each second a sharp reminder of the impending deadline looming like a storm cloud on the horizon. I'd been battling against time, grappling with my own inadequacies as I revised my manuscript for what felt like the hundredth time. Each keystroke echoed a mix of determination and despair, a constant tug-of-war between my ambitions and the suffocating weight of expectation.

The familiar aroma of fresh coffee filled the air, a brief comfort amidst the mounting pressure. I took a sip, the warmth spreading through my chest like a gentle hug, but it couldn't drown out the whispers of self-doubt that had taken up residence in my mind. I closed my eyes, inhaling deeply, trying to recapture the spark of inspiration that had driven me to write in the first place. The scenes I had crafted felt less vivid, the characters more distant, and the passion that once fueled my creativity now felt like a flickering candle in a raging wind.

But it wasn't just the deadline gnawing at my sanity; it was Evan. His laughter still echoed in my ears, a melody I couldn't escape. Memories of our late-night talks, filled with dreams and laughter, mingled with the bitter taste of regret. The weight of our last encounter hung heavy, like a thick fog that blurred the lines between hope and despair. The thought of losing him gnawed at me more than any missed deadline ever could. What if he couldn't see past my shortcomings? What if he decided I wasn't worth the trouble?

With each passing hour, my anxiety spiraled further. The bright lights of the city outside my window transformed into a blur, flickering like the flickering embers of a dying fire. As night draped its velvet cloak over the world, the city seemed to pulse with life, but I felt trapped in a vacuum, suffocated by my own doubts. The glow of the streetlamps outside cast long shadows on my walls, and I couldn't shake the feeling that those shadows were my fears, lurking just out of reach yet always present.

The following day unfolded with an air of dread. I was supposed to meet my editor, Rebecca, to finalize the last of my revisions. Her sharp wit and keen eye for detail had guided me through the maze of publishing, but today I felt like an imposter in my own skin. As I navigated through the bustling streets of Chicago, the chatter of pedestrians faded into a dull hum. I couldn't help but feel the city's pulse quickening in rhythm with my own racing heart, but it was a tempo I couldn't match.

When I arrived at the café, Rebecca was already seated, a steaming cup of herbal tea cradled in her hands. Her brows furrowed slightly as she looked up, concern etched across her features. I could sense her scrutiny, and it only deepened the pit in my stomach. The weight of her expectations felt like an anchor dragging me into the depths of despair.

"I hope you've made some progress," she said, her voice laced with a blend of encouragement and disappointment.

I nodded, forcing a smile that felt like a mask over my real emotions. "Yeah, I've been working on it. It's just—"

"Just what?" she prompted, setting her cup down and leaning forward, her gaze piercing through the veil I had tried to put up.

"It's a lot, you know? The edits, my personal life—everything feels so chaotic." The words spilled from my lips before I could rein them in, the dam of my emotions cracking under the pressure.

Rebecca regarded me for a moment, her expression softening. "I understand. But you have to prioritize what's important. Don't let the noise drown out your voice."

Her words resonated deeply, but all I could think about was the news I had received the night before. The stark reality that my childhood home had been sold, the very place that had cradled my dreams and my memories, hit me like a punch to the gut. I had always envisioned returning there, a sanctuary where I could escape the chaos of adulthood. Now, it was just another ghost from my past, a reminder of all I was losing.

Frustration bubbled inside me, and before I could stop it, I lashed out. "You don't understand! This isn't just about deadlines; it's about everything falling apart. My home is gone, my heart is a mess, and I'm terrified I'm going to lose Evan too!"

The words hung in the air, heavy with truth. Rebecca's eyes widened slightly, but before she could respond, I stood up, the chair scraping against the tiled floor. "I can't do this," I choked out, the tears I had fought so hard to contain spilling over.

I stormed out of the café, the cool air of the street hitting me like a rush of clarity, but it didn't erase the turmoil within. I walked aimlessly, the world around me a blur of colors and sounds, my heart racing as thoughts of Evan invaded every corner of my mind. What if he chose to leave? What if I pushed him away with my chaos?

Just as I rounded a corner, I froze, the familiar figure of Evan standing there, bathed in the warm glow of the afternoon sun. The world around me fell silent, the rush of city life fading into the background. In that moment, it was just the two of us, suspended in time. The emotions I had buried deep surged to the surface, raw and unfiltered. I wanted to run to him, to wrap my arms around him and spill every fear and hope, but I stood there, paralyzed by uncertainty.

His gaze met mine, and the vulnerability in his eyes mirrored my own. It was a moment charged with a thousand unspoken words, a collision of hearts that begged for honesty. I took a step forward, the distance between us shrinking, and in that instant, I knew that whatever we were facing, I couldn't let fear dictate my actions any longer.

The moment our eyes locked, the world around me faded into a blur, the noise of the bustling city dimming as if we were ensconced in a bubble of our own making. Evan stood there, his hair tousled by the wind, an expression of concern etched on his face that mirrored the turmoil churning within me. I felt a magnetic pull, an invisible thread weaving us together despite the chaos of my mind. Every step I took felt monumental, laden with the weight of everything left unsaid between us.

"What happened?" His voice was low, laced with a tenderness that threatened to unravel the carefully constructed walls I had built around my heart.

I opened my mouth, struggling to articulate the whirlwind of emotions that swirled within me. How could I explain the suffocating loss of my childhood home, the sense of being unmoored, and the fear that had settled in my bones? Instead, I took a step closer, the distance evaporating as I let the tide of vulnerability wash over me.

"I... I don't know how to do this," I admitted, my voice barely above a whisper. The confession hung in the air, a fragile admission that exposed the cracks in my façade.

Evan shifted slightly, his eyes searching mine, and I could feel the warmth radiating from him like a lifeline amidst the storm. "You don't have to do it alone. You've never had to," he reassured me, his hand reaching out, brushing against mine. The contact sent a shockwave of warmth through me, igniting a flicker of hope I had thought extinguished.

For a moment, we stood there, our hands intertwined as if we were grounding each other, a quiet acknowledgment of the chaos swirling around us. The realization washed over me that in our shared silence, there was an understanding that ran deeper than words. Yet, beneath the warmth, the insecurities still festered.

"What if I'm not enough?" I asked, the fear spilling out in a tremor, my eyes searching his for the answers I desperately needed. "What if all this—my writing, my life—pushes you away?"

His gaze softened, and he took a step closer, eliminating the last barrier between us. "You're more than enough," he said firmly, his voice unwavering. "I see you, all of you, even the parts you're afraid to show. That's what I care about."

As those words sank in, I felt a surge of emotions crashing over me like a tidal wave—relief, longing, and the realization that vulnerability was not a weakness but a strength. I had been so terrified of losing him that I had failed to see that the very act of letting him in could create a bridge, a way to navigate through the storm together.

"I've been so caught up in my own fears that I've pushed you away," I confessed, tears blurring my vision. "I didn't want to burden you with my chaos."

Evan's expression hardened slightly, determination etching deep lines on his forehead. "You think I wouldn't want to be here for you? That I wouldn't want to share the burdens, the joys, everything? You're not a burden; you're a partner, and we can face this together."

The sincerity in his words enveloped me, wrapping around my heart like a soft blanket, soothing the raw edges of my fear. I took a deep breath, grounding myself in this moment of clarity, feeling the weight of expectation lift just a fraction. We stood at a crossroads, and the direction we chose would shape our journey.

"Then let's figure it out," I said, determination bubbling up within me. "Let's confront everything that's been holding us back."

He smiled, a radiant light breaking through the clouds that had obscured my vision for far too long. In that smile, I saw hope, and with it, the possibility of something beautiful rising from the ashes of my uncertainty.

As we walked together down the street, the bustling life of the city surged around us. The sun peeked through the clouds, illuminating the pathway ahead with a golden hue. I felt lighter, each step carrying away the weight of my past, each breath filling me with newfound courage.

"Where do we start?" Evan asked, glancing sideways at me, his expression a mix of curiosity and warmth.

I thought for a moment, the gears of my mind spinning in sync with the vibrant energy of the city. "Let's revisit the places that shaped us," I proposed, excitement bubbling within me. "Let's go back to the spots that hold our memories, our dreams."

His eyes sparkled with mischief. "Like our first coffee date?"

"Exactly," I laughed, feeling a spark of joy flicker to life. "But let's not stop there. We can explore the city, let each place remind us why we're fighting for this."

With a nod, we set off on our impromptu adventure, weaving through the lively streets of Chicago, the rhythm of the city matching the newfound beat of my heart. We visited the café where we first met, the cozy little nook filled with the aroma of freshly ground coffee and laughter echoing from the walls.

"Remember when we spent hours talking about nothing and everything?" Evan mused, his voice a comforting melody that wrapped around me like a hug.

I chuckled, the memory flooding back. "I thought you were going to order a black coffee and just sit there in silence!"

He feigned offense, his eyes sparkling with laughter. "I am a man of depth! But I guess you saw through my coffee shop charade."

As we shared stories and laughter, I felt a wave of gratitude wash over me. Each memory we uncovered, every shared smile, began to heal the fractures within me. The past no longer felt like a heavy weight but rather a canvas painted with both joy and sorrow, each stroke defining the masterpiece of our journey.

From the café, we wandered through the bustling streets, our fingers still entwined, exploring the vibrant murals that adorned the walls, their colors bursting forth like the emotions surging within us. Each piece of art told a story, and as we paused to admire a mural depicting two figures embracing against a backdrop of swirling stars, I felt a profound sense of connection, as if the universe was urging us to embrace our own journey, imperfections and all.

With every step we took, I realized the power of presence, the importance of acknowledging the past without letting it define our future. I was not just a writer grappling with self-doubt; I was a woman rediscovering the strength within herself, the resilience that had been there all along, waiting to be embraced.

In that moment, I made a silent vow: to fight for us, to nurture the love that had blossomed amidst the chaos, and to write not just about my dreams but to live them, one day at a time, hand in hand with the person who believed in me even when I struggled to believe in myself.

The city felt alive around us, each bustling street and honking taxi weaving into the tapestry of our newfound resolve. As Evan and I meandered through Chicago, the weight of my earlier despair began to lift, replaced by the electricity of possibility. The buildings loomed tall and proud, their glass facades reflecting the sunlight like diamonds sparkling on a crown. It was as if the city itself was cheering us on, urging us to embrace this moment, to carve out our own place amidst the urban symphony.

We made our way to the riverwalk, the gentle lapping of the water beneath the bridge providing a soothing soundtrack to our conversation. The scent of blooming magnolias and the sweet tang of the nearby food stalls filled the air, creating a feast for the senses that invigorated my spirit. With each step, I felt lighter, my heart buoyed by the warmth of Evan's presence, the quiet strength radiating from him like a comforting light.

"Have you ever wondered about the stories hidden in the city?" Evan mused, his eyes scanning the vibrant skyline as if searching for secrets buried within its concrete walls. "Every building has a tale, every street corner a memory."

I nodded, feeling a kinship with his sentiment. "It's like a living storybook," I replied, my voice imbued with a newfound excitement. "And we're just characters navigating the plot."

He chuckled, his laughter bubbling up like a spring, infectious and genuine. "So, what's our plot twist? Do we run into an old friend, or perhaps an unexpected adventure awaits?"

A playful grin spread across my face. "Let's make it a quest for the best pizza in the city. I know a place that's supposed to be legendary."

With a nod, Evan matched my enthusiasm, and we set off, weaving through the throngs of people, sharing snippets of our lives like scattered breadcrumbs along the way. I recounted the chaos of my writing process, punctuating my stories with exaggerated gestures and dramatic flair, while Evan listened intently, a grin plastered on his face that made my heart race.

We arrived at the pizzeria, a cozy little joint tucked away between two towering office buildings, its neon sign flickering invitingly in the late afternoon sun. The aroma of baked dough, rich tomato sauce, and melted cheese wafted through the air, drawing us in like a moth to a flame. Inside, the ambiance was warm and inviting, decorated with memorabilia that told tales of the city's history—a relic from its past nestled in the heart of the bustling metropolis.

As we waited for our order, I felt a sense of comfort in the rhythm of our conversation, the banter flowing easily between us like a well-rehearsed duet. I could see the remnants of my earlier fears dissolve into laughter, our shared humor creating an invisible thread that stitched our hearts closer together. I had entered this day with a heart heavy with uncertainty, but with each moment spent in Evan's presence, I felt the burdens ease, replaced by a sense of belonging.

When the pizza arrived, it was a masterpiece—a bubbling medley of colors and textures, the golden crust promising the perfect balance of crunch and tenderness. The first bite sent a shockwave of flavor exploding in my mouth, and I closed my eyes in pure bliss, savoring the moment. "This is incredible!" I exclaimed, my voice muffled as I took another enthusiastic bite.

Evan grinned, his eyes sparkling with mirth. "Told you it was legendary. This place is an institution." He leaned back in his chair, a content smile stretching across his face as he watched me indulge.

As the meal progressed, the conversation shifted from playful banter to deeper reflections. We spoke of our dreams and aspirations, the places we longed to explore, the stories we yearned to tell. Evan shared his vision of becoming a photographer, capturing the world through his lens, while I revealed my desire to write stories that resonated, tales that would linger in the hearts of readers long after they'd turned the last page.

"I want my words to inspire," I admitted, the vulnerability of the moment electrifying the air between us. "To evoke feelings and create connections."

Evan's gaze intensified, the warmth in his eyes igniting a flame of determination within me. "You're already doing that, you know. Your work has the power to change lives. You just have to believe in it, and in yourself."

His words settled into the crevices of my heart, wrapping around the insecurities I'd carried for far too long. The more he spoke, the more I could feel the dam of self-doubt begin to crack, each word a gentle push against the walls I had built.

As we finished our meal, I felt an unshakable bond forming, a shared understanding that went beyond the surface. It was in the way we looked at each other, the soft smiles that danced on our lips, and the unspoken promises hanging in the air. We were in this together, navigating the complexities of life, love, and our own intertwined destinies.

With the sun beginning to set, casting a warm glow over the city, we made our way back to the riverwalk, our fingers entwined as if they belonged together. The gentle lapping of the water mirrored the rhythm of my heart, each beat syncing with the serenity of the moment.

"Let's promise to always face our fears head-on," Evan suggested, his voice steady, grounded. "No matter how overwhelming they seem, we'll tackle them together."

I felt a swell of emotion rise within me, and I squeezed his hand tighter, the warmth of his touch igniting a fire of hope deep within. "Agreed. Together, we can conquer anything."

As the last rays of sunlight dipped below the horizon, painting the sky in hues of orange and purple, we stood at the water's edge, the city alive around us, a kaleidoscope of dreams and possibilities. I inhaled deeply, the crisp evening air filling my lungs with a renewed sense of purpose.

"Can you hear that?" I asked, tilting my head slightly, as if listening for the whispers of the universe.

"What?" Evan looked at me quizzically, a smile still lingering on his lips.

"The sound of everything coming together," I replied, a smile breaking across my face. "It feels like the world is conspiring in our favor."

Evan laughed, the sound resonating in the air like a joyous melody. "If this is what a quest for pizza leads to, I'd say we're on the right track."

With a shared laugh, we turned back towards the city, a tapestry of lights twinkling like stars come to earth. It was more than just a beautiful city; it was a testament to resilience, to dreams fulfilled, and to love that could weather any storm.

Hand in hand, we walked into the night, our hearts open to whatever awaited us. The journey ahead would be filled with challenges, but with Evan by my side, I knew we could face anything. Together, we would carve our own path through the complexities of life, weaving our dreams into the fabric of reality, and writing our story one vibrant moment at a time.

Chapter 10: Echoes of Yesterday

The sun casts a warm golden glow across the mosaic of leaves, each one a brushstroke in nature's vibrant masterpiece. I take a deep breath, filling my lungs with the brisk, invigorating air, as I step onto the winding path of Central Park. The crunch of dried leaves beneath my boots is a symphony, punctuating the soft rustle of branches swaying in the gentle breeze. The world around me buzzes with life; children's laughter dances through the air, mingling with the distant sound of a street musician strumming a guitar. It feels as if the city is alive, pulsing with energy, and yet here I am, wrapped in my thoughts, tethered to Evan, who walks beside me.

As we wander deeper into the park, I catch a glimpse of his profile, illuminated by the dappled sunlight filtering through the branches above. There's a playful glint in his eyes that evokes the carefree days of our youth. It's hard to believe how quickly time has flown by, and yet in this moment, it feels like nothing has changed. We banter about everything and nothing, our words flowing effortlessly, as if we've never been apart. I can't help but recall the mischief we conjured in those halcyon days—sneaking into the local cinema, our hearts racing with the thrill of rebellion, sinking into plush red velvet seats to lose ourselves in the magic of silver-screen adventures. The films transported us to far-off places, igniting dreams and shaping our imaginations, and in their glow, we found a bond that felt unbreakable.

I let a soft chuckle escape my lips as I recount the time we smuggled in homemade popcorn and ended up with kernels strewn all over the theater. He laughs too, the sound a melody that warms the chill in the air. Each shared memory stitches our pasts together, and with every laugh, I feel those protective barriers around my heart beginning to falter. There's a sweetness in these moments, a reminder of the innocent connection we once had.

But as the laughter fades, an undercurrent of unspoken words hangs heavy in the air. It's there, lingering like the last notes of a forgotten song, nudging at the corners of my mind. I glance at him, and for a heartbeat, I catch the shadow of doubt flickering in his gaze. What unspoken truths lie between us, waiting for the right moment to unravel? The warmth of our connection feels fragile, as though it could shatter with the slightest touch.

We stroll past the shimmering waters of the lake, the surface a canvas reflecting the sky's brilliant hues. The gentle lapping of the water against the shore creates a rhythmic lullaby that draws me in. I pause for a moment, captivated by the sight of a pair of swans gliding gracefully across the surface, their elegance contrasting sharply with the chaos of city life just beyond the park's embrace.

"Remember when we used to chase ducks here?" I ask, my voice a soft thread against the backdrop of chirping birds and distant laughter.

Evan turns, a smirk playing on his lips. "I seem to recall you being more interested in scaring them than actually feeding them."

I roll my eyes, feigning annoyance, but I can't suppress a smile. "I was simply asserting my dominance in the animal kingdom."

"Dominance? More like an exhibition of sheer clumsiness." His laughter bubbles up, and for a moment, it's just us—two friends enveloped in the warm embrace of nostalgia, the troubles of the world forgotten.

As the sun dips lower in the sky, casting long shadows on the path ahead, the laughter dims, and a silence drapes over us. It's a silence that begs to be filled with the truths we've avoided. I can feel my heart racing, each beat echoing in the hollow space between us. The weight of unresolved emotions clings to the air, threatening to smother the joy we've briefly recaptured.

"Evan," I start, hesitating as the words claw at my throat. "There's something we need to talk about."

He shifts, the lightness in his demeanor faltering as he meets my gaze. "I know," he replies, his voice quiet yet resolute. "I've felt it too."

The acknowledgment hangs between us, a fragile thread that could either weave us closer together or unravel everything we've just begun to rebuild. The autumn leaves dance around us, swirling in a playful gust, and for a fleeting moment, I wish we could escape this moment, evade the conversation that lies ahead.

But we're not children anymore, and running away won't solve the complexities of our lives. The sunlight catches in his hair, illuminating the contours of his face, and I see the boy I used to know, but also the man he's become—someone who has faced his own battles, someone who still holds pieces of my heart.

"I never meant for things to get complicated," I murmur, the vulnerability in my voice betraying the bravado I've tried to maintain. "I just—"

"I just want to understand," he interjects softly, taking a step closer, his presence anchoring me amidst the swirling uncertainty. "I don't want to lose you again."

His words resonate deep within me, sending a tremor through the walls I've so carefully constructed. My heart swells with a mix of longing and fear, the familiar ache surfacing again, a reminder of the bond we've shared and the scars that linger.

"Neither do I," I confess, my voice barely above a whisper, yet it feels like the most powerful declaration. The truth hangs between us, shimmering with potential, daring us to take that leap into the unknown, to embrace the echoes of yesterday while forging a path toward tomorrow.

The golden hues of the setting sun seep through the branches, casting a warm glow on Evan's face, softening the sharp lines of worry etched across his brow. He takes a breath, and for a moment, the air is thick with unspoken words, each one weighing down the potential of our reunion. I wish I could sweep away the uncertainties that cling to us like autumn's last remnants, but some things refuse to be brushed aside, no matter how fervently I wish they would vanish.

"I remember the first movie we watched together," I say, breaking the tension with a fond reminiscence, hoping to recapture the lightness we shared moments ago. "It was that ridiculous superhero film, and you insisted on wearing your mom's old cape. You thought it would help you fly."

Evan chuckles, a sound rich and full, wrapping around me like a warm blanket. "That was an embarrassing day," he replies, a teasing glint returning to his eyes. "You were the one who tried to be my sidekick, but I still think you wanted the popcorn more than to save the world."

"It was a heroic mission," I counter with mock seriousness. "We couldn't let the villain win, could we?"

As laughter lingers between us, it feels as though the world around us has melted away, leaving only the two of us, suspended in a cocoon of shared history. But I feel the tension thrumming beneath the surface, a reminder that while our past may be filled with laughter, the present is tangled in unresolved complexities. I can see it flicker across Evan's expression, that blend of warmth and wariness, the desire to leap forward shadowed by the weight of what we left behind.

"Do you think we were happier then?" I venture, the question slipping out before I can rein it back. The park seems to quiet around us, the wind stilled as if waiting for his response.

He hesitates, eyes drifting toward the lake, where the swans glide in their serene dance. "Maybe," he finally replies, his voice contemplative, laced with a hint of nostalgia. "But we were also kids—naive to the realities of life. It was easier to dream then."

"Is that what we're doing now? Dreaming?"

His gaze shifts back to me, a flicker of challenge lighting up his expression. "Maybe it's time to stop dreaming and start living those dreams."

The sincerity in his words strikes a chord deep within me. Life has a way of smothering our dreams beneath layers of responsibility, fears, and expectations. The city hums with the rhythm of busy lives, people racing past with their own stories, and I find myself longing for something simpler—something real.

I step closer, the magnetic pull between us stronger now. "Evan, what do you want?"

He searches my face, his brow furrowing as though I've posed an impossible question. "I want..." He pauses, gathering his thoughts, and I can feel the energy crackling in the space between us. "I want to figure things out—to understand where we stand. I don't want to go back to being just friends if we can be more."

The vulnerability in his admission is disarming, and my heart skips a beat. There it is, laid bare between us—the raw honesty that feels as refreshing as the autumn air. I search his eyes for a flicker of uncertainty, but all I see is determination, a desire to bridge the gap that life has carved between us.

"I feel the same," I whisper, the words spilling out before I can second-guess myself. "But what does that mean for us?"

He exhales slowly, his breath visible in the cool air, and for a moment, I can almost hear the gears turning in his mind. "It means taking a risk," he says finally, a hint of bravado creeping into his voice. "It means trusting that we can be honest with each other, that we can explore this...whatever this is."

I nod, the concept swirling around us like the leaves that drift lazily down from the trees. Trust is a fragile thing, built on the foundations of shared experiences and honesty, yet often shattered by fear and misunderstanding. The thought sends a shiver down my spine, and I glance toward the horizon where the sun kisses the skyline, illuminating the city in hues of orange and pink.

"We have so much to navigate," I say softly, my heart heavy with the weight of the past. "What if we mess it up? What if we lose this connection again?"

He steps closer, his warmth enveloping me, and in that moment, I feel anchored in the storm of uncertainty. "Then we pick up the pieces together," he replies, a fierce determination burning in his gaze. "I'm not going anywhere."

The sincerity of his promise wraps around me, chasing away the chill that had crept into my heart. I want to believe him, to trust that this time, we can weather whatever storms life throws our way. "Okay," I finally say, my voice steadier than I feel. "Let's try. Let's be brave together."

A smile breaks across his face, one that reaches his eyes and lights up the shadows that had lingered there. "Bravery looks good on you," he teases gently, and I can't help but laugh, the sound bursting forth like a refreshing breeze.

As we continue our walk through the park, the world around us resumes its vibrant rhythm—the laughter of children, the distant sounds of city life, the rustle of leaves dancing in the wind. We are two souls navigating a winding path, ready to embrace whatever comes next, together. Each step feels lighter, the weight of the past loosening its grip, and I allow myself to imagine a future where we can explore this new terrain, where laughter mingles with the promise of something deeper.

And as the sun sinks lower in the sky, casting its last rays upon us, I know that this moment is just the beginning—an echo of yesterday merging with the infinite possibilities of tomorrow. Together, we can step into the unknown, hand in hand, ready to craft a story of our own, a narrative woven with threads of hope, laughter, and a courage that blooms anew with every shared glance.

The vibrant hues of the setting sun cast an ethereal glow on the park, each leaf seeming to catch fire as the day slipped into twilight. With every step we took, the crunch of foliage beneath our feet sounded like a muted applause, celebrating the unspoken promises lingering between us. Evan's presence felt like a tether, grounding me in a whirlwind of emotions. As we ventured deeper into the park, the laughter of children echoed around us, but it was the distant sound of a saxophonist playing smooth jazz that infused our surroundings with an unmistakable warmth, creating a perfect backdrop for what was to come.

"Let's sit," I suggested, motioning toward a weathered bench overlooking the lake. The water shimmered like liquid gold, reflecting the fiery sky above. As we settled into the worn wood, I felt the rush of nostalgia flooding back—this was our spot, the very bench where we had shared dreams and fears, plotting our escape from the mundane realities of life.

Evan turned toward me, his expression serious, yet his eyes sparkled with something deeper. "I think we both know there are things we need to confront," he began, his voice steady but tinged with uncertainty. "Things we've been avoiding since we started talking again."

The weight of his words hung in the air, thick and tangible. I swallowed hard, feeling the tension wrap around us like an invisible cloak. "What if we're not ready?" I replied, the question escaping as a plea. The thought of unearthing the past was as daunting as stepping into a deep, dark ocean without knowing how to swim.

"Then we take our time," he offered, his tone gentle yet firm. "But I don't want to tiptoe around it forever. We've both changed—grown—and it's okay to acknowledge that. I want to understand who you are now, just as much as I want you to know me."

I nodded slowly, allowing his words to sink in. The truth was, I felt lost in the labyrinth of my own life. The years had molded me into someone different—perhaps more guarded, certainly more cautious. But there was an undeniable longing inside me, a yearning for connection that only he could fulfill.

"What do you want to know?" I asked, my heart racing at the prospect of baring my soul.

He leaned in, an earnestness radiating from him. "Everything. What's kept you up at night? What dreams did you have that got sidelined? Who are you now when you're not the person everyone expects you to be?"

With each question, I felt the walls around my heart tremble, as though they were ready to collapse under the weight of my truth. I took a deep breath, gathering my thoughts like scattered leaves in the wind. "I think..." I began, my voice steadying, "I think I lost myself along the way. I got caught up in what everyone else wanted me to be—the dutiful daughter, the reliable friend, the perfect employee. I forgot about what I wanted, about the dreams I had when we were kids."

His gaze remained unwavering, and I felt a warmth spread through me, the knowledge that he was genuinely listening, truly invested in the conversation. "And what about now?" he asked softly. "What do you want?"

The question hung in the air, heavy yet liberating. I had spent so much time avoiding the answer, fearing it might lead me down an uncertain path. "I want to rediscover myself," I admitted, the words tumbling out before I could hold them back. "I want to create, to travel, to feel alive again. I want..." I hesitated, my heart pounding as I faced the vulnerability of my desires. "I want to be brave enough to pursue my passions, whatever they may be."

Evan nodded, a soft smile breaking across his face. "That's a beautiful desire. And you're already being brave by just saying it out loud."

I felt my cheeks flush, a mix of embarrassment and gratitude. His acceptance felt like a salve to the wounds I had carried for far too long. "What about you?" I pressed, eager to turn the focus back to him. "What do you want?"

For a moment, he looked away, lost in thought. "I want to stop living in the shadows of my own expectations," he finally confessed. "I want to create something meaningful, to take risks without fearing the outcome. I want to reclaim the dreams I buried beneath responsibilities."

As he spoke, I noticed the flicker of determination in his eyes, the same spark that had drawn me to him all those years ago. The idea that we both stood at the precipice of rediscovery filled me with an intoxicating sense of hope.

"I think we can help each other," I suggested, feeling a rush of excitement course through me. "If we're brave enough to take that leap, to support each other, maybe we can carve out new paths together."

His smile widened, and the warmth radiating from him felt like sunlight breaking through clouds. "I would love that," he replied, his voice steady. "Let's be each other's cheerleaders, holding each other accountable while we chase those dreams."

As we spoke, the sun dipped below the horizon, painting the sky in shades of indigo and deep violet, as if nature itself was celebrating our newfound resolve. The air turned cooler, but a cozy warmth settled around us, cocooning us in the hope of fresh beginnings.

"Let's promise to meet here, regularly," I proposed, my heart swelling with anticipation. "We can share our progress, our setbacks, and everything in between."

"I promise," he replied, sincerity lacing his words. "I'll be here, right where it all began."

As the last light of day surrendered to the encroaching night, I felt a surge of gratitude for this moment, for this connection. The bustling city felt distant, almost like a dream, as the park enveloped us in its tranquil embrace.

We lingered for a while, side by side on that familiar bench, our fingers brushing against each other, sending sparks of electricity coursing through my veins. The night deepened, wrapping the world in shadows, but it also ignited a flicker of something bright within me—hope, connection, and the promise of new beginnings.

With the stars beginning to twinkle overhead, I knew this was more than just a moment of reconnection; it was a declaration. A promise that we wouldn't shy away from the ghosts of our pasts, but instead face them head-on, ready to forge a future infused with laughter, adventure, and perhaps even love.

As we rose to leave, I felt lighter, as though I had shed layers of doubt and fear. The road ahead was uncertain, but with Evan beside me, I felt ready to embrace the unknown. Together, we would navigate this vibrant world, filled with echoes of yesterday and the promise of tomorrow, hand in hand, heart to heart, ready to create a story uniquely our own.

Chapter 11: The Ghost of Regrets

The city was awash in a velvet twilight, the kind that wrapped around the buildings like a comforting shawl, yet reminded me of all the warmth I could lose. I sat at my cluttered desk, the glow from my laptop casting a soft light that felt both inviting and isolating, a flickering flame battling the encroaching shadows of doubt. My apartment, a quirky little haven nestled in the heart of downtown Chicago, was alive with memories. Each creak of the floorboards whispered tales of late-night laughter and long conversations, punctuated by the vibrant nightlife thrumming just outside my window. Yet, despite the rhythm of life surrounding me, an uneasy silence loomed in the corners of my heart, echoing the uncertainty that had nestled in the depths of my being since Evan reentered my life.

The romantic film I was editing, a montage of fleeting glances and bittersweet moments, mirrored my turmoil with unnerving accuracy. As I scrolled through frames of lovers entwined in passionate embraces and bittersweet farewells, I felt a pang of envy coupled with dread. Their stories, woven with the threads of hope and despair, became a reflection of my own tangled narrative. Every lingering shot of a soft touch or a whispered promise resonated with the fear that my own heart was bound to the shackles of the past. I desperately wanted to lose myself in the art, but my mind continually drifted back to him, the magnetic pull of Evan's presence in my life reminding me of the fragility of happiness.

The air was thick with the scent of freshly brewed coffee, remnants of my third cup that evening, a lifeline to keep my exhaustion at bay. Outside, the hustle of the city pulsed like a heartbeat, neon lights flickering in sync with the rhythm of my thoughts. I let my gaze wander to the window, where the world outside was draped in hues of indigo and gold, the distant sounds of laughter and music drifting in like an intoxicating lullaby. It was a reminder that life moved on, relentlessly, while I remained trapped in a web of fears that clung to me like a second skin.

"Are you in there?" The voice was soft yet filled with warmth, a melody I could recognize anywhere. I turned to see Evan leaning against the doorframe, a smirk playing at the corners of his lips. He had a way of sneaking up on me, catching me off guard just when I thought I had my walls firmly in place. His dark hair, tousled yet intentional, framed a face that held the kind of familiarity that felt like coming home. The warmth of his gaze grounded me, a lifeline in a sea of chaos.

"Just drowning in the world of love stories," I replied, attempting a lightheartedness I didn't fully feel. He crossed the room, the air between us crackling with an unspoken tension that had become our new normal. Each interaction was a dance of vulnerability and guardedness, a balance between wanting to be close and fearing the potential heartbreak.

"Do you need a distraction?" he asked, his tone teasing yet sincere. I glanced at the montage on the screen, the characters caught in their own struggles, and felt a rush of emotions that I couldn't quite articulate. The last thing I wanted was to bring him into my mess, yet the thought of him leaving—of losing him again—sent a chill spiraling through me.

"Maybe," I murmured, biting my lip as I searched for the right words. I wanted to share my fears, but the words felt stuck in my throat, an echo of the regrets that threatened to spill over. Instead, I gestured toward the couch, inviting him to join me in the soft glow of the screen, the warmth of his presence a welcome distraction from the chaos in my mind.

As he settled beside me, our shoulders brushed, igniting a familiar spark that ignited a warmth in my chest. We fell into a comfortable silence, the montage continuing to play as I subconsciously leaned closer, drawn to him like a moth to a flame. I wanted to lose myself in the moment, to forget the tangled web of my thoughts, but the underlying fear of loss clawed at the edges of my mind.

"Have you ever regretted something so much it keeps you awake at night?" I asked, the words spilling out before I could stop them. It was a vulnerability I hadn't intended to reveal, yet there it was, raw and unfiltered. Evan's brow furrowed slightly as he considered my question, the light from the screen casting a gentle glow on his face, illuminating the depths of his expression.

"Every day," he replied, his voice low and sincere. "But I've learned that regrets are part of life. They shape us, mold us into who we are meant to become." There was a wisdom in his words, a calm assurance that I longed to absorb. He turned to me, his gaze penetrating, as if he could see right through the barriers I had carefully constructed. "What's haunting you, really?"

The question hung in the air, heavy with significance. I took a breath, feeling the weight of my unspoken fears pressing against my chest like an anchor pulling me deeper into the abyss. I glanced back at the screen, where a couple shared a heart-wrenching goodbye, and for a fleeting moment, I felt that same sense of impending loss wrapping around my heart. Would I, too, find myself at a crossroads, forced to confront the consequences of my past?

"I'm just scared," I confessed, my voice barely above a whisper. "Scared of losing you again, of letting my past mistakes dictate my future." The admission felt like a release, a crack in the armor I had built around my heart, allowing the light to seep in, albeit cautiously.

Evan's expression softened, his hand finding mine, our fingers intertwining in a gesture that felt both grounding and electrifying. "You won't lose me," he promised, his voice steady and reassuring. "We all have ghosts from our past. But it's how we confront them that defines who we become."

As his words hung in the air, a flicker of hope ignited within me, battling against the shadows of regret that had threatened to consume my spirit. Perhaps, in this moment, amidst the swirl of vibrant memories and the soft glow of the screen, I could begin to confront the truths I had buried deep within. I could redefine my narrative, one frame at a time, and maybe, just maybe, reclaim the happiness I so desperately craved.

The warmth of Evan's hand lingered on mine like a whispered promise, a tangible reassurance against the tumult swirling within me. I stole a glance at him, his features softened by the flickering light from the laptop, casting shadows that danced across his jawline, making him appear almost ethereal. The montage continued, weaving together moments of joy and heartbreak that felt alarmingly familiar, each frame striking a chord within my heart. But it was in the comfort of his presence that I felt a flicker of courage, the kind that could pierce through the gloom of my uncertainties.

"I've spent so long running from my past," I confessed, my voice barely above a murmur, as though I were afraid to disturb the fragile peace we had found. "Every time I think I've moved on, it feels like I'm tethered to my regrets. They cling to me like shadows, refusing to fade away." I paused, searching his face for understanding. "I don't want them to creep into what we have now."

Evan turned fully towards me, his dark eyes reflecting a mix of empathy and determination. "You don't have to carry that weight alone," he said, his tone earnest, a lifeline in a sea of self-doubt. "Facing our ghosts doesn't mean we have to do it all at once. It's about taking those small steps towards understanding." The softness of his words wrapped around me, encouraging me to peel back the layers of my guarded heart.

I inhaled deeply, feeling the heaviness of my past pressing against my chest, yet a part of me was drawn to the idea of unpacking it. The film played on, yet the plot blurred as I became lost in my own thoughts, imagining the ghostly figures of my regrets, each one flickering into view like the grainy footage of a forgotten film reel. There was the ghost of a career choice made in haste, the shadows of friendships that had frayed and faded, and most haunting of all, the memory of love lost too soon. Each memory was a thread woven into the fabric of my identity, a tapestry that had been stitched together with both pain and beauty.

Evan squeezed my hand gently, snapping me back to the present. "You're not defined by those choices. They're part of your story, not the entire narrative," he said. "What matters is how you choose to move forward. Embrace those lessons and let them guide you, not haunt you."

His words echoed in my mind like a soothing balm, and for the first time in a long while, I felt a flicker of hope. Maybe it was possible to rewrite my story, to allow the past to inform my future without controlling it. A smile crept onto my lips, a wry acknowledgment of the complexity of emotions swirling within me. "You make it sound so easy," I replied, a teasing note in my voice. "Just embrace the lessons and let it go? Sounds simple enough."

"Life rarely is," he countered, his smile infectious, lightening the atmosphere as the montage shifted to a scene of a couple sharing an intimate dance. The camera captured every subtle movement—the way their bodies swayed in harmony, the gentle laughter that punctuated their moments. Watching it, I felt a pang of longing, not just for romance, but for connection, for a shared experience that felt genuine and transformative.

As I leaned into Evan, letting the warmth of his presence seep into my bones, I was struck by the realization that he embodied that connection I craved. He was here, willing to share this journey with me, ready to face the ghosts together. "What if I took those small steps?" I pondered aloud, allowing the idea to settle into the spaces between us. "What if I actually confronted the parts of my past that terrify me?"

Evan's expression brightened, and he nodded encouragingly. "Let's start with one. Maybe something manageable, something you can explore without feeling overwhelmed." The challenge hung between us, ripe with potential. It felt like standing on the precipice of a cliff, ready to leap into the unknown, the wind whispering promises of freedom and growth.

I closed my eyes, picturing the ghosts I would face. Perhaps it was time to revisit the choices I had made, to sift through the tangled mess of my experiences and understand what they had taught me. One memory stood out like a beacon amid the fog: the choice to leave my hometown in search of something greater, the bittersweet farewell to friendships that had shaped my youth. That decision had seemed so clear-cut then, yet in retrospect, it felt like the first crack in the foundation of who I was.

"Okay," I said, my voice steadier now, fueled by the connection we shared. "Let's start there. I want to understand why I made that choice, how it changed me." The admission felt liberating, a first step into a journey that promised self-discovery.

"Good," Evan replied, his voice rich with encouragement. "I'll be right here with you." There was a warmth in his eyes, a promise of support that settled over me like a comforting blanket, chasing away the lingering chill of fear.

As the film played on, the soundtrack shifted to a haunting melody, enhancing the emotion of the montage. I felt the weight of my past pressing against my chest, but it no longer felt suffocating. Instead, it felt like an invitation—an invitation to explore, to understand, to redefine what my past meant for my future.

"Let's talk about it," I suggested, a new sense of determination blossoming within me. "I can start by recalling the night I left, the moment I decided to chase my dreams. I want to remember everything—the laughter, the tears, the fear. It was a part of me, after all."

Evan leaned back, attentive, ready to guide me through the labyrinth of my memories. "And I'll be here to listen," he assured me.

As I began to weave my story, the memories surged forth like a tide, bringing with them a mixture of nostalgia and melancholy. I could feel the vibrant energy of my hometown, a small place where the streets echoed with laughter and the scent of summer barbecues lingered in the air. I remembered the friends who had stood by me, their faces glowing with the innocence of youth, their laughter a balm against the world's challenges.

But with each cherished recollection, shadows began to creep in—hints of unresolved tensions, the lingering guilt of leaving them behind. The ghosts of my choices fluttered around me like restless spirits, urging me to confront the complexities of my decision. Yet here, in this moment with Evan by my side, I felt the strength to face them. It was no longer a journey I had to undertake alone. The prospect of opening up about my past ignited a fire within me, a spark that promised transformation.

"Let's do this," I murmured, my heart racing with anticipation. I was ready to shed the weight of my regrets and embrace the lessons they held, knowing that each step taken with Evan would lead me closer to the person I was meant to become. Together, we would navigate the delicate dance of vulnerability, armed with the understanding that in confronting my past, I would be carving a path toward a future filled with hope, connection, and the possibility of love unbound by the shadows that once held me captive.

In the days that followed, the autumn air shifted outside, crisp and vibrant, casting the city in a palette of amber and gold. Each leaf that fluttered to the ground seemed to echo the fleeting nature of time, a reminder of all that I had experienced and all that lay ahead. As I sat at my desk, the faint rustle of leaves filtering through my open window, the city hummed with life. Laughter floated up from the street below, where people darted in and out of cozy cafes, wrapped in scarves, their cheeks flushed from the cool breeze. It was a scene of warmth and connection, and yet, I felt oddly detached, like an observer in my own life.

Evan had left a mark on me that was as undeniable as it was complicated. Our conversations had sparked something deep within—a hunger for authenticity that I had long ignored, buried beneath layers of self-doubt. The montage I had been editing now felt like a mirror reflecting not just the characters' journeys but also my own. I was no longer just piecing together the fragments of others' stories; I was weaving together the threads of my own, desperately trying to make sense of the chaos.

One evening, after a long day of editing, I decided to take a stroll along the lakefront. The sun was dipping below the horizon, painting the sky in shades of purple and orange, and as I walked, the soft crunch of gravel beneath my feet was grounding. I felt the wind tugging at my hair, teasing it out of place, as if urging me to let go of my carefully constructed facade. This was my sanctuary, a place where I could reflect on the moments that had led me to this point.

I approached a weathered wooden bench overlooking the water, the surface slick with the remnants of a recent rain. Sitting down, I let out a slow breath, watching the ripples dance across the surface of the lake, each one a reminder of how life was always in motion. It was in this serene moment of solitude that the memories came flooding back—the decisions I had made, the paths I had chosen, and the people I had left behind.

I thought of my childhood friends, those steadfast companions who had walked with me through the highs and lows. We had shared dreams and secrets under the starlit skies of our small town, but with every step I took towards my career, I felt those ties loosening, stretching thin like threads of a fragile tapestry. I had yearned for adventure, for the promise of something greater, but at what cost? My heart ached with the weight of that realization, a pull that gnawed at the edges of my conscience.

With the water glimmering under the fading light, I could almost hear their laughter echoing in my mind, mingling with the laughter of those I now surrounded myself with. But where did that leave me? I had chased my dreams, and yet, with each achievement, I had carved out a piece of myself, relinquishing those connections that once defined me. Would I always be caught between two worlds, forever searching for a place to belong?

The thought of Evan anchored me in the present. I was terrified that my past choices would drive a wedge between us, that the shadows of my decisions would rise up and shatter the delicate bond we were beginning to forge. It was a fear that tightened around my chest, yet I felt a strange sense of clarity. I was ready to confront those ghosts—not just in the context of my past but in relation to the future I craved.

Determined, I returned home with a newfound resolve. I fired up my laptop and opened the editing software once more. The footage from the montage flickered to life, each frame capturing moments that resonated with my own fears and desires. I envisioned a narrative that explored the theme of confronting one's past to embrace the present. With each cut and transition, I infused my emotional journey into the film, transforming my pain into art. I could feel the weight lifting as I poured my heart into the project, crafting a story that reflected the power of vulnerability and healing.

The next day, I invited Evan to watch the nearly completed montage. My heart raced as I arranged the cozy atmosphere of my living room—dimmed lights, soft pillows, and a bowl of popcorn at the ready. I wanted him to see not just the film but also the journey I was embarking on. The air was thick with anticipation as he arrived, a familiar smile spreading across his face, lighting up the room and my spirit.

"Ready to be amazed?" I teased, playfully nudging him as I hit play.

The film unfolded, and I could feel Evan's presence beside me, his focus unwavering as he absorbed each scene. The characters' struggles mirrored my own, their journeys echoing my desire for acceptance and understanding. I watched him react, his eyes widening at the poignant moments, his expressions shifting as the storyline revealed the power of confronting one's past. It was as if the film was a vessel for my soul, exposing the intricacies of my heart and the lessons I had learned along the way.

As the final scene faded to black, a silence enveloped us. I glanced at Evan, his eyes shimmering with emotion. "That was... incredible," he said, his voice thick with sincerity. "You poured your heart into this."

I smiled, feeling the warmth of his praise wash over me. "Thank you. It's more than just a film to me. It's a part of my journey, a way to confront what I've been running from."

His gaze held mine, and in that moment, I felt a connection deepen—a shared understanding that transcended the boundaries of our individual experiences. "You're not alone in this," he assured me, reaching out to squeeze my hand gently. "We all have ghosts we're trying to outrun. But it's in facing them that we truly live."

The truth in his words settled within me, igniting a spark of hope that I hadn't dared to embrace before. "I want to keep facing them," I confessed, the vulnerability in my voice mingling with a sense of determination. "I want to learn from them and move forward, not just for me but for us."

Evan nodded, his expression serious yet encouraging. "Then let's do it together. Whatever you need, I'm here."

The weight of his promise enveloped me like a comforting embrace, infusing me with the courage to explore the depths of my soul. I felt ready to shed the layers of regret and reclaim the vibrant, authentic self I had been stifling for far too long.

As we moved through the montage, discussing its nuances and the feelings it evoked, the room filled with laughter and introspection. The dialogue flowed effortlessly between us, weaving a bond that felt both exhilarating and terrifying. I realized that I no longer had to navigate my journey in solitude; I had found a partner willing to step into the light with me, illuminating the path toward healing and acceptance.

With each moment shared, the past began to lose its power over me, transforming from a haunting specter into a teacher imparting wisdom. I could feel the burdens lifting, replaced by a lightness that allowed me to breathe deeply for the first time in ages. I was ready to write a new chapter, one where the ghosts of regrets would no longer define my identity but would serve as reminders of resilience and growth.

As we sat there, the evening stretching before us, I could see the potential for something beautiful—an ever-evolving story filled with laughter, challenges, and love. And as the credits rolled on our evening, I realized that I wasn't just editing a montage; I was reshaping my life, and in doing so, I was allowing Evan to become a part of my narrative in ways I had never dared to imagine before. Together, we would confront the past and embrace the future, one frame at a time, forging a bond that would endure, no matter what ghosts lay in wait.

Chapter 12: The Confrontation

Sunflowers brighten the cramped, urban space of my apartment, their cheerful yellow petals a stark contrast to the muted hues of my life. They sway slightly as if dancing to the rhythm of my heartbeat, which seems to echo in the silence that envelops us. Evan, with his tousled hair and those deep-set, expressive eyes that have always managed to melt my defenses, stands awkwardly in the middle of my living room. I catch a hint of nervousness in his smile, a flicker of uncertainty that makes my heart clench. The bouquet is vibrant and alive, a token of hope, yet it feels laden with the unspoken weight of everything that has come before us.

The city outside my window pulses with life, its cacophony of horns and chatter a distant murmur, somehow both familiar and alien. I take a moment to inhale deeply, savoring the scent of fresh flowers mixed with the faint aroma of the coffee I brewed earlier. It fills the room with warmth, a fragile comfort as I grapple with the tangled web of emotions swirling within me. I motion for Evan to sit beside me, the couch creaking beneath our shared weight, an almost ominous sound echoing my unease. I curl my fingers around the edge of the cushion, grounding myself as I glance sideways at him, caught off guard by the intensity of his gaze.

"Why now?" I finally ask, the words spilling out before I can second-guess them. "You could have come by any time, but it had to be today." The question hangs in the air, thick and heavy. It feels like a challenge, but also an invitation for honesty, something we had both shied away from in the past.

He leans forward, elbows resting on his knees, an earnest look in his eyes that pulls me in, holding me captive. "Because I miss you," he replies, his voice low and steady. The simplicity of his words ignites a warmth in my chest, a spark that dances dangerously close to hope.

"And I've been thinking about us. About what we could be if we tried."

His admission sends my mind racing. Memories flood back—laughter echoing through late-night conversations, shared secrets, the kind of intimate moments that felt like they were woven into the fabric of my being. Yet, underneath it all lies the fear, the haunting specter of our shared history that looms larger than life. What if this was just a fleeting whim for him, a momentary lapse of judgment? I blink hard, trying to shake off the thought.

"I've been grappling with my own fears too," I confess, feeling the truth of my vulnerability bare itself before him. "We have so much to untangle. It's not just about the chemistry; it's about trust, about whether we can really change."

A flicker of concern passes across his features, and I can see him wrestling with the weight of my words. This isn't just a romantic reunion; it's a confrontation with our past selves, the mistakes and miscommunications that built a wall between us. The tension in the room thickens, the air crackling with unspoken words, and for a moment, I wonder if we will ever truly bridge the gap.

As I search his eyes for reassurance, the sudden, sharp knock at the door jolts us both from the fragile cocoon of our intimacy. I feel a pang of frustration, the interruption an unwelcome reminder of the world outside—one that seems intent on shattering the delicate moment we were trying to create. I exchange a glance with Evan, a silent communication that says everything and nothing at once. It feels like the universe is conspiring against us, tossing obstacles in our path when all I want is a chance to explore the connection that has always simmered just beneath the surface.

With a reluctant sigh, I rise from the couch, the sunflowers catching the light and casting playful shadows against the walls, as if they too are anxious about what lies beyond the threshold. I walk to the door, the wooden frame solid and grounding beneath my palm. I take a deep breath, steeling myself for whatever awaits me outside.

I pull the door open, revealing a familiar face, one that I never expected to see standing there—Sarah, my best friend since childhood. Her eyes are wide, sparkling with a mixture of excitement and urgency, and her hair flutters in the breeze like a wild halo. She stands there, a whirlwind of energy, clutching a handful of bags, her enthusiasm palpable.

"Sorry to interrupt!" she beams, her presence bright and chaotic, a stark contrast to the charged atmosphere inside. "I thought you could use a little surprise, maybe some ice cream and gossip?"

I force a smile, but inside, I feel my heart sinking. This was not how I envisioned this moment unfolding. Evan is still seated on the couch, his expression unreadable as he watches the scene unfold. I can sense the tension creeping back into the room, the potential for something beautiful slipping away like sand through my fingers.

"Of course," I reply, trying to mask my disappointment. "Just give me a second." I turn back to Evan, who is leaning against the couch, arms crossed, his expression shifting from hope to resignation.

The conversation I'd been so desperate to continue hangs in the air, tantalizingly close yet frustratingly out of reach. I wonder if I'll ever have the courage to breach those depths with him, to strip away the layers of doubt and insecurity that have held us captive for far too long. But as I invite Sarah in, the door swings shut behind me, sealing our fate, at least for now. The warmth of Evan's presence begins to fade, overshadowed by the vibrant chaos of the life I've built, one that may not have room for the love I crave.

The door swings open to reveal Sarah, her exuberance filling the air like confetti. With bags in tow, she spills forth a cascade of energy that swirls through my apartment, displacing the fragile moment I had hoped to nurture with Evan. "I brought your favorite!" she exclaims, brandishing a container of mint chocolate chip ice cream like a trophy. Her eyes glimmer with mischief, and I can't help but chuckle, even as a part of me wishes we could retreat back to the conversation that had just been interrupted.

Evan shifts in his seat, the light in his eyes dimming slightly as he takes in the scene. My heart sinks a little. I see the way his posture tightens, the playful ambiance that had begun to envelop us now replaced with a palpable tension. Sarah prattles on about her day—work dramas, hilarious mishaps, the usual delightful chaos that draws me in like a moth to a flame. I'm grateful for her distraction, yet I can't shake the weight of what had just been said, the intimacy of our shared vulnerability still lingering in the air, like the scent of those sunflowers.

As she unpacks her haul—ice cream, cookies, and a mystery bag that seems to be bursting with other treats—I find myself slipping into the familiar rhythm of our friendship. We settle onto the couch, Sarah's laughter bubbling over as she shares snippets of her life, painting vivid pictures of absurd encounters and spontaneous adventures. I can feel the joy of her presence wrapping around me, but every now and then, my gaze flickers to Evan, who sits somewhat apart, an observer to this vibrant whirlwind.

"Are you going to just sit there, Evan? Join us!" Sarah beckons, her infectious energy urging him to step into the light. He hesitates, his eyes darting between us, a silent conflict playing across his features. I watch as he pushes himself off the couch and joins us, the tension still thick between us, but masked beneath Sarah's enthusiasm.

"Alright, what's the gossip?" he asks, a playful smirk creeping onto his face, but I can see the uncertainty lurking beneath the surface. Sarah dives into the details of her recent escapades, and Evan listens with an attentive ear, offering comments here and there, attempting to integrate himself into the buoyant atmosphere. It's as if he's trying to merge two worlds—my history with him, fraught with complexities, and the uncomplicated bond I share with Sarah, rooted in years of shared secrets and laughter.

Yet, as the ice cream melts and the cookies crumble, I can't shake the feeling of something unresolved, hovering just beneath the surface like a heavy fog. My heart flutters with unease as I realize that while Sarah's stories are amusing, they are also a clever disguise, keeping me from confronting the real questions that swirl in my mind.

"Okay, enough about my chaos," Sarah suddenly declares, tilting her head toward Evan with a playful glint in her eye. "What about you two? What's happening with this connection? I mean, you guys were practically radiating chemistry when I walked in." Her words hang in the air, both a jest and an honest inquiry that pierces through the joviality of the moment.

I freeze, my spoon hovering above the bowl of ice cream, the playful chatter silenced by her pointed observation. Evan looks at me, a mixture of apprehension and hope flickering in his gaze. I can almost hear the gears turning in his mind, the questions he wants to ask but doesn't dare to voice. It feels as if the universe has conspired to peel back the layers of our situation in front of my closest friend, and suddenly, I'm standing on the precipice of an emotional cliff.

"I...we were just talking about how complicated things have been," I admit, the words escaping me before I can fully comprehend the implications. "It's not just about chemistry. It's about trust, about what we've both been through."

Evan nods slowly, his expression serious as he meets my eyes. "I've made mistakes, and I know I hurt you. I never wanted to come back into your life without acknowledging that." His voice is steady, yet the weight of his admission hangs in the air, echoing through the space between us like a reminder of the fractures that had formed in the past.

Sarah shifts, her excitement giving way to a more somber understanding. "It sounds like you both need to communicate better," she offers gently, her tone shifting from playful to supportive. "But you also need to trust each other. That's how you build a connection."

The room feels suddenly smaller, the walls closing in around us as her words resonate. I can feel the heat rising in my cheeks, the truth of her statement ringing loud and clear. Communication had always been our stumbling block, the one issue that had led us astray. I glance at Evan, who appears lost in thought, the moment stretching uncomfortably as we navigate the choppy waters of our shared history.

"Maybe we can start fresh," I suggest, the words tumbling out, fueled by a mix of vulnerability and determination. "Maybe we can give ourselves a chance to rediscover who we are together." I can feel the flutter of hope igniting within me, a tiny flame daring to break through the shadows of our past.

Evan's face lights up with a tentative smile, and I watch as a sense of relief washes over him, the weight on his shoulders lifting just a bit. "I'd like that," he replies softly, his sincerity evident as he looks at me, his gaze unwavering.

For a moment, time seems to stretch and weave a delicate tapestry of possibility between us, the promise of something beautiful emerging from the wreckage of what once was. But just as quickly as it ignites, it's interrupted by the blare of Sarah's phone, her face lighting up with a new notification.

"Oh, hang on," she says, fumbling for her phone, her excitement breaking the spell we had woven. I feel the warmth dissipate, the delicate threads of connection loosening as the outside world intrudes once more.

Evan glances at me, a silent understanding passing between us as Sarah dives back into her digital universe. I can't help but chuckle at the irony of it all—just when I think we've made strides in bridging the gap, reality comes rushing back in, reminding me that nothing is ever truly straightforward.

Yet, as I watch Sarah animatedly scroll through her messages, I know that this moment isn't lost. It's merely a pause, a deep breath before the plunge into the unknown waters of what could be. As I look back at Evan, I see the flicker of hope reflected in his eyes, and for the first time in what feels like forever, I allow myself to believe that perhaps, just perhaps, we might find our way back to each other after all.

As Sarah scrolled through her phone, I stole glances at Evan, whose expression oscillated between hopeful and contemplative. The tension in the room felt like a taut string, ready to snap at the slightest touch. I could see that he was grappling with a whirlwind of emotions, the remnants of our earlier conversation still hanging in the air. I wanted nothing more than to pull him back into that space of honesty, where our fears could meld into understanding, but Sarah's infectious enthusiasm painted over our fragile moment, drawing us back into the familiar chaos of our lives.

"Did I mention I found a great new coffee shop?" Sarah's voice sliced through the silence, her excitement bouncing off the walls. "It's this quaint little place on 5th Street, just opened last week. The barista is adorable, and they have the best avocado toast!" She launches into a detailed account of her outing, weaving the tale with all the vividness of a master storyteller. I can almost see the green of the avocado, the crunch of the toast, and the smile of the barista in my mind's eye.

Evan leans back, his posture relaxing slightly as he engages with Sarah's enthusiasm. I watch as he laughs at her antics, the warmth of their interaction washing over him. It's comforting to see him let his guard down, but I can't help but feel a twinge of frustration. I want to shout at the universe, to demand it allow us a moment of peace to unearth the truth between us. But here we are, nestled in the chaos of friendship, skirting around the edges of our deeper emotions.

"Honestly, you should join me next time," Sarah says, glancing between us, her gaze teasing but laced with genuine camaraderie. "We could turn it into a fun little outing—girl talk and sunshine. Just don't get mad if I hog the avocado toast."

Evan grins, the corners of his eyes crinkling with mirth. "I'll have to make sure to bring my own meal then, just in case," he replies with a playful wink, and I can feel the warmth returning to the room, the energy shifting ever so slightly.

But as the conversation flows, I feel the pull of reality gnawing at me. This lightness, while a balm to the tension, is also a distraction, and my heart aches for the raw honesty I had momentarily tasted. I glance at Evan, who seems to be caught in the same paradox—a longing for connection tangled with the reluctance to delve into the depths of our shared history.

As the evening stretches on, the ice cream dwindles, and Sarah's stories evolve into animated discussions about future plans. She discusses weekend getaways and new restaurants she's eager to explore, her enthusiasm infectious. Evan nods along, his laughter ringing out like a bell, and I find myself swept up in the warmth of our shared friendship. Yet, beneath it all lies a quiet storm brewing—a tempest of unspoken words that lurks just out of reach.

Finally, the evening winds down, the remnants of ice cream and cookie crumbs littering the table like the scattered thoughts in my mind. Sarah glances at the clock, her eyes widening. "Oh, wow! I didn't realize how late it was! I've got an early morning tomorrow," she exclaims, the surprise in her voice cutting through the lingering haze of our earlier conversations. "But we'll definitely plan that coffee outing soon, right?"

I nod, forcing a smile, my heart heavy with the unspoken promise of what remains uncharted. "Absolutely. Let's do it."

Once she's gone, the apartment falls into a comfortable silence, the soft hum of the city outside filtering in through the window. I feel the void that Sarah's absence leaves, yet there's also a weight—an expectation lingering in the air. I turn to Evan, who remains seated on the couch, his gaze fixed on a distant point, as if contemplating the very fabric of our shared reality.

"We didn't get to finish earlier," I finally say, my voice steady despite the flutter in my chest. "What were you going to say?"

He shifts, his brow furrowing as he turns to face me fully, a spark of determination igniting in his eyes. "I was going to say that I want to be honest with you," he starts, his tone serious but gentle. "I've been struggling with how to approach you since I came back. I've missed you, but it's not just about longing for what we had. It's about recognizing the mistakes I made and wanting to make them right."

His sincerity washes over me like a wave, both soothing and unsettling. I feel the tension unraveling slowly, the threads of fear loosening just enough to let in a glimmer of hope. "I need you to know that I'm willing to work through it," he continues, his voice dropping to a whisper, as if the very act of confessing his feelings could shatter the delicate peace we had created.

"What if I'm not ready?" I counter, my heart racing at the thought of navigating those treacherous waters. "What if we try and it doesn't work?"

"I think that's a risk we both have to take," he replies, his eyes never wavering from mine. "I'd rather face that uncertainty with you than live in a world where we never try. I believe we can be better. We can grow from this."

As the words hang between us, I feel a rush of emotions swelling within me—fear, hope, apprehension. It's terrifying to think of opening myself up again, of exposing my vulnerabilities to someone who has the power to hurt me. But as I look into Evan's eyes, I see something more—an echo of the person I once cherished, the friend I thought I'd lost forever.

"Okay," I breathe, the admission slipping past my lips before I can fully comprehend it. "Let's try."

A smile breaks across Evan's face, genuine and bright, illuminating the shadows that had lingered for far too long. "Thank you," he whispers, his relief palpable, wrapping around me like a warm embrace. "I promise I won't take this for granted."

We sit there for a moment, the weight of our decision settling comfortably around us. The city outside hums with life, the faint sounds of laughter and distant music filtering through the window, an unintentional backdrop to our quiet revelation. It's as if the world is celebrating our tentative steps towards healing, and I find solace in that.

For the first time in what feels like an eternity, I allow myself to envision the possibilities—imperfect, messy, and real. It's a chance for a new beginning, a delicate dance toward rediscovery, and as I glance at Evan, the air thick with unspoken promise, I can almost believe that we might just find our way back to each other, one step at a time.

Chapter 13: The Unwelcome Visitor

The door creaked open, revealing Sophie, her luminous smile instantly piercing through the cozy warmth of my living room. The walls, lined with soft yellow paint that echoed the sun's embrace, suddenly felt too bright, too cheerful for the mood that quickly enveloped us. A rich tapestry of memories fluttered between us—images of carefree summers spent chasing fireflies and late-night secrets shared beneath the stars. Yet now, with her poised presence, those sweet memories twisted into something bitter. I couldn't ignore the weight of the history she carried with her, an unwelcome shadow looming in the corners of our rekindled connection.

Sophie swept into the room with an effortless grace, her laughter spilling out like an effervescent tide, washing over the carefully arranged serenity of my space. She had a way of transforming the mundane into the magical, her charm radiant and intoxicating. Her tousled curls danced playfully as she twirled, her sundress swirling around her like a watercolor painting coming to life. I felt the air grow heavy, the warmth that once enveloped Evan and me shrinking under her playful, yet calculated attention.

Evan stood frozen at the threshold, a frown tugging at the corners of his lips as he processed the scene unfolding before him. I glanced at him, searching for a glimmer of reassurance, but his gaze was locked on Sophie, that same unfurling tension from our earlier conversations now morphing into something far more complex. I had invited him back into my life, believing that we could forge a new beginning. But Sophie's arrival felt like a sudden thunderstorm, dark clouds blotting out the sun.

"Surprise!" she chimed, and I caught a hint of mischief in her voice, as if she were a magician revealing her grandest trick. The way she sauntered over to him, tossing her hair back with a casual flick of her wrist, ignited a fire within me that I had thought extinguished long ago. The old memories of their relationship flared up, feeding on my insecurities, rekindling the jealousy I had hoped to leave behind.

"So good to see you, Evan!" she purred, leaning into him, her body language rife with familiarity that felt almost intimate. The knot in my stomach twisted tighter as I watched him respond with a polite smile, yet something in his eyes hinted at discomfort. It was as if he were caught between two worlds: the past, where Sophie had undoubtedly cast a long shadow, and the present, which I desperately wanted to shape alongside him.

I forced a laugh, trying to anchor myself to the conversation, but it came out awkward and brittle, like a poorly crafted glass ornament teetering on the edge of a table. "What a surprise, indeed! I didn't know you were back in town." I leaned against the counter, arms crossed defensively, hoping to shield my vulnerability. The bright yellow of the kitchen walls felt suffocating as I stared into the depths of her eyes, searching for a hint of malice beneath her surface charm.

"Oh, just for a short visit," Sophie replied, her voice dripping with sweetness. "I thought it might be fun to catch up with some old friends." She glanced at me, her expression unreadable, as if she were appraising a rival. "I didn't realize you two were... back together." The implications hung heavy in the air, leaving an acrid taste in my mouth. I wanted to scream that we weren't "back together," that we were merely trying to navigate the choppy waters of a complicated relationship, but instead, I swallowed my words like bitter pills.

Evan's eyes flickered to me, a silent plea for understanding, as if he could sense the turmoil brewing inside. "It's complicated," he murmured, the weight of the truth lingering in the room like an uninvited guest. But Sophie didn't seem to care for the nuances; she thrived on the chaos, weaving in and out of the conversation like a skilled dancer, drawing attention to herself with each playful remark.

"Complicated can be fun," she quipped, her laughter ringing out like chimes in the wind, bright but hollow. "I always loved a good challenge." She leaned closer to Evan, her shoulder brushing against his, igniting the spark of jealousy within me anew. The reality of their past crashed over me like a wave, relentless and overwhelming. How many times had I sat in this very spot, sharing secrets and dreams with Evan, while she occupied the space of his memories like a ghost?

The evening unraveled into a peculiar dance, an uncomfortable game of one-upmanship where I found myself floundering to reclaim the narrative. With every story Sophie shared, every laugh that seemed too easy and too familiar, I felt myself sinking deeper into a quagmire of doubt. Could I hold onto this fragile connection with Evan while navigating the currents stirred up by her presence? It was like trying to keep a candle lit in a hurricane.

Evan's laughter mingled with hers, and my heart clenched at the sight. In that moment, the space I had once thought of as ours felt like a battleground, a place where I was left to defend my stake while grappling with the encroaching shadows of their shared history. I shifted in my seat, searching for the right words, the ones that would convince me of my place in this complicated web. But all I could muster was silence, the cacophony of emotions within me swirling and crashing like a tempest against the walls of my heart.

As the evening wore on, I could feel the boundaries of our fragile reality bending under the weight of unspoken words and hidden agendas. The lively conversation felt like a masquerade, each laugh and flirtation concealing deeper intentions, leaving me to wonder if I had truly opened the door to welcome an old friend or if I had inadvertently invited a tempest into the sanctuary I had sought to create with Evan. The atmosphere shifted with every interaction, each glance exchanged holding the promise of a future that seemed more uncertain with each passing moment.

The evening stretched on, an endless loop of laughter that felt more like a calculated performance than genuine mirth. Sophie's voice flowed like a sweet melody, wrapping around Evan as she spun stories of their past, each one steeped in nostalgia that felt achingly familiar. I could almost hear the strains of a love song in the background, a haunting serenade that underscored the tension pulsating beneath the surface. As she recounted tales of spontaneous road trips and moonlit picnics, I watched Evan, a storm brewing behind his calm exterior, as if he were battling a tempest of his own.

I busied myself in the kitchen, attempting to create a semblance of normalcy amidst the chaos. The clatter of plates became my refuge, each sound a tiny distraction from the whirlwind of emotions swirling around me. I poured wine into glasses, the deep red liquid swirling like the confusion in my heart. I caught a glimpse of Sophie through the doorway, her laughter tinkling like wind chimes, and my heart twisted with a mixture of longing and jealousy. I was acutely aware of the past she carried with her, a shimmering veil draped over her every word.

"Remember that time we got lost on our way to the lake?" she giggled, her eyes sparkling as she nudged Evan playfully. "You thought we could just follow the stars. It took us hours to find our way back!"

He chuckled, a sound that sent ripples of warmth through me, but it was tainted with a hint of unease. "Yeah, I thought I was some kind of navigator," he replied, his smile faltering as he met my gaze. I felt an electric pulse pass between us, a silent acknowledgment of the uncomfortable truth that lingered in the air like a thick fog.

"Those were the days," I said, forcing a smile to mask the tightening in my chest. "But hey, I have a map now!" I waved a flimsy piece of paper in the air, trying to inject some levity into the atmosphere, but it fell flat as Sophie flashed me a knowing look. The corners of her mouth turned up in a way that felt less playful and more predatory, as if she relished the uncertainty blossoming between us.

"Maps are overrated," she quipped, leaning closer to Evan, her shoulder brushing against his. "Adventure is all about spontaneity, don't you think?" The way she tilted her head, her voice dropping to a conspiratorial whisper, made my skin crawl. It was a subtle game, one where I felt hopelessly outmatched, and the realization left a bitter taste in my mouth.

As the evening progressed, I found myself retreating further into the kitchen, the room feeling like a sanctuary, albeit a fragile one. I arranged fruit on a platter with meticulous care, the vibrant colors stark against the white china. Strawberries, bursting with sweetness, seemed to mock my plight, while the tangy citrus slices reminded me of the sharpness of my own insecurities. Each fruit felt like a metaphor for the choices we make—the sweetness of moments shared overshadowed by the acidity of betrayal lurking just beneath the surface.

Evan's laughter drifted in from the living room, an alluring sound that beckoned me to return, but I hesitated, trapped in a web of my own making. It was absurd, really, the way I felt like a character in a play I had not auditioned for, surrounded by actors who knew their lines far better than I did. Just as I was about to rejoin them, Sophie's voice rose above the rest, her tone tinged with a touch of challenge. "So, Evan, tell me, what's it like being back in town? Any regrets?"

The question hung in the air like a heavy fog, thick and suffocating. I could feel Evan's hesitation radiating from the other room, and the answer felt like a knife poised to cut. I took a deep breath, steeling myself for whatever fallout was about to occur. I was tired of feeling like an intruder in my own life, tired of the way Sophie's presence cast shadows on everything we had started to build.

Before I could second-guess myself, I stepped into the living room, a resolute smile plastered on my face. "Regrets? He should have plenty!" I interjected, my voice light but laced with an undertone of steel. "After all, he did leave the best part of town behind." I met Sophie's gaze, holding it steady, my heart racing. For a moment, I felt the tide shift, the laughter receding as we stood at an impasse.

Evan looked at me, surprise flickering in his eyes, and I sensed the weight of my words settling between us, a fragile bond strengthened by my willingness to stake my claim. Sophie's expression hardened, the playful glint replaced by something sharper, more calculating. "Ah, but every journey has its moments," she replied, her voice dripping with feigned sweetness. "Some just choose to forget them."

The tension in the room escalated, a palpable charge that ignited something primal within me. My heart raced as I squared my shoulders, unwilling to back down. "True, but some moments shape who we are," I countered, my gaze never wavering from hers.

In that instant, I could almost hear the collective breath being held around us, the atmosphere thickening with the weight of unsaid words. The battle lines were drawn, and I could feel the stakes rising, the stakes of friendship, loyalty, and the heart. Sophie's laughter faded into silence, replaced by an edge of something darker, a silent acknowledgment of the new dynamic.

"Is that so?" she finally replied, her tone cool and measured. "I suppose we all have our paths to walk, don't we?"

Evan's gaze darted between us, a silent plea for peace lingering in his eyes. I could sense his discomfort, the way the air between us crackled with the electricity of past emotions colliding with present desires. Yet as Sophie leaned in closer to him, I could feel the flicker of something shifting within me, a burgeoning confidence igniting as I remembered why I had invited him back into my life in the first place. I was here to reclaim my narrative, to not only exist in the shadows of their history but to redefine my role as the leading lady in this complicated story.

I took a step closer to Evan, brushing against his arm as I felt the warmth radiating from him. "We can make new moments, you know," I said softly, glancing at Sophie, my voice steady despite the storm raging inside. "On our own terms." The words hung in the air, a promise wrapped in defiance, a flicker of hope igniting the darkness that threatened to consume us.

Sophie's laughter hung in the air, a tinkling sound that had once felt like music but now felt like discord. She twirled effortlessly around the room, her sundress brushing against the furniture as if it belonged to a world far removed from my own. I stood rigid, trapped in an invisible web of emotions, watching her weave a narrative with Evan that felt both enticing and devastating. Each word she uttered dripped with familiarity, evoking memories I had tried so hard to push aside. The evenings we spent together, with her laughter echoing in the warm summer nights, suddenly felt like a betrayal to the woman I was becoming.

In an attempt to reclaim my ground, I plastered a smile on my face and stepped closer to the two of them. "Sophie, tell us about your new job," I chimed, injecting a brightness into my tone that I didn't quite feel. I desperately wanted to shift the focus, to steer the conversation away from their shared past, but she merely grinned, unfazed, as though she sensed the precarious balance of power shifting beneath her feet.

"Oh, it's nothing as glamorous as being a graphic designer," she said, her voice light yet deliberately mocking. "I'm just working at a small startup, but the energy is infectious. We're all about innovation, and trust me, we're changing the world, one project at a time." Her eyes sparkled with enthusiasm, but I could detect an underlying motive—a subtle challenge embedded within her words, as if she was daring me to question the validity of her success.

"Sounds amazing," Evan replied, his voice tinged with genuine admiration. I caught the way his eyes brightened at her mention of "changing the world," and my heart sank deeper. Here we were, standing at the intersection of old flames and new beginnings, and I felt the weight of expectations crashing down around me.

As the evening progressed, I tried to engage with Sophie, sharing snippets of my life, tales of mundane office antics and late-night creative bursts. Yet, with every word I uttered, her laughter would crescendo, swallowing my voice whole, drowning out my attempts to be seen. I began to feel like a ghost in my own home, relegated to the background while Sophie took center stage, her charisma lighting up the room like a thousand fireflies flitting through the night.

"Remember the camping trip when we tried to start a fire and nearly burned the whole forest down?" I ventured, hoping to evoke a shared memory that would draw us closer rather than push us apart. Evan chuckled, the sound warm and inviting, and for a moment, I felt a glimmer of hope flicker within me. But Sophie's reaction was instantaneous; she leaned into Evan, her laughter ringing out like a bell, while I sat there, an uninvited bystander.

"Of course! You always had the worst luck with fires, didn't you, Evan? Or was it just that you didn't want to admit you didn't know how to light one?" she teased, her tone light but sharp. I winced at her jibe, the way she wielded it like a weapon, cutting into the fabric of our shared experiences.

"Hey, I can light a fire now," Evan defended, his smile fading slightly as he met my gaze, trying to gauge my reaction. The unspoken words hung heavily between us, a tether pulling me closer while also fraying at the edges.

"Well, maybe we should have a bonfire soon," I suggested, my voice steadier than I felt. "I can demonstrate my impeccable fire-starting skills."

"Oh, I'm sure it'll be a magnificent display," Sophie replied with a smirk, her eyes twinkling with mischief. "Just don't forget the marshmallows; otherwise, what's the point?"

I forced a laugh, trying to match her energy, but the bitterness in my throat made it difficult. I felt trapped in a paradox, yearning to connect with Evan while battling the undeniable chemistry crackling in the air between him and Sophie. It was a delicate dance, and I was desperate to avoid stepping on the wrong toes.

As night descended, the shadows lengthened, casting an eerie glow over the room. The flickering candlelight painted our faces in shades of gold and gray, each contour revealing hidden fears and unspoken truths. I caught Evan's gaze, searching for reassurance, but he appeared lost, caught between two worlds that were colliding in front of him.

"I think I'll take a walk," I announced suddenly, the words tumbling from my lips before I could second-guess myself. The walls felt as though they were closing in, suffocating me with their memories. I needed air, a chance to breathe, to think beyond the stifling atmosphere thickened with tension.

"Do you want company?" Evan asked, his concern palpable.

"No, I'll be fine. Just need to clear my head," I replied, waving away his offer with a dismissive gesture. I needed this moment to gather my thoughts, to sift through the chaos of my emotions before confronting the reality of our situation.

Stepping outside, the cool night air enveloped me like a balm, washing away the heaviness that had settled in my chest. I walked down the path, the gravel crunching beneath my feet, each step pulling me further away from the intoxicating chaos of the living room. The moon hung high in the sky, casting a silver glow over the yard, illuminating the world in a tranquil beauty that felt so distant from the turmoil I had just left behind.

I found solace under the expansive canopy of stars, breathing deeply, allowing the crisp night air to fill my lungs. It was a stark contrast to the vibrant warmth of the living room, and I felt my heart begin to steady. Here, surrounded by nature's quiet embrace, I could finally confront the reality of what had been brewing inside me.

A soft rustle behind me interrupted my thoughts, and I turned to see Evan stepping out onto the porch, his silhouette framed against the light spilling from the house. He approached cautiously, as if he were stepping into a fragile dream. "I thought you might need company after all," he said softly, his breath visible in the cool air.

"I'm sorry for running off," I admitted, my voice barely above a whisper. "I just... I felt overwhelmed."

He stepped closer, the tension between us shifting once again. "I get it. This is all a lot to handle." He hesitated, glancing back towards the house before returning his gaze to me. "Sophie has a way of making everything feel complicated, doesn't she?"

I nodded, the weight of his words resonating deep within me. "She does. It's like she knows how to press all the right buttons."

"I don't want you to feel threatened," he said, his tone earnest. "What we have is real to me. I'm here for you."

"I know," I replied, meeting his gaze. "But the past is a heavy shadow, Evan. I can't help but feel like I'm always going to be competing with it."

"Maybe it's time to stop thinking of it that way," he suggested, taking a step closer, our fingers nearly brushing. "What if we carve out our own space, our own memories? Something that can't be overshadowed?"

His words hung in the air like a promise, a lifeline thrown into the swirling sea of uncertainty. As I stood under the vastness of the night sky, I felt the stirrings of hope ignite within me. Perhaps I could shed the weight of the past, redefine my own narrative alongside him. Maybe, just maybe, we could create a story uniquely ours, filled with laughter, warmth, and new beginnings.

The tension that had weighed heavily on me began to dissolve, replaced by the warmth of his presence, and I could finally see the path ahead illuminated by possibility. The moonlit night whispered secrets of new beginnings, urging me to embrace the unknown and walk boldly into the future we could create together.

Chapter 14: A Heart Divided

Sophie's presence lingers like a specter in my mind, making it impossible to focus on anything else. I throw myself into editing, but the footage blurs together as my thoughts drift back to Evan and his interactions with her. It's as if a relentless tide has swept in, dragging with it the memories of laughter shared, secrets whispered under the stars, and promises that felt unbreakable. Instead of the rush of creativity that usually accompanies my work, I find myself adrift in a sea of doubt.

The studio is a cacophony of sounds, a hum of voices merging with the click of cameras and the whirr of machines. Yet, in this bustling space, I feel achingly alone. It's ironic how surrounded I am by my colleagues, yet they seem a world away, their laughter muffled like echoes in a vast canyon. I steal glances at Evan, who is engrossed in conversation with Sophie. Their chemistry dances in the air, sparking a jealousy that ignites in the pit of my stomach. Every laugh she tosses his way feels like a dagger, sharp and precise, finding the tender spots of my insecurities. What do they share that I don't?

I shake my head, trying to dispel the dark clouds gathering overhead. "Focus," I murmur to myself, pushing a stray hair behind my ear as I refocus my gaze on the monitor. But the images before me blur into a haze. I can't help but picture them together—Evan's easy smile directed at her, his eyes sparkling with a light I fear I might never see again. He was my anchor once, but now it seems that anchor is caught in a current that pulls him away from me.

With each passing day, my insecurities compound, and I begin to doubt the strength of our rekindled connection. I can't shake the feeling that I'm competing against a ghost of our past—a version of Evan that I never truly knew. It gnaws at me, the idea that maybe this bond we've worked to reignite is built on shaky ground, a mere flicker in the shadow of memories that remain untouched by the passage of time.

As the sun begins to set, painting the sky in hues of orange and lavender, I retreat to my apartment, seeking solace in the dim light and familiarity of my space. The walls, once vibrant with dreams and laughter, feel like they're closing in on me, constricting my breath and suffocating my spirit. The air carries the faint scent of lavender from the candles I burn, their soft glow attempting to pierce through the thick fog of uncertainty that surrounds me.

I slide onto my worn couch, the fabric soft against my skin, and pull out my journal—a place where I can bare my soul without fear of judgment. The pages have seen my triumphs and heartbreaks, each scribbled word a testament to my journey. Tonight, however, feels different; tonight, I'm not just documenting my life. I'm searching for clarity, yearning to untangle the web of emotions that threaten to ensnare me.

I pen my thoughts, letting the ink flow freely across the page. I write about my fear of losing Evan to memories that shine brighter than our present. I describe how Sophie seems to embody everything I've ever been afraid of—the effortless charm, the beauty that steals the breath away, and the ease with which she navigates the world. Each stroke of my pen is cathartic, releasing the tension built up in my chest. I write about the moments we've shared—the stolen glances, the electric touches, and the way his laughter wraps around me like a warm embrace.

Yet, with every word, I realize that I need to confront not only my fears but also the unspoken tension between Evan and me. It looms like an uninvited guest at a party, filling the space with awkward silences and unanswered questions. I set the pen down for a moment, my heart racing as I consider the weight of my next thought: Do I have the courage to ask him about Sophie? To voice the insecurities that claw at my insides and demand recognition?

The wind whispers through the trees outside my window, a gentle reminder of the world continuing beyond my worries. I rise, pacing my small living room as I consider my next steps. My reflection in the mirror catches my eye, and for a fleeting moment, I catch a glimpse of the woman I once was—a woman unafraid to speak her mind, to stand her ground. I long to reclaim that version of myself, the one who chased her dreams and believed in love without hesitation.

With a deep breath, I return to my journal, pouring out my fears, my dreams, and the uncertainty that lingers like a shadow. I craft a letter—no, a declaration—of my feelings, determined to face whatever truth lies ahead. My hands shake slightly as I write, each word a promise to myself to be honest, to seek answers rather than wallow in doubt.

As I finish the final sentence, the sky outside deepens to a velvety blue, stars beginning to dot the canvas overhead. I close my journal and glance at the clock. It's late, but I know that sleep won't come easy tonight. Not until I confront Evan, not until I lay my heart bare before him and face the possibility of either healing or heartbreak.

With a determined heart, I rise and make my way to the door, feeling the cool air wrap around me like a reassuring embrace. The night is alive with sounds—the distant hum of traffic, the rustle of leaves, the soft laughter of neighbors. As I step outside, I'm filled with a sense of purpose, ready to face whatever awaits me on the other side of the door.

The cool night air wraps around me like a soft, familiar shawl as I step outside, my heart racing in a rhythm that echoes my resolve. The streets of our city are alive with a gentle hum, the kind that makes the pulse of life seem both exhilarating and daunting. Streetlights flicker like distant stars, illuminating the sidewalk in warm halos that guide my path. I tread carefully, my thoughts flitting between hope and anxiety, each step taking me closer to a confrontation I've both craved and dreaded.

I arrive at Evan's apartment building, a charming brick structure adorned with ivy that climbs its facade like a lover's embrace. Memories swirl in my mind, each moment spent here laden with laughter, shared dreams, and the sweet taste of first love. The entrance door, a weathered oak that bears the marks of time, feels heavy in my hand, as if it guards the secrets that lie within. With a deep breath, I push it open, the familiar creak echoing my internal hesitation.

The elevator ride up to his floor is almost surreal, the sensation of rising evoking a mix of anticipation and dread. I run my fingers over the worn metal panel, counting the floors as they tick by, my heart beating in tandem with the mechanical sounds. Each ping of the elevator resonates in my chest, the weight of what I'm about to do almost unbearable. When the doors slide open, I step out into the hallway, which is softly illuminated by flickering sconces that cast playful shadows.

I approach his door, a mixture of exhilaration and trepidation flooding my senses. Before I can knock, the door swings open, revealing Evan. He stands there, casual and unassuming, in a worn T-shirt and sweatpants that hang low on his hips. The sight of him, so effortlessly handsome, strikes a chord deep within me, a reminder of why I fell in love with him in the first place. But there's something else in his eyes—an uncertainty that mirrors my own.

"Hey," he says, a smile breaking through the tension, but I can see the flicker of surprise at my unexpected appearance. It's both comforting and alarming, as if he's taken aback by the intensity of my unplanned visit.

"Hi," I reply, my voice steadying as I step inside, the scent of his cologne mingling with the faint aroma of coffee lingering in the air. His apartment feels like a sanctuary—a blend of memories, soft lighting, and the intimacy of our shared history. I take a moment to absorb the atmosphere, the walls lined with photographs that tell our story in fragments.

"Want some coffee?" he offers, moving toward the kitchen. I nod, but my thoughts swirl, drowning out the comfort of familiarity. As he busies himself with the coffee maker, I lean against the counter, the cool surface grounding me as I gather my thoughts. The sound of water bubbling and the rich aroma of brewing coffee fill the air, but they can't mask the unease that looms between us.

"Thanks for inviting me to your screening last week," he begins, his casual tone not quite matching the weight of the moment. "I really enjoyed it."

I force a smile, though it feels fragile. "I'm glad you could come." The words feel insufficient, a mere whisper of the tempest of emotions I'm trying to articulate.

The coffee machine beeps, and he pours two steaming mugs, the rich liquid swirling with promise and comfort. As he hands one to me, our fingers brush, and for a fleeting moment, the world around us fades away, leaving just the two of us. But reality comes crashing back, and I know I can't let this moment slip into casual banter.

"Evan, we need to talk." The words spill out before I can second-guess myself. He looks up, surprise flashing in his eyes, but there's a flicker of understanding there too, as if he's been waiting for this moment to arrive.

"Yeah, I figured as much," he replies, his voice low and steady. "What's on your mind?"

I take a deep breath, my heart pounding as I search for the right words. "It's about Sophie." The name hangs in the air between us like an uninvited guest, thickening the atmosphere. I watch as his expression shifts, the relaxed demeanor giving way to a seriousness that pulls at my insides.

"I know she's been around a lot lately," I continue, my voice trembling slightly. "And I can't help but feel... threatened by her presence."

He nods slowly, a furrow forming in his brow. "I understand. She's a friend, someone from my past, and I didn't expect it to impact you like this." His honesty disarms me, but I can't let that be the end of this conversation.

"It's not just her being around," I confess, my heart racing. "It's that I feel like I'm competing against a version of you that I don't know—the Evan who knew her before, who shared things with her that you haven't shared with me."

A silence stretches between us, the weight of my words settling heavily in the air. I can see the gears turning in his mind as he processes what I've said. "I never meant to make you feel that way," he replies, his voice earnest, laced with concern. "You're my priority, not her."

"Then why does it feel like she's come back to reclaim what once was?" I challenge gently, hoping to unravel the truth buried beneath our past.

Evan steps closer, his eyes earnest and unwavering. "Because she's part of my history, and I can't erase that. But I want to build a new history with you, one that's stronger and deeper than anything I had with her."

His words wash over me, a wave of relief mingled with lingering uncertainty. I see in his gaze the sincerity I crave, the promise of a future we can craft together if only we're brave enough to face the shadows. "I need to know that you want this, Evan. That you want me."

"I do," he says firmly, reaching out to take my hands in his, warmth radiating between us. "You're the one I want to be with, and I need you to trust that."

The connection between us feels palpable, a thread woven through our shared history and the uncertain path ahead. As I search his eyes, I find not just the comfort of familiarity but the spark of something new, something worth fighting for. In that moment, the ghost of Sophie seems to recede, leaving space for the living, breathing love that exists between us—one filled with possibilities, laughter, and the beauty of rebuilding.

With a renewed sense of hope, I lean closer, allowing the walls that once held me captive to crumble. In the midst of uncertainty, I see a future unfolding before us, vibrant and alive, a story waiting to be written anew.

The warmth of Evan's hands envelops mine, a comforting anchor in the midst of my swirling thoughts. He steps closer, the air between us charged with a blend of tension and promise, like a tightly strung bow ready to unleash its arrow. I can see the earnestness in his gaze, a reflection of the heartache and hope we've both carried since we last navigated these emotional waters. With a breath that feels like a small act of courage, I lean into the moment, feeling the edges of my uncertainty begin to soften.

"I want to believe you," I admit, my voice barely above a whisper, trembling with vulnerability. "But it's hard to shake this feeling of inadequacy." My words spill out, raw and unfiltered, revealing the cracks in my carefully constructed facade. "What if I'm just a placeholder while you figure out your feelings for her?"

Evan's brow furrows, the warmth in his expression shifting to concern. "You're not a placeholder, and I don't want to keep bringing her up, but I need you to understand that my past with Sophie doesn't compare to what we've built together." He pauses, squeezing my hands gently. "You're my present and my future. I need you to trust that."

Trust. The word hangs between us, heavy with significance. It's not just a feeling; it's a fragile thread woven into the fabric of our relationship, one that needs care and nurturing. I search his eyes for reassurance, feeling the weight of unspoken histories. The memory of our shared laughter, late-night talks, and stolen kisses flood back, all competing with the ghost of Sophie.

"Let's make new memories," he suggests suddenly, the spark of inspiration lighting up his features. "Something that's just ours. No past, no shadows. Just you and me."

The idea is intoxicating. I can almost taste the sweet nectar of possibility on my tongue—a chance to redefine our relationship, to step away from the echoes of the past. I feel my heart rate quicken as I nod slowly. "What did you have in mind?"

"Adventure," he replies with a playful grin, the glint of mischief dancing in his eyes. "How about we take a spontaneous trip? Just us. Somewhere we can explore, laugh, and let go of everything that's holding us back."

"Spontaneous? You mean like a weekend road trip?" I laugh softly, my heart lifting at the thought. The idea of escape, of immersing ourselves in a new environment, feels like exactly what we need—a reset button, if you will.

"Exactly!" He beams, his enthusiasm infectious. "We can hit the coast, maybe visit a few small towns. I've always wanted to check out that quirky beachside diner that claims to have the best milkshakes in the state."

The image of us cruising down the coastline, the wind whipping through our hair, fills me with a giddy excitement. "Alright, then. Let's do it. We can leave tomorrow morning."

As we finalize our plans, the tension between us begins to ebb, replaced by a shared exhilaration. The laughter that spills from our lips feels like the first rays of sunlight breaking through a heavy fog. We talk late into the night, exchanging stories and dreams, weaving our hopes into a tapestry that feels uniquely ours. In those moments, the specter of Sophie recedes, leaving space for the vibrant reality we are creating together.

The following morning dawns with a golden glow, the sunlight filtering through my curtains like the gentle brush of a lover's hand. I'm filled with an electric anticipation as I gather my belongings—swimsuits, sundresses, and snacks that promise to be devoured during the journey. Each item I pack feels like a piece of our new adventure, a tangible step toward a brighter future.

Evan arrives just as I finish loading the car, his playful spirit shining through as he tosses his duffel bag into the backseat. "Ready for the best road trip of our lives?" he asks, his eyes sparkling with excitement. I can't help but smile back, feeling a sense of possibility blooming in my chest.

As we pull onto the highway, the city quickly fades into a blur of concrete and steel, giving way to the lush greens of the countryside. I roll down the window, the fresh air rushing in and filling the car with a sense of freedom. The sun shines brightly, casting a warm glow that bathes us in its embrace. Evan reaches for the radio, his fingers dancing over the buttons until he finds a station that plays our favorite playlist. The familiar melodies wrap around us, echoing the laughter we share as we sing along, our voices mingling with the music.

The miles slip away beneath the tires, each passing town a new opportunity for exploration. We stop at a roadside fruit stand, the vibrant colors of fresh strawberries, peaches, and cherries beckoning us to indulge. The vendor greets us with a warm smile, sharing stories of the local harvest and recommending the best treats. We sample the fruit, sweet juices dribbling down our chins, laughter bubbling up between us like the effervescence of champagne. In those simple moments, the weight of insecurity feels light, the promise of new memories overshadowing the past.

As we drive, the landscape shifts from rolling hills to breathtaking vistas overlooking the ocean. The coastline stretches out before us, a tapestry of blues and greens, the waves crashing against the rocks like the heartbeats of the earth. I lean against the window, my heart swelling with gratitude and joy. "This is incredible," I whisper, awed by the beauty that surrounds us.

Evan glances over, his gaze tender as he takes in the sight of me. "Just wait until you see the beach. I've heard it's like something out of a postcard."

When we finally arrive, the sun hangs low in the sky, casting a warm, golden hue over everything. The beach is a hidden gem, fringed by dunes and wildflowers, the sound of the surf calming my restless spirit. We set up our towels, kicking off our shoes and running towards the water, the cool waves lapping at our feet. Laughter escapes my lips as the surf splashes against my legs, sending shivers of exhilaration through me.

Evan grabs my hand, pulling me deeper into the water, and together we dive into the embrace of the ocean. In that moment, I'm buoyed by the joy of our shared laughter, the way the sunlight dances on the water, and the exhilarating rush of being alive. As we emerge, gasping for breath, our faces are lit with the kind of happiness that transcends words, a promise of new beginnings and uncharted adventures.

We spend the day exploring the beach, collecting shells, and constructing sandcastles that quickly crumble under the gentle onslaught of the waves. Each moment we share, from the playful splashes to the quiet walks along the shore, feels like a thread stitching our hearts closer together. The specter of Sophie fades further into the background, overshadowed by the reality of the connection we are rekindling.

As the sun sets, painting the sky in vibrant hues of pink and orange, we sit side by side on the sand, our fingers intertwined. The horizon stretches endlessly before us, a promise of the future and all its possibilities. I lean against him, soaking in the warmth of his body, the rhythmic sound of the waves soothing my heart.

"I never want this to end," I murmur, my voice barely a whisper as the first stars begin to twinkle overhead.

"It doesn't have to," he replies, turning to face me. The sincerity in his eyes sends a rush of emotion coursing through me. "We can take this moment and make it last. We just need to keep choosing each other, every day."

His words resonate deep within me, igniting a spark of hope. In the shadow of uncertainty, I see the glimmer of a love that can flourish, unfurling like the petals of a flower in spring. The past may shape us, but it doesn't have to define our future. With Evan by my side, I feel ready to embrace whatever comes next, knowing that together we can forge a path illuminated by trust, love, and the promise of endless possibilities.

Chapter 15: Fractured Trust

The theater's atmosphere envelops me, a cocoon of dark velvet and dim light, where the flickering images on the screen seem to dance in time with the quiet thunder of my heartbeat. I sink deeper into the plush seat, the familiar scent of popcorn mingling with the crispness of soda, wrapping around me like a warm blanket. Yet, warmth is the last thing I feel as I glance sideways at Evan. His presence is magnetic, but in the flickering glow, it feels almost tethered to Sophie, who occupies the seat just two rows down. The moment I stepped into this world, I sensed the shift, like the air before a storm, thick with unsaid words and potential chaos.

Evan leans in, whispering something that should be sweet, but I barely hear it. Instead, my focus darts back to Sophie, her silhouette sharp against the screen's glow. She's beautiful, in that effortlessly striking way that makes it seem like she's just stepped off a magazine cover—perfectly styled hair, a vintage dress that hugs her figure, and an air of confidence that makes me feel frumpy in my own outfit. The radiant warmth of her smile is an affront to my insecurities, especially as she casts her gaze toward Evan, her eyes sparkling with unspoken challenge.

As the film starts, I try to anchor myself in the plot, a meandering story of love lost and found, but the narrative dissolves into a distant hum, overshadowed by the tension thrumming in my chest. I've never been one to shy away from confrontations, but this uncharted territory of jealousy feels foreign and intimidating. Each time the film flickers through scenes of passion, I find myself caught in a different kind of drama—one fueled not by the actors on screen, but by the pulsing energy of my own emotions. I can see it—the way Evan laughs at something Sophie whispers, the lightness in his eyes that I thought was reserved for me.

The film shifts to a quiet moment, the protagonist lost in a moment of solitude, a scene that mirrors my own heart's stillness amid the noise around me. In the shadowy theater, I feel every heartbeat as if it echoes against the walls. I can't help but question everything—the easy intimacy that once felt like home between Evan and me now feels precarious, like glass perched on the edge of a table.

When the credits roll, the dimmed lights feel almost blinding as they pierce through the haze of uncertainty. I take a deep breath, steadying myself for the impending conversation, but my resolve is waning. The soft chatter of fellow moviegoers fills the space, yet I feel utterly isolated in my thoughts. As we rise, Evan turns to me, his face a mixture of warmth and curiosity, and I force a smile, though it feels brittle on my lips.

"Did you enjoy it?" he asks, and I can't help but think of how different his voice sounds when he's talking to me versus Sophie. There's an inflection, a lilt of familiarity that drapes over his words like silk, contrasting sharply with my own discomfort. I nod, attempting to summon genuine enthusiasm, but the corners of my mouth seem to betray me.

"Let's grab a drink," he suggests, oblivious to the chaos spiraling within me. I glance at Sophie, who is laughing too loudly, her attention still firmly fixed on Evan. The way she holds her glass, poised and confident, ignites an ember of resentment in me. I want to shout at the universe for putting us in this scenario, for making me feel small and overshadowed.

As we step out into the bustling street, the cool night air greets us, carrying the scent of roasted nuts from a nearby vendor. The city feels alive, a cacophony of laughter and chatter, but I'm lost in my head, an island adrift in a sea of doubt. I can hear Evan's voice weaving through the crowd, but it's as if I'm listening from underwater, each word distorted and muffled. He seems so at ease, his laughter ringing out with the sound of tinkling bells, and I can't help but wonder when I stopped being the source of that joy.

We settle at a small bar, the ambiance cozy with low-hanging lights and eclectic decor. The atmosphere is warm, but a chill settles in my bones as I watch Evan's gaze wander, catching snippets of conversation with other patrons. Sophie approaches, her laughter breaking through the barriers of my thoughts. "Mind if I join?" she asks, her voice syrupy sweet, as if her presence can dissolve the tension like sugar in tea.

Evan looks at me, searching for a cue, and I can feel the weight of his gaze, the expectation shimmering between us. I could easily ask her to leave, to reclaim the evening as ours, but something holds me back—a part of me that recognizes the futility in asserting dominance over what is inherently complex. Instead, I smile, a thin veneer of politeness, and nod. "Of course," I manage, my voice steadier than I feel.

As she settles beside Evan, I force myself to engage, though every word feels like an uphill battle. The banter flows around me, light and airy, while my own contributions feel like stones weighing down the conversation. I catch snippets of their shared memories, inside jokes floating like confetti, and I'm reminded that trust, once fractured, creates a rift that can swallow even the brightest moments whole. The laughter bounces around the table, echoing in my mind, and I know I have to find my voice amid the noise.

The laughter flows around us like a vibrant current, drawing me in and pushing me away in equal measure. Evan and Sophie seem to have an effortless connection, as if they've known each other for lifetimes. The ease with which she leans into his shoulder, her laughter bubbling forth like a sparkling brook, makes my heart clench in my chest. I can feel the heat of their shared moments, illuminating the space between them, while I sit anchored to my own discomfort, as if tethered by invisible strings that pull tighter with every passing second.

"Do you remember that time we got lost in New Orleans?" Sophie's voice dances lightly in the air, and I can't help but feel the weight of her words pressing against my defenses. The mention of a city so alive with history and music evokes images of vibrant streets, jazz spilling from open windows, and the sweet scent of beignets wafting through the air. But rather than warmth, the memory is sharp, a reminder of the places I've never been with Evan, the adventures I can't claim as my own. I take a sip of my drink, the icy burn of whiskey grounding me momentarily, as if I can freeze time and hold onto this moment before it slips away.

"What a disaster that was!" Evan chuckles, his voice deep and rich, echoing through the bar with a resonance that makes me shiver. He glances at me, searching for an ally in our shared history, but I can see the flicker of connection in his gaze directed at Sophie. It's a subtle shift, barely noticeable, yet it looms larger than the wooden bar top separating us. "We ended up at that little voodoo shop, remember?"

"Yes! And you tried to buy that ridiculous talisman!" Sophie's laughter bubbles up again, and I feel a pang of envy at how easily they slip into memories, their shared laughter knitting a bond that seems impenetrable. I can't shake the feeling of being an outsider in a conversation meant for two.

"Hey, at least I was trying to ward off bad luck!" Evan retorts, and there's a lightness to his tone that makes it clear he's enjoying this dance with Sophie. I can't help but wonder if he's aware of the impact of his words, the unintentional dagger they plunge into my chest.

"Bad luck is just another term for adventure," I finally interject, my voice steady despite the turmoil swirling beneath the surface. The moment hangs in the air, and I can see the surprise in both their eyes.

It's as if I've crashed their party, but I refuse to retreat, no matter how uncomfortable it feels.

"Exactly!" Sophie replies, her smile brightening the dim space between us. "Life's too short to take seriously all the time, right?"

"Right," I echo, though my heart beats in defiance, drowning out the agreement. I swallow hard, reminding myself that I've never been one to shy away from a challenge. "I'm all for a little chaos."

Evan grins at me, the warmth returning to his gaze, but I can see the moment he shifts back to Sophie, his attention drawn like a moth to a flame. The bittersweet taste of my drink turns sour as I navigate the landscape of our shared history, the trails of our past winding in and out of view, obscured by the fog of unresolved feelings.

The conversation flits from one topic to another, an erratic dance I struggle to keep up with. As they reminisce, I find myself grasping for the threads of our own shared experiences, desperate to weave myself back into the fabric of our relationship. Yet, the memories feel distant, like photographs faded by time, while Sophie's vibrant tales breathe new life into Evan's laughter.

The chatter of the bar fades into the background as I turn inward, grappling with the realization that I'm at a crossroads. It's not just about Sophie; it's about the unsteady ground I stand on. With every shared story, I feel the weight of our past shifting, an intricate puzzle I'm no longer certain I can solve. I take a deep breath, filling my lungs with the heady mix of spirits and stories, as I force myself to remain present.

"Let's take a picture!" Sophie suggests, her enthusiasm infectious as she pulls out her phone. The world around me blurs as they huddle together, a perfect tableau framed by the soft glow of the bar lights. I force a smile, feeling like an outsider peering through a window into a scene where I no longer belong. But when they pose, their faces glowing with laughter, I can't resist the urge to join them.

"C'mon! You too!" Sophie gestures me closer, and I squeeze in beside them, trying to embrace the moment despite the unease twisting in my stomach. I manage a genuine smile, the kind that lights up my eyes even as my heart trembles.

As the camera clicks, capturing a moment that feels both fleeting and eternal, I wish I could hold onto this feeling. I want to believe that there's still a place for me in Evan's world, a space where Sophie's vibrant energy doesn't eclipse my own. But deep down, I know I'm fighting against the current, trying to swim upstream while the tide pulls me away.

After the photo is taken, the momentary excitement fades, and the atmosphere shifts again, the air thick with unspoken words. I look at Evan, hoping to see a glimmer of reassurance in his eyes, but the warmth has dimmed, clouded by Sophie's presence. It feels as if we're treading water in a deep sea of uncertainty, and I'm not sure how to break the surface.

"What about you, though? Any good tales from your adventures?" Sophie asks, turning her attention back to me, the curiosity in her voice both inviting and tinged with a hint of competition.

"I've had my fair share of chaos," I say, forcing myself to smile, the words rolling off my tongue like honey, though they taste like ash. I dig deep, seeking a story that will bring us closer rather than push us further apart. "Last summer, I went hiking in the Rockies and ended up lost for a few hours. I thought I'd stumbled into a bear's den!"

Evan laughs, and I can feel a hint of genuine interest ignite in his gaze. "What happened?"

"I ended up finding my way back by following a family of deer," I say, my laughter mingling with theirs. It's a good story, but the shadow of doubt lingers. I want to be part of this moment, but the specter of Sophie's laughter echoes in my ears, a reminder that I'm vying for space in a world where I once felt secure.

As the evening progresses, the conversation flows more easily, yet the specter of unease remains, a constant reminder of the unspoken tensions between us. I take comfort in the camaraderie, yet a fragile thread weaves through my thoughts, binding me to the uncertainty of what lies ahead. With every shared smile, I can't help but wonder if this fragile moment of connection will shatter under the weight of my own insecurities, leaving me adrift in a sea of unfulfilled promises and fractured trust.

The laughter fades into a low murmur as the bar begins to hum with late-night energy, patrons settling into their own worlds of conversation, drinks, and the vibrant pulse of life. I clutch my glass a little too tightly, feeling the cold seep into my skin, a physical manifestation of the chill that runs through me. Despite the warmth of the whiskey coursing through my veins, my stomach churns with uncertainty. I watch Evan and Sophie, their chemistry palpable, as if they are part of an intricate dance that I was never meant to join. The flicker of their shared laughter creates an illusion of intimacy that cuts deeper than any words could.

As the evening stretches on, I search for a foothold in this strange new landscape. I lean in, determined to reclaim some semblance of connection, channeling every ounce of strength into making my presence felt. "So, Sophie," I say, forcing a smile that feels more like a grimace, "do you ever get tired of running the art gallery? It seems like a dream job, but I imagine it can be exhausting."

She tilts her head, her expression playful. "Exhausting is an understatement! You wouldn't believe the number of egos I have to wrangle daily. But then again, what's art without a little chaos?" Her laughter is infectious, and I feel the corners of my mouth lift involuntarily.

"Is that where you two met?" I ask, trying to navigate the conversation toward common ground, my voice steadying as I find my footing.

"Ah, yes! Evan was one of my very first patrons. He walked in, looked at a piece, and then turned to me and said, 'I don't get it, but I want to!'" Sophie rolls her eyes dramatically, her smile bright enough to light the dimly lit bar. I can't help but appreciate her spirited nature; it's a quality that makes her both alluring and intimidating.

Evan chuckles, leaning back in his chair, his gaze warm as he recalls the memory. "I'll never live that down, will I? But I meant it! I just love how art can make you feel something even if you don't understand it." There's a sincerity in his voice that sends a ripple through me. I want to reach across the table and grasp that sentiment, to dive into the shared passion he so effortlessly conveys.

"I think that's the beauty of it, though," I chime in, eager to contribute to the conversation. "Art has a way of touching people without needing a manual." I find my stride, fueled by the momentary connection, but the electric tension still lingers, tethering me to the uncertainty of our dynamic.

As the night deepens, the energy shifts, and the trio of us becomes a quartet when another friend of Evan's, a tall man with tousled hair and a disarming grin, joins our table. His presence adds a different kind of energy, and the conversation flows seamlessly, bouncing from stories of past escapades to shared opinions about local art exhibits. I can see the camaraderie building, a safety net that feels tantalizingly close yet slightly out of reach.

But amid the banter, I feel Sophie's gaze frequently flit back to Evan, like a hummingbird drawn to the most vibrant flower in the garden. Each look exchanged between them is a reminder of my precarious position. I can't help but notice how easily they slip into their own rhythm, weaving tales that seem to have been etched in memory long before I arrived.

As the laughter rings out around me, I cast my gaze out the window, where the city lights twinkle like distant stars against the night sky. The streets below pulse with life—cars honking, people moving, and music spilling from nearby clubs. It's a world filled with possibilities, yet here I sit, wrestling with insecurities that feel like anchors dragging me into the depths of uncertainty.

"Hey, what's on your mind?" Evan's voice breaks through my thoughts, pulling me back to the moment. His brow is furrowed in concern, and the warmth in his eyes contrasts with the tightness in my chest. For a moment, I wonder if he can see the storm brewing beneath my exterior, but I shake my head, a soft smile gracing my lips.

"Oh, just lost in thought, I guess. This city has a way of making you feel small, doesn't it?"

"Sometimes it's nice to feel small," Sophie interjects, her eyes dancing with mischief. "It reminds you of the bigger picture." There's a knowing look between them, an unspoken bond that pulses with history and depth.

"True," I reply, though a shadow lingers behind my smile. The moment stretches, heavy with unspoken words and uncharted territories. I can feel the unsteady ground beneath me, the knowledge that this evening is an exercise in navigating the fragile landscape of relationships.

As the night begins to wane and the bar starts to thin out, the three of us share one last round of drinks. I watch Evan as he engages with Sophie, his laughter ringing like music, a melody I can't seem to join. I want to reach out, to pull him into my orbit, but I can feel the space between us widening like a chasm filled with doubt and fear.

Sophie's laughter is bright, slicing through the atmosphere, and I catch a glimpse of the two of them leaning closer together, a shared moment that feels electric. The recognition washes over me, igniting the fire of jealousy that simmers beneath my skin. I can't shake the feeling that I'm grasping at straws, trying to hold onto a relationship that may no longer exist in the way I desire.

The clock on the wall ticks steadily, a reminder that time is slipping away, but in that moment, I feel a surge of defiance. "Okay, let's do something crazy," I declare, my heart racing at the unexpected boldness of my words. "How about we head to that rooftop bar? I hear the view of the skyline is breathtaking at night."

The suggestion hangs in the air for a moment, and I can see the surprise in both their expressions. "You're on," Evan says, his eyes sparkling with enthusiasm. Sophie raises her glass in agreement, and I can't help but feel a flicker of hope ignite within me.

As we step out into the cool night air, the city opens up before us like a canvas waiting to be painted. The skyline is alive, illuminated by the soft glow of lights reflecting off glass and steel, creating a breathtaking tapestry of dreams and possibilities. I inhale deeply, the crisp air filling my lungs as we make our way through the streets, my heart beating in rhythm with the pulse of the city.

The rooftop bar is just a few blocks away, and the excitement buzzes in the air as we ascend to the top floor. The atmosphere shifts once more as we step out onto the terrace, where the wind tousles our hair and the stars shimmer like diamonds against the velvet sky. The view is nothing short of breathtaking—a panoramic vista of the city sprawling beneath us, each light a flickering promise of stories yet untold.

Evan stands beside me, his gaze sweeping across the horizon, and for a moment, I catch a glimpse of the man I fell in love with. He seems lost in thought, and I wonder what memories are conjured in his mind as he gazes into the distance. But before I can delve deeper into my musings, Sophie breaks the silence, her laughter ringing out like a clear bell.

"This place is magical!" she exclaims, spinning around with her arms outstretched as if she could embrace the entire city. I can't help but smile, the infectious joy lighting a spark within me.

"Absolutely," I agree, stepping closer to the edge, my heart racing with exhilaration. The city feels alive in this moment, a beautiful tapestry woven from laughter, dreams, and unspoken desires.

As we raise our glasses to toast, I take a deep breath, allowing the moment to wash over me. It's a fragile peace, a fleeting connection that feels both exhilarating and terrifying. But as I look at Evan, the warmth in his gaze ignites a flicker of hope within me. Maybe, just maybe, there's still a path forward, a way to reclaim the trust that feels fractured yet not beyond repair. The night stretches ahead, full of promise and uncertainty, and for now, I'm willing to embrace it all.

Chapter 16: The Breaking Point

The lobby of the historic Beacon Theater was suffused with a chaotic energy, a whirlwind of laughter and the echoes of clinking glasses from the bar as patrons mingled after the screening. Ornate chandeliers dangled from the ceiling like polished jewels, their soft light illuminating the glistening marble floors. I could almost taste the champagne in the air, a reminder of the evening's celebratory vibe, yet all I felt was the icy grip of anxiety tightening around my chest. The vibrant hum of conversation buzzed around me, but it was the silence looming between Evan and me that screamed the loudest.

My heart raced, each beat an urgent call to action as I spotted him across the room. He stood there, hands shoved deep in the pockets of his tailored blazer, an effortless picture of charisma. But the easy smile he wore was not meant for me; it was for someone else—a flash of blonde hair that flickered like a flame, illuminating memories I desperately wished to extinguish. I could feel the anger boiling inside, a potent blend of jealousy and frustration that had reached a breaking point.

With determination coursing through my veins, I crossed the room, my heels clicking sharply against the marble, each step an act of defiance against my wavering resolve. I could feel the warmth of the crowd as they swirled around me, yet the space between Evan and me felt like a chasm I had to leap across. When I finally reached him, the air thickened, charged with unspoken words and emotions begging to be unleashed.

"Evan," I said, my voice trembling but resolute, drawing his attention. He turned, surprise flickering in his eyes as if he hadn't expected me to approach. "We need to talk."

His brow furrowed, concern etching deeper lines across his forehead. He stepped closer, his presence both a comfort and a reminder of the distance I felt. "Is everything okay?"

"Is everything okay?" I echoed, my voice rising slightly. "How can everything be okay when you're still tangled up in whatever that was with Sophie?" My heart raced, the familiar burn of tears threatening to spill. "I can't just stand by while you drift back into your past like it was nothing."

He looked taken aback, and for a fleeting moment, I feared I had crossed a line I shouldn't have. But as his expression softened, I felt a flicker of hope that maybe my vulnerability could pierce through the walls he had built around himself.

"Jenna," he began, his voice low, almost a whisper. "Sophie is part of my past. You have to believe me. What we have—"

"What we have?" I interrupted, frustration bubbling over. "It feels like you're keeping one foot in the past while you're trying to build something with me. How can I compete with memories that you seem to cherish?" The words came tumbling out, raw and unrefined, and I hated myself for showing him how deeply his connection to her affected me.

His expression shifted, the softening replaced by a deeper intensity as he stepped even closer. The subtle scent of his cologne, a mix of cedar and something distinctly him, enveloped me, grounding me even as my emotions threatened to spiral out of control. "Jenna, you're not competing with anyone. Sophie was part of my life at a different time. I've moved on."

I inhaled sharply, my breath hitching as I gazed into his eyes, searching for the truth hidden beneath his words. They held a warmth that ignited something within me, but lingering doubts whispered cruelly, taunting me with visions of a future where I was merely a placeholder, a convenient distraction from a love he thought he had lost.

"You say that, but then I see you with her, and it's like I'm not even there. It's hard for me to trust that you're not still entangled in your feelings for her." The lump in my throat grew larger, but I refused to back down. I was standing here, baring my soul, and I needed him to see just how serious I was.

His gaze locked onto mine, an electric connection crackling between us. "I get it," he said, his voice tinged with urgency. "But you have to know that my heart belongs to you. It's always been you. I can't change the past, but I can promise you that I'm here, right now, with you."

My breath caught, the sincerity in his voice pulling at the frayed edges of my heart. "But what if she comes back? What if she wants you again?"

Evan stepped back slightly, taking a moment to compose himself. "Then I'd remind her that my life is with you. You're the one I want, Jenna. I need you to trust me. This is a journey, and we need to navigate these waters together."

I felt the weight of his words pressing down on me, mingling with the swirling uncertainty inside. Could I really trust him? The path before us was fraught with obstacles, each twist a potential pitfall that could send us spiraling back into the darkness of old wounds. Yet, as I looked into his earnest eyes, I felt the tentative threads of hope weaving themselves into a fragile tapestry of possibility.

"Okay," I said finally, the word barely escaping my lips. "I want to trust you. I do." The tears threatened to spill, but I fought them back, wanting to appear strong even as I felt the delicate balance of our relationship hanging in the air.

"Then let's take this one step at a time," he replied, reaching out to brush a strand of hair behind my ear. The simple gesture sent shivers down my spine, igniting a spark of warmth amid the cold doubt that had taken root in my heart. "We'll figure it out together. Just promise me you won't shut me out."

With a tentative smile breaking through the tension, I nodded. The path ahead was still uncertain, but as I stood there, enveloped in the warmth of his presence, I realized I was willing to embrace the journey, no matter how daunting it may be. Together, we would navigate the murky waters of love, trust, and the haunting shadows of the past, striving for a brighter future that I dared to believe was within our reach.

The warmth of Evan's hand on my cheek lingered long after he had pulled away, leaving me with a curious mix of hope and lingering doubt. I stood there, surrounded by the thrumming energy of the theater lobby, yet feeling as though we existed in our own bubble—an oasis carved out amid the chaos of chattering voices and clinking glasses. The faint scent of popcorn hung in the air, mingling with the more intoxicating aroma of Evan's cologne, creating a concoction that stirred something deep within me, something that reminded me why I had risked so much to confront him.

As I gazed into his eyes, the earnestness reflected in his expression began to soothe the sharp edges of my insecurity. "I want us to be real," I confessed, my voice barely above a whisper. The words felt heavy yet necessary, a bridge I hoped would lead us to solid ground. "I can't live in the shadows of someone who no longer exists in your life."

His brow furrowed as he considered my words. "Then let's create our own light," he replied, his tone firm yet gentle, as if he were making a promise that would bind us together in a new way. The determination in his voice stirred something within me, a flicker of courage against the backdrop of uncertainty.

We moved through the throng of patrons, weaving past clusters of friends and couples, laughter cascading around us like confetti. My heart raced with each step, not just from the confrontation, but from the anticipation of what lay ahead. As we exited the theater, the cool night air hit me like a refreshing wave, grounding me as I tried to process everything I had just laid bare. The streets were alive with the hum of New York City—cars honking, street vendors calling out, the distant sound of a saxophonist playing a soulful tune beneath the flickering neon lights.

"Do you want to grab a drink?" Evan asked, his voice cutting through the din of the city. The way he looked at me, with a hint of uncertainty mingled with eagerness, made my stomach flutter. I nodded, my earlier hesitation dissipating as the thought of sharing a quiet moment with him began to sound like the perfect remedy for the tension we had just navigated.

We found ourselves in a cozy bar just a block away, its dim lighting casting soft shadows across the wooden beams. The rich scent of aged whiskey wafted through the air, mingling with the sweetness of mixed cocktails being prepared behind the bar. I slid onto a barstool, the leather cool against my skin, and watched as Evan settled beside me, a reassuring presence that felt both familiar and thrilling.

"Two old fashions, please," he ordered with a confident ease that made me smile. There was something so effortlessly charming about him in moments like this, when the weight of the world faded away, leaving just the two of us in our own private universe. As the bartender expertly mixed our drinks, I felt a surge of gratitude wash over me. We had faced the shadows, and now we were carving out our space amidst the lights.

"I've been thinking," I said as Evan turned to me, his drink in hand, the ice clinking softly against the glass. "About us. About how I want to make this work." My heart raced, not just from the drink but from the vulnerability of my admission. "I don't want to be someone you compare to your past. I want to be the reason you look forward, not back."

He took a sip of his drink, his eyes never leaving mine, as if he were searching for something hidden beneath the surface of my words. "I don't want that either," he replied, his voice steady. "You're not a comparison to anyone. You're... unique." The sincerity in his tone wrapped around me like a warm blanket, chasing away the ghosts that had loomed over us.

"Sometimes I feel like I'm just trying to outrun memories," I admitted, my fingers nervously tracing the rim of my glass. "Like I'm trying to prove something to you. To myself."

Evan leaned closer, the warmth of his body radiating toward me. "You don't have to prove anything. Just be you. That's who I fell for in the first place." His words danced between us, weaving a thread of connection that felt almost palpable.

The conversation flowed effortlessly, like a well-worn rhythm that had been waiting for us to find it. We talked about our dreams, our fears, and the future we longed to build together. With each revelation, the walls between us crumbled further, revealing a foundation of trust that I hadn't realized we were laying.

"Do you remember that time we went to that little Italian restaurant?" Evan asked suddenly, a playful smile spreading across his face. "You ordered that ridiculously large plate of pasta, and I thought you were going to roll out of there."

I laughed, the sound echoing through the bar, brightening the dim space. "How could I forget? You were so shocked that I actually finished it. I swear I could've run a marathon afterward."

He chuckled, the memory lighting up his features. "It was impressive, but I had to wonder where you put it all. I still don't understand how you could eat that much and look so good doing it."

My cheeks flushed, a mix of embarrassment and joy flooding me at his compliment. "It's a gift, I suppose. I just enjoy food." The shared laughter felt like a balm, smoothing over the raw edges of our earlier conversation.

We sipped our drinks, the world around us fading into a blur as we focused on each other. The soft glow of the bar lights danced off his features, creating a halo effect that made him seem almost ethereal. In that moment, I could envision a future woven from these threads of connection and understanding. The ghosts of our pasts felt a little less daunting, transformed into stepping stones leading us forward rather than anchors holding us back.

As the night wore on, we ventured deeper into conversations about our aspirations and how we might blend our lives together. I could see the flicker of possibility in his eyes, reflecting my own burgeoning hope. Maybe, just maybe, we were crafting something beautiful—a tapestry of shared experiences, woven tightly together.

When we finally left the bar, the city felt different, the air electric with the promise of new beginnings. I clutched Evan's hand, the warmth of his fingers intertwined with mine, guiding me through the bustling streets. In the glow of the streetlights, I could see the way his expression softened when he looked at me, the affection in his gaze kindling a warmth within my chest.

As we walked, a sense of calm settled over me, a quiet reassurance that we were facing this journey together. With each step forward, the echoes of the past began to fade, and the future, once shrouded in uncertainty, started to reveal itself—a vivid panorama painted with the colors of hope, laughter, and an unwavering commitment to each other.

The night wore on, each moment infused with the kind of electric anticipation that could ignite even the most mundane of experiences. As Evan and I strolled through the vibrant streets of New York, the city pulsated around us—a cacophony of sounds, colors, and scents swirling in a symphony of urban life. The smell of roasted chestnuts and warm pretzels wafted through the air, mingling with the faint perfume of rain-soaked asphalt from earlier in the day. Neon signs flickered overhead, casting playful reflections that danced on the pavement beneath our feet, illuminating a path forward that felt increasingly promising.

Evan's hand fit perfectly in mine, each squeeze a silent reassurance that he was firmly anchored in the present, despite the shadows of his past. I glanced at him, trying to read the nuances in his expression, which shifted between laughter and contemplation as we navigated the lively streets. His laughter felt like music to my ears, rich and warm, echoing in harmony with the pulse of the city, but even in the lighthearted moments, a flicker of something more serious lay beneath. I sensed the same uncertainty that bubbled beneath my own surface, an unspoken agreement that we were both still grappling with our feelings.

"Have you ever wondered what our lives would be like if we hadn't crossed paths?" he asked suddenly, a hint of playfulness in his voice, yet the question bore the weight of genuine curiosity. The moon hung low in the sky, casting a silver glow over his face, making his features appear almost angelic.

"Like some sort of alternate reality?" I replied, a teasing lilt in my tone as I tilted my head, pondering the possibilities. "I can picture it. You'd probably still be brooding over old photos and I'd be stuck in a cycle of dating bad coffee and bad boys."

Evan laughed, a rich sound that vibrated through the air. "That sounds about right. You'd be the queen of coffee dates, pouring your heart out over lattes that never quite meet your expectations."

I nudged him playfully with my shoulder, and he feigned a dramatic stagger, pretending to be knocked off balance. "Okay, okay, but what about you? What would you be doing?"

"Honestly?" I paused, searching for an answer that felt true. "I'd probably be sitting at my favorite café, scribbling my thoughts into a notebook and wondering when I'd finally make something of myself."

His brow furrowed slightly, the laughter dimming as he turned to face me more fully. "But you have made something of yourself. You're incredible, Jenna. You're out here, living your life, and pursuing your dreams. It takes guts."

The warmth of his words flooded over me, igniting a spark of something deep within. "Thank you," I murmured, a genuine smile breaking through my earlier doubts. "That means a lot coming from you." I felt a swell of gratitude for this moment, a fleeting snapshot of clarity amid the chaos of my emotions.

We continued down the sidewalk, the hum of the city fading into a comforting backdrop, creating a pocket of intimacy where it felt like just the two of us existed. We passed art galleries and vintage bookstores, their windows glowing like lanterns in the night. Each step we took felt like a small victory, a building block in the foundation we were trying to lay. As we wandered, I couldn't shake the feeling that we were both building toward something monumental—if only we could find a way to bridge the gaps between us.

As the evening deepened, we found ourselves standing before a quaint little ice cream shop, its cheerful exterior inviting us in with promises of sweet delights. The bell above the door jingled softly as we entered, the cool air inside a refreshing respite from the lingering warmth of the streets. The shop was adorned with colorful pastel decor, reminiscent of an earlier time, and the scent of waffle cones wafted through the air like a siren's call.

"What's your favorite flavor?" Evan asked, peering over the glass counter at the array of choices, each more tempting than the last.

"Definitely mint chocolate chip," I replied without hesitation, grinning as I recalled the countless summer nights spent indulging in the icy treat. "It's a classic."

"Interesting choice," he mused, nodding thoughtfully. "I'd have pegged you for a cookie dough kind of girl."

"Ah, cookie dough is my guilty pleasure," I admitted with a playful smirk. "But mint chocolate chip? That's my soul in a cone."

We ordered our ice creams, laughter bubbling between us as we savored the first delightful bites. I watched him, entranced by the way he focused intently on the flavors, his brows furrowing in concentration as if he were conducting an intricate tasting. The playful banter resumed, and in those moments, the weight of our earlier conversation seemed to lift, replaced by a lightness that felt like a balm to my spirit.

Evan was animated as he recounted silly anecdotes from his childhood, his passion for storytelling illuminating the space between us. I found myself drawn into his world, the details of his life unfolding like pages in a book I desperately wanted to read. His words painted vivid pictures of days spent exploring the parks, afternoons filled with laughter and adventure, and nights gathered around the dinner table with family.

As he spoke, I felt a twinge of longing to know everything about him—the corners of his mind I hadn't yet explored, the dreams he held close to his heart. "What about you? What's your favorite memory?" he asked, turning the spotlight back on me, the curiosity in his eyes sparkling with genuine interest.

I took a moment, the memories swirling in my mind like the melting ice cream in my hand. "I think I'd have to say the summers spent with my grandmother," I replied, a smile breaking across my face as I remembered the warmth of her kitchen. "She'd bake cookies every weekend, and we'd sit on the porch, watching the world go by. It was simple, but those moments felt magical."

"Magic is found in the simplest things," he said softly, a thoughtful look crossing his face. "Those are the moments that shape us."

I nodded, the warmth of his understanding wrapping around me like a cozy blanket. We continued sharing stories, our laughter mingling with the soft sounds of the bustling street outside, creating a tapestry of connection that felt ever more intricate. With each shared piece of ourselves, I sensed that we were threading together a new narrative, one that could potentially eclipse the shadows of our pasts.

As we finished our ice creams, I looked up at the night sky, the stars twinkling above like distant whispers of hope. "You know," I said, a spark of inspiration igniting within me, "I want to create more moments like this—more memories that are just ours."

Evan's expression brightened, and I could see the gears turning in his mind. "Then let's make it happen," he replied, his voice steady and filled with conviction. "We'll fill our lives with experiences that shape us, that define who we are together."

The weight of those words settled over us, and in that instant, I felt a profound shift. The path ahead was still cloaked in uncertainty, but I could see glimmers of light peeking through. Together, we would forge ahead, armed with the stories of our pasts and the promise of what could be.

With a renewed sense of purpose, we stepped out of the ice cream shop and into the night, hand in hand. The city around us pulsed with life, a vivid backdrop to the unfolding narrative we were determined to write together. As we walked, the laughter and warmth flowed between us, a tangible thread binding our hearts and aspirations into a tapestry rich with possibility.

The road ahead would undoubtedly have its challenges, but we were ready to face them—together. And as the first hints of dawn began to light the horizon, I felt an exhilarating sense of freedom, the kind that comes from knowing that while the past might shape us, it would not define our future. Together, we would embrace whatever awaited us, writing our story one step at a time.

Chapter 17: Unearthing Secrets

The air in the library is thick with the scent of aged paper, a heady concoction of wisdom and the whispers of stories long told. Dust motes dance lazily in the shafts of light streaming through the tall, stained-glass windows, casting a kaleidoscope of colors upon the hardwood floor. As I walk among the towering shelves, my fingers brush the spines of books that seem to hum with secrets. Each one holds a universe within, and I wonder how many lives have been touched by their pages.

I've always found solace here, amidst the stacks, where time loses its grip and the outside world fades away. But today, the familiar embrace of the library feels different. My heart beats in sync with the ticking of the antique clock mounted high on the wall, each tick a reminder of the unresolved tension that lingers like smoke in the air. My mind drifts to the heated confrontation with Evan—the way the words fell like heavy stones between us, shifting the very foundation of what we had built over years. I thought I could drown my worries in my film project, yet here I am, restless, the flicker of inspiration extinguished under the weight of unspoken truths.

I wander deeper into the library's labyrinth, searching for something to spark my creativity, something to pull me from this fog. The shelves seem to stretch endlessly, each turn revealing new titles and forgotten tales. My fingers dance over the spines, seeking out the promise of adventure, but all I feel is the cold ache of nostalgia. I remind myself that I am here to unearth inspiration, not to dwell in the past, but the past has a way of creeping back in, like shadows at dusk.

Then, tucked away in a dim corner, I spot a hidden alcove, its entrance framed by heavy velvet drapes that hang like ancient guardians. Curiosity tugs at me, and I push the curtains aside, the fabric brushing against my skin like a lover's caress. Inside, the air is stale yet charged, as if the spirits of countless writers linger in anticipation of the next dreamer to pass through. I squint at the sight before me: shelves filled with old scripts, notes, and forgotten manuscripts that seem to call out to me, their voices barely above a whisper yet undeniably potent.

I step forward, drawn in by the allure of history, and my heart skips when I spot a familiar cover peeking out from the depths of a nearby shelf. I pull it free, a rush of recognition flooding over me—the script I had penned with Evan all those years ago, the one that had been our shared dream, our escape from the mundane chaos of high school life. The pages are yellowed, the ink faded, yet every word feels vibrant, alive, as if it had only been written yesterday.

As I flip through the script, the memories crash over me like a tidal wave, dragging me back to a time when everything seemed simpler, more magical. I remember the thrill of sneaking into his garage, the smell of motor oil and old pizza mingling with the sweet promise of creativity. We would stay up late, fueled by pizza and soda, sketching out scenes and crafting characters that felt like extensions of ourselves. Our laughter would echo off the walls, a symphony of youthful ambition.

But that was then. Now, the weight of unfulfilled promises sits heavily on my chest. I feel a twinge of guilt for how things turned out, for how we drifted apart, letting life and its relentless demands steer us into separate orbits. What could we have created if we had stayed true to our dreams, our partnership? The thought sends a chill through me, and I close my eyes, letting the memories wash over me.

A part of me yearns to reach out to Evan, to rekindle that spark, but another part—the practical part—cautions against it. He has moved on, and I don't even know if he remembers our dreams, our script. Would he even want to revisit that time? The questions swirl in my mind, blurring the lines between what was and what could have been.

The allure of the script begins to morph into something more profound. It's not just a relic of the past; it's a mirror reflecting our growth, our transformation. I run my fingers over the faded pages, tracing the words we had crafted together. The characters we created, infused with pieces of ourselves, begin to take on new meanings. Their struggles echo my own. Their triumphs—our unyielding hope—feel like a call to action.

With renewed determination, I set the script down and grab my notebook from my bag, flipping to a fresh page. As I begin to jot down ideas, I feel the energy shift. The words spill out, fueled by a mixture of nostalgia and a fierce desire to reclaim my voice. I can feel Evan's spirit within the lines, urging me forward. This is not just about the film project anymore; it's about us, about the raw truth of our journey.

As I scribble, the library fades into the background, the world outside becoming a distant echo. I can almost hear Evan's laughter, the sound of his voice guiding me through the chaos of my thoughts. It's a bittersweet symphony of longing and resolve. I realize then that the weight of our past can either anchor me down or propel me forward. I choose to let it lift me, to use it as fuel for the fire that had been smoldering within me, waiting for the right moment to ignite.

Lost in my thoughts, I write until my hand aches, and the sun begins to dip low in the sky, casting golden hues across the library's interior. It feels like a new beginning, the dawn of something that transcends the heartache of yesterday. With each stroke of my pen, I weave together the threads of memory and aspiration, crafting a tapestry rich with possibility. And just like that, the weight lifts, and I am reminded that the journey is not just about the destination but also the connections we forge along the way, both past and present.

The hum of the library surrounds me, a gentle symphony of whispers and the rustle of turning pages. I immerse myself deeper in the pages of our old script, letting the world around me blur into insignificance. With each line I read, the bond Evan and I once shared comes alive, vivid and intoxicating. I can almost hear the echo of our youthful laughter and the clatter of our ambitions, reminiscent of a time when dreams felt boundless, unrestrained by the sharp edges of reality. It's as if I can feel Evan beside me, his vibrant spirit woven into every word, guiding me back to the essence of who we once were.

The pages tell a story that seems suspended in time, filled with hopes and aspirations that were never quite realized. I wonder if Evan remembers those late nights spent plotting plots and crafting characters. Perhaps he, too, feels the pull of nostalgia, or maybe he's moved on, blissfully unfettered by the ghosts of our past. The uncertainty gnaws at me, feeding the fire of my anxiety. I long to reach out, to bridge the chasm that has formed between us, yet fear holds me captive, a cruel reminder of the words left unspoken.

As I flip to the final pages, a crumpled note slips out, fluttering to the ground like a fallen leaf. I kneel to pick it up, unfolding it carefully, my breath hitching as I recognize Evan's familiar handwriting. The note is a playful list of "Top 10 Reasons Why Our Script Will Win an Oscar," complete with exaggerated doodles and laughable quips. Reading it, I can hear his voice teasing me, his mischievous grin lighting up his face. It's a snapshot of our youth, capturing the essence of our partnership, a time when the world felt limitless and every day held a promise of adventure.

A smile spreads across my face, illuminating the shadows of doubt that had crept in. I tuck the note into my pocket, a tangible reminder of the joy we once found in our collaboration. That spark ignites something within me, a flicker of courage. Perhaps it's time to reconnect, to reframe our narrative. The notion that we could create again feels like a breath of fresh air, invigorating my spirit and clearing the fog of hesitation. I can almost hear the distant hum of possibility thrumming in my veins.

With my mind racing and my heart pounding, I gather my things and make my way to the exit, the script tucked under my arm. The golden light of the setting sun spills into the library, bathing the space in a warm glow that feels like a benediction. I step outside, the cool air enveloping me like a soft embrace, and I take a moment to breathe in the fading day. The world is alive with color—the rustling leaves, the laughter of children playing in the park, the distant sound of music drifting from a nearby café. It's a vibrant tapestry of life, a reminder that while I may have been lost in reflection, the world continues to turn, and my story is still being written.

I wander through the neighborhood, my mind whirling with thoughts of Evan, our shared past, and the possibilities that lay ahead. The streets are lined with familiar sights, each corner evoking memories—our favorite coffee shop with its eclectic décor and aroma of freshly brewed coffee, the old theater where we'd spent countless evenings lost in the magic of film. I realize that this place is not just a backdrop; it's a character in my story, a silent witness to our journey.

As I approach the café, the door swings open, releasing a burst of laughter and warmth. Inside, the chatter of friends and the clinking of cups create a comforting ambiance. I step in, scanning the room, and my heart skips a beat when I spot him—Evan, seated at a corner table, his head bent over a script, the light catching the unruly curls that frame his face. He looks just as I remember, but time has added a layer of maturity, a quiet confidence that intrigues me. The sight of him stirs a whirlwind of emotions, nostalgia intertwining with a hesitant thrill.

Gathering my courage, I make my way toward him, each step a mix of exhilaration and trepidation. As I approach, he looks up, and our eyes lock. The world around us fades, leaving just the two of us suspended in time. For a moment, the air thickens with unspoken words, the weight of our shared history hanging in the balance.

"Hey," I say, my voice barely above a whisper, laden with a mixture of hope and uncertainty.

"Hey," he replies, a smile breaking across his face, transforming his expression into something radiant. "It's been a while."

"It has," I agree, feeling the warmth of connection seeping into the spaces between us. "I found something today." I pull the script from under my arm, my fingers trembling slightly as I present it to him.

Evan glances down, surprise flickering in his eyes before recognition dawns. "Our script!" he exclaims, a grin spreading across his face. The joy in his voice sends a rush of adrenaline through me, the barriers of time and distance dissolving in an instant. "I thought I'd lost this forever."

"I was hoping we could maybe... work on it again?" The words tumble out, a leap of faith that feels both exhilarating and terrifying. The prospect of collaboration reignites a flame within me, a longing for that creative bond we once shared.

He studies my face, his expression contemplative, a flicker of uncertainty crossing his features. "Are you sure? It's been so long, and life has taken us in different directions."

"Exactly," I reply, the conviction in my voice surprising even me. "But maybe we can find our way back. We've grown, we've experienced so much. What if we bring all of that into this?"

Evan's gaze softens, and a hint of a smile plays on his lips. "You might be onto something. I've missed this." The sincerity in his tone fills me with a warmth that is both familiar and new.

In that moment, the weight of the past shifts, no longer a burden but a foundation upon which we can build something even more beautiful. As we dive into conversation, sharing ideas and laughter, the world around us recedes once more, the vibrant hum of life continuing its rhythm while we embark on a journey of rediscovery together.

A charged silence lingers between Evan and me as we exchange glances, the air thick with the weight of possibilities. The café hums around us, yet we exist in our own world, bound by the fragile thread of nostalgia and unspoken aspirations. I watch as he turns the pages of the script, his brow furrowing in concentration. Each line of dialogue evokes laughter and camaraderie, the essence of our youthful dreams resonating within those faded words. It's as if the script breathes life into our shared past, rekindling the flickering embers of a connection that had almost extinguished.

"What if we set it in a place that feels as alive as the characters themselves?" I suggest, the idea blooming in my mind like spring flowers bursting through winter's last grasp. "A vibrant backdrop where the stakes feel as real as our own struggles." The thought pulls me further into the realm of our imagination, sparking excitement in my chest.

Evan's eyes light up, and I see the flicker of his creative spark reignite. "What about a carnival? All those colorful tents, the laughter, and the chaos. It would mirror the ups and downs we faced, right?" His enthusiasm is infectious, and I can almost see the scenes playing out in my mind—the laughter of children, the haunting melodies of distant rides, and the thrill of chasing dreams amidst a backdrop of swirling lights.

"Yes!" I nod vigorously, the idea solidifying into something tangible. "The carnival could represent not just the fun and freedom of youth, but also the unpredictability of life. Our characters could navigate the complexities of love and ambition, just like we did." The vision dances vividly in my thoughts, and I can almost hear the distant calliope music, its sweet tones underscoring the chaos of emotions swirling within me.

Our conversation flows like a river, meandering through various ideas, each twist and turn revealing deeper layers of our shared experience. The initial trepidation dissolves as we lose ourselves in the creative process, the familiar rhythm of collaboration washing over us. I find myself captivated not just by the story we're crafting but by the rekindling of our friendship. Every laugh we share feels like a delicate stitch binding our past to the present, weaving a tapestry rich with the colors of our youthful exuberance.

With each new idea, I feel the walls I had built around my heart begin to crumble. Evan's presence is grounding, and the connection we once shared feels like a forgotten melody, now revived. It's as if time has melted away, leaving only the essence of who we are, stripped of the burdens we've carried. For the first time in weeks, I feel free to dream again.

As dusk settles, the café lights flicker to life, casting a warm glow over our table, illuminating the spark of creativity between us. I reach for my notebook, a habit formed over years of capturing fleeting thoughts and inspirations. As I scribble down ideas, I catch a glimpse of Evan watching me, his expression thoughtful, almost wistful. The intensity in his gaze sends a shiver down my spine, igniting a complex mix of emotions that I can't quite place.

"What is it?" I ask, curiosity piquing as I look up from my notes.

He hesitates for a moment, the weight of unspoken words lingering in the air. "I was just thinking about how different we are now compared to back then. It's like... we've both grown in ways I didn't expect." His tone is introspective, and I sense a vulnerability that tugs at something deep within me.

"Yes, but that doesn't mean we can't reconnect," I reply, my voice steady, the conviction in my words surprising even myself. "We've changed, yes, but the core of who we are—the passion for storytelling, the dreams we once shared—those haven't vanished. If anything, they've evolved."

The honesty between us feels electric, charging the space with unspoken potential. Evan leans back in his chair, a thoughtful expression crossing his face. "What if we explore that evolution? Not just in the story but in how we tell it, how we convey our growth through our characters? It could make for something incredibly rich and layered."

His suggestion resonates with me, and I nod vigorously, excitement bubbling up inside. "Absolutely! We can draw on our experiences—what we've learned about love, ambition, and even the pain of loss. The characters can reflect our journeys, navigating their own paths of self-discovery amid the colorful chaos of the carnival."

As the evening deepens, we delve into the intricacies of our plot, weaving in themes of resilience, passion, and the bittersweet nature of dreams. I find myself lost in the rhythm of our collaboration, the banter flowing freely, laughter spilling out like confetti. The world outside the café fades into a blur, the neon lights from passing cars casting a kaleidoscope of colors against the window, illuminating the possibilities that lie ahead.

Hours slip away unnoticed, and soon, the café begins to empty, the chatter dwindling to a hush. It's just us now, two old friends revisiting the depths of their dreams, reigniting a spark that had almost flickered out. I glance at the clock, surprise washing over me. "We've been here for hours," I say, a mixture of awe and contentment filling my voice.

"Feels like no time has passed at all," he replies, his smile warm and genuine. "It's rare to feel this kind of connection again."

A soft blush creeps into my cheeks, and I take a moment to absorb the weight of his words. There's a truth in what he says, a thread of understanding that runs deeper than mere friendship. I realize that this moment is about more than just revisiting our past; it's about creating something new, something that can transform our shared experiences into art.

As we prepare to leave, a sense of excitement envelops me, a fluttering sensation in my chest that speaks of endless possibilities. We step outside into the cool night air, the stars twinkling above us like scattered diamonds across the velvet sky. The carnival lights are still visible in the distance, vibrant and inviting, a symbol of the adventure that awaits.

"Let's do this," I say, turning to Evan, my eyes bright with determination. "Let's take this script and breathe new life into it. We owe it to ourselves—and to the dreams we once had."

His laughter rings out, bright and infectious, cutting through the night. "You know what? I think we can pull this off."

In that moment, under the vast expanse of the universe, I feel a shift within me. The uncertainty that had clung to me like a shadow begins to dissolve, replaced by a burgeoning sense of hope. The carnival, with its chaotic beauty and vibrant promise, reflects the path we're about to embark on together. The road ahead may be fraught with challenges, but as long as we walk it side by side, I know we can face whatever comes our way.

As we stroll through the neighborhood, laughter echoing into the night, the lines of our story begin to weave together anew, a narrative rich with color and emotion, reflecting the depth of our past and the vibrancy of our present. Together, we step into the unknown, hand in hand with our dreams, ready to craft a tale that is as wild and beautiful as the life we aspire to live.

Chapter 18: Tides of Change

A drizzle lingered in the air, casting a soft veil over the bustling streets of New York City, where the neon lights flickered like restless fireflies amidst the muted grays of an early autumn morning. I stepped into the diner, its familiar red vinyl booths and chrome accents wrapping around me like a warm embrace. The faint clinking of silverware and the hum of quiet conversations provided a comforting soundtrack, enveloping me in nostalgia as I made my way to the counter. The smell of freshly brewed coffee intertwined with the sweet, buttery scent of homemade apple pie, a fragrance that always reminded me of my grandmother's kitchen.

As I slid into a booth, the light from the window cast a gentle glow on the weathered script resting on the table. Its pages were creased and yellowing, the ink a little faded but the words still pulsed with life. This script, once a beacon of our dreams, now felt like a relic of a time when my best friend Evan and I believed we could conquer the world with our stories. I couldn't help but smile as I traced the familiar lines with my fingers, memories rushing back like a tidal wave.

Evan had been my partner in crime, the one who understood my wild ambitions and whispered secrets of creativity into the cool night air. We spent countless nights at this very diner, our laughter rising above the clatter of dishes as we plotted our take on the world. With every shared dream, we crafted a tapestry of hope, interwoven with the threads of youthful exuberance and unyielding determination. Now, here I was, hoping to reignite that same passion.

He arrived with a hesitant smile, the kind that hinted at vulnerability and nostalgia all at once. I watched as he entered, his hands buried deep in the pockets of his worn leather jacket, a relic from our youth. The years had etched their marks on him—slightly tousled hair, a shadow of stubble along his jawline, and an undeniable weariness in his eyes. Yet, beneath that exterior, there still flickered a spark that reminded me of the boy who once dreamt so fervently alongside me.

"Hey," I greeted, my voice barely above a whisper as I slid the script across the table. He took a moment to absorb the sight, the weight of our shared past hanging between us like an old ghost reluctant to depart.

"Wow," he murmured, his fingers brushing against the pages, and I felt my heart leap. "I can't believe you still have this."

"Of course I do. It's a piece of us," I replied, my voice thick with emotion. "I thought maybe we could... revisit it?"

He raised an eyebrow, a playful challenge dancing in his gaze. "Revisit? You mean write something new?"

"Why not?" I smiled, an idea blossoming in my mind. "It could be a celebration of who we've become—what we've learned since those days."

As he read through the first few lines, I watched his expression shift from nostalgia to inspiration, the barriers we'd erected over the years beginning to crumble with every word he absorbed. We reminisced about the late-night brainstorming sessions that turned into dawn, the way we would sip coffee as if it were liquid inspiration, fueling our passion for storytelling.

"Remember that one night?" he chuckled, leaning back as if the weight of the past had momentarily lifted. "We wrote a whole scene in the middle of a thunderstorm. I think I ended up soaked to the bone."

"I do," I laughed, the memory brightening my spirit. "And you insisted on saving your notebook. You were like a drenched cat clutching onto a piece of paper."

He grinned, and for a moment, the years fell away, leaving just the essence of who we were—a pair of dreamers lost in the vibrant chaos of creativity.

Our conversation flowed seamlessly, punctuated by laughter and shared glances. As the diner filled with the midday crowd, it felt as if we had carved out our own sanctuary in that booth. I could see the recognition in his eyes as he recalled the joy we once felt, the ambitions we shared. The weight of our past struggles began to shift, replaced by a burgeoning hope that perhaps we could tap into that energy once again.

But there was something more—a profound sense of healing. We no longer carried the burdens of our past like leaden weights. Instead, they had transformed into stepping stones, guiding us toward the present, where possibility thrived. Our dynamic, once marred by unspoken grievances and regrets, felt rejuvenated. The pain of our past was still there, lingering just beneath the surface, but now it served as a reminder of how far we had come.

"Do you think we could actually do it?" Evan asked, leaning forward, his voice a mix of excitement and uncertainty.

I nodded, the vision crystal clear in my mind. "We've grown so much. This time, we'll write from a place of strength, not fear. We know what it means to stumble, and we've learned how to rise."

He smiled, a genuine expression of hope sparking between us. "I'd like that. I really would."

In that moment, amidst the aromas of coffee and pie, the past faded into a backdrop of vibrant colors, and the future shimmered with potential. It felt like the beginning of a new chapter, a chance to reclaim our voices and share the stories we had tucked away. I could feel the tides of change washing over us, a gentle but firm reminder that while we had once been lost, we were now on the brink of rediscovering our purpose.

The afternoon sun streamed through the diner's windows, casting a golden glow on our table, as if the universe itself conspired to highlight this pivotal moment. The steam from our coffee mugs curled into the air, mingling with the sweet scent of apple pie and the savory aroma of the diner's famous meatloaf. I leaned in, a spark of excitement igniting in my chest, eager to explore the depths of our old script together.

Evan flipped through the pages with a mixture of reverence and nostalgia, his brow furrowing as he encountered the raw, unpolished lines we had penned in fits of inspiration. "I can't believe we thought this was ready for the stage," he chuckled, his laughter warm and infectious, like the sun piercing through a winter's chill.

"Naïve, weren't we?" I grinned, memories flooding back of our late-night discussions, punctuated by too much coffee and the thrill of dreaming big. "But there's something beautiful about that naïveté, don't you think? It was unfiltered, pure enthusiasm."

He nodded, the weight of the past lifting slightly as we reminisced. "I remember how we used to brainstorm at the park, watching the city pulse with life around us. Those ideas flowed like the river—sometimes calm, sometimes raging, but always alive."

I recalled those afternoons vividly, sitting cross-legged on the grass, surrounded by the laughter of children and the rustle of leaves overhead. Those moments had felt infinite, filled with possibilities. Now, that same energy danced in the air as we revisited our long-forgotten dreams.

"What if we turned this into something different?" I proposed, my heart racing at the thought. "What if we weave in our experiences, the lessons we've learned? We can create something that speaks to who we are now."

Evan's eyes brightened with intrigue, and I could see his mind racing ahead, envisioning a tapestry of narratives woven together by our growth. "You mean, like a coming-of-age story for adults?"

"Exactly!" I exclaimed, the excitement bubbling over. "We've both been through so much—heartbreak, triumphs, the whole spectrum of life. Let's write from that place, where vulnerability meets strength."

He leaned back, contemplating, and for a heartbeat, the air crackled with potential. The thought of crafting a story that intertwined our pasts with our present ignited something profound within us. It was more than just nostalgia; it was a chance to reclaim our narrative and mold it into a reflection of who we had become.

"I love it," he said, nodding slowly. "But how do we start?"

"Let's dive in," I suggested, the enthusiasm radiating from me. "Let's brainstorm. What themes resonate with us now?"

The diner, once a mere backdrop, transformed into our creative sanctuary as we began to scribble ideas on napkins, the scent of cinnamon mingling with the ink. We bounced thoughts off one another, weaving through our memories like a delicate dance. The booth felt like a cocoon, shielding us from the world outside, where the hustle and bustle of city life continued unabated.

Evan leaned in, excitement brimming in his eyes. "What about love? Not just romantic love but the love between friends, the love of self?"

I smiled, warmed by the notion. "And the love of stories. The characters we create mirror our experiences and desires, revealing pieces of ourselves."

"Yes! Like those moments when we felt lost, and then, unexpectedly, we found our way," he added, his voice softening, a hint of vulnerability creeping in.

As we scribbled, the memories cascaded like autumn leaves, each one telling its own story of growth and resilience. The laughter, the tears, and everything in between formed a tapestry rich with texture. I could feel the momentum building, the words spilling out as our shared creativity ignited a fire within us.

We took turns recalling the pivotal moments that shaped us—the heartbreaks that shattered our illusions, the failures that taught us humility, and the successes that propelled us forward. Each revelation felt like a brick removed from a wall we had built around ourselves.

"Do you remember that summer we decided to go on a road trip?" I asked, a grin spreading across my face. "The one where we got hopelessly lost and ended up at that tacky roadside diner?"

He laughed heartily, a sound that felt like home. "How could I forget? You were convinced the map was wrong, and I was adamant about the directions!"

"And we ended up sharing that oversized milkshake while laughing at our own stupidity," I added, warmth flooding my chest as I recalled the joy of those carefree moments.

"Those spontaneous adventures made us who we are," he said, his voice rich with emotion. "They taught us to embrace the unexpected."

The conversation flowed seamlessly, each idea sparking another, the words falling into place like pieces of a jigsaw puzzle. I could sense the shift in our dynamic—once burdened by the weight of unspoken tensions, we now found ourselves buoyed by laughter and the thrill of creation.

As the sun began to dip below the skyline, casting long shadows across the diner, I felt a sense of urgency mixed with exhilaration. This was our chance—not just to rekindle our passion for storytelling, but to redefine our narratives and infuse them with authenticity.

"What if we wrote a scene together?" I suggested, my heart racing at the thought of collaborating once more. "Something spontaneous, like we used to do."

Evan's eyes sparkled with mischief. "Alright, but only if it involves a road trip."

"Deal," I replied, feeling the thrill of youthful rebellion rush through me.

With that, we tossed aside our carefully curated notes and let our imaginations run wild. Words flowed like the river we once dreamed of—sometimes messy, sometimes lyrical, but always alive. In that quaint diner, surrounded by the warmth of coffee and the sweet smell of pie, we reclaimed our joy, channeling our journeys into a tapestry of stories that mirrored the lives we had led.

And as we wrote, we discovered something profound: we were not just retelling our past; we were embracing the beautiful, chaotic symphony of our lives, and for the first time in a long while, it felt like we were exactly where we were meant to be.

As our laughter mingled with the ambient sounds of clinking dishes and hushed conversations, I felt a palpable sense of liberation. Each shared memory transformed into a thread in the tapestry of our collaboration, and the diner morphed into our sacred space—an altar to our ambitions and dreams. With each word, our old script evolved into something vibrant and new, a vessel for our growth and understanding.

"Let's bring in elements from our lives," I suggested, my mind racing with ideas. "The characters should be flawed yet relatable, much like us."

Evan nodded, his eyes glimmering with inspiration. "What about a character who is navigating a tumultuous relationship with their own expectations? They want to be someone, but they're torn between who they are and who they think they should be."

"Yes! Like an artist who's lost their muse," I replied, eager to flesh it out. "We could reflect our own struggles, the times we felt adrift, questioning everything. It resonates with so many people."

He leaned closer, scribbling furiously on a napkin, and I couldn't help but feel a surge of affection for this man who had once shared my dreams so unconditionally. "What if we set it in a city that feels as alive and chaotic as the characters? A place where dreams collide with reality?"

"New York," I said, the name slipping off my tongue like a well-worn secret. "It's the backdrop of our youth, filled with ambition and despair. A character navigating the subway at rush hour could symbolize the chaos of pursuing dreams."

"Yes! And perhaps their journey involves unexpected friendships with strangers they meet along the way," he added, his voice rising with excitement. "Each encounter can teach them something new, peeling back layers of their identity."

We spent hours immersed in this creative whirlpool, each idea sparking another. The sun sank lower in the sky, casting a warm, golden hue that illuminated the diner's retro decor. The clatter of dishes began to fade as the evening crowd shifted, but we were lost in our world, oblivious to the passage of time.

"What if we introduce a secondary character, someone who embodies the spirit of adventure?" I suggested, the thought bubbling up like champagne. "They could challenge the protagonist to step out of their comfort zone, to confront their fears."

Evan grinned, clearly energized. "An artist, maybe? Someone who plays by their own rules, unafraid of failure. They could become the catalyst for change."

"Exactly! And through their interactions, our protagonist can begin to unravel their own insecurities," I mused, feeling the narrative take shape in my mind. "This adventure can symbolize not just the pursuit of artistic fulfillment but the journey toward self-acceptance."

The thrill of creation surged through us, a palpable energy that crackled in the air. It felt as if we were piecing together a puzzle, each fragment a reflection of our lives. I reveled in this sense of purpose, in the way our past experiences had shaped our perspectives, enriching our story.

As we continued to brainstorm, the words flowed with an ease that felt almost miraculous. We mapped out scenes filled with laughter and heartbreak, moments where the characters would stumble but ultimately rise, just as we had. It was exhilarating to consider how our own journeys had prepared us for this—how every setback had been a stepping stone, propelling us to this moment.

The sun finally dipped below the skyline, casting long shadows and bathing the diner in a soft twilight glow. The light outside turned golden, giving everything a surreal quality as if we were caught in a dream. I glanced at Evan, his silhouette framed by the window, and for a moment, I felt a wave of gratitude wash over me. This wasn't just about writing; it was about reconnecting, rediscovering the bond that had once felt unbreakable.

"Let's make a pact," I proposed, my heart racing. "No matter where life takes us, we'll always return to this. We'll keep creating, keep dreaming. Even when it's hard."

His eyes locked onto mine, filled with a sincerity that pierced through the playful banter. "I promise. This isn't just a story; it's our legacy."

A comfortable silence enveloped us, filled with the weight of our unspoken promises. I couldn't help but wonder what other chapters awaited us in this journey of rediscovery.

After a while, we decided to take a break, allowing the creative whirlwind to settle. I stood to grab us a couple of slices of that infamous pie, savoring the small joys that punctuated our lives. The warmth of the kitchen embraced me as I watched the baker roll out dough with deft fingers, his concentration palpable as he transformed simple ingredients into comfort. I imagined our characters savoring this very pie, sharing it amidst laughter and revelations, deepening their connections just as we had.

When I returned to the booth, Evan was lost in thought, his brow furrowed. I slid the slice of pie in front of him, breaking the tension that had momentarily clouded his expression. "Here's a taste of inspiration," I quipped, nudging him playfully.

He chuckled, the heaviness lifting, and as we dove into our slices, I couldn't help but notice the way the pie's sweetness mirrored the richness of our conversation. "You know," he said, licking a crumb from his lip, "there's something magical about revisiting our roots. It's like unearthing buried treasure."

"Yes! Every character we create carries a piece of us," I replied, my mind racing. "They are reflections, mirrors that show us our fears, our hopes, and even the parts we've tried to bury."

"And in sharing those stories, we help others feel less alone," he added, a glint of understanding in his eyes. "Isn't that what art is all about?"

We spent the rest of the evening crafting character arcs and plot twists, the diner's atmosphere enveloping us like a warm hug. The walls resonated with the echoes of countless stories shared over coffee and pie, and it felt as though we were weaving our own tale into that rich tapestry.

As we wrapped up for the night, the city outside buzzed with life, a constant reminder of the dreams that danced just out of reach. But this time, I felt armed with purpose and clarity. Our connection—rooted in shared history and renewed dreams—would propel us forward, guiding us as we navigated the intricate maze of creativity.

Walking out of the diner, the cool evening air nipped at my cheeks, and I breathed in deeply, tasting the promise of adventure. The world stretched before us, vast and inviting, a canvas awaiting our brushstrokes. I glanced at Evan, who walked beside me, the warmth of our renewed partnership radiating between us. In that moment, I knew that together, we could craft something extraordinary—a story that would not only honor our past but embrace the limitless potential of our future. The city sparkled around us, a reminder that every ending was simply a new beginning, and we were ready to embrace whatever came next.

Chapter 19: The Turning Tide

The diner exuded a nostalgic warmth, its neon sign buzzing softly like a firefly in the thick evening air. I could hear the sizzling of bacon and the dull clattering of plates, mingling with the gentle hum of laughter and low conversations, each voice wrapping around me like a favorite old sweater. The place was a tapestry of stories, woven together by the regulars who inhabited it, their lives unfolding over cups of coffee and greasy slices of pie. This was our sanctuary, a slice of Americana where dreams simmered alongside milkshakes, and where the bright red vinyl booths held whispers of secrets shared.

Sitting across from Evan, I felt the comfort of his presence, the way his smile ignited the very room around us. He had a way of making the mundane feel magical, as if even the chipped Formica tabletop held treasures of its own. I leaned forward, fully absorbed in the rhythm of our conversation, sharing tales of our days—his humorous anecdotes from the radio station, my latest forays into the world of freelance writing. We laughed, our voices blending with the clinks of cutlery and the distant jingle of the doorbell announcing new arrivals. It felt perfect, like the world had settled into a harmonious melody, one that I desperately wanted to last.

But then, just like that, the atmosphere shifted. The door swung open, and in she strode—Sophie, with her confident stride and an air of effortless charm. The flicker of the neon lights caught in her tousled hair, illuminating her like a movie star stepping into the limelight. She glided over to our booth with a disarming smile, her eyes sparkling with mischief, and slid into the seat opposite us without so much as a greeting. I felt an involuntary tightening in my chest, the easy warmth of the diner turning icy as she settled in, her presence a stark contrast to the jovial comfort that had enveloped us moments before.

"Well, well, look who it is," she said, her voice smooth as silk but laced with something sharper underneath. I could sense the tension in the air, thickening like the fog rolling in from the nearby bay. It wrapped around me, making my heart race as I exchanged a glance with Evan, his expression shifting from surprise to something unreadable. The easy rhythm we had established moments ago faltered, the melody turning discordant.

Sophie turned her attention to Evan, leaning in just a fraction too close, her laughter bright and infectious, drawing him into her orbit with a practiced ease. I felt small, like a leaf caught in a whirlwind, as my earlier confidence began to slip through my fingers like sand. The pang of jealousy was sharp and immediate, but this time, I swallowed it down. I took a deep breath, focusing on the space we had carved out together, willing the warmth of our connection to radiate back into existence.

"So, what are you two up to? Getting all cozy in here?" she teased, a playful glint in her eyes. I clenched my jaw, feeling the tension spiral around us. The lighthearted banter felt heavy now, weighted by her presence, but I refused to let her intrusion steal my thunder.

I forced a smile and redirected the conversation, recalling a story about my recent escapade at a local book signing where I had accidentally spilled coffee on my favorite author. The way I animatedly recounted the chaos drew Evan's laughter back, a sound like music to my ears. He leaned in, his eyes brightening, and for a moment, Sophie's hold on him wavered.

"Oh really? You did what?" he asked, his laughter infectious, warming me from the inside out. I shared the details, describing the author's horrified expression, how I had scrambled to clean up the mess while turning an embarrassing situation into a comical encounter. I could feel Sophie's annoyance simmering just beneath the surface, her playful smile faltering as she realized I wasn't about to let her dominate our evening.

As I spoke, I noticed the flicker of annoyance in her eyes, a fleeting reminder that I was no longer willing to play the passive role she expected of me. I was determined to reclaim my place in Evan's life, to remind him—and myself—that I was worthy of his attention. The tide was turning, and I was ready to swim against the current, to assert my presence in this complicated dance.

Sophie tried to interject with her own tales, but I maintained the momentum, leaning into the joy that bubbled between Evan and me. Our conversation flowed effortlessly, punctuated by shared glances and laughter that came easily, each moment reclaiming the space we had built. I sensed Sophie's frustration grow, the way her posture stiffened, her smile faltering as she fought to reestablish her position.

Just when I thought I could breathe a little easier, she switched tactics, her voice dripping with feigned sweetness. "Evan, I've been meaning to ask—how's that project going at the station? I heard some exciting changes are coming your way," she said, a calculated tone creeping into her words, the underlying intention clear as day.

Evan looked caught off guard, his attention faltering for a split second. But I seized the moment, eager to remind him of the vision we had discussed earlier, the dreams we had shared over countless coffees. "Oh, he's been absolutely crushing it! Just last week, he shared this incredible idea for a community outreach program. You should hear about it!" My enthusiasm flowed like a river, hopeful and vibrant, drowning out Sophie's calculated attempt to sway him.

As I spoke, I could see the moment Evan's eyes lit up again, his passion bubbling to the surface, feeding off my excitement. I felt a surge of triumph, a reminder that I held my own power. In that cozy diner, amidst the hum of laughter and the clinking of dishes, I was no longer just a spectator in a game that had once felt rigged against me. I was reclaiming my narrative, rewriting the story of us one word at a time, ready to navigate the uncertain waters ahead with courage and conviction.

The laughter between Evan and me mingled with the familiar sounds of clattering silverware and the soft chatter of other diners. I could feel the warmth of our shared humor wrapping around me like a well-worn blanket, grounding me amidst Sophie's invasive presence. The air was thick with the scent of coffee and cinnamon, making my heart swell with the comfort of this small, vibrant world. I kept my focus on Evan, noticing the little things that drew me to him—the way he tucked a loose strand of hair behind his ear when he was amused, or how his laughter had a way of lighting up even the dimmest corners of the diner.

Sophie leaned back in her seat, arms crossed, observing us with an intensity that felt almost predatory. The shift in her demeanor had transformed from playful to calculating, and I was acutely aware of the games she was playing. With a determined smile, I raised my cup, the steam swirling upward, a tangible reminder of my resolve.

"Did I tell you about the time I almost set my kitchen on fire?" I asked, a teasing glint in my eye. Evan's face lit up with intrigue, and I could see the familiar ease returning as he leaned in, forgetting Sophie for the moment. I launched into the tale, recounting the disaster of an ambitious baking attempt gone awry, complete with the smoke alarms blaring and my panicked attempts to salvage what was left of my pride. Each twist in the story elicited laughter from Evan, and the more animated I became, the more I felt the bonds of our connection strengthen.

Yet, Sophie was not one to be easily dismissed. "Sounds like a real disaster," she interjected, her tone laced with feigned concern. "But I'm sure you've learned your lesson. Some of us just have more natural talent in the kitchen." Her words dripped with a sweetness that felt more like poison than sugar, and I could see the way Evan's expression shifted, the lines of amusement tightening ever so slightly.

I met Sophie's gaze head-on, refusing to let her jibe derail me. "Oh, I've definitely learned a thing or two," I replied, my voice steady and bright. "For instance, I now know that smoke detectors make for very effective timers." I winked at Evan, who chuckled, clearly appreciating the lightheartedness. Sophie's facade of confidence wavered, and I felt a flicker of triumph—this was my moment to reclaim my narrative.

As we continued our banter, I could see the tide shifting. Sophie, though still attempting to claw her way back into the conversation, couldn't quite match the electric energy that crackled between Evan and me. He was fully engaged, his laughter infectious, pulling me further into our own little world where the din of the diner faded into a gentle hum. I was riding the wave of exhilaration, relishing every moment as I wove our shared history into the narrative, reminding him of the countless adventures we had embarked on together.

"I remember the last time we tried to make that ridiculously complicated soufflé," I said, nudging Evan playfully. "I think we spent more time picking egg shells out than actually cooking." The memory brought a grin to his face, and I felt a rush of warmth as our eyes locked, a silent acknowledgment passing between us—this was our story, rich and layered, and Sophie couldn't rewrite it.

She leaned forward, attempting to regain the spotlight. "I've been working on my culinary skills too," she said, her tone light but her eyes glinting with an underlying challenge. "Maybe we should have a cook-off one of these weekends. It could be fun!" The smile she wore was disarming, yet it masked the tension simmering just below the surface.

Evan's brows furrowed, clearly caught off guard by the suggestion. "That could be interesting," he replied cautiously, glancing at me. I could feel the weight of the moment hanging in the air, thick with unspoken words. There it was again—the tug-of-war for his attention, a game that had gone on far too long.

I took a deep breath, my heart racing. "Absolutely! Just remember, I bring the fire extinguisher," I shot back, my voice bright, my smile wide. The laughter erupted between us once more, and I could see Evan relax, that familiar ease settling back into his shoulders.

As the conversation continued, I could see the tables around us casting curious glances, drawn into the energy we were generating. I realized, in that moment, that I didn't just want to reclaim my place; I wanted to bask in it, to revel in the warmth of what we had. The diner was filled with life, each booth a small world of its own, yet here we were, crafting our own universe, distinct and resilient against the intrusion of outside forces.

Eventually, Sophie leaned back, her demeanor shifting as she crossed her arms again, a subtle but undeniable sign of defeat. The flicker of annoyance returned to her eyes, and I felt a rush of exhilaration; I had turned the tide, refusing to be swept away by her currents.

"So, what's next for you two?" she asked, her tone now bordering on condescension, as if trying to trap us in the web of her disinterest.

Evan's response was quick, vibrant. "We're planning to explore that new bookshop that opened downtown. They have a whole section on local authors. You should check it out, Sophie!" The invitation hung in the air, and I could see the shift in her expression, a momentary flash of discomfort that made my heart race with exhilaration.

"Sounds... quaint," she replied, a practiced smile on her lips. "I suppose that's what you two are into, huh?" The way she said it, as if it was a mere afterthought, only fueled my determination.

I turned to Evan, excitement bubbling within me. "It's a fantastic spot! They have an open mic night every Thursday, and I think you'd love it. It's all about showcasing local talent." I glanced back at Sophie, my heart thumping with a mixture of defiance and glee. "Who knows? Maybe I'll even read a few passages from my latest piece."

Evan's eyes sparkled at the thought, and I could feel the warmth of the moment enveloping us once again. We were creating our own path, and I was ready to walk it hand in hand with him, undeterred by the shadows of anyone else's presence. I was no longer an outsider in my own life, and the flicker of triumph in Evan's eyes told me that he recognized it too.

As the evening wore on, the chatter in the diner swelled and receded, but within our booth, time seemed to slow, expanding the moments into something profound. The laughter, the shared stories, the subtle glances—it was all weaving a tapestry of connection that felt invincible. In that cocoon of laughter and the familiar sounds of the diner, I knew that I was reclaiming not just my place, but a future intertwined with Evan's, bright and limitless.

The atmosphere in the diner pulsed with a renewed energy, the air thick with the aromas of frying eggs and freshly baked pie. As I continued to weave our narrative, I noticed the way Evan leaned in, drawn closer by the warmth of shared laughter and the comfort of familiarity. It was as though the chaotic swirl of life outside those red vinyl booths faded into an unimportant backdrop. Our conversations flowed with ease, each laugh and light-hearted jab pulling us deeper into the orbit we had created together, defying the gravitational pull of Sophie's unwelcome intrusion.

Sophie, with her polished demeanor, tried to interject again, but it was clear the spell she sought to cast was beginning to wane. Her attempt at a casual question fell flat, lost amidst the rhythm of our repartee. I reveled in the moment, feeling the tension in her posture shift slightly, the confident facade starting to crack. Each flicker of annoyance that crossed her face ignited a quiet thrill within me—a reminder that I wasn't just a passive player in this game of hearts. I had a voice, a story worth telling, and I was more than ready to reclaim my narrative.

"Tell me more about your radio show, Evan. I heard your last segment was a hit!" I encouraged, knowing how much he loved to share his passion. His face lit up, the spark igniting his eyes as he dove into the details of his latest on-air adventures. The way he described the conversations he had with local artists, each word imbued with his enthusiasm, was captivating. I watched as his passion painted vivid images in the air between us, a canvas of dreams and aspirations that echoed through the diner.

The dim light of the diner glinted off the silverware, casting tiny reflections like stars in a night sky, and for a moment, it felt as if we were the only two people in the universe. I drank in every detail: the slight flush in his cheeks, the way he gestured animatedly, his fingers tracing the air as he built his narrative. I leaned forward, encouraging him with nods and playful interjections, each moment drawing us closer, pushing the uncertainty and tension of Sophie's presence into the background.

Yet, as Evan's words flowed, Sophie shifted in her seat, the impatience radiating off her like waves of heat. "You really should consider diversifying your interests, Evan. There's a whole world outside this little diner," she remarked, a sharp edge cutting through her playful tone. Her attempt to redirect the conversation was transparent, a last-ditch effort to reel him back into her orbit.

But I refused to let her overshadow our moment. "True, but sometimes the best stories come from the places we least expect," I countered, my voice steady, a deliberate choice to affirm our connection in front of her. I glanced at Evan, whose expression remained engaged, his focus unwavering. In that fleeting moment, I felt a surge of triumph, the sense that I was holding my ground and refusing to yield to her insidious charm.

With a well-timed change of topic, I reached into my bag and pulled out a stack of freshly printed flyers for the local community event I was organizing. "Speaking of stories, I've been planning a fundraiser to highlight local authors and their work. We could use someone like you to help spread the word, Evan! You're such a natural with your connections," I suggested, my excitement bubbling over as I placed the flyers in front of him. The vibrancy of my enthusiasm was palpable, a breath of fresh air sweeping through our booth.

Sophie's expression darkened, her carefully cultivated smile faltering as she glanced at the flyers. "Oh, that's nice, but do you really think you can pull that off?" she questioned, her tone dripping with skepticism. It felt like a jab, a well-placed dart aimed to deflate my spirit, but I could sense Evan's protectiveness simmering beneath the surface.

"Actually, I think it's a fantastic idea," he replied, his voice firm, filled with conviction. "You should give it a shot. There's a lot of talent in this community that deserves to be showcased." The way he looked at me then was a silent promise, a reassurance that he stood with me, ready to help me fight back against the shadows of doubt Sophie sought to cast.

As the evening continued, the atmosphere began to shift, the initial tension slowly dissipating. The chatter from other booths blended into a soothing background hum, the rhythmic clinking of coffee cups creating a comforting symphony. The diner felt alive, each patron contributing their own story to the tapestry we were creating together.

I glanced out the window, where the dimming light of dusk cast a soft glow over the streets, transforming the mundane into something almost magical. The vibrant neon sign of the diner flickered, its reflection dancing on the rain-slicked pavement outside, a beacon of warmth amid the gathering shadows. I felt a swell of gratitude for this moment, for the sanctuary we had carved out for ourselves amidst the chaos of life.

Sophie leaned back, her interest waning as she observed us from a distance, her attempts to manipulate the narrative gradually falling flat. It was as if the very air around us thickened with a sense of inevitability. I could sense the shift, an unspoken agreement that our world was no longer hers to navigate.

Evan's laughter broke through the silence, a sound so genuine it sent a jolt of joy through me. "And remember the time we tried to make a podcast?" he recalled, and the memory flooded back, igniting a fresh wave of laughter between us. We were two adventurers navigating uncharted waters, each mishap and misstep only drawing us closer.

The conversation flowed effortlessly, an intricate dance of words and glances, each moment laden with meaning. I could feel the warmth of Evan's presence, a steady flame igniting my heart, as we began to envision what lay ahead. A world filled with potential, where our dreams could flourish beyond the confines of the diner's neon-lit walls.

As Sophie sat silently across from us, her attempts at distraction dwindling, I felt a sense of liberation. The tide had indeed turned, and I was no longer on the periphery, waiting for my moment to arrive. I was in the center of it all, surrounded by laughter and warmth, ready to forge ahead, hand in hand with Evan.

With every laugh shared, every story told, I felt the invisible chains of uncertainty slip away. The connection we were nurturing was profound, unyielding, and as the diner buzzed with life around us, I knew that this was just the beginning of our journey together—a beautiful, messy, and vibrant adventure waiting to unfold.

Chapter 20: The Spark of Inspiration

The clatter of silverware and the murmur of conversation enveloped me like a warm embrace as I settled into my usual corner booth at the diner, its well-worn vinyl a comforting presence beneath me. This place, with its flickering neon sign and the aroma of frying bacon mingling with freshly brewed coffee, had always felt like home. The walls were adorned with black-and-white photographs, each capturing a moment in time—laughter shared over a milkshake, families gathered for Sunday brunch, lovers stealing a kiss under the gentle glow of overhead lights. Today, however, my heart raced for reasons beyond the usual comfort. I could still feel the weight of Evan's gaze from our last encounter, a haunting blend of nostalgia and unspoken promises that echoed in my thoughts.

With my laptop open and a half-eaten slice of pie beside me, I lost myself in the world I was creating. The café hummed with life, the low chatter blending into a backdrop that fueled my creativity. I ran my fingers over the keyboard, each click a note in the symphony of my thoughts. Scenes unfolded like petals blooming in spring—vivid, layered, and intricately beautiful. I imagined characters that danced through the narrative, each movement infused with the essence of what I felt for Evan, a reminder that love could bloom even amidst the chaos of life.

As I edited, I became a conductor of emotions, orchestrating every frame with care. I could see the protagonist—her spirit fiery yet tender—mirroring my own journey. She traversed the landscapes of love and loss, grappling with the same fears and desires that had plagued me. In her, I found solace, a reflection of my struggles, my triumphs. The café's ambiance enveloped me, and for those precious hours, I forgot the world outside. I was not just crafting a film; I was weaving my heart into each scene, allowing the pixels to transform into a tapestry of raw emotion.

It wasn't long before the diner's door swung open, and the familiar chime heralded Evan's arrival. He strode in, his presence commanding the attention of the room, even amid the bustling crowd. There was something magnetic about him—his tousled hair catching the light, those deep-set eyes that seemed to hold secrets of their own. My heart fluttered as he approached, the weight of our shared history hanging between us like an invisible thread, taut yet fragile.

"Mind if I join you?" he asked, a teasing grin playing on his lips. I gestured to the seat across from me, a smile breaking free as the remnants of hesitation melted away. His mere presence sparked something deep within me, a blend of creativity and longing that filled the air around us. We fell into conversation effortlessly, our words weaving a tapestry of laughter and shared memories, rekindling the chemistry that had once burned so brightly between us.

"So, what's the project you've been working on?" Evan leaned in, genuine curiosity dancing in his eyes. I hesitated for a moment, feeling a mix of vulnerability and excitement. Sharing my work felt like exposing my soul, yet there was a strange thrill in inviting him into this part of my life.

"It's a film about love—its complexities, the beauty in vulnerability," I explained, my passion spilling over as I detailed the narrative arc and character development. Evan listened intently, nodding along, his enthusiasm palpable. With each word I spoke, I could see the flicker of inspiration igniting in his gaze, and it emboldened me to delve deeper.

"And you've captured it all in this little laptop?" he teased, his laughter ringing like music, a balm to my creative nerves. "I can only imagine how you've managed to turn your experiences into such a vivid portrayal."

We spent hours dissecting ideas, brainstorming plot twists, and developing characters, our imaginations intertwining in a dance of inspiration. With every passing moment, the spark of our shared creativity illuminated the diner, our laughter blending with the clink of coffee cups and the sizzle of the grill. I couldn't help but marvel at how easily our minds synced, as if we had been crafting stories together for a lifetime.

As the sun dipped below the horizon, painting the diner's windows with hues of gold and crimson, I felt an exhilarating rush. We were no longer just friends rekindling old flames; we were collaborators, each stroke of our conversation fanning the flames of ambition. I sensed a shift in the air, a promise of what could be if we dared to embrace this connection.

"Why don't we do this more often?" I asked, my heart racing at the prospect. "You have so many ideas, and I could use the extra perspective." Evan's expression brightened, a spark of mischief in his eyes as he leaned back, considering my offer.

"I'd love that," he replied, his voice low, filled with sincerity. "I've always admired your vision, and collaborating sounds like a dream. Plus, it gives me an excuse to spend more time with you."

As the night deepened, we exchanged stories—fragments of our lives that shaped us, making us who we were today. I shared tales of late-night drives along the Pacific Coast Highway, where the ocean met the sky in an eternal embrace. He recounted adventures from his travels, each destination a new chapter that painted his world with colors I longed to see. The more we shared, the more I realized how intertwined our journeys had been, both marked by moments of serendipity and longing.

With the diner's neon lights flickering above us like distant stars, I knew we stood on the brink of something extraordinary. Our collaboration felt like the beginning of a new chapter, one where our passions intertwined, creating something greater than ourselves.

The thought filled me with a warmth that pulsed through my veins, igniting my creative spirit. I was not just telling a story; I was living it, breathing life into the characters that reflected our journey—a testament to the magic of second chances and the undeniable spark of inspiration that could light the way, even through the darkest of nights.

The following days unfolded like a symphony, each moment building upon the last, creating a harmonious blend of ideas and inspiration. The sun spilled through my apartment windows, casting warm golden rays that danced across my cluttered desk, illuminating sketches and storyboards I had painstakingly crafted. Every inch of the space radiated creativity; the walls, adorned with posters from films that had shaped my childhood, bore witness to my artistic ambitions. I often found myself losing track of time, immersed in a world that felt both familiar and exhilaratingly new.

Evan became a fixture in my daily routine, his laughter echoing through the halls of my apartment as we bounced ideas off one another like a pair of kids in a candy store. We settled into a comfortable rhythm, the kind that felt as if we had been doing this forever. Over the faint sound of the city outside, we would argue over the best plot twists or hash out character arcs, our discussions evolving into a delightful tapestry woven with banter and mutual admiration. There was a playfulness in our creativity, a sense of lightness that made it easy to forget the weight of the world outside.

One afternoon, while we sat cross-legged on the floor, surrounded by stacks of notes and half-finished storyboards, I noticed a flicker of excitement in Evan's eyes as he sketched out a particularly ambitious scene. His fingers moved deftly, bringing to life a visual I had only begun to imagine. It was as if each stroke of his pencil captured a part of him—his passion, his vision—and I couldn't help but be captivated by the way he brought ideas to life.

"Picture this," he said, his voice animated, "the protagonist stands on the edge of a cliff, overlooking the ocean at sunset. It's a moment of reckoning, a decision that could change everything. The waves crash below, mirroring the turmoil inside her." He paused, his gaze fixed on the horizon outside the window. "This isn't just about the story; it's about the release. We all have our cliffs, don't we?"

I nodded, feeling a wave of inspiration wash over me. "Exactly! It's about facing those fears head-on, finding the courage to leap into the unknown. It's exhilarating and terrifying at the same time."

As the words tumbled out, I realized that what we were crafting was more than just a film; it was a reflection of our journeys, our struggles, and the hopes we dared to harbor. In that moment, surrounded by scattered notes and coffee cups, I could feel the invisible thread that bound us together growing stronger. Our shared vulnerabilities poured into the narrative, transforming our collaboration into something deeply personal.

The city outside pulsed with life, its heartbeat syncing with the rhythm of our creativity. The chatter of passersby floated in through the open window, a reminder of the world beyond our bubble. On particularly inspired days, we would take breaks, stepping outside to let the energy of the streets fuel our imagination. The vibrant chaos of street vendors hawking their wares, artists painting murals on crumbling brick walls, and laughter ringing out from cafes painted a colorful backdrop to our burgeoning story.

One evening, as we strolled through the bustling streets, the sun dipped below the skyline, painting the sky in shades of violet and crimson. I could feel the buzz of excitement crackling in the air, as if the universe itself was cheering us on. We paused in front of a small gallery, its windows showcasing vibrant pieces that seemed to beckon us inside.

"Let's take a look," Evan suggested, his eyes alight with curiosity. Inside, the walls were adorned with canvases that captured the essence of humanity—the beauty, the pain, the rawness of existence. Each piece resonated deeply, drawing me in as I lost myself in the colors and forms that spoke of stories untold.

"Art has this incredible ability to connect people," I mused, glancing at Evan. "It's like a bridge that allows us to understand each other on a deeper level."

He nodded, studying a piece that depicted two figures reaching for one another across a chasm, their hands almost touching. "Exactly. It's a reminder that even in our struggles, we're not alone. There's a thread that ties us all together."

As we moved through the gallery, I felt a sense of clarity wash over me. The emotions evoked by the artwork mirrored what I was striving to convey in my film. The stories were all around us, waiting to be captured and shared, and our mission felt more vital than ever.

Afterward, we found ourselves back in my apartment, the weight of the day transformed into a bubbling sense of possibility. We sprawled on the floor, surrounded by sketches and notes, the atmosphere charged with creativity. I reached for my laptop and began typing, the words flowing freely as Evan chimed in, enhancing the narrative with his insights.

Hours melted away as we crafted a sequence that captured the essence of our discoveries—the beauty of connection, the complexity of choices, and the power of vulnerability. It felt exhilarating, a perfect blend of our voices merging into something beautifully unique. As the clock ticked past midnight, I could hardly believe how far we had come, how much our collaboration had grown.

"Can you believe how amazing this is?" I asked, looking up from the screen, my heart racing. "We're really doing this. We're creating something that means something, something that could resonate with people."

Evan met my gaze, his expression serious yet playful. "Absolutely. But just remember, it's only the beginning. There's so much more to explore, to discover."

The thrill of the unknown sparkled between us, igniting a shared ambition that pushed us forward. I could feel the world opening up before us, the possibilities endless as we ventured deeper into this creative journey. It was exhilarating, terrifying, and everything in between—like standing on the edge of that cliff, ready to leap into the vast expanse of our dreams.

With every brainstorming session, with every late-night editing spree, I began to believe that the magic we were weaving together was more than just a film; it was a testament to the power of connection and the beauty of taking risks. In that moment, I knew we were not just artists, but explorers navigating the uncharted territory of our hearts and minds. And as we moved forward, I felt a sense of purpose igniting within me, a spark that promised to illuminate even the darkest corners of our journey.

The more we immersed ourselves in the project, the deeper the layers of our collaboration unraveled, revealing intricate details that breathed life into the story. The apartment transformed into our sacred creative space, littered with coffee cups, sketches, and an ever-growing stack of screenplays. Each evening, the golden glow of the lamps created a cozy cocoon, shielding us from the outside world as we dove into the depths of our imaginations.

One chilly evening, wrapped in blankets, we found ourselves lost in conversation about the heartbeat of our narrative—the protagonist's journey through love and loss. The streets outside were slick with rain, the soft patter against the window creating a rhythmic backdrop to our brainstorming session. I leaned back against the couch, thoughts swirling like the steam rising from our mugs.

"Let's give her a flaw that makes her relatable, someone who struggles to let go," I suggested, my voice barely rising above the soothing sounds of the rain. "Something that reflects our fears about vulnerability."

Evan nodded, his brow furrowed in concentration. "Absolutely. Maybe she's been hurt in the past, leading her to push people away, even those who truly care for her." He leaned forward, excitement lighting up his eyes. "And then she meets someone who challenges her to confront those fears. It's the push and pull of intimacy."

As the words flowed between us, I could see the character taking shape—a vivid figure of strength and fragility, much like us. I imagined her standing on that metaphorical cliff Evan had described, peering into the abyss of her own insecurities while yearning for connection. I thought of the moments in my life that mirrored her struggles, the time I hesitated to share my dreams with others for fear of failure, the times I let opportunities slip through my fingers.

"Let's give her a moment of clarity," I proposed, my voice taking on a more passionate tone. "A scene where she stands on that cliff, looking out at the horizon, and realizes that sometimes, the greatest risk is not taking one at all."

Evan's face lit up with inspiration, and he grabbed a nearby notepad, furiously jotting down notes. "Yes! That's where we can really pull at the audience's heartstrings. We can juxtapose her fear with the beauty of what lies beyond the edge—a metaphorical leap of faith."

The rain continued to drum softly against the window, and with every idea that sparked between us, I could feel the story solidifying. The air around us crackled with creativity, as if the universe itself was conspiring to bring our visions to life.

As the days rolled on, we began to envision the supporting characters, a colorful ensemble that would enrich our narrative tapestry. Each one came alive with quirks and dreams, blending seamlessly into the protagonist's world. I imagined a wise yet eccentric mentor, an old filmmaker who recognized the fire within our protagonist, and a loyal best friend who would stand by her through thick and thin, offering comic relief and sage advice.

One afternoon, we decided to venture out for inspiration, the air crisp with the scent of autumn leaves. We strolled through the nearby park, the trees ablaze with hues of gold and crimson, their branches swaying gently in the breeze. The laughter of children playing nearby mingled with the rustling leaves, and I couldn't help but feel that we were walking through a living canvas, one that echoed the beauty of our own budding narrative.

"Nature has a way of reminding us of life's cycles," Evan mused, kicking a fallen leaf as we wandered down a winding path. "It's all about growth, letting go, and embracing change."

"That's it!" I exclaimed, my eyes lighting up. "What if we incorporate elements of nature into the story? The changing seasons can mirror her emotional journey, representing the stages of her growth."

Evan grinned, his enthusiasm infectious. "And each season can bring a different lesson—spring for renewal, summer for passion, autumn for reflection, and winter for introspection."

As we continued our walk, ideas blossomed like the flowers peeking through the frost. I could see the protagonist moving through these seasons, her transformation paralleling the world around her, each shift reflecting her internal battles.

Returning home that evening, we collapsed onto the couch, surrounded by sketches and notes that now looked more like a patchwork quilt than mere ideas scattered across the floor. I felt a thrill run through me, a blend of excitement and anxiety. The story was evolving, becoming more than just a film; it was a piece of our souls, a testament to our vulnerabilities and aspirations.

We dove into the editing process once more, meticulously piecing together scenes that captured the essence of our journey. Every frame resonated with meaning, and I could see glimpses of myself in the protagonist—her fears, her hopes, her relentless pursuit of authenticity. I felt a profound connection to her, as if she were an extension of my own heart.

One night, as we worked late into the hours, the weight of the world faded away, leaving only the hum of creativity. The city outside twinkled with life, but inside our bubble, time stood still. I looked over at Evan, his focus unwavering, a slight smile playing at the corners of his lips as he adjusted a scene. There was something comforting in the way he devoted himself to our work, his passion igniting the air between us.

"Do you ever wonder where this journey will take us?" I asked, my voice soft, breaking the stillness that enveloped us. "I mean, what if we actually finish this? What if it resonates with people?"

Evan turned to me, the warmth of his gaze steadying my racing heart. "I think it will. We're pouring everything we have into this, and authenticity always finds a way to connect. People crave real stories, the kind that touch the soul."

His words hung in the air, a promise of what lay ahead. The flickering candlelight danced across his features, highlighting the determination etched in his brow. In that moment, I felt an overwhelming sense of gratitude wash over me. Here we were, two souls entwined in a creative pursuit, wrestling with our dreams and fears, and forging something magnificent together.

The following weeks saw us navigating the peaks and valleys of the creative process, our laughter mingling with moments of frustration and triumph. The story unfolded in ways we never anticipated, each twist and turn a delightful surprise. Late nights transformed into early mornings, fueled by caffeine and the exhilarating pull of inspiration. Our discussions grew deeper, exploring not only the narrative but the themes that resonated with us—the power of love, the importance of vulnerability, and the necessity of embracing change.

As we neared the completion of our project, I couldn't shake the feeling that we were standing at the precipice of something monumental. The film had become a mirror reflecting our journeys, our growth, and our shared experiences. It was as if we had poured our hearts into a vessel, ready to set it afloat into the world, a testament to the magic that can arise when two creative souls unite.

And in that moment of clarity, amidst the chaos of our shared space, I realized that whatever awaited us on the other side—success, failure, or something in between—what truly mattered was the journey itself, the connections we had forged, and the way we had breathed life into our dreams together.

Chapter 21: Shifting Currents

The air in the room felt electric, charged with the unspoken words lingering between Evan and me, like a tightly wound spring waiting for release. Each late-night editing session had transformed into an unexpected ritual, a delicate dance of camaraderie that danced around the edges of something deeper. Our laughter echoed softly against the walls, punctuated by the rustle of papers and the gentle tap of keys as we meticulously dissected each line of our collaborative project. Yet, it was the shared glances that lingered longer than necessary, the accidental brushes of our fingers, that sent ripples of warmth through me, a spark that ignited my imagination in ways I had never anticipated.

Evan was everything I admired—intelligent, with a wit that could cut through the heaviest of silences, and a kindness that enveloped me like a warm blanket. He wore his dark hair slightly tousled, as if he had just rolled out of bed after a restless night spent thinking of me, which felt like a lovely fantasy I cherished even when I knew it wasn't entirely true. His blue eyes were a clear sky after a storm, captivating and often reflecting the complexity of his thoughts, making me wonder what lay behind them. It was as though I could see entire galaxies in the depths of his gaze, each twinkle illuminating the spaces we dared not traverse.

We spent those evenings in my cramped apartment, an eclectic blend of mismatched furniture and overflowing bookshelves that teetered under the weight of stories yet to be told. The smell of coffee hung thick in the air, mingling with the scent of old paper and ink. I often lost myself in the warmth of the moment, the way the soft glow of the lamp cast a golden hue over everything, painting our conversation in rich, vivid colors. My heart raced, a chaotic orchestra in my chest, as I found myself wanting more than just shared ideas and creative breakthroughs; I longed for a deeper connection that simmered just below the surface.

It was on one such night, as the city outside my window bathed in the light of a thousand flickering stars, that the atmosphere shifted. We had just wrapped up a particularly intense session, our laughter mingling with the rhythmic tapping of rain against the window. I watched as Evan leaned back in his chair, running a hand through his hair in that way that made my heart flutter. The moment felt charged, and I dared to linger on his lips for a heartbeat too long, my thoughts racing with the possibilities of what lay ahead. Just then, the phone shattered the delicate silence, its shrill ring slicing through the warmth like a cold winter wind.

The moment I saw my mother's name flash on the screen, a chill gripped my heart. I answered with a tentative "Hello," each syllable laced with a growing sense of dread. My mother's voice, usually so steady and reassuring, trembled with an urgency that set my mind spiraling. My father's health had taken a turn for the worse, a sudden decline that left me breathless. Each word felt like a stone dropped into the still waters of my newfound happiness, sending ripples of anxiety and uncertainty crashing against the shores of my heart.

As I hung up the phone, the warmth of the room faded, replaced by a cold reality that settled heavily on my shoulders. I could feel the weight of my father's absence looming like a dark cloud, threatening to swallow the brightness I had found with Evan. My heart raced as I glanced at him, his expression shifting from curiosity to concern as he sensed the change in the atmosphere. I wanted to shield him from my turmoil, to protect the fragile connection we had nurtured in those intimate hours, but I could feel the tears welling up, my defenses crumbling.

"I have to go back home," I managed to whisper, my voice barely above a breath.

His gaze softened, and I could see the questions swirling in his mind. The unspoken fear of losing what we had barely begun to build weighed heavily between us. "What happened?" he asked, his voice low and gentle, like a balm on a fresh wound.

"My dad," I replied, the words catching in my throat. "He's... he's not doing well." The admission felt like a confession, raw and exposed. My heart thudded painfully in my chest, the thought of returning to the town I had escaped from clashing violently with the memories I had buried deep within. The prospect of facing my past, of unraveling the threads of my childhood, filled me with dread, yet I knew I had no choice.

Evan reached across the table, his hand enveloping mine in a comforting grip that sent shockwaves of warmth through me, a reminder of the connection we had forged. "I'm here for you," he said, his voice steady, offering a lifeline in the storm that raged within me. But I couldn't help but feel that the promise of support came with the weight of uncertainty, a tether that could just as easily pull us apart as it could bind us together.

As I prepared to leave, the thought of returning to that familiar yet suffocating place haunted me. The streets of my hometown were lined with memories, some sweet, others bitter, and the thought of facing them again made my stomach churn. I could already picture the small, quaint diner where I spent countless afternoons with my father, his laughter echoing against the backdrop of clinking cutlery and sizzling burgers. Now, the thought of returning to that booth, where I once felt safe and cherished, now felt like stepping into a whirlwind of conflicting emotions.

Tears brimmed at the corners of my eyes as I stole one last glance at Evan, the realization that I might be leaving behind more than just a budding romance crashing over me like a tidal wave. Our connection, so vibrant and alive, suddenly felt like a fragile dream at the mercy of my inevitable return to the past. The promise of what we could be lingered in the air, tantalizing yet tainted with the knowledge that I was about to step into a reality that threatened to unravel everything I held dear.

The drive back to my hometown felt like traversing a familiar yet foreboding landscape, each mile stretching my anxiety thin as I navigated the winding roads that led to a place once filled with laughter and love but now seemed steeped in shadows. The trees lining the highway stood tall and solemn, their branches swaying gently in the wind, as if whispering secrets of those who had walked this path before me. With each passing glance, I was reminded of memories I had tried so hard to tuck away—the summer days spent on the banks of the river, the scent of blooming wildflowers, and my father's hearty laughter echoing through the air like a cherished melody. Yet, those joyful notes were now accompanied by an ominous undertone, a reminder of the gravity that loomed over me.

As I approached the familiar outskirts of town, the first signs of civilization appeared: the crumbling brick of the old general store, the park where I had learned to ride my bike, and the white picket fences that encased houses filled with stories and lives long forgotten. Each landmark felt like a poignant reminder of who I once was—a girl filled with dreams and the innocent hope that life would always carry the sweetness of summer. But now, I was returning not as that carefree child but as a woman burdened with the weight of reality, ready to confront the ghosts of my past.

Pulling into the driveway of my childhood home, I took a moment to gather myself. The house stood as a testament to time, its paint peeling and the garden overgrown, mirroring the state of my emotions. A bittersweet nostalgia enveloped me, swirling like the autumn leaves that danced around my feet as I stepped out of the car. The familiar creak of the gate echoed in my ears, a sound so ordinary yet layered with years of memories—distant laughter, arguments, and those quiet moments of contentment shared over cups of steaming tea.

My mother greeted me at the door, her eyes filled with a mixture of relief and worry that cut through me like a knife. She enveloped me in her embrace, and I could feel the warmth of her body, yet there was an undeniable tension in her grip, a silent acknowledgment of the gravity of our circumstances. "He's in the hospital," she whispered, her voice thick with emotion, as if speaking too loudly might shatter the delicate bubble we were both trying to maintain.

The hospital felt sterile, the scent of antiseptic wafting through the air like a bitter reminder of the fragility of life. I walked through the corridors, my heart heavy with the weight of uncertainty, each step resonating against the linoleum floor. The muted conversations of nurses and the soft beeping of machines filled the air, creating an atmosphere charged with anxiety. It felt surreal, stepping into a place where time seemed suspended, as if each moment held the potential for both hope and despair.

When I finally entered my father's room, I was unprepared for the sight before me. He lay in the bed, a frail shadow of the man I remembered, his face gaunt and his breaths shallow. The room was dim, the only light coming from a small window where the sun filtered through, casting soft shadows that danced across the walls. I felt a rush of emotions surge through me—fear, sadness, and an overwhelming sense of helplessness. This was the man who had taught me how to ride a bike, who had cheered the loudest at my graduations, who had made me believe in magic with his tales of adventure. And now, he was reduced to this—stripped of his vitality and spirit, leaving behind an ache that settled deep within my chest.

I approached the bed slowly, as if afraid to disturb the fragile moment. "Dad," I whispered, my voice trembling. His eyes fluttered open, and for a brief moment, clarity flickered within them, a spark of recognition that sent a rush of warmth through my veins. "I'm here." I grasped his hand, the familiar warmth still present despite the chill that permeated the room.

"Sweetheart," he croaked, his voice a mere whisper, "you shouldn't have come." The words hung heavy in the air, a quiet testament to his unwavering desire to shield me from pain, even as he lay vulnerable before me.

"Of course, I had to come," I replied, squeezing his hand, trying to infuse my warmth into him. "You mean everything to me." The truth of my words poured out, an unfiltered declaration that surged through the haze of fear and uncertainty. In that moment, nothing else mattered—just the bond between us, the love that transcended the circumstances.

As the days unfolded, I settled into a rhythm, balancing my time between the hospital and my childhood home. I took refuge in the small things that once brought me joy: the comforting scent of my mother's cooking wafting through the air, the gentle rustle of leaves outside my window, and the memories that whispered through the halls of the house. Yet, there was an underlying tension that gnawed at me, the gnawing ache of the life I had left behind—the late-night conversations with Evan, the laughter we shared, and the burgeoning connection that felt like a flickering flame ready to ignite.

Even as I devoted myself to my father's care, I couldn't shake the feeling of longing that wrapped around my heart like a vine, entangling me in a bittersweet embrace. I found myself reaching for my phone, wishing I could bridge the distance between us, to share my fears and anxieties with Evan, to seek comfort in the familiarity of his voice. But the reality of my situation weighed heavy on my conscience, reminding me that the life I had built was on pause, suspended in the limbo of my father's illness.

One afternoon, as I sat by my father's bedside, the sun streaming through the window, I felt a sudden surge of determination. I would be there for him, fighting through every moment of darkness, but

I also had to keep a piece of my heart alive for myself. I picked up my phone, hesitant but resolute, and typed out a message to Evan, letting him know I was thinking of him, that I missed our late-night discussions, and that I would return to the life we had begun to forge together. In that moment, it felt like an act of rebellion against the current that threatened to sweep me away, a small affirmation that love, in all its forms, was worth holding onto, no matter the storm raging around me.

The hospital room became my sanctuary and my prison, a juxtaposition of hope and despair. I spent countless hours by my father's side, absorbing every word he spoke, cherishing the moments of clarity that flickered across his face like a passing storm cloud. Despite his condition, there were glimmers of the man I adored—his humor surfacing unexpectedly, a wry comment about the hospital's bland food or a shared memory that could momentarily lift the pallor that shadowed his features. "Remember the fishing trip when you caught that tiny fish and insisted it was the biggest?" he chuckled weakly, his laughter an echo of a time when life felt infinitely brighter. I nodded, the warmth of nostalgia flooding my heart, a reminder of simpler days and the bond we shared.

Yet, as days stretched into weeks, an ache settled in the pit of my stomach. Each moment spent in this sterile bubble made me acutely aware of the life I had pressed pause on. The conversations with Evan, once a vibrant source of joy, turned into a bittersweet longing. I found myself recalling our late-night discussions, the way he listened as if I were the only person in the world, the way his laughter ignited a warmth within me that I hadn't known I craved. With each passing day, I missed him more—his quick wit, his kindness, and that spark of connection that had begun to weave itself into the fabric of my life.

On one particularly quiet afternoon, as I sat by my father's bedside, my fingers instinctively reached for my phone, my heart racing at the thought of hearing Evan's voice. I sent a message, pouring my heart into the screen: I miss you. Things are tough here. Just wanted you to know you're on my mind. The seconds felt like hours as I waited for a response, each heartbeat a reminder of my vulnerability and the gaping distance between us.

As evening settled in, the sky painted with hues of orange and violet, my phone buzzed, breaking the stillness. Evan's message flickered to life, a warm embrace across the miles. I'm here for you. Let me know when you need me. His words were simple yet packed with sincerity, wrapping around me like a lifeline in turbulent waters. A smile broke through my worries, illuminating the darkness that had been creeping in on me.

With newfound resolve, I decided I would share with him the intricacies of my experience here—my father's strength, the love that enveloped us like a protective shield, and the ache of nostalgia that threatened to drown me. I wanted him to know that even in this haze of uncertainty, he had become a light guiding me back to myself.

The days began to blur together, but I held onto the moments that mattered—the laughter shared with my father, the sweet anecdotes that painted vivid pictures of our past. Yet, the specter of my decision loomed over me, an unshakable weight pressing against my chest. I couldn't ignore the sense of urgency that tugged at me, a whisper that insisted I must reconcile the pieces of my life before it was too late.

With each passing day, my father's condition shifted like the tide, a constant reminder of life's fragility. I watched as my mother stood vigil by his side, her unwavering strength both inspiring and heartbreaking. It was in those moments that I recognized how deeply love could run, binding us together in the face of adversity. I found myself drawing strength from their bond, marveling at the way they navigated this storm hand in hand.

One evening, as the sun dipped below the horizon, casting a golden glow across the room, my father turned to me with a newfound clarity. "You need to live, sweetheart," he said, his voice steady but soft. "Don't hold back because of me." His words hung in the air, a gentle push against the walls I had built around myself.

"I want to," I replied, the ache in my chest surfacing again. "I just don't know how to balance it all."

"Love is worth the risk," he said, his gaze unwavering, as if he were imparting the most vital lesson of my life. "You've got to fight for it."

Those words resonated within me, echoing through the labyrinth of my thoughts. It was a reminder that life was fleeting, that each moment was precious and ought to be embraced rather than feared. I realized then that I couldn't let my father's illness define my happiness or my love for Evan.

As I stepped outside the hospital, the night air was crisp, carrying with it the promise of change. I looked up at the stars, each twinkle a reminder of all the possibilities waiting for me beyond these walls. With every inhale, I breathed in hope, determination swelling within me like the tides. I made a promise to myself that I would not only support my father but also return to Evan—to nurture the budding relationship that felt so promising.

The next day, I took a leap of faith, reaching out to Evan once more. I explained everything—the bittersweet moments spent with my father, my mother's resilience, and the small victories that brightened our days. I spoke of the laughter that echoed through the hospital corridors, how it reminded me that love could flourish even in the bleakest of circumstances. I poured my heart into every word, hoping he would feel the depth of my longing and the sincerity of my intentions.

His response was swift, filled with understanding and warmth. I'm here, no matter what. We'll figure it out together. Reading his words, I felt the tension in my chest begin to ease, as if a dam had broken, allowing the flood of emotions to flow freely.

As I returned to the hospital, my heart felt lighter. I began to look for ways to bring joy into my father's room. I would read to him, choosing books filled with adventure and laughter, hoping to transport us both to distant lands far removed from the sterile walls of the hospital. I brought in photos from my life, snippets of joy and warmth that brought a smile to his face, anchoring him in the love that surrounded us.

Each evening, as I settled into the rhythm of caring for him, I made it a point to talk about Evan, sharing our stories, our hopes, and the connection we had built. I saw the flicker of recognition in my father's eyes, a spark of understanding that he encouraged me to embrace wholeheartedly. "Love is what matters most, my girl," he whispered one night, his grip on my hand firm yet gentle. "You've got to hold onto that, even when it feels uncertain."

In that moment, I realized I was at a crossroads, one foot planted firmly in my past, the other stepping forward into a future painted with possibilities. As I leaned in closer to my father, the warmth of his presence wrapped around me like a protective cloak, and I vowed to cherish every moment—both with him and with Evan. I understood that while the storm may rage on, the love we shared would always light the way forward, guiding me through the darkness and into the light.

Chapter 22: Homecoming

Returning to my childhood home feels like stepping into a time capsule, each familiar corner stirring memories long buried. The heavy wooden door creaks open, a familiar protest echoing through the silence of the entryway, and I am engulfed by the scent of my mother's baking wafting from the kitchen. It's an aroma that wraps around me like a soft, warm blanket, transporting me back to lazy Sunday afternoons spent sprawled across the living room floor, flour dusting my small hands as I helped her mix batter for the sweetest of cakes. Those moments felt infinite then, untouched by time and the complexities of adulthood.

I venture deeper into the house, my heart aching for the warmth of family. The walls, once vibrant with laughter and love, now feel heavy with the weight of absence. The family portraits lining the hallway, each frame a testament to moments frozen in time, remind me of a life once lived in a whirlwind of joy. There's a picture of me at my eighth birthday, cake smeared across my face, my eyes alight with pure, unfiltered happiness. The girl in the photo is a stranger now, a ghost of who I once was, lost beneath layers of adult worries and the weight of expectation. But it's here, within these four walls, that I hope to rediscover that spark, to remember what it feels like to be unencumbered by the burdens I've carried.

With each step, I can feel the echoes of my childhood reverberating through the air. The creaky floorboards groan beneath my weight, a familiar symphony that plays a melancholy tune. I linger in the living room, where my father and I spent countless evenings watching baseball games, the glow of the television illuminating our shared silence. The couch is still in its corner, the fabric faded and worn, yet it remains steadfast, a testament to resilience and time. I sink into it, the cushions enveloping me, and for a moment, I allow myself to breathe, to let the memories wash over me.

But beneath the nostalgia lies an undeniable current of tension, a stark reminder of the unresolved issues waiting to surface. My father is in the hospital, battling demons of his own, and I can't shake the feeling that this visit is more than just a homecoming; it's a reckoning. The weight of our fractured relationship looms like an uninvited guest, lurking in the shadows, ready to disrupt the fragile peace I've managed to find. I often replay our conversations in my mind, a chaotic collage of unfiltered emotions that shift from light-hearted reminiscing to gut-wrenching honesty. Each word is a step toward understanding, yet also a reminder of how far we've drifted apart.

The hospital room feels sterile, a stark contrast to the warmth of my childhood home. The smell of antiseptic fills the air, mingling with the faint scent of my father's cologne, a bittersweet reminder of the man I used to know. He lies in the bed, frail and pale, the once sturdy figure reduced to a shadow of himself. The machines beep and hum around him, a rhythmic backdrop to our silent standoff. I can see the weariness etched on his face, the weight of regret and unspoken words heavy in the air between us.

"Hey, Dad," I manage to say, my voice barely above a whisper, thick with unshed tears. He turns his head slowly, his eyes meeting mine with a flicker of recognition, followed by a myriad of emotions that play across his features—surprise, sadness, and something that resembles hope. The silence stretches, thick and suffocating, as we both grapple with the enormity of this moment.

"Thought you'd never come back," he finally replies, his voice gravelly, tinged with the exhaustion of countless battles fought in silence. Each word feels like a dagger, a reminder of the years lost to misunderstandings and missed opportunities.

"I had to," I respond, the truth spilling from my lips before I can rein it in. "I needed to see you." I can feel my heart pounding in my chest, a relentless drumbeat echoing the conflicting emotions swirling within me—anger, sadness, and an aching desire for connection.

As our conversations ebb and flow, we navigate through the memories like skilled dancers, hesitant yet desperate to find our rhythm. We talk about the old days—the fishing trips that ended in laughter, the family vacations filled with bickering yet underscored by love. Each story pulls us closer to the surface, a fragile bridge spanning the chasm of our differences. But just when I think we're making progress, a misstep sends us tumbling back into the depths.

"Why didn't you ever just tell me?" I ask, the question bursting forth like a dam breaking under pressure. The hurt and confusion of my youth flood back, a torrent of feelings I've tried to bury. "Why did you keep everything so bottled up?"

His gaze drops, a flicker of shame crossing his features. "I thought I was protecting you," he replies, his voice thick with remorse. "But in doing so, I only pushed you away."

I want to scream, to lash out at the man who stood as my rock yet became a ghost in my life. But beneath the anger lies a deeper yearning—a desire to understand, to unearth the complexities that make him who he is. The fear of losing him weighs heavily on me, a constant reminder that time is not on our side. With every tick of the clock, I am reminded that our moments are limited, and I crave the chance to forge a new bond, one built on honesty rather than silence.

And so, we sit together in that sterile room, the sounds of the outside world fading away as we grapple with the enormity of our shared past. It is not easy, and there are moments of tension that threaten to unravel us, but beneath it all lies a glimmer of hope, a promise that perhaps, just perhaps, we can bridge the gap and find our way back to each other.

The sun filters through the hospital window, casting a soft golden glow on my father's frail form. Shadows dance around us, shifting like our unsteady conversation, while the rhythmic beeping of the monitor punctuates the silence. I trace the contours of his weathered hands, fingers once strong and capable, now trembling slightly as they rest on the crisp white sheets. It's a poignant reminder of time's relentless march, each wrinkle a testament to stories untold and battles fought.

"What do you remember about your own father?" I ask, hoping to peel back the layers of his guarded heart. The question hangs in the air, delicate yet heavy, like the weight of an unfinished letter. He glances at me, eyes clouded with a mixture of nostalgia and pain.

"Not much," he replies, his voice low, almost a whisper. "He was a good man, but..." He hesitates, and I can see the struggle behind his eyes, as if the words are caught in a net of unprocessed emotions. "He never spoke much about feelings, you know? It was always work, responsibility. I thought that's how I should be."

A flicker of understanding ignites within me. I can't help but wonder how much of his silence is rooted in the legacy of his father. Perhaps it's an unspoken rule passed down through generations, a code of stoicism that has stifled our family's ability to communicate. "Dad, it's okay to talk about feelings," I urge gently. "We're all human."

He lets out a rough chuckle that's tinged with bitterness, and it cuts through the air. "It's easy to say, but harder to do. You think I wanted to be this way? I wanted to protect you from my burdens." There's a raw honesty in his voice, a vulnerability I've rarely seen.

"But you didn't protect me," I reply, a sense of urgency rising in my chest. "You pushed me away. I needed you, and you were just... gone." The words feel cathartic, spilling out like a long-held breath. The air around us thickens with the weight of confession, and I can almost hear the walls of our shared history creaking in response.

He looks at me, the softness in his gaze cutting through the tension, and I feel a shift, a subtle cracking in the fortress he's built around himself. "I'm sorry," he murmurs, his voice barely audible. "I didn't know how to be what you needed."

The admission hangs between us, a fragile thread connecting two souls that have long drifted apart. I can feel the tears pooling in my eyes, the overwhelming swell of empathy washing over me. In this moment, we are both exposed—vulnerable yet resilient, bound by the very imperfections that have shaped us. "It's okay, Dad," I whisper, my heart aching for both of us. "We can figure this out together."

As the afternoon light dims, we delve deeper into the past. Our conversations swirl around cherished memories, reliving moments that spark joy and sorrow in equal measure. I remember the laughter echoing from the kitchen as my father tried, and often failed, to cook a decent meal. He would joke about his culinary disasters, the smoke detector serving as our uninvited dinner guest, while I would giggle, my stomach tight with laughter.

"Remember the time you set the spaghetti on fire?" I ask, a grin breaking across my face. The heaviness that hung in the air begins to lift, replaced by the warmth of shared laughter.

"Ah, yes, the infamous spaghetti fiasco," he chuckles, a glimmer of mischief returning to his eyes. "I thought I was being adventurous. Turns out, I was just foolish."

Our laughter rings through the sterile hospital room, a soothing balm that eases the sharp edges of our past. Each story we share serves as a thread, weaving a tapestry of connection and understanding. Yet, even as we reminisce, I can feel the shadows lurking, waiting for their moment to re-enter the fray.

Eventually, our laughter gives way to silence, the kind that is both comforting and daunting. The weight of unspoken words presses against my chest. "Dad," I start hesitantly, "is there anything you regret? Anything you wish you could change?"

He takes a deep breath, his eyes drifting to the window where the fading light casts long shadows. "So many things," he says, his voice heavy with remorse. "But what's done is done. All I can do now is try to make amends."

"Amends?" I echo, my heart racing. "What do you mean?"

He turns to me, the lines on his face deepening with emotion. "I want to be better—better for you, for myself. I want to be present. But I need your help. I can't do this alone."

A swell of hope rises within me, mingling with the uncertainty of our new path forward. "I'll help you, Dad. We can start fresh," I say, my voice steady. "But it's going to take work. I need you to be honest with me, even when it's hard."

"I can try," he replies, the flicker of determination igniting in his eyes. "I've spent so long hiding behind walls; it's time to take them down."

In that moment, something shifts within the confines of the hospital room. It feels as though the air has grown lighter, filled with the potential of what could be. I see my father not just as the man I have resented but as a fellow traveler on this winding road of life, someone capable of change, just as I am.

As the shadows deepen outside, I find comfort in the realization that we are embarking on a journey together—one fraught with challenges but also brimming with possibilities. I take his hand, the warmth of our connection grounding me amidst the chaos of emotions swirling within. The hospital may be a place of healing, but it's also a place of transformation—a space where two souls can begin to mend the threads of their fractured bond.

And as we sit there, the fading light spilling across the room, I know that we are not just facing the remnants of the past; we are stepping toward an uncertain but hopeful future, a homecoming that holds the promise of new beginnings.

The night deepens, casting a soft blanket of darkness across the hospital grounds, the fluorescent lights flickering like stars in a subdued sky. My father's breathing has steadied, a rhythm that lulls the tension in the room. I sit beside him, the quiet punctuated only by the occasional beeping of the machines monitoring his vitals. As I watch him, I'm struck by how vulnerable he appears—this man who once towered over me, filled with strength and certainty, now reduced to a fragile figure. The realization washes over me like a cold wave, stirring up a whirlwind of emotions that I struggle to contain.

"Do you remember the treehouse?" I ask, my voice barely above a whisper, hoping to evoke a smile. His eyes flicker with recognition, and I can almost see the memories dancing in the depths.

"Of course," he replies, a faint smile playing on his lips. "I was convinced it would be the best fort in the neighborhood."

"It wasn't exactly the Taj Mahal, Dad," I tease lightly, savoring this moment of connection. "But it was ours. The floor was creaky, and I think a squirrel lived in one of the walls."

He chuckles softly, the sound tinged with nostalgia. "You always had the best imagination. I wanted to give you a place where you could be a queen, if only for a little while."

His words hang in the air, a gentle balm that soothes the ache of the past. I remember climbing the rickety ladder, feeling invincible as I reached the top, my crown of wildflowers perched precariously on my head. Those carefree days were a treasure trove of innocence, unmarred by the complexities of adult life. "It felt like a castle back then," I say, lost in the memory of sunlit afternoons spent in our wooden sanctuary, the world far below us.

"Maybe it was," he muses, "just a different kind of castle."

The laughter that bubbles between us is a fragile thread, binding us together. Yet, beneath that lightness lies an undercurrent of unspoken truths, waiting to surface. "Dad, I want to understand," I say, the weight of my sincerity pressing down on us. "What made you so distant? Why did you feel you had to protect me from your life?"

He closes his eyes for a moment, gathering his thoughts as if summoning the courage to unravel years of silence. "It wasn't just you I was trying to protect. It was me. I thought if I didn't let you see my struggles, you'd never have to bear them." His voice cracks, revealing a vulnerability that feels raw and fresh.

"Didn't you see that I wanted to share those burdens?" I reply, my heart racing with the intensity of my feelings. "I needed you to be real with me."

The silence stretches between us, heavy with the weight of understanding and regret. "I was afraid, my girl," he finally admits, his voice trembling. "Afraid of letting you down. Afraid of showing you the cracks in my armor."

"Dad, we all have cracks," I assure him, my voice steady. "Those imperfections are what make us human. We're not perfect, and we don't have to be. I just want you here with me, flaws and all."

He nods, a single tear slipping down his cheek. In that moment, I see the man beneath the father, the man who has endured heartache and loss, yet still yearns for connection. I reach for his hand, the warmth of our touch igniting a flicker of hope within me. "We can figure this out together," I say, my heart swelling with determination.

As the night deepens, we share stories—some that bring laughter, others that cradle the bittersweet ache of regret. He speaks of his childhood, revealing snippets of his life that I had never known. I learn of the games he played in the backyard with his brothers, the music that filled their home, and the dreams he once harbored before life's burdens overshadowed them.

"I wanted to be a musician," he confesses, a hint of longing lingering in his voice. "But life took me in a different direction."

The admission stirs something within me. "You still can, Dad," I encourage gently. "It's never too late."

"I don't know," he sighs, the weariness in his voice palpable. "Sometimes I feel like I've lost my chance."

"No," I insist, my heart racing at the thought. "You just need to believe that you can take those steps again. It's okay to chase your dreams, even now."

He meets my gaze, and for the first time, I see a glimmer of something I hadn't noticed before—possibility. "Maybe," he murmurs, a tentative smile teasing the corners of his lips.

We continue to talk, our words weaving an intricate tapestry of vulnerability and hope. As the hours slip by, I find myself sharing my own dreams, my aspirations tangled with the pain of uncertainty. I tell him about the writing projects that have kept me up at night, my passion ignited by the stories yearning to be told.

"I've always wanted to write a book," I admit, my cheeks flushing with the vulnerability of sharing that dream. "But I've always felt like I wasn't good enough."

"You are good enough," he asserts, his voice firm yet tender. "Don't ever let fear hold you back."

With those words, the night unfolds like a story of its own—one of healing, understanding, and the delicate dance of reconnecting. I watch as he slowly shifts, revealing pieces of himself that had long been buried. The room, once a sterile cage of silence, has transformed into a sanctuary of acceptance.

As dawn breaks, the first rays of light spill through the window, casting a golden hue over everything, illuminating the shadows that once loomed so large. In that quiet moment, I realize we are both beginning anew. The past no longer holds us captive; it merely serves as the foundation upon which we will build a new relationship—one that embraces imperfection, vulnerability, and the beauty of second chances.

In the days that follow, I visit him regularly, and our conversations deepen like the roots of the trees that once towered over our backyard. He shares his regrets, his hopes, and the dreams he thought he had buried. I listen, weaving my own aspirations into the fabric of our dialogue, both of us discovering strength in each other.

Our laughter fills the sterile room, the memories we create together mingling with the scent of antiseptic, transforming the hospital into a home. I watch as he begins to reclaim parts of himself, picking up a guitar that had languished untouched, the strings whispering stories of his youth. Each note he plays resonates within me, a reminder that it's never too late to chase the melodies of our hearts.

And as the sun sets behind the horizon, I hold onto the knowledge that while our past may have shaped us, it does not define us. We are not merely products of our history; we are architects of our future, building bridges where once there were walls. With every visit, every shared smile and tear, we continue to carve out a new narrative—one that embraces our shared flaws, celebrates our triumphs, and honors the bond that connects us, a bond that is stronger than the shadows of our past.

Chapter 23: Echoes of the Past

The sun dipped low on the horizon, casting a golden hue over the familiar streets of my hometown, where each corner whispered echoes of laughter and echoes of heartache. As I strolled through the narrow lanes, the scent of warm pretzels wafted through the air, intertwining with the rich aroma of freshly brewed coffee spilling out from the quaint café on the corner. The soft glow of streetlights flickered on, illuminating the worn cobblestones beneath my feet, each stone a silent witness to the stories that unfolded here—our stories.

My fingers brushed against the weathered surface of the brick walls as I made my way past the old cinema, its marquee now faded and peeling but still radiating an air of nostalgic charm. I remembered the thrill of slipping into its dimly lit confines with Evan, popcorn in hand, sharing whispers and stolen glances that lingered long after the credits rolled. The silver screen had been our escape, a portal to distant lands where heroes triumphed, and love conquered all. I could almost hear the haunting notes of our favorite soundtrack, a melody that played in my heart even now.

I paused at the entrance, where a flickering neon light buzzed like a distant memory. The ghosts of my past swirled around me—laughter and late-night debates about film plots, the thrill of our first kiss beneath the stars. The girl I had been felt like a stranger now, lost in the chaos of adulthood. In this moment, nostalgia swept over me like a tide, pulling me back to a time when the world was simpler, and love felt eternal.

With a sigh, I stepped away from the cinema and headed towards the park, a sprawling green oasis that had been the backdrop of so many pivotal moments. The swings creaked softly in the evening breeze, a melodic reminder of carefree days spent with friends, where the biggest worry was whether we'd have enough time to chase fireflies. I settled onto one of the benches, the worn wood familiar beneath me, and let the warmth of the setting sun bathe me in its glow.

As I sat there, I spotted a figure in the distance—Mark, Evan's childhood friend, making his way towards me with an easy gait that spoke of years filled with camaraderie. His smile was disarming, a beacon of the past that cut through the haze of my memories. We exchanged greetings, and the warmth of his presence brought back a flood of shared moments. Mark had always been the life of the party, the kind of guy who could lift spirits with a joke or a well-timed quip.

"Can you believe it's been so long?" he asked, settling onto the bench beside me. The question hung in the air like the last note of a song, reverberating through the quiet park. I nodded, suddenly feeling the weight of the years that had slipped away unnoticed.

"Yeah, it feels surreal. This place hasn't changed much, has it?" I glanced around, taking in the familiar sights—the old oak tree that stood as a sentinel, the pond that glimmered under the fading light, and the laughter of children echoing in the distance.

Mark chuckled, a sound rich with the warmth of fond memories. "Nope, same old park. Just like us, I suppose. Though I hear you've been living the high life in the city."

I smiled sheepishly, memories of late nights and bustling streets flooding my mind. "It has its moments. But there's something special about being back here, you know? It feels... grounding."

He turned serious, his gaze searching mine. "Have you seen Evan?"

The mention of his name sent a ripple through my heart, stirring emotions I had long buried. "Not yet. I didn't come back for that," I replied, my voice steadier than I felt.

Mark hesitated, as if weighing his words. "He's been through a lot since you left. I think it's hard for him, still. He often talks about you."

The revelation pierced through the shield I had built around my heart. My mind raced back to the last time I had seen Evan—the tear-streaked faces, the promises made and broken. I had chosen to walk away, believing it was what was best for both of us, but the ache of regret clung to me like a second skin.

"Yeah?" I whispered, almost afraid to hear more. "What do you mean?"

Mark leaned in, his voice low and earnest. "He struggled for a while, you know? Losing you hit him hard. But he's been working on himself, getting back on his feet. He's even started a small business—something he's passionate about. It's impressive, really."

A flutter of pride swelled within me, mingled with the bittersweet taste of longing. Evan had always had that fire inside him, a spark that drew people in and left them wanting more. I had admired his dreams, the way he could talk about them with such fervor. Knowing he was finding his way again reignited the warmth I had thought extinguished.

Mark continued, recounting tales of Evan's resilience, his determination to rise above the challenges life had thrown at him. I listened, captivated by the narrative unfolding before me, a story of growth and transformation that mirrored my own. The shadows of our past intertwined with the light of their present, weaving a tapestry of connection that felt both familiar and foreign.

As twilight draped its silken veil over the park, I realized that the past was never truly gone; it lingered, shaping us in ways we often failed to see. The memories of Evan, the laughter we shared, the dreams we dared to chase—these were the threads that connected us, regardless of the distance or time that separated our lives. The warmth of nostalgia wrapped around me, beckoning me to revisit those moments, to face the remnants of our love that still danced in the corners of my heart.

A shiver danced along my spine as the last traces of daylight surrendered to the encroaching night, enveloping the park in a comforting embrace of twilight. The laughter of children faded, replaced by the rustling leaves whispering secrets to the wind. I found myself lost in thought, contemplating the life I had chosen, one that took me far from this town, yet rooted me to it in ways I hadn't fully understood until now.

Mark's voice pulled me back to the moment, a steady stream of warmth amidst the chill of nostalgia. "You know," he continued, a hint of mischief in his tone, "he still thinks you were right to leave. He admires your courage. But deep down, I think he wonders what could have been."

Those words hung in the air, heavy yet hopeful, stirring a tempest of emotions within me. Courage? I had never felt that way about my choice. It had been easier to run than to confront the complexities of love—our love. I felt the weight of Mark's gaze, searching for a reaction, but my heart was a jumble of confusion and yearning.

"Does he still play guitar?" I asked, hoping to tread lightly through the minefield of emotions we were navigating.

Mark chuckled, the sound rich with memories. "Like he's possessed. You know how he was with that thing, right? Spent hours strumming away, writing songs that he thought would change the world."

The image of Evan hunched over his guitar in that little corner of my heart flickered to life, the passion radiating from him like the first rays of dawn. I could almost hear the lilting notes that spilled from his fingertips, melodies that lingered in the air long after the music had stopped. He had woven his soul into those songs, capturing moments of joy and sorrow with the stroke of a string.

"Is he still doing that?" I found myself asking, the question trembling on my lips like a delicate flower on the brink of blooming.

Mark's expression softened. "Yeah, he's performing again. Not at big venues yet, just some open mic nights and local gigs, but he's got a following. People remember him."

A swell of pride unfurled within me, warming the corners of my heart that had long been left unlit. Evan was carving his path, finding his voice in a world that had felt stifling for so long. I was filled with a strange mix of elation and sorrow. The happiness for his success was dulled by the ache of my absence in those moments.

"Have you seen him perform?" I asked, my curiosity piqued, a flicker of hope igniting in the pit of my stomach.

"Once or twice," Mark replied, his eyes alight with recollections. "He was electric. You could feel the energy in the room. The way he looked at the crowd, it was like he was searching for someone in the sea of faces. I think he was hoping you'd show up."

A lump formed in my throat, the bittersweet taste of longing swirling within me. I had chosen distance, believing it would allow us both to heal, yet here I was, shackled by what-ifs and regrets. The truth was a shadow that followed me, a haunting presence I couldn't shake.

As the darkness thickened around us, the stars began to twinkle like distant hopes, dotting the sky with promise. I drew in a deep breath, the cool air invigorating my senses. "Maybe I should go to one of his gigs," I mused, more to myself than to Mark. The thought sparked a thrill deep within me, intertwining with the tendrils of nostalgia.

Mark nodded encouragingly. "I think you should. It might be just what you need—to see how far he's come. And who knows? Maybe it'll help both of you find closure, or a new beginning."

A new beginning. The phrase lingered in the air, a tantalizing notion that was both terrifying and exhilarating. What if there was still something left between us, something worth exploring in the soft glow of night and the warmth of shared dreams?

I shifted on the bench, excitement battling apprehension within me. "You really think he'd want to see me again?"

"Of course," Mark replied, his tone earnest. "You two had something special. It's not just something you forget. It changes you."

With every word, my heart raced faster, beating a rhythm of hope against the backdrop of the night. The idea of seeing Evan again felt monumental, a collision of past and present that could lead to unforeseen possibilities. My mind was a flurry of thoughts, images flashing through like a film reel—his laugh, the way his eyes sparkled when he spoke about his passions, the warmth of his hand in mine.

"Maybe I'll surprise him," I said, the thought crystallizing into determination.

Mark's smile widened, a spark of encouragement radiating from him. "I can help set it up. There's an open mic night next week at that little café downtown. I can get you a spot."

The rush of adrenaline was intoxicating. I could already envision it—the dim lights, the cozy ambiance filled with the scent of brewed coffee, and Evan standing there, lost in his music, just a few feet away.

With newfound excitement coursing through me, I realized that reconnecting with the echoes of the past didn't have to mean reliving old wounds. Instead, it could be an opportunity to bridge the gap, to allow the once-shattered pieces of our story to intertwine again, perhaps even more beautifully than before.

The park around us began to empty as families made their way home, but I felt anchored in that moment, buoyed by the warmth of friendship and the flickering flame of possibility. The stars above twinkled like promises waiting to be fulfilled, and I knew deep down that this wasn't just a return to my hometown; it was a return to myself, a rediscovery of who I was and who I might still become.

In the distance, I could hear the soft strumming of a guitar, its melody drifting through the night air like a beacon of hope, calling me back to the heart of what truly mattered—connection, love, and the courage to embrace the unknown.

The days that followed my conversation with Mark were a whirlwind of anticipation and self-reflection, each one wrapped in a cocoon of nostalgia and the burgeoning hope of what could be. The air was thick with promise, the streets of my hometown shifting underfoot like a familiar but distant dream, urging me to let go of past insecurities and embrace the unfolding narrative. I felt buoyed by the whispers of the past, each memory a delicate thread weaving a tapestry that shimmered with possibility.

As the date of the open mic night drew closer, I found myself drawn to the café where it would be held, a charming little spot nestled between a bookstore and an antique shop, its windows adorned with twinkling fairy lights that danced in the evening breeze. The café was a haven, filled with the rich aroma of freshly ground coffee mingling with the sweet scent of pastries. Inside, the atmosphere buzzed with creative energy, an eclectic mix of artists, writers, and dreamers, each sharing their passions over steaming mugs and laughter that spilled into the air like musical notes.

I spent hours there, my fingers tracing the edges of my notebook as I scribbled down lyrics, desperate to capture the essence of what I felt. Words flowed through me like water, sometimes clear and sometimes murky, revealing the struggle of a heart caught between past and present. With every line I penned, I felt a bittersweet connection to Evan, a reminder of the times we had spent here, sharing dreams over coffee and trying to write the soundtrack of our lives. The idea of performing in front of him sent a thrill coursing through my veins, accompanied by an undercurrent of fear that threatened to stifle my creativity.

The night of the open mic arrived, draped in a cloak of anticipation that felt electric. I stood before the café's entrance, my heart hammering against my ribs as I took in the sight of familiar faces mingling with new ones. The warm glow of the interior beckoned me, each flickering candle casting playful shadows on the walls. I could hear the sound of laughter mixed with the strumming of a guitar, and for a moment, I hesitated, uncertainty gripping me like a vice.

Mark appeared at my side, his presence grounding me amidst the whirlwind of emotions. "You ready for this?" he asked, a knowing smile illuminating his face.

I nodded, though the tremor in my voice betrayed my confidence. "Ready as I'll ever be."

As we entered the café, the atmosphere wrapped around me like a soft embrace. The cozy seating areas were filled with clusters of people, their faces alight with enthusiasm. I scanned the room, my pulse quickening when I spotted Evan on the far side, his back turned to me as he chatted animatedly with a group of friends. He looked different yet achingly familiar, his hair tousled just so, a hint of mischief dancing in his posture. The sight of him sent a rush of warmth through my veins, igniting the embers of feelings I thought I had buried.

"Let's get you a drink to calm those nerves," Mark suggested, guiding me to the counter. I ordered a cappuccino, the foam swirling in delicate patterns that seemed to mirror my swirling thoughts. As I waited, I caught snippets of conversations around me—stories of love and loss, of dreams realized and dashed. Each tale was a reminder of the shared humanity that connected us all.

When it was finally my turn to take the stage, I felt a surge of adrenaline coursing through me, drowning out the initial wave of apprehension. Mark gave me an encouraging nod, and I stepped into the spotlight, the warmth of the lights washing over me. My heart raced as I glanced at Evan, who turned, his eyes widening in recognition.

The microphone felt foreign in my hand, yet oddly comforting, like a lifeline thrown into turbulent waters. I cleared my throat, the noise drawing the attention of the audience. A hush fell over the café, anticipation hanging thick in the air as I gathered my thoughts, letting the silence wrap around me.

With a deep breath, I began to strum my guitar, the familiar chords anchoring me in the present moment. The first notes spilled forth, tentative yet full of emotion, carrying the weight of all I had wanted to say over the years. I closed my eyes and let the music guide me, transforming the café into a sanctuary of shared experience, where my voice intertwined with the memories of laughter and heartache.

As I sang, I could feel Evan's gaze on me, the intensity of his presence igniting a fire within. Each verse unfolded like a story, a reflection of our journey, the highs and lows intertwined in a delicate dance. The audience swayed, some tapping their feet in rhythm, while others nodded along, captivated by the raw honesty of the moment.

I poured my heart into the performance, each lyric a testament to the love we had shared, the distance we had traveled, and the lingering echoes of what still remained. I sang of dreams chased and lost, of laughter that once filled empty spaces, and of the hope that whispered in the dark.

As I reached the final chorus, I opened my eyes, locking onto Evan's gaze. In that instant, everything fell away—the crowd, the café, the past. It was just him and me, suspended in a moment that felt both fragile and infinite. His expression was a tapestry of emotions, a mirror reflecting the journey we had taken separately yet together, each note a bridge connecting our hearts once more.

When the last chord faded into the air, a hush enveloped the room before the applause erupted like a wave crashing against the shore. The sound washed over me, a blend of relief and exhilaration, but all I could focus on was Evan, his smile radiant, eyes shining with unspoken words.

As I stepped off the stage, the world spun around me, the warmth of the café enveloping me like a blanket. Mark clapped me on the back, a grin plastered across his face. "You were amazing! That was incredible!"

But my focus was entirely on Evan, who stood waiting for me, his hands tucked into the pockets of his jeans, an expression of awe etched on his face. The space between us was charged with a thousand unsaid things, and as I approached, every step felt monumental, each heartbeat echoing in the silence that enveloped us.

"Wow," he finally said, his voice low and full of warmth. "You still have that gift."

The compliment sent a ripple of warmth through me, a soft light breaking through the haze of uncertainty. "Thank you. I just... I wanted to share what I felt."

Evan nodded, a softness in his eyes that spoke of understanding and connection. "You captured it perfectly."

In that moment, the past and present wove together, threads of shared history intertwining with the hopes of what could still be. The air crackled with possibility as we stood there, two souls once entangled in a dance of love, now taking tentative steps towards a future that felt both familiar and exhilaratingly new.

As the music continued to play softly in the background, I realized that the echoes of our past were not merely reminders of what had been lost but also the foundation for what could still flourish. The love we had once shared was not extinguished; it had merely transformed, waiting patiently for us to embrace it once more.

Underneath the soft glow of café lights, with the laughter of friends and strangers swirling around us, I took a step closer to Evan, the weight of unspoken words hanging between us, ready to be released into the world. The evening was just beginning, and with it, the promise of new beginnings beckoned like the dawn of a beautiful day.

Chapter 24: Crossroads

The sterile scent of antiseptic hung in the air, mingling with the faint, metallic tang of medical instruments. The fluorescent lights above flickered intermittently, casting an unflattering glow on the faded blue-green walls that surrounded me, reminding me of a hospital waiting room stuck in a time warp. My father lay still in the bed, a tangle of wires and tubes snaking from his frail frame, his chest rising and falling with the slow, labored rhythm of machines that echoed the uncertainty of his condition. Each beep of the monitor felt like a heartbeat, a relentless reminder of the time slipping away between us.

As the hours stretched into nights, the silence grew heavy, punctuated only by the occasional shuffle of nurses and the distant murmurs of anxious families. I found myself at the crossroads of despair and hope, caught between the warmth of cherished memories and the sharp sting of impending loss. The hospital room had become a capsule, isolating us from the vibrant world outside—a world of city lights, bustling streets, and dreams deferred.

The shadows lengthened as twilight seeped through the small window, casting an ethereal glow across the room. I sat by my father's bedside, the cold plastic chair unyielding beneath me, clutching his hand as though the simple act of holding on could somehow tether him to this world. My fingers traced the familiar lines on his palm, roughened by years of labor and sacrifice. I recalled the countless times he had wrapped his arms around me, promising that everything would be okay, the warmth of his embrace a fortress against life's storms. Yet now, he was the one in need of shelter, and I felt powerless.

It was one of those suffocating moments, when the weight of unspoken words hung in the air like an impending storm. I could see the struggle in his eyes, the flicker of a man caught in the web of his own regrets, yet still trying to reach for clarity. With a deep, ragged breath, I encouraged him to speak. I could feel the tension coiling within me, a mixture of fear and longing swirling in my chest. His voice, gravelly yet earnest, broke through the silence like a whispered prayer.

"I always wanted the best for you, you know," he murmured, his gaze drifting to the window, as if seeking answers from the fading light. "But I never knew how to show it. I was too wrapped up in my own world, my own failures."

My heart twisted at his admission, a tempest of emotions crashing over me. The ache of missed opportunities surged within, and I blinked back tears, desperate to articulate the whirlwind of feelings swirling around us. It was a moment fraught with vulnerability, a bridge built of honesty that stretched across the chasm of our shared history.

"You did the best you could," I replied softly, my voice trembling with a mixture of tenderness and resolve. "But I need you to understand that I've spent too long feeling like I wasn't enough. You didn't fail me. Life just... got complicated."

He turned to me, the flicker of recognition igniting in his eyes as the shadows of past misunderstandings began to dissolve. "I wanted to protect you from my mistakes," he confessed, his voice barely above a whisper. "But in doing so, I pushed you away. I never wanted you to feel alone."

The tears that had threatened to spill over finally fell, cascading down my cheeks as I surrendered to the weight of the moment. It was cathartic, a release that echoed through the sterile confines of the room. The air felt lighter, as if we were shedding layers of unspoken fears, weaving a fragile tapestry of understanding between us. The unsteady beeping of the heart monitor became a melody of reconciliation, each note resonating with the promise of healing.

"I don't want to dwell on what's lost," I said, squeezing his hand tighter, as if infusing my warmth into his frail fingers. "I want to focus on what we can still share. We have now, Dad. We can start fresh."

His smile was faint but genuine, a flicker of the man I had always admired, now softened by the weight of his vulnerability. "I'd like that," he replied, a hint of hope threading through his words. "Life is too short to let the past dictate our future."

In that fleeting moment, the chaos of the hospital faded away, leaving only the two of us in our fragile sanctuary. The world outside continued to spin, oblivious to the pivotal shift that had occurred within those four walls. I could almost hear the laughter of children playing in the park down the street, the distant hum of traffic blending with the songs of city life. New York, with its relentless energy and possibility, called to me like a siren, urging me to reclaim my narrative.

As I sat there, enveloped in the warmth of my father's frail presence, I made a silent vow. The threads of our shared story, tangled and frayed, could be rewoven into something beautiful. I would return to the city that had become a mosaic of dreams and heartaches, and I would fight for the love I had rekindled with Evan. No longer shackled by fear or regret, I would step into the vibrant tapestry of life, ready to embrace every moment, knowing that the fragility of existence only heightened its beauty.

The realization settled over me like a soft embrace—my journey was not defined by the shadows of loss, but rather by the radiant potential of love and connection. In that hospital room, amidst the beeping machines and sterile air, I discovered a profound truth: every ending is but a prelude to a new beginning, and the heart is resilient enough to carry us through even the darkest of times.

The city that never sleeps pulsed with life as I stepped into the familiar chaos of its streets, the vibrant energy electrifying the air around me. The autumn sun hung low in the sky, casting golden rays over the urban landscape, illuminating the crimson and amber leaves that clung to the trees like fiery confetti. I inhaled deeply, savoring the mingled aromas of roasted chestnuts, warm pretzels, and the crisp scent of fall, all blended with the distant notes of jazz drifting from a nearby café. New York was alive, and so was I—reborn from the shadows of uncertainty.

Each step on the sidewalk felt like a heartbeat, a reminder that I was here, fully present in a world where possibilities sprawled before me like an uncharted map. My heart raced, not just with the thrill of returning to the city but with the realization that I had unfinished business. Evan's face flashed through my mind, his laughter an intoxicating melody that had woven itself into the fabric of my days. The memory of his smile warmed me as I navigated the thrumming crowds, each person a brushstroke in the vibrant tapestry of life.

I found myself at a quaint coffee shop on the corner of 14th and 8th, a place I used to frequent during my student days. Its windows were framed with blooming flowers that danced in the gentle breeze, while the sound of the espresso machine created a comforting symphony against the backdrop of hushed conversations. The scent of freshly brewed coffee wrapped around me like a familiar hug, and I stepped inside, eager to momentarily escape the frenzy outside.

As I settled into a corner table, my fingers traced the rim of the steaming mug in front of me, my thoughts swirling like the foam atop my cappuccino. The café was a haven of warmth, a cozy retreat where I could gather my thoughts and summon the courage to confront Evan. I could almost see him across the room, his boyish charm alive in the flicker of candlelight. The thought sent butterflies dancing in my stomach, a mixture of excitement and fear.

With each sip, I reflected on our journey—how we had stumbled back into each other's lives like two wayward stars drawn together by gravity, each moment a brushstroke in a larger masterpiece. The laughter we shared, the whispered secrets under the night sky, and the bittersweet farewell that had lingered in the air like the last notes of a song. The realization that I wanted more than just fleeting encounters surged within me, a tide that could not be contained.

Before I could overthink it, I pulled out my phone, the screen lighting up with the world that lay just a click away. I typed out a message, my fingers hesitating momentarily over the keys. The words flowed, a stream of consciousness spilling forth: "Hey, Evan. I'm back in the city. Can we talk?" My heart raced as I hit send, the message disappearing into the ether, leaving me with a sense of both anticipation and dread. What if he didn't respond? What if I had returned only to find the door to our connection firmly shut?

Minutes felt like hours as I waited, my gaze drifting around the café. A couple nearby was lost in their own world, their laughter punctuating the air as they shared a pastry. A mother chased after her toddler, who squealed with delight as he dodged between tables, the innocence of childhood echoing in his giggles. I longed to feel that carefree spirit again, to let go of the burdens I carried, even if just for a moment.

Just as I began to lose hope, my phone buzzed against the table, and my heart jumped into my throat. I opened the message, and there it was: "Of course! Where do you want to meet?" Relief washed over me, mingling with a rush of giddiness. He wanted to see me; he hadn't turned away.

With renewed purpose, I replied, suggesting a park not far from the café. It was a place that had held its share of our memories, where we had shared lazy afternoons and stolen kisses beneath the trees. I envisioned us there, the leaves falling like confetti around us, laughter echoing in the crisp air as we bridged the gap that had separated us for far too long.

When I arrived at the park, the sun hung low, casting a golden glow that filtered through the branches, creating a dappled pattern on the ground. I spotted Evan leaning against a tree, his posture relaxed yet alert, as if he had been waiting for this moment for eternity. The sight of him stirred something deep within me—a mix of nostalgia and yearning that swept through my veins like wildfire.

He looked up, and our eyes locked, a spark igniting the air between us. The warmth of his smile melted away the last remnants of doubt that clung to my heart. I could see the man I remembered—the boy who had chased dreams with unyielding determination. Time had changed us both, but in that instant, we were once again the two who had dared to dream together.

"Hey," he said, his voice smooth like honey, laced with an undercurrent of emotion that sent shivers down my spine.

"Hey," I echoed, my voice barely above a whisper as I stepped closer, the distance between us shrinking like the twilight shadows around us.

We stood there for a moment, the world around us fading as the gravity of our reunion settled in. The laughter of children faded into the background, the rustling leaves a mere whisper as we took in the magnitude of what this meeting could mean.

"I missed you," I confessed, my heart racing as the words tumbled out, raw and unguarded.

"I missed you too," he replied, his gaze steady, unwavering, like an anchor in the storm of emotions swirling within me.

In that shared moment, under the kaleidoscope of fading light, I realized that I was no longer the girl defined by her past or shackled by fears of loss. I was ready to embrace whatever came next, ready to explore the depths of what we could become. The city around us thrummed with life, and I felt a renewed sense of belonging.

With Evan by my side, the road ahead no longer seemed daunting. Instead, it appeared as an adventure waiting to unfold, a path illuminated by the warmth of rekindled love and the promise of new beginnings.

The warmth of Evan's presence enveloped me as we stood beneath the trees, our surroundings a symphony of colors painted by the setting sun. The golden light filtered through the leaves, casting playful shadows on the ground, where fallen foliage crunched softly beneath our feet. It felt like the world had paused, just for us, creating a sacred space where the weight of our past could be laid to rest. I looked into his eyes, those deep pools of emotion that had always held the promise of something more, and I could feel the unspoken words hanging in the air, waiting to be released.

As we began to walk side by side, the park came alive around us. A dog bounded past, its owner laughing as it chased a rogue squirrel, while a couple on a nearby bench shared a quiet moment, fingers intertwined like threads of a tapestry. I felt an overwhelming urge to capture this moment, to etch it into my memory—a time when everything felt right, a time when I was reminded of the beauty that lay in the vulnerability of reconnecting with someone I had once loved deeply.

"I've thought about you a lot since... everything," Evan said, breaking the silence that enveloped us. His voice was steady, but I could hear the slight tremor of uncertainty laced within it. "When you left, I felt like I lost a part of myself. I didn't know how to make sense of it."

I nodded, a rush of emotions flooding my senses. "I felt the same way. Leaving was the hardest thing I've ever done. I kept telling myself it was for the best, but it felt like a betrayal." I paused, searching for the right words to bridge the gap that had formed between us during our time apart. "But I realized I was running away from what mattered most."

He stopped walking, turning to face me fully, his expression earnest. "So what do we do now? What do you want?"

His question hung in the air, the weight of it palpable. I took a deep breath, letting the crisp autumn air fill my lungs, feeling invigorated yet vulnerable. "I want to be honest about what I feel," I replied, meeting his gaze with unwavering sincerity. "I want to fight for us. For what we had. I don't want to let fear dictate my choices anymore."

Evan's smile returned, and it felt like the sun breaking through a storm. "You have no idea how relieved I am to hear you say that. I've been scared to reach out, afraid of what you might say."

"Why were you scared?" I asked, my curiosity piqued.

"Because sometimes it feels easier to hold onto memories than to risk creating new ones," he admitted, a shadow flickering across his face. "I didn't want to ruin what we had by trying to rekindle it. But now I see how foolish that was."

Our conversation flowed effortlessly, weaving between the threads of our shared past and the potential for a future. Each revelation felt like peeling away layers of armor we had both donned to shield ourselves from hurt. The park, with its swaying trees and laughter in the distance, transformed into our confessional, a sanctuary where we could explore our truths without the fear of judgment.

"I remember the way you would laugh at my terrible jokes," Evan said, the warmth of nostalgia brightening his eyes. "Even when I bombed them, you always found a way to make me feel like a genius."

"That's because you have this incredible way of seeing the world," I replied, my heart swelling with affection. "You always turned the mundane into something magical, and I loved that about you."

A moment of silence passed, heavy with the unvoiced acknowledgment of everything we had lost and gained. The leaves rustled above us, as if nature itself were urging us forward, encouraging the seeds of hope we were planting in the fertile ground of possibility.

"Let's not waste time," he suggested, his voice low and earnest. "Let's find a way to make this work. Together."

The thought sent a rush of exhilaration coursing through me. Together. The word echoed in my mind, filling the spaces where doubt had once lingered. I could picture it—the two of us navigating the bustling streets of New York, laughing, sharing late-night conversations over mugs of coffee, exploring the hidden gems of the city that had once felt so big and intimidating.

"I want to do that, but I also need to focus on my career," I said, the weight of reality settling in. "I've spent so long in the shadow of uncertainty, and I can't let my professional aspirations slip away again. I want to build something for myself."

Evan nodded, understanding reflected in his gaze. "I get it. We'll figure it out together. You don't have to choose one over the other. You're strong enough to balance both. And I'll be right there beside you, cheering you on."

His encouragement wrapped around me like a warm embrace, banishing the remnants of my fears. I had spent so long worrying about what it meant to choose love, to prioritize my heart over ambition. But standing here, with Evan by my side, I began to understand that love wasn't a distraction from my dreams; it could be a source of strength, propelling me forward rather than holding me back.

As twilight descended, painting the sky in hues of lavender and indigo, we found a bench near the water's edge. The reflections of the city's skyline shimmered like a thousand diamonds on the surface, the lights twinkling in harmony with our own flickering hopes. We sat side by side, the distance between us no longer defined by fear or misunderstanding but by a palpable connection that felt destined to flourish.

"I can't help but think about everything we've been through," I mused, my voice barely above a whisper as I gazed out at the water. "How we drifted apart, how it felt like a lifetime ago."

"It did," Evan agreed, his tone reflective. "But maybe we needed that time apart to grow. To understand ourselves better. I know I'm not the same person I was back then."

"Neither am I," I admitted, turning to face him fully. "I've learned that life is too fragile to waste on what-ifs. I want to make choices that lead to love and joy, not regret."

His smile was infectious, brightening the dusk around us. "Then let's start right now. Let's create memories that we'll cherish. We can take this one step at a time, no pressure. Just two people trying to find their way."

The sincerity in his voice filled me with a sense of peace I hadn't realized I'd been searching for. As the first stars began to twinkle above us, I reached for his hand, our fingers intertwining in a gesture that felt both familiar and new. The warmth of his touch anchored me, reminding me that we were embarking on this journey together.

In that moment, I understood that love, like the city around us, was a living entity—vibrant, unpredictable, and full of potential. We were ready to weave our story anew, embracing the twists and turns that awaited us. The challenges ahead would be met with courage and laughter, as we learned to dance through life's uncertainties hand in hand. With each breath, we exhaled the burdens of the past and inhaled the promise of a future bursting with possibility, where our hearts could soar free amid the chaos of existence.

With every beat, my heart echoed the resounding truth: together, we would build something beautiful, a love that could withstand the tests of time and circumstance. As the city hummed with life around us, I felt an unshakeable conviction that we were exactly where we were meant to be.

Chapter 25: The Journey Back

The cacophony of New York City surrounds me as I step off the train, the familiar sounds of honking cabs and distant sirens melding into a symphony of urban life. Each pulse of the city feels electric, sending a shiver of excitement down my spine. I inhale deeply, savoring the scent of roasted chestnuts and pretzels wafting from nearby vendors, a comforting reminder of countless moments spent wandering these bustling streets. Yet beneath the vibrant exterior lies an unsettling knot in my stomach, a weight born from the complexities of family ties and my father's precarious health.

As I navigate through the throng of people, I can't help but notice the kaleidoscope of faces, each one etched with stories of their own. A woman in a bright yellow raincoat hurries by, clutching a bouquet of daisies, perhaps a gesture of love or gratitude. A street performer strums a soulful tune on his guitar, his voice weaving through the air, a momentary reprieve from the city's relentless pace. This city thrives on its contrasts; the beauty and chaos coexist in a dance as old as time itself.

My mind races with thoughts of Evan as I make my way to our apartment. I can almost feel the warmth of his smile enveloping me, soothing the jagged edges of my anxieties. He has been my anchor, a steady presence in a world that often feels tumultuous. But with each step I take, I grapple with the enormity of my father's situation, the lingering frustration of our conversations, and the unresolved tension that hangs like a shadow over my heart.

The moment I arrive home, the familiar scent of sandalwood and lavender envelops me, a soft embrace that speaks of comfort and safety. I push open the door, and there he is—Evan, leaning against the kitchen counter, his hair tousled and a hint of worry creasing his brow. The moment our eyes meet, something inside me shifts.

His expression transforms from concern to joy, and suddenly, all the chaos of the past weeks seems to fade into the background.

I rush into his arms, the world around us blurring into nothingness as he pulls me close. The warmth of his body seeps into my bones, erasing the chill of my worries, if only for a moment. "I missed you," he murmurs, his voice a low, soothing balm that calms my restless heart. I bury my face in the crook of his neck, inhaling the scent of his cologne, a blend of cedar and spice that feels like home.

The rush of emotions spills forth, and I find myself sharing everything—the weight of my father's illness, the conversations laced with unspoken words, the fear of losing something I never truly understood until now. Evan listens intently, his eyes reflecting the flicker of hope I desperately cling to. Each word I speak feels like a thread weaving us closer together, and as I recount my journey, the distance between us shrinks until it almost disappears.

He cups my face, his thumb tracing the line of my jaw with a tenderness that sends a shiver down my spine. "We'll get through this together," he says, his voice steady and filled with conviction. It's a promise, a lifeline tossed into the turbulent waters of my heart, and I can't help but believe him. For the first time in weeks, I feel a glimmer of optimism, a light breaking through the clouds of uncertainty.

As we move to the couch, the city continues to pulse outside, a vibrant backdrop to our shared moment. The golden glow of the streetlights filters through the windows, casting playful shadows across the room. I lean back against the cushions, grateful for this small oasis amid the chaos. I watch as Evan rummages through the kitchen, returning with two steaming mugs of cocoa topped with fluffy marshmallows. The sight brings a smile to my lips; this simple act of caring encapsulates the essence of who he is.

With each sip, the sweetness washes over me, melting away the last remnants of doubt. I take a moment to observe him, the way the soft light plays off his features, illuminating the lines of worry etched into his forehead. There's a strength about him, an unwavering commitment that draws me in like a moth to a flame. I realize how profoundly I have missed this—the comfort of his presence, the familiarity of our routines, the laughter that fills the silences.

"What's next for us?" I ask, my voice barely above a whisper. The question hangs in the air, heavy with implications, as the weight of my father's health and the complexities of our relationship intertwine.

Evan's expression shifts, a thoughtful look passing over his face. "I think we need to be honest with each other, more than ever," he replies, the gravity of his words settling between us. "Life is too unpredictable. We can't afford to hold back anymore." His sincerity strikes a chord within me, echoing the tumultuous emotions I've carried back from my visit home.

Nervously, I nod, feeling a surge of vulnerability wash over me. The walls I had so carefully constructed begin to crumble, piece by piece. It's terrifying, but in the same breath, it feels liberating. In this moment, I am reminded that real love is forged in the fires of honesty and vulnerability, and I can't afford to shy away any longer.

As the night deepens and the city outside glimmers like a sea of stars, we sit together, cocooned in our little sanctuary. The worries of the world seem to fade, leaving only the two of us, ready to face whatever comes next. The air crackles with unspoken promises, a sense of possibility blossoming in the spaces between our words. And for the first time in what feels like an eternity, I believe that perhaps we can navigate the complexities of life together, stronger than we ever imagined.

The evening air in New York is thick with the scents of impending autumn; the crispness has begun to weave its way through the bustling streets, mingling with the rich aroma of roasted coffee and the ever-present hint of asphalt warmed by the day's sun. Evan and I sink deeper into the comfort of our living room, the faint sound of the city's heartbeat outside, a reminder that life continues, relentless and unwavering. The soft glow of the lamp casts golden shadows on the walls, creating an intimate cocoon where the worries of the outside world seem to dissolve.

"I've been thinking about us," I say, breaking the comfortable silence that had settled over us like a favorite blanket. My heart races at the vulnerability of my admission. It's a moment that feels as monumental as the skyline outside, where dreams are etched into every towering structure.

Evan's gaze sharpens, a mix of anticipation and concern flickering in his eyes. "What's on your mind?" He leans forward, his elbows resting on his knees, the tension in his posture betraying the casual demeanor he tries to project.

"Everything," I reply, my voice trembling slightly. "My father's health has made me realize how fleeting life can be. We spend so much time caught up in the minutiae, the noise, when what truly matters is right in front of us." I gesture between us, my hand hovering in the space that holds both our fears and our hopes.

He nods, a slow understanding dawning on his face. "I get that. We've both been so wrapped up in our own lives, our careers... It's like we forgot to nurture this—us."

"Exactly. I don't want to look back one day and see a series of missed opportunities, unspoken words." I lean back against the plush couch, allowing the soft fabric to cradle me, yet the weight of my words hangs heavy in the air.

Evan shifts closer, his fingers brushing against mine, igniting a spark that travels up my arm. "So, what do we do about it? How do we change?" His voice is steady, but I can hear the urgency in his tone, the desire to bridge the gap that has been silently widening between us.

I take a deep breath, gathering my thoughts, as if the very act of breathing can clear the fog clouding my mind. "Maybe we need to start with honesty—really sharing our fears and dreams, not just the surface stuff." The thought of peeling back those layers sends a shiver down my spine. It's terrifying yet exhilarating.

Evan meets my gaze, the vulnerability in his eyes mirroring my own. "I want that. I want to know every part of you, the good and the bad." His admission hangs between us, a fragile thread woven with trust and longing. I nod, feeling a warmth spread through me, igniting a flicker of hope that perhaps we can truly begin anew.

"What if we made a list of everything we want?" I suggest, a playful smile creeping onto my lips. "Places to go, things to try—adventures we've always talked about but never taken."

Evan chuckles, a rich sound that dances through the air, lightening the mood. "You know I'm always up for an adventure. But I might hold you to that list."

"Deal," I reply, grinning. The thought of creating something tangible to hold us accountable feels refreshing.

As the night unfolds, we start to share our aspirations, our voices intertwining like a melody. The conversation flows easily, each revelation bringing us closer, igniting the embers of connection that had dimmed in the tumult of our lives. I tell him about my dream to explore the rugged beauty of the Pacific Northwest, to breathe in the scent of pine trees and listen to the whispers of the ocean. He shares his wish to revisit New Orleans, to lose himself in the vibrant streets and let the music guide him, just like we did on that impromptu trip last year.

"Remember that jazz club?" he asks, a nostalgic smile illuminating his face. "We danced until dawn, didn't care that we had an early flight the next morning."

I laugh, the memory flooding back in vivid detail—the sultry night air, the rhythm of the saxophone, and how the world seemed to fade away as we swayed together, lost in our own universe. "We were so reckless," I say, a playful lilt in my voice.

"Or maybe just free," he counters, his expression thoughtful. "That's what I want us to feel again. Unburdened, just living in the moment."

I can feel the warmth of his words wrapping around me, a promise of what we could become. "Then let's make that our goal. We need to carve out time for us, no distractions, just exploring who we are together."

His smile widens, and for a moment, the room feels charged with potential, a promise that we could break free from the chains of our routines. "How about this weekend? A little getaway—somewhere we can rediscover that spark?"

My heart leaps at the suggestion. "I love that idea. Just you and me, no phones, no work—just us."

As we continue to brainstorm, the outside world fades, the sirens and laughter becoming a distant hum. With every word, we weave a tapestry of dreams, desires, and possibilities, the lines of our individual lives blurring into a shared vision.

Hours slip by, unnoticed, until we find ourselves sprawled across the couch, the city lights flickering outside like a thousand tiny stars. A comfortable silence envelops us as I rest my head on Evan's shoulder, feeling the steady rhythm of his heartbeat beneath me—a soothing reminder that we are in this together.

"I never want this to end," I whisper, my voice barely breaking the stillness.

"Neither do I," he replies, his fingers threading through my hair, sending shivers of comfort coursing through me.

In that moment, I realize that the journey we are embarking on isn't just about exploring the world outside; it's about delving deep into the beautiful chaos of each other. The road ahead may be uncertain, marked with challenges and heartaches, but as long as we navigate it together, I know we will be okay. The weight on my shoulders begins to lift, replaced by a buoyant hope that blossoms in the crevices of my heart. And for the first time in a long time, I truly believe in the magic of new beginnings.

In the days that follow, New York reveals itself in all its splendor and chaos, a kaleidoscope of experiences that shape our new beginning. The sun filters through the towering buildings, casting long shadows that dance across the pavement, a reminder that life is never static. Each morning, I awaken to the soft symphony of the city: the distant wail of sirens, the rhythmic clatter of construction, and the muffled laughter from the café below. I breathe it all in, allowing the vibrant energy to infuse me with renewed purpose.

Evan and I decide to take our exploration beyond the confines of our cozy apartment. One particularly crisp Saturday morning, we venture to Central Park, the sprawling green oasis nestled amid the concrete jungle. The leaves are beginning to turn, splashes of amber and crimson painting the landscape in a glorious display of autumn. The air is cool and invigorating, carrying with it the scent of damp earth and freshly fallen leaves.

As we stroll hand in hand along the winding paths, the cacophony of the city fades into a gentle hum, replaced by the laughter of children, the rustling of leaves, and the occasional bark of a dog chasing after a fallen acorn. I watch as Evan's eyes light up when he spots a cluster of children flying kites, their colorful tails flitting against the azure sky like the very embodiment of freedom.

"Let's join them," he suggests, a hint of mischief dancing in his eyes. Before I can respond, he's off, tugging me behind him, laughter bubbling up within me. The park comes alive as we find ourselves in the midst of spontaneous joy. We grab a kite from a nearby vendor—a bright yellow one shaped like a dragon, its eyes wide and mischievous.

As we run, the wind catches the kite, pulling it upward into the expansive blue. I can hardly contain my laughter, the sheer delight of this simple activity washing away any lingering concerns about my father or our future. Evan's enthusiasm is infectious, and as we take turns launching the kite higher into the sky, it feels as though we're not just flying a toy, but also our dreams, letting them soar without fear.

We collapse onto the grass, breathless and exhilarated, the dragon kite dancing above us like a playful spirit. I lean back, allowing myself a moment to relish the warmth of the sun on my face, the soft rustle of grass beneath me. "This is what I needed," I say, my voice a contented murmur.

Evan turns to me, his expression tender and contemplative. "You know, sometimes the simplest moments are the ones that matter most. They remind us to be present." His gaze is steady, and I can see the sincerity etched into his features. "And to not take each other for granted."

Those words resonate within me, settling into the crevices of my mind. We've both been so consumed by our individual challenges that we nearly lost sight of the beauty of just being together. The thought sends a pang through my heart; it's a reminder of how fleeting time can be, how quickly life can shift beneath our feet.

As the sun begins to dip low on the horizon, painting the sky in hues of pink and gold, I suggest we visit a quaint little bistro I've always loved, tucked away in a quiet corner of the Upper West Side. It's one of those places that feels like a well-kept secret, with its rustic charm and inviting aroma of baked bread wafting from the kitchen.

Evan agrees enthusiastically, and we set off, our hands intertwined as we navigate the vibrant streets. The warm glow of shop windows illuminates our path, casting a spell that feels both comforting and exhilarating. The city seems to thrum with life around us—street musicians serenade passersby, artists showcase their works on the sidewalks, and the scent of roasted chestnuts wafts from a nearby cart.

We settle into a cozy corner of the bistro, the ambiance intimate with its flickering candlelight and soft jazz playing in the background. The walls are lined with eclectic artwork, each piece telling a story of its own. I order a warm butternut squash soup, its velvety texture promising comfort, while Evan opts for a classic croque monsieur.

As we share bites and banter, the conversation flows effortlessly, our laughter mingling with the clinking of glasses and the soft murmur of other patrons. With each passing moment, I feel more at ease, the shadows of my father's illness receding further into the background. Evan's presence feels like an anchor, grounding me in the present, reminding me that I am not alone.

"Do you remember that time we tried to cook together?" Evan's eyes twinkle with mischief, and I can't help but chuckle at the memory of our kitchen disaster, the kitchen counter smeared with flour and the smoke alarm blaring in protest.

"How could I forget? We nearly set the apartment on fire," I reply, shaking my head at the absurdity of it all. "But we ended up laughing so hard that we forgot about dinner altogether."

He leans in closer, his expression earnest. "That's what I love about us. No matter how chaotic things get, we can always find a way to laugh."

His words wrap around me like a warm embrace, igniting a spark of affection that brightens my heart. The past few weeks may have been filled with uncertainty, but moments like this remind me of the strength of our bond, the unwavering support we provide one another amidst life's trials.

As we finish our meal, the world outside darkens, the city sparkling like a constellation of stars. The streets are alive with nightlife, and as we leave the bistro, I can feel the pulse of the city urging us forward, inviting us to explore the vibrant tapestry of experiences that await.

We wander down to the river, the soft lapping of water against the shore creating a soothing rhythm that mirrors the beat of my heart. The skyline looms above us, a breathtaking silhouette against the moonlit sky, each building a testament to dreams realized and yet to be chased.

Evan stops, turning to face me, the glow of the city casting a warm halo around him. "Can we make a pact?" he asks, his expression serious yet filled with warmth.

I nod, intrigued. "What kind of pact?"

He takes a deep breath, his gaze steady. "Let's promise to always prioritize moments like this. To be present for each other, no matter what life throws our way. We need to cherish the time we have, even if it's just a simple evening out."

My heart swells at his words, the weight of them resonating deeply. "I promise," I reply, my voice firm yet tender. "I want that, too."

And as we stand there, under the vast expanse of the New York sky, I realize that this journey—both the one I'm on with Evan and the one I'm navigating with my father—is about more than just facing challenges. It's about the love and laughter that fill the spaces in between, the small moments that weave the fabric of our lives into something beautiful and meaningful.

With the city lights twinkling around us, I take a step closer to Evan, feeling the warmth of his body next to mine. Together, we stand on the precipice of new adventures, ready to embrace whatever comes next, hand in hand, hearts open to the infinite possibilities that lie ahead.

Chapter 26: The Confession

The park stretches before us, a vibrant tapestry of amber and crimson, as though the trees have donned their finest attire for this momentous occasion. Each step feels both exhilarating and surreal, the familiar path winding through the foliage like a secret invitation to relive our past. The air is crisp, tinged with the earthy scent of damp leaves and a hint of nostalgia that wraps around us like an old, well-worn blanket. I can feel the weight of my emotions—a delightful mix of joy and trepidation—swirling inside me like the gusts of wind that playfully tug at the stray strands of my hair.

His hand feels warm and reassuring in mine, a silent promise that we are no longer navigating this journey alone. Every brush of our fingers sends a jolt of electricity up my arm, igniting a long-forgotten flame that dances in my chest. I catch glimpses of our laughter etched into the bark of the trees and feel the whispers of our shared secrets floating on the breeze. This park has witnessed our youthful dreams and naive hopes, and now it stands as a witness to our second chance, a sacred ground for confessions yet to come.

As we find our way to a secluded bench, nestled beneath a sprawling oak that cradles our memories, I can't help but admire the play of sunlight filtering through the leaves, casting dappled shadows on the ground. The tranquility envelops us, offering a refuge from the chaos of the world outside. My heart thumps wildly against my ribcage, each beat echoing the unspoken truths that hang between us, thick as the air before a storm. I glance at him, the sun catching the gold flecks in his brown eyes, and I wonder how I ever let fear eclipse what has always felt so beautifully right.

"Do you remember that time we got lost here?" I ask, a teasing lilt creeping into my voice as I attempt to deflect the gravity of the moment. His laughter, warm and rich, fills the space between us, chasing away my nerves like the sun dispersing morning fog.

"How could I forget?" he replies, shaking his head with mock seriousness. "You insisted on taking the path less traveled. I thought we'd never find our way back."

"That was part of the adventure!" I laugh, the sound echoing against the backdrop of rustling leaves. "I remember thinking that even if we were lost, I wouldn't have wanted to be anywhere else."

The weight of those words settles between us, and I feel a tingle of something profound—a shared understanding that stretches beyond time. The laughter fades into a comfortable silence, and I can feel the moment shifting, the atmosphere thickening with anticipation.

Taking a deep breath, I focus on his face, tracing the contours of his features with my eyes. There's a softness there, an openness that encourages me to dive into the depths of my feelings. It's time. I draw my fingers away from his, feeling the chill of the air seep into the space where warmth had lingered, and with a tremor in my voice, I start.

"I've been thinking a lot about us," I begin, the words tumbling out like the first drops of rain before a downpour. "About everything we went through and how it led us back here, to this moment."

He nods, his expression earnest, encouraging me to continue. "I never wanted to lose you, you know. I was scared—scared of what it all meant. But the truth is... I've loved you for a long time."

The confession hangs between us, a shimmering thread woven from our past. I see the realization flicker across his face, a beautiful blend of surprise and understanding. His eyes widen, and for a brief moment, the world around us fades, leaving only the two of us suspended in a bubble of honesty and hope.

"I've waited for this," he murmurs, his voice barely above a whisper, rich with emotion. "I've always known, deep down. I just didn't know how to say it."

The words settle in my heart like warm sunlight breaking through the clouds, illuminating all the shadows of doubt that had clouded my mind. There's a beauty in vulnerability, a power in laying one's heart bare, and as he leans closer, I feel as though we are orbiting around something sacred, something meant to be cherished.

In that shared breath, the air thick with unspoken promises, I lean in, drawn by an invisible force, and our lips meet in a hesitant, tentative kiss. It's as if time has paused, allowing us to savor the sweetness of this moment. The world around us fades into insignificance—the laughter of children playing nearby, the distant hum of traffic, the rustle of leaves—all becomes a distant echo as I lose myself in the warmth of his embrace.

As our kiss deepens, a surge of warmth floods through me, igniting every nerve ending, awakening a fire that had lain dormant for too long. It's a kiss that speaks of all the words left unsaid, of the pain we've endured, and of the joy that now fills the spaces between us. I pull away slightly, gazing into his eyes, searching for the reassurance that this isn't just a fleeting moment but the beginning of something new and profound.

"I've missed this," I confess, my heart swelling with gratitude for the chance to rediscover what we once had. "I've missed you."

His smile is bright, a beacon of hope that lights up the autumn sky, and I realize then that this park, once a mere collection of memories, has transformed into a landscape of promise, where love is not just a fleeting emotion but a tangible force that can mend even the deepest of wounds.

The kiss lingers in the air, a gentle reminder of the electric connection we've rediscovered. It feels like the world around us has come alive, each rustle of leaves and distant laugh echoing the joy we've found in each other once more. I lean back slightly, taking in the details of his face, the way the afternoon sun casts a warm glow across his features, illuminating the soft smile that dances upon his lips.

In that moment, the worries of the past—the misunderstandings, the silences that grew like weeds between us—seem to dissipate into the crisp autumn air. I remember the lonely nights spent missing him, each tick of the clock a reminder of what could have been. But now, standing here, I feel the delicate threads of fate weaving us back together, tighter and more resilient than before.

"Do you think we can really do this?" I ask, the weight of my question hanging in the air. "Can we move forward without the shadows of what happened?" My voice trembles slightly, betraying the uncertainty that lurks in the corners of my heart.

He takes a moment, searching my eyes as if to map the landscape of my fears. "I believe we can," he replies, his voice steady, filled with an assurance that settles the storm within me. "We've always been stronger together. It's just about being honest, right? With ourselves and with each other."

I nod, feeling a flicker of hope ignite within me. This is the foundation we need—the courage to confront our past while daring to dream of a future. The sun sinks lower in the sky, painting the horizon in hues of gold and crimson, a vibrant backdrop that echoes the warmth blooming in my chest.

We settle into the comforting rhythm of conversation, reminiscing about the little moments that once defined us. I tell him about the coffee shop that opened up down the street from my apartment, where the barista remembers my order and often slips in an extra pastry just because. He laughs, his laughter a rich melody that harmonizes with the sound of leaves rustling in the breeze.

"Do you remember that time we tried to make pancakes and ended up with a disaster?" he asks, his eyes sparkling with mirth.

"Oh, God, how could I forget?" I reply, laughing at the memory of our flour-covered kitchen and the way we'd both collapsed in laughter over our failed attempts. "I still don't understand how we managed to set off the smoke alarm."

His smile broadens, and I can't help but lean closer, wanting to capture every moment of joy as if it might slip away again. "That was the best breakfast ever," he says, his gaze fixed on me with an intensity that sends shivers down my spine. "Not because of the pancakes but because of us."

The tenderness in his words envelops me like a warm hug, and I realize how much I've missed this—this easy banter that flows between us, as natural as breathing. There's a beautiful rhythm in our exchanges, a dance of words and laughter that feels both familiar and new.

As the sun dips lower, painting the world in a dusky hue, I turn serious again, feeling the moment shift. "What if we face more challenges?" I ask, vulnerability threading my voice. "What if we can't overcome everything that's been said and done?"

He leans forward, his elbows resting on his knees, grounding us in the gravity of the moment. "Every relationship has its challenges," he replies, his tone earnest. "But if we're both willing to put in the work, to be honest and transparent, I believe we can navigate anything together. We just have to keep talking."

His words resonate deep within me, and I feel the tension that had coiled tightly around my heart begin to unfurl. It's a promise—a commitment to openness, to vulnerability, to forging a bond that could withstand the tests of time.

The golden light fades, and the park transforms into a realm of shadows and whispers. The laughter of children has turned into the soft chirping of crickets, serenading the night that wraps around us like a gentle cloak. I take a deep breath, inhaling the scent of damp earth and fading leaves, and let my mind wander to the possibilities that lie ahead.

"What do you see for us?" I ask, my heart racing at the thought of the future, filled with both hope and uncertainty. "Where do you want this to go?"

He takes a moment, contemplating my question, and in the stillness, I can feel the weight of his thoughts. "I see us taking our time," he finally says, his voice low and steady. "I want to build something real, something lasting. I want to travel together, explore new places, and create memories that are ours alone."

The vision he paints feels like a tapestry unfurling before my eyes—colorful, intricate, and filled with moments of laughter, adventure, and connection. "And what about home?" I ask, my heart swelling with the thought of a shared space filled with our combined quirks and dreams.

He smiles, a soft, knowing smile that warms my insides. "Home can be anywhere we are together," he replies. "Whether it's a cozy apartment in the city or a little cottage by the beach, as long as we're there, that's where I want to be."

His words hang in the air, a beautiful promise that reverberates through my entire being. A vision of a life intertwined with his unfurls in my mind, each thread vibrant and shimmering with potential. I can see us—cooking together in a cramped kitchen, bickering over who has the better taste in music, and sharing quiet evenings wrapped in each other's arms, enveloped in the soft glow of lamplight.

Suddenly, I'm overwhelmed by a rush of emotion, and my voice quivers as I speak. "I want that too. I want to build a life with you, a future filled with laughter and love."

As I look into his eyes, I can see the warmth of his affection reflected back at me, a mirror of the love that has blossomed anew. In that moment, the fears and uncertainties that once loomed large seem to shrink away, replaced by a beautiful sense of clarity. We are embarking on a journey, hand in hand, ready to face whatever comes our way.

The last traces of sunlight dip below the horizon, and stars begin to twinkle overhead, a million tiny beacons lighting the path ahead. We sit together in comfortable silence, our hands entwined, as the world transforms around us. The park, once a repository of memories, becomes a canvas for our dreams—a place where we can paint our future, stroke by delicate stroke.

As twilight descends, casting a soft veil over the park, the world around us morphs into a symphony of shadows and flickering lights. The last golden rays of sunlight bleed into a palette of indigo and violet, painting the sky with the promise of new beginnings. The air grows cooler, but the warmth radiating between us wraps around me like a snug shawl, providing comfort against the encroaching chill. I shift slightly on the bench, the old wood creaking beneath us, a familiar sound that echoes the laughter of our past.

Our conversation flows like a gentle stream, the topic drifting from our dreams to the quirks that have always made us uniquely us. "Remember that time you tried to teach me how to skateboard?" I ask, a grin spreading across my face at the recollection.

"Oh, don't remind me! I was convinced I could turn you into a pro in one afternoon," he laughs, his eyes sparkling with mirth. "What a disaster that was! I think we spent more time laughing than actually skating."

I chuckle at the memory—the way he had teetered on the edge of the board, demonstrating the perfect stance, only to take a tumble that sent him sprawling onto the grass. The echo of our shared laughter fills my heart with warmth, reminding me of those days when everything felt simpler, lighter.

"Sometimes, I think we're still those kids, trying to figure it all out," I muse, my tone softening. "But maybe that's the beauty of it.

We're still learning, still falling, but now we have each other to help us get back up."

He nods, the sincerity of his gaze anchoring me in the moment. "Exactly. I don't want to just relive our past; I want to create new memories, build on what we have. It's not about perfection; it's about enjoying the ride together, even when it gets bumpy."

With a sudden surge of boldness, I turn my gaze toward the shimmering stars emerging above us, pinpricks of light that flicker like dreams waiting to be grasped. "What's one dream you've always had but never dared to pursue?"

He takes a moment, his brow furrowed in thought. "I've always wanted to travel across the country, maybe take a road trip to the Grand Canyon," he admits, his voice brimming with a sense of longing. "To see it in all its glory, to stand at the edge and just soak in the vastness of it all."

A smile creeps across my face, and my heart races at the thought of sharing that adventure with him. "Let's do it," I say, the words spilling out before I can second-guess myself. "Let's plan a trip, just you and me. We can drive, stop wherever we want, make spontaneous detours. I want to see you stand at that edge, feeling as small as you've always dreamed."

His eyes widen with excitement, and I can see the thrill of possibility dancing in his gaze. "Really? You'd want to do that?"

"Absolutely. Life is too short for regrets, and we've spent too long apart already," I reply, feeling the weight of my own convictions. "Let's make every moment count."

The prospect of the journey ahead swells in my chest, intertwining with the warmth of our rekindled connection. I can almost hear the hum of the tires on the road, feel the wind tousling our hair as we laugh over bad playlists and the random snacks we'll inevitably hoard.

As the darkness deepens, a delicate hush settles over the park, broken only by the rustle of leaves and the distant sound of laughter echoing from a nearby playground. The atmosphere feels charged with unspoken possibilities, a magical bubble where time seems to stand still. I lean back on the bench, my heart racing with anticipation as I study his profile, the way the moonlight dances across his features, illuminating the corners of his smile.

"Hey," I whisper, pulling his attention back to me. "What if we made a list of things to do together? Adventures we've always wanted to try?"

He raises an eyebrow, intrigued. "A bucket list?"

"Exactly! Let's fill it with all the things we've missed out on, things we can do together now that we have this second chance," I suggest, my voice bubbling with enthusiasm. "Like hiking through the mountains, stargazing at the beach, or even just cozying up on the couch with a stack of movies."

"I love that idea," he replies, leaning in closer, his eyes alight with excitement. "We can make it a living document, adding things as we go. It'll be our guide to a life filled with laughter and love."

I can feel the warmth of his breath on my skin, a tender reminder of our closeness, and I can't help but smile. "I'm serious about the road trip, though. Let's make it happen, sooner rather than later."

He nods, determination written across his face. "I'll start planning. I want to take the scenic route, hit all the quirky roadside attractions along the way. You know, the giant ball of yarn, the world's largest rubber band ball..."

"Perfect! I've always wanted to see the world's largest anything," I tease, and we both laugh, the sound mingling with the gentle whispers of the night.

As we sit beneath the sprawling branches of the oak tree, I feel a sense of belonging wash over me, a powerful affirmation that we are exactly where we need to be. The worries that had clouded my mind begin to dissipate, leaving space for dreams to take root. This moment, this park, has become our sanctuary—a place where we can lay bare our hopes and fears, rebuilding the foundation of our love brick by careful brick.

With the stars twinkling overhead like a million tiny eyes watching over us, I feel a profound sense of gratitude wash over me. It's as if the universe has conspired to bring us back together, allowing us to grow from the lessons of our past while embracing the promise of what lies ahead.

I squeeze his hand, the connection electric and grounding all at once. "No matter what happens, I want you to know that I'm here. I'm all in."

His eyes soften, a warmth enveloping us that feels like a sacred vow. "And I'm all in too. Together, we'll face whatever comes our way. This is just the beginning."

With those words, the weight of the past transforms into a canvas for the future, painted in bold strokes of hope and love. As the moon rises high above, casting a silvery glow over the park, I lean my head on his shoulder, letting the moment wash over me. In the quiet serenity of the night, surrounded by the whispers of the wind and the rustling of leaves, I realize that we are ready to embark on this journey together—one filled with laughter, adventure, and the kind of love that grows deeper with each shared experience. And in that realization, I know that everything we've ever wanted is not just a dream; it's within our grasp.

Chapter 27: Tides of Change

The sun dipped below the horizon, painting the sky in hues of burnt orange and deep indigo, as I sat in the quaint coffee shop on the corner of 15th and Vine. The air was thick with the rich aroma of freshly ground beans, mingling with the faint sweetness of vanilla and caramel wafting from the barista's counter. My laptop flickered to life, casting a soft glow across the polished wooden table, its surface marked by countless scribbles and the occasional coffee ring—remnants of previous patrons whose dreams, hopes, and caffeine-induced epiphanies lingered in the air like ghosts.

As I took a sip of my latte, the warmth enveloping my hands, I couldn't help but feel a swell of excitement coursing through me. The weight of my feelings for Evan had shifted overnight from a burden to a buoyant exhilaration. The thrill of what we'd confessed to each other, those electrifying admissions that had hung between us like fragile silk threads, had morphed into something more—an intricate tapestry woven with trust, vulnerability, and a spark that ignited every moment we spent together.

Evan had become my muse, an unexpected catalyst for my creativity. Every time I closed my eyes, I could picture him—his dark curls tousled, his eyes glinting with mischief, and that enchanting smile that threatened to unravel my composure. Our late-night editing sessions had transformed the sterile confines of my cramped apartment into a vibrant studio filled with laughter and inspiration. As we dissected each scene of the film project, the room hummed with our shared enthusiasm, and I found myself lost in the rhythm of our collaboration.

"Did you see how the light dances in this shot?" I exclaimed, my heart racing as I clicked through the frames. "It's like the sun is whispering secrets to the trees. We have to emphasize that!"

Evan leaned closer, his shoulder brushing against mine, sending ripples of warmth coursing through me. "Absolutely. Let's amplify that moment. It'll draw the audience into the magic of the woods."

The synergy between us felt electric, crackling with an energy I had never known before. Every glance shared, every laugh exchanged, only deepened the connection. It was as if we were two stars on a collision course, and with each passing day, the gravitational pull grew stronger, threatening to pull us into a cosmic dance neither of us could escape. Yet, amid this joy, a shadow loomed—a constant reminder of Sophie. Her specter lingered at the edges of my thoughts, an unwelcome whisper that tugged at my heart.

I glanced up from my screen, stealing a moment to watch Evan as he focused on his edits, his brow furrowed in concentration. He had an intensity about him, a fierce dedication that inspired me to dig deeper into my own work. But I could see it, too, the flicker of uncertainty that crossed his features whenever we mentioned her name or when silence draped itself over our conversations. I knew that while our relationship had transformed, the past wasn't ready to let go. It wrapped around us like a fog, refusing to dissipate even as we stepped into this new chapter.

With the buzz of the coffee shop swirling around us, I felt a sudden resolve. We had to address the elephant in the room, the unresolved tension that hung between us like a delicate balance waiting to tip. "Evan," I ventured, my voice soft yet firm, "we need to talk about Sophie."

He paused, the warmth of his gaze faltering for just a second. "Yeah, I know," he replied, his tone laced with a hint of trepidation. "It's hard, isn't it?"

"Hard doesn't begin to cover it," I admitted, my heart pounding in my chest. "But we can't keep ignoring it. I want this," I gestured between us, "but I need to understand where you stand with her. It's like we're dancing on a tightrope, and I don't want to fall."

His expression shifted, vulnerability flickering across his face. "Sophie was a part of my life for so long, but it's different now. I thought I could compartmentalize my feelings, but you've brought something into my life that I never expected."

The sincerity in his eyes sent a shiver down my spine, a mixture of fear and hope battling within me. "I feel that too," I replied, my voice trembling. "But if we're going to make this work, we need to be honest with each other, even if it's uncomfortable."

We sat there in the dim light, the chatter of the coffee shop fading into the background as we waded through the murky waters of our pasts. The clinking of cups and the faint jazz music provided a soothing backdrop, but all I could focus on was the raw honesty emerging between us, each word stripping away the layers of fear that had kept us apart. As we laid our feelings bare, I found solace in the notion that this was a necessary step—one that could either solidify our bond or drive us apart.

When the conversation waned, I felt a weight lift, a tentative peace settling between us. I realized that navigating this emotional terrain wouldn't be easy, but it was essential. As the sun continued its descent, casting long shadows through the shop's windows, I couldn't shake the feeling that change was upon us—like the tide shifting, ebbing and flowing, promising a new beginning that would require trust, patience, and perhaps a little magic.

The sun's final rays dipped beneath the horizon, casting a warm golden light that filtered through the coffee shop windows, illuminating the dust particles dancing in the air like tiny fairies celebrating our newfound connection. I watched as Evan leaned back in his chair, his fingers raking through his curls, revealing the weariness that had settled in from late nights and early mornings spent wrestling with our shared vision. There was a depth to his eyes, a hint of vulnerability that made my heart ache with a fierce affection.

"Why don't we take a break?" I suggested, wanting to shift the energy and give him a moment to breathe. "We could go for a walk. The park is just a few blocks away."

His eyes lit up with a spark of mischief. "You know I can't resist a good outdoor adventure. Plus, I could use some fresh air to clear my mind before we dive back in."

As we stepped outside, the evening air wrapped around us like a soft blanket, tinged with the sweet scent of blooming jasmine that drifted from nearby gardens. The vibrant chatter of the city enveloped us, punctuated by the laughter of couples walking hand in hand and the distant sound of a street musician strumming a heartfelt melody. We walked side by side, our fingers brushing occasionally, igniting little sparks that sent thrills racing up my arm.

"Isn't it funny how the city changes with the light?" Evan mused, glancing around as we made our way down the sidewalk. "Everything feels more alive at night, as if the buildings themselves breathe a sigh of relief."

I smiled, caught up in his infectious enthusiasm. "You're right. It's like a secret world comes alive, revealing all its hidden treasures. We could film an entire sequence here—just capturing the essence of the night."

Evan nodded, his gaze drifting to a nearby street lamp casting a halo of light onto the pavement. "We should. I want to create something that feels authentic, something that resonates with the audience."

Our conversation flowed effortlessly, like a river finding its course, until we reached the park, its lush greenery a stark contrast to the concrete jungle surrounding us. We meandered along the winding path, the gentle rustle of leaves and the distant sounds of children playing weaving a soothing melody. I took a deep breath, letting the scent of freshly cut grass and earthy soil fill my lungs, grounding me in this moment with him.

As we approached a secluded bench nestled beneath a grand oak tree, I hesitated, feeling a wave of vulnerability wash over me. "Evan," I began, the words tumbling out before I could stop them, "do you ever think about the impact of our pasts on our present? I mean, I can't shake the feeling that we're still tethered to it, even as we step forward."

He sat down beside me, his expression contemplative. "All the time. It's like trying to run with a weight tied to your ankles. But I also believe that confronting those shadows can be liberating. It's messy, but isn't that what life is? A series of beautifully chaotic moments?"

His insight struck a chord within me, resonating like a note struck perfectly on a well-tuned piano. "You're right. It's just... I want to be fully present with you, without the ghosts of our past overshadowing what we could have."

Evan turned to me, his eyes earnest. "We can't erase what's happened, but we can choose how it shapes us moving forward. I'm committed to being honest with you. I don't want Sophie's memory to hang over us like a storm cloud."

A sense of relief washed over me, mingling with the tension that had wound tightly in my chest. "Thank you. That means everything to me. I want us to build something real together, grounded in trust and open communication."

As night fell deeper around us, the park transformed into a serene oasis, the moon casting silvery light across the grass. I could hear the soft whispers of the wind through the trees, as if the universe itself was listening, urging us to take the next step.

Evan reached for my hand, intertwining our fingers with a gentle confidence that sent shivers of warmth coursing through me. "I promise to keep the lines of communication open. You deserve that, and so do I."

We lingered there, enveloped in the soft glow of the moonlight, each heartbeat echoing the promise we were forging. The past may have shaped us, but it no longer dictated our path. We would navigate this uncharted territory together, hand in hand, weaving our stories into a tapestry that celebrated both our joys and our scars.

As we strolled back, a comfortable silence settled between us, punctuated only by our laughter and the soft rustle of leaves. I felt lighter, as if I had shed the burdens I had carried for far too long. The tension that had lingered like a specter was replaced by a shared excitement for what lay ahead—a blank canvas waiting for us to splash it with the colors of our emotions.

When we reached my apartment, I turned to Evan, my heart fluttering like a delicate butterfly. "Let's finish editing tonight. I think we have something special brewing."

He grinned, that captivating smile igniting a spark of anticipation within me. "Absolutely. Let's make magic."

As we settled back into our editing sanctuary, the world outside faded away. The soft glow of the computer screen illuminated our faces, highlighting the determination in his eyes as we worked side by side, breathing life into our film. Each frame we crafted felt like a step toward solidifying our connection, as if every cut and edit brought us closer to unveiling a story that was uniquely ours.

The hours slipped away, punctuated by bursts of laughter and the occasional playful banter. With each shared moment, I felt the weight of the past ease a little more, making room for the exhilarating uncertainty of our future. And in that bustling city, under the watchful gaze of a billion stars, I realized that we were not just crafting a film; we were writing our own narrative, one that defied the shadows and celebrated the brilliance of new beginnings.

The clock on the wall ticked softly, a rhythmic reminder that the world outside continued to spin while we immersed ourselves in our own little universe. Each keystroke felt like an incantation, transforming raw footage into something magical, something alive. I sat beside Evan, our shoulders brushing against one another as we sifted through the kaleidoscope of clips we had captured during our time together.

The vibrant city had become our backdrop, each street corner a canvas, each face a story waiting to unfold. We had filmed in bustling markets, where the laughter of children mingled with the enticing aroma of sizzling street food, and in serene parks, where sunlight filtered through leaves, creating a dappled effect that danced across the ground. With every shot, I poured my heart into the narrative we were crafting, weaving elements of hope and healing into the fabric of the film.

"Look at this," I said, excitement bubbling in my voice as I clicked on a clip of a sunset over the skyline. The fiery colors mirrored the warmth blossoming in my chest. "This needs to be our opening shot. It sets the tone perfectly."

Evan leaned in closer, his breath warm against my ear as he murmured his agreement. "It's stunning. It captures that feeling of possibility, don't you think? Like anything can happen."

The intimacy of the moment wrapped around us, a cocoon of shared dreams and aspirations. Yet, as I glanced at the footage, a lingering thought prickled at the back of my mind. I turned to Evan, my heart racing as I steeled myself for another deep conversation. "I think we should add a scene where we address the past—where we acknowledge the things that tried to hold us back."

His brow furrowed in thought, the light from the screen reflecting in his eyes. "That could work. But how do we do that without it overshadowing the rest of the film?"

I pondered his question, my fingers brushing over the keyboard as ideas swirled in my mind. "What if we incorporate subtle hints? Like moments where the characters reflect on their struggles—images of shadows, perhaps, or glimpses of people walking away. It'll signify the burdens we carry, but also show that we're moving forward."

Evan's expression shifted from uncertainty to intrigue. "I like that. It feels honest."

We continued to edit, each clip bringing us closer to the heart of our story. The film was more than a project; it became a metaphor for our relationship, a testament to the healing power of creativity. As we pieced it together, I felt a surge of gratitude for this journey, for the way it forced us to confront our insecurities while simultaneously fostering an undeniable bond.

With every hour that passed, our late-night sessions morphed into something more profound. Laughter punctuated the air as we snacked on popcorn and shared stories of our lives. Evan recounted his awkward teenage years, complete with the time he had accidentally joined the chess club instead of the debate team. "I thought it would be a suave move," he chuckled, shaking his head at the memory. "But all I got was a crown and a lot of confused looks."

"Hey, a king among pawns! That's not so bad," I teased, nudging him playfully.

And then it was my turn. "You think that's bad? I once wore mismatched shoes to an important presentation."

He leaned back, his eyes gleaming with curiosity. "What happened?"

"It was a disaster, obviously. But the funniest part? No one noticed until I pointed it out. I was the only one who thought I was a walking catastrophe."

Our laughter filled the room, a melody that chased away the lingering shadows of our pasts. Yet, in the stillness that followed, I felt the familiar weight return, a reminder that we still had unspoken truths to face. The delicate thread of tension remained, a silent acknowledgment of Sophie's lingering presence in our lives.

Later that night, as the clock ticked toward midnight, the atmosphere shifted. I paused the footage and turned to Evan, my heart thumping in my chest. "Evan, can we talk about Sophie again? I need to understand more about her place in your life."

He nodded slowly, his expression serious. "I've been thinking about it too. I want to be honest with you. I thought moving forward meant forgetting, but it's not that simple."

Taking a deep breath, I searched for the right words. "I get that. But we can't let her define what we're building together. I don't want her to be a ghost haunting our future."

Evan's eyes softened, filled with understanding. "You're right. Sophie was part of my past, but she's not my future. I care about you, and I want to be fully present with you, not lost in memories."

The sincerity in his voice struck a chord deep within me, and I felt a sense of relief wash over me. "I want that too. I want to support you, to help you move past what you've been through."

As we spoke, a sense of clarity emerged. Our vulnerabilities became a bridge, connecting us in a way that transcended the shadows of our histories. We were no longer just two individuals fumbling through the darkness; we were partners, ready to embrace whatever lay ahead.

When we finally wrapped up for the night, I couldn't shake the warmth of his words from my mind. As we walked to the door, the cool night air greeted us, crisp and invigorating. "Let's celebrate," I suggested. "How about ice cream?"

Evan grinned, his enthusiasm infectious. "You read my mind. There's that little shop down the street that has the best flavors."

We strolled through the city, the moonlight illuminating the path ahead, illuminating our way forward. As we approached the ice cream shop, the inviting glow of neon lights beckoned us closer. The air was thick with the sweet scent of waffle cones and chocolate, a siren call that was impossible to resist.

Standing in line, I felt a sense of normalcy wash over me—a moment of joy nestled within the chaos of our lives. We chose our flavors, a silly contest of who could pick the most outrageous combination. I settled on lavender honey, while he opted for a wild raspberry basil that made me giggle.

With our cones in hand, we wandered back into the night, our laughter echoing against the city's backdrop. I savored the creamy sweetness, the flavors mingling on my tongue, while Evan teased me about my 'grandma flavor' choice.

"This is all part of my plan," I declared dramatically. "Lavender is known for its calming properties. I'm just trying to keep our relationship zen."

Evan threw his head back and laughed, a rich sound that made my heart soar. "Well, you've certainly succeeded in calming my chaotic spirit. I feel like we could conquer the world right now."

As we walked beneath the flickering streetlights, I realized that, in this moment, we were not merely editing a film or sorting through our pasts. We were crafting a life together, one filled with sweetness and laughter, bound by a shared commitment to growth and understanding.

The city pulsed around us, a living, breathing entity filled with stories, dreams, and the vibrant energy of possibility. With every step we took, I felt the weight of the past lighten, replaced by the thrill of anticipation for what lay ahead. Hand in hand, we stepped forward into the unknown, ready to embrace the tides of change, confident in the knowledge that we would navigate them together, side by side.

Chapter 28: Shadows of Doubt

I stood at the edge of the bustling film festival, a world of flashing lights and laughter unfurling before me like the vibrant ribbons of a parade. The scent of buttered popcorn wafted through the air, mingling with the subtle tang of summer rain lingering on the pavement outside. Glowing banners swayed gently in the breeze, heralding the arrival of cinematic masterpieces and the artists behind them. I gripped the strap of my satchel, a tether that seemed to ground me in this electric atmosphere. Each face was a tapestry of excitement and expectation, yet my heart pounded a different rhythm, a discordant beat resonating with doubt.

Evan stood a few paces away, his silhouette outlined by the kaleidoscope of colors spilling from the grand marquee. His eyes sparkled with enthusiasm as he chatted animatedly with a group of festival-goers, effortlessly charming them with stories that felt almost cinematic in their own right. I had fallen for him the way one falls into a dream: slowly, then all at once, until he became the focal point of my waking hours. But dreams can be fragile, and as I watched him laugh, a sense of unease threaded through my chest.

The crowd surged, drawing my gaze away from Evan, and in that moment, Sophie emerged like a scene-stealer in the movie of my life. Her hair, a cascade of sunlit curls, caught the light as she moved with an ease that was both intoxicating and infuriating. She had that effortless allure, the kind that turned heads and made hearts skip a beat. It was a talent I had seen before, and one that I knew all too well. There was an unspoken pact in this moment: she was here to reclaim the spotlight, and Evan, standing unsuspectingly at its center, was the perfect target.

Sophie approached him with the grace of a gazelle, her laugh ringing out like music. I could see the flicker of recognition in Evan's eyes, a warm glow that ignited the air between them. My heart clenched as they exchanged pleasantries, the chemistry between them palpable. I took a deep breath, but it felt like inhaling shards of glass. This was not the reunion I had envisioned when I first set foot in this festival. I had hoped for shared moments, laughter, and perhaps a whispered promise beneath the stars, but instead, I felt like an interloper in my own story.

The crowd moved around us, a wave of bodies thrumming with anticipation for the next screening, but I felt rooted in place, caught in a vortex of conflicting emotions. I reminded myself that Evan had reassured me time and again of his commitment, that our shared moments had been filled with sincerity and warmth. Yet, watching him with Sophie, the insecurities I had worked so hard to bury began to bubble up to the surface, threatening to engulf me in a tide of doubt.

Sophie leaned in closer to Evan, her voice low, whispering something that elicited a grin from him. I felt my stomach knot as I strained to hear the words that fluttered like moths around a flame, tantalizing yet forbidden. The intimacy of their exchange felt like a dagger to my confidence, a reminder of how easily connections could shift and change. What if her charm wrapped around him like vines, suffocating our budding relationship? What if I was merely a fleeting chapter in his story, one easily replaced by her dramatic flair?

I watched as Sophie lightly touched Evan's arm, a gesture that felt too familiar, too intimate. A shiver of jealousy raced through me, colder than the rain-drenched air. In that moment, the laughter and chatter surrounding us faded into a dull roar, leaving only the two of them and the looming shadow of my insecurities. I could feel the walls I had built beginning to tremble, threatening to crumble under the weight of my apprehension. It was as if the universe had conspired to place her directly in our path, a reminder of all I feared losing.

With each passing second, I could sense the balance we had fought to establish wobbling precariously, as if on a tightrope strung between the promise of new beginnings and the ghosts of old relationships. Memories of our late-night talks, the way his eyes lit up when he spoke about his passions, and the way he would reach for my hand as if to tether me to him flooded my mind. Yet, here stood Sophie, the embodiment of everything I felt I was not—confident, vibrant, and utterly magnetic.

I took a step back, a natural instinct born from the fight or flight that surged within me. I couldn't bear to witness their connection grow, and yet part of me felt anchored to the spot, a spectator in this drama that threatened to unfold. The neon lights twinkled above like stars, indifferent to my turmoil, and I wrestled with the urge to pull him back into my orbit, to remind him of the universe we had created together.

But as I shifted my weight, preparing to retreat, I caught Evan's gaze across the throng of people. His eyes locked onto mine, and in that instant, the noise faded away, leaving only the two of us in a bubble that pulsed with unspoken understanding. There was something in his expression—a mixture of surprise and concern—that made my heart flutter. He excused himself from Sophie, taking a few strides toward me, and as he drew closer, I could feel the rush of relief flooding my veins, washing away the remnants of doubt that had threatened to consume me.

"Hey," he said, his voice warm, yet edged with urgency. "I didn't see you. I've been looking for you."

The sincerity in his tone ignited a spark of hope within me, igniting the remnants of my courage. I took a deep breath, willing the uncertainty to fade as I prepared to reclaim the narrative of our shared story, to ensure it didn't spiral into something I feared. I wasn't ready to let the shadows of doubt dim the vibrant world we had begun to build together.

Evan's eyes sparkled with a blend of surprise and delight as he approached me, slicing through the murky waters of my anxiety like a warm beam of sunlight. I could sense the electricity in the air, a crackling connection that seemed to weave around us, pulling me back into our shared reality. As he closed the distance, the noise of the festival faded into a muffled hum, each person fading into mere background characters in our scene.

"What are you doing here?" he asked, the corners of his mouth tugging into that familiar, boyish grin that always made my heart skip a beat. The concern etched in his brow only deepened my resolve to shake off the shadows lurking behind me.

"I wanted to see what all the excitement was about," I replied, my voice steady, though my heart raced. "Looks like I caught the opening act." I gestured to Sophie, who was now engaged in animated conversation with another festival-goer, her laughter rising like the effervescent bubbles in a glass of champagne. I could almost feel her vivacious spirit spilling into the space around her, filling it with an energy that both fascinated and intimidated me.

Evan followed my gaze, and for a moment, I feared I would see a flicker of longing in his eyes, the kind of gaze that signaled an inevitable pull back toward the familiar warmth of someone he once cherished. Instead, he turned his focus back to me, and I found solace in the sincerity of his expression.

"I'm really glad to see you," he said, his voice low, almost a whisper. "I didn't want you to feel left out. Sophie... she can be a bit much sometimes." There was an edge to his words, a protective undertone that wrapped around me like a cozy blanket on a chilly evening. I could feel the sincerity radiating from him, warming my skin, yet the anxiety bubbling within me refused to dissipate entirely.

"Much?" I echoed, a slight laugh escaping my lips to mask the tremor of insecurity beneath. "You mean over-the-top? Like fireworks at a funeral?"

He chuckled, a deep, melodic sound that resonated within me. "Something like that."

We stood there, enveloped in a shared moment that felt precious amidst the clamor of the festival. The cacophony of laughter and chatter surged around us, but here, it was just the two of us, standing together under the glow of neon lights that cast a warm hue over everything. I could feel the corners of my mouth tugging upward in response to his presence, and I let the warmth of his hand brush against mine, a subtle reassurance.

"Shall we escape?" he asked, tilting his head toward the less crowded area where the strings of lights twinkled like stars. "There's a quieter spot just around the corner, perfect for a little... cinematic retreat."

I nodded, feeling a sense of adventure bubble within me. Together, we slipped through the throngs of people, the world shifting around us in a dizzying blur. The laughter faded, replaced by a distant melody that echoed through the air—a soft, enchanting tune that wrapped itself around our shoulders like an embrace.

As we stepped into the alcove, the atmosphere transformed. Here, the sounds of the festival faded to a gentle whisper, replaced by the serene rustle of leaves in the cool evening breeze. Fairy lights strung overhead blinked like tiny constellations, creating a pocket of intimacy in a night filled with chaos. I leaned against the weathered wooden railing, taking a moment to breathe in the tranquility, the soft scent of night-blooming jasmine weaving through the air.

Evan turned to me, his expression softening as he studied my face, as if trying to decipher the intricate tapestry of emotions woven into my features. "You okay?" he asked, his tone laced with concern. "I know Sophie can be... distracting."

"Distracting?" I scoffed, attempting to inject humor into the tension that hung like an unwelcome guest. "More like a hurricane in a teacup."

He laughed, the sound lightening the air around us. "You've got a point there. But listen," he continued, stepping closer, his gaze steady and earnest. "I'm not here for her. You know that, right? What we have... it matters to me."

In that moment, a spark ignited within me, dispelling the shadows that had lingered since Sophie's arrival. I nodded, letting his words settle around me like a warm embrace. "I know. I just... I can't help but feel like I'm competing with a version of you that I can't quite measure up to."

Evan reached out, his fingers grazing my arm, sending a pleasant shiver up my spine. "You don't have to compete with anyone. I chose you, remember?"

His sincerity wrapped around me like a protective barrier against the storm of self-doubt that had threatened to consume me. I felt the warmth radiating from his hand seep into my skin, igniting a flicker of confidence that had been dimmed. "You're right. I know you chose me. It's just... sometimes it feels like I'm standing in the shadow of someone who shines a little brighter."

"Then let's change the lighting," he replied, his gaze intense and unwavering. "You deserve to stand in the spotlight too."

With a newfound determination, I straightened my shoulders, allowing his words to bolster my resolve. I wanted to be brave, to shed the layers of insecurity that clung to me like a heavy cloak. In this moment, with the stars twinkling overhead and the distant laughter echoing like a sweet serenade, I decided to embrace the chaos, to welcome the uncertainty that came with loving someone as vibrant as Evan.

"I guess I just need to remember that our story is unique," I said, the words flowing freely as I found my voice within this fragile space we'd carved out together. "Sophie may be a bright star, but you and I... we have our own constellation."

His smile widened, lighting up his face, and I felt the warmth of it wash over me, banishing the last remnants of doubt. "Exactly. And who knows? Maybe we'll outshine her."

With that, the tension began to dissipate, replaced by laughter and the shared anticipation of the festival. We stepped back into the lively world beyond our quiet alcove, hands intertwined, the electric connection between us reigniting with each pulse of excitement around us. I realized that the flicker of jealousy I had felt was merely a passing storm, one I was more than capable of weathering. Together, we could navigate the winding paths of uncertainty, bound by a love that flourished in the face of adversity, determined to embrace whatever

As we slipped back into the festival's vibrant throng, a sense of resolve blossomed within me, a defiance against the shadows of doubt that had threatened to encroach upon the fragile landscape we'd built together. The air hummed with anticipation, a palpable energy that felt like the electric crackle before a summer storm. Evan's hand was a steadying force in mine, the warmth of his grip grounding me as we navigated the swirling masses of festival-goers who floated from screening to screening, their laughter ringing out like a symphony.

"Let's find some popcorn," Evan suggested, his eyes dancing with a mischievous light. "I hear it's practically a festival requirement."

"Is that so?" I quipped, a smile breaking across my face despite the remnants of insecurity still clinging to my thoughts. "What about nachos? I hear they're the real culinary stars of any film event."

"Careful now, we wouldn't want to start a culinary war in the middle of a cinematic celebration," he shot back, his laughter infectious, drawing me further into the lightness of the moment. We maneuvered through the crowd, sidestepping enthusiastic patrons brandishing festival pamphlets and drinks, the air rich with the aroma of buttered popcorn and roasted almonds mingling with the scent of summer blooms from nearby flower stalls.

At the popcorn stand, the vendor, an elderly man with twinkling blue eyes and a wide grin, poured fluffy kernels into a paper cone, their golden surfaces glistening under the festival lights. I couldn't help but feel a sense of warmth watching him work; his joy in serving was palpable, almost contagious. I turned to Evan, who was already grinning widely, his enthusiasm infectious.

"What's the verdict?" I asked, wiggling my fingers in excitement.

"Perfectly buttery, just like my taste in films," he replied, plucking a piece from the cone and tossing it playfully into my mouth. I caught it effortlessly, the burst of buttery flavor mixing with the sweet aftertaste of my lingering anxiety. It felt like a small victory in a world that seemed determined to challenge us at every turn.

As we made our way back into the festival grounds, we passed by a large screen showing a montage of clips from the films to be screened that evening. The images flickered like memories being unearthed, each one eliciting a gasp or cheer from the crowd. The energy was electric, and I felt the knots in my stomach slowly loosening.

"Did you see that one?" Evan pointed to a particularly emotional scene, his eyes alight with excitement. "I heard it's a tear-jerker. We should totally catch that one together."

"Are you trying to make me cry?" I teased, nudging him with my elbow.

"Only if you promise to bring the nachos," he countered, his eyes sparkling with mischief.

In that moment, the doubts that had clung to me like a shadow began to dissolve into the background, overshadowed by the warmth of our connection and the laughter that seemed to flow so easily between us. We settled onto a grassy knoll, the ground beneath us warm from the day's sun, the fabric of the world around us fading into a canvas of bright colors and joyous sounds.

The festival unfolded like a kaleidoscope, people flitting about, their faces animated with joy, their stories intertwining for a fleeting moment before they vanished into the crowd. I felt a sense of belonging seep into my bones, the comfort of being near Evan providing a shield against the chaos.

Just as we began to relax, a familiar voice sliced through the revelry—a melodic laugh that danced through the air like music. Sophie appeared at the edge of our grassy refuge, her presence as commanding as a leading lady entering a scene. She was flanked by a couple of friends, their expressions equally animated as they scanned the crowd. My heart raced, not from the thrill of the festival but from the familiar pang of insecurity that welled up in my chest.

"Evan!" Sophie called out, her voice cutting through the ambient sounds like a siren's call. "I was just looking for you! We're about to head over to the new screening, want to join us?"

Evan's eyes flicked toward me, a silent question lingering between us. I could feel the tension coiling back into the space, a taut string ready to snap. It would be so easy for him to slip back into the familiar orbit of her charm, to be drawn into her world where I felt I could never quite measure up.

"Actually," he said, his voice steady, "I promised I'd catch up with her first." He gestured toward me, his hand still holding mine, anchoring me in this moment. "We're having a little festival date over here."

The corners of Sophie's mouth tightened for just a fraction of a second, a crack in her flawless facade, before she plastered on that radiant smile. "Oh, how cute," she replied, the sweetness in her tone laced with a hint of condescension. "You two really are a couple now, huh?"

I felt my cheeks flush, the heat of embarrassment rising. I hated the way she could twist the words, making them feel sharp and barbed. "Just enjoying the festival," I replied, my voice steady despite the churning in my stomach.

"Well, if you change your mind, you know where to find us," Sophie said, casting a glance at Evan, a flicker of something unspoken passing between them. "We'll be at the front row, living the cinematic life."

As she turned to leave, I felt Evan's grip tighten around my hand, grounding me once more in our shared reality. "You okay?" he asked, his voice low, concern etched into his features.

"I will be," I assured him, though the weight of her presence lingered like a ghost. "Just trying to shake off the echoes of her shadow."

With a gentle squeeze, he drew me closer, enveloping me in the warmth of his presence. "You don't have to be anyone but yourself," he whispered, his breath warm against my ear. "That's who I'm here for."

The shadows of doubt flickered but did not extinguish, for they were part of me, just as much as my desire to embrace this budding relationship. Yet, in that moment, with Evan by my side, I realized I didn't have to chase away every lingering insecurity. Instead, I could allow them to exist, a bittersweet reminder of my journey, while forging ahead into the unknown with the knowledge that I was not alone.

We settled back onto the grass, the festival unfolding around us like a vibrant tapestry of life, each thread weaving our story into the greater narrative. I felt the pulse of excitement thrumming through my veins, a reminder that I was here, present and alive, ready to embrace whatever challenges lay ahead. As the sun dipped lower in the sky, casting a golden glow over everything, I leaned into Evan, allowing the warmth of his body to wash over me, igniting a spark of hope that felt as boundless as the starry night to come.

Chapter 29: The Breaking Point

The air hung thick with the remnants of laughter and the lingering scent of fried dough, mingling with the earthy aroma of the autumn leaves that crunched beneath my feet. The festival had been a kaleidoscope of color, a vibrant tapestry woven from the heartbeats of a small town alive with tradition and joy. Under the twinkling lights strung from tree to tree, the whole world had felt alive and electric, filled with the heady promise of possibilities and whispered dreams. Yet, even amidst the laughter and clinking glasses, a dark cloud had settled over my heart, heavy and foreboding. I could no longer ignore it, not when Evan's laughter rang out a little too brightly as he conversed with Sophie, her carefree demeanor a sharp contrast to my own simmering turmoil.

Now, as the festival's remnants faded into the night, I felt that turmoil coalescing into something fierce and unstoppable. The moon hung low, casting silvered shadows on the pavement, and in the quiet aftermath of the celebration, I caught up to Evan outside the town hall, where the final notes of the band faded away. He was leaning against the wooden railing, his gaze lost in the darkened expanse of the park, the glow of the fairy lights dimming behind him.

"Evan," I called, my voice a tremor on the cool night air, weaving through the remnants of my festering discontent. He turned, and the look in his eyes—a mixture of surprise and concern—sent a rush of heat to my cheeks. But I couldn't back down now; the pressure had built to a point where I could no longer hold it inside.

"Why were you so close to Sophie?" The words burst from my lips like a dam breaking, each syllable saturated with pent-up frustration. I stepped closer, the wood beneath my feet creaking, mirroring the cracking sound of my resolve. "You seemed so... happy with her."

Evan's brow furrowed, his brow furrowing deeper as confusion clouded his features. "What? Are you serious?" He stepped toward me, the distance between us dissipating like fog in the morning sun. "She's just a friend, Cassie. You know that."

"Do I?" I shot back, my heart racing, the taste of desperation seeping into my tone. "Because the way you look at her—like she's the only person in the room—it makes me question everything." The words spilled out, raw and unfiltered, the weight of insecurity anchoring them to my soul.

His jaw tightened, and I could see the gears turning in his mind, the struggle etched across his face as he searched for the right words. "I don't look at her like that, and you know it. I thought you trusted me." The hurt in his voice echoed my own, but I couldn't let it deter me. The ache in my chest was overwhelming, and I was on the brink of breaking.

"I want to trust you, Evan, but I'm scared. Scared that you'll slip away, scared that I'm not enough. Every time I see you with her, it's like a reminder of my own shortcomings." The floodgates opened, and the tears I had fought so hard to hold back began to spill over, tracing hot paths down my cheeks. "I don't want to lose you again."

He reached out, brushing a thumb beneath my eye, and the tenderness of his touch sent a shiver down my spine. "You won't lose me, Cassie. I promise. My heart belongs to you. Sophie is just..." His voice trailed off, frustration palpable in the way his hands ran through his tousled hair. "A distraction? A friend?" I could hear the conflict in his words, the effort to convince me intermingling with his own feelings of frustration.

"It doesn't matter!" I nearly shouted, the words erupting from the pit of my stomach. "I don't want to hear about her. I want to know that you're here, with me, completely."

For a moment, silence enveloped us, thick and suffocating. The world around us seemed to fade—the rustle of leaves, the distant laughter from the festival, the sound of our own hearts beating in tandem, caught in this moment of turmoil. I could feel the weight of our history pressing down on us, memories of our previous separations flaring up like wildfire, threatening to consume everything we had fought for.

"I know," he finally whispered, the vulnerability in his voice a soothing balm to my frayed nerves. "But we need to talk about this, all of it—about us, our past. If we're going to move forward, we can't keep letting these shadows control us."

The realization struck me then, a profound truth amidst the chaos: the shadows were not just specters of our past; they were the insecurities I had nurtured like a twisted vine, wrapping tightly around my heart and squeezing until I could hardly breathe. I took a deep breath, the cool air filling my lungs, and nodded slowly, feeling the gravity of the moment settle over us like a heavy cloak.

"Then let's talk," I said, my voice steadier now, the fire of my anger giving way to the flickering light of hope. "But I need you to promise me one thing—no more secrets."

"Never," he replied, a soft smile breaking through the tension. "We're in this together, Cassie. Always."

In that moment, as we stood on the precipice of our fears, the night sky above us opened up like a vast canvas, dotted with stars that shone brightly despite the darkness around them. The realization that we were willing to confront our past, together, ignited a warmth in my chest. Perhaps, just perhaps, we were not too far gone to salvage what we had built. As the crisp night air wrapped around us, I felt a flicker of hope, a glimmer of light breaking through the shadows, and I knew that our journey was just beginning.

With our promises lingering in the cool night air, we made our way down the dimly lit path leading from the town hall, the vibrant echoes of the festival fading behind us. The crunch of leaves beneath our feet punctuated the silence, a rhythmic reminder of the weight of our shared history. I felt a twinge of guilt wash over me as I glanced sideways at Evan. His hands were shoved deep into his pockets, the tension radiating off him like heat from a flame. I wanted to reach out, to hold him close and banish the shadows that lurked between us, but the fear of what lay ahead made my feet feel leaden.

"Let's walk," he said suddenly, breaking the stillness that enveloped us. His voice was soft yet resolute, carrying a hint of determination that sparked something within me. As we strolled along the familiar streets of our town, with its quaint houses lined like old friends, memories swirled around us—snapshots of laughter, whispered secrets, and quiet moments under starlit skies.

"How did we get here?" I finally asked, my voice barely above a whisper. "How did everything become so complicated?" I knew the answer lay in the tangled web of emotions we had woven, a tapestry of past heartaches and lingering doubts.

Evan stopped and turned to me, his blue eyes piercing through the dark. "Life happened, Cassie. We got caught up in it, and I guess I didn't realize how much those shadows could linger." His honesty pierced me like an arrow, a sharp reminder that we had both been guilty of running from the truth.

"I tried to be strong," I confessed, looking away as a flush crept up my cheeks. "But it's exhausting. Some days, it feels like I'm barely holding it together, and when I see you with her..." My voice faltered, and I took a steadying breath, trying to gather the pieces of my vulnerability. "It's like I'm losing you all over again."

"Cassie, I'm right here," he said, stepping closer, the warmth radiating off him a welcome reprieve from the chill of the night. "I never left. I'm just as scared of losing you, but I need you to see that. I've always wanted you."

His words hung in the air, heavy with promise and regret. I wanted to believe him, to accept that the insecurities gnawing at my heart were unfounded. But the scars of our past ran deep, etched into my soul like graffiti on a forgotten wall. "How do we move forward?" I asked, searching his gaze for answers that felt as elusive as the stars above.

"We face it," he replied simply. "We confront the past—together." There was a raw sincerity in his voice that ignited a spark of hope within me. The flickering flame was small, but it was there, and I clung to it like a lifeline.

We resumed our walk, the night wrapping around us like a soft blanket, and with each step, I felt the tension easing between us, little by little. The town lay in a hush, the vibrant chaos of the festival a distant memory. We ventured to the park where we had spent countless evenings, stealing kisses beneath the old oak tree, the very same tree that now stood sentinel over us, its leaves rustling gently in the breeze as if urging us to move forward.

"I remember when we used to sit right here," Evan said, gesturing to a worn bench under the sprawling branches. "You'd always tease me about how I could never find the right words to say what I felt."

A soft laugh escaped my lips, laced with nostalgia. "You had a way of making the simplest things sound profound, though. It was charming."

"Maybe I should channel that charm again," he said with a playful smirk. But the moment was fleeting; the underlying seriousness of our conversation crept back in like a shadow.

"What if we can't fix this?" I asked, my voice barely above a whisper. "What if we're just prolonging the inevitable?"

Evan's expression shifted, a flash of determination crossing his features. "We can't think like that. We owe it to ourselves to try." He reached for my hand, intertwining our fingers, and in that simple gesture, the warmth of his skin against mine filled the cold spaces in my heart.

"I want to try," I admitted, squeezing his hand tighter. "But it's hard. I feel like I'm standing on the edge of a cliff, afraid to jump."

"That's okay," he replied, his thumb brushing against the back of my hand. "I'll be right there with you. We'll jump together."

As the words hung in the air, I felt an unexpected sense of calm wash over me, as if the fears that had once threatened to consume us were receding like the tide. Perhaps this was the moment we needed, a chance to turn our shared pain into something beautiful, something strong.

The night deepened around us, the stars twinkling like diamonds scattered across velvet. With the gentle rustle of leaves and the distant sounds of the festival behind us, it felt as if time had slowed, allowing us to linger in this fragile moment of connection.

"Do you remember that night when we made that ridiculous pact to never let anything come between us?" Evan asked, a smile creeping across his face.

"How could I forget?" I chuckled, the memory lighting up my heart. "We were so young and naive, thinking we could conquer the world with nothing but our dreams."

"Naive, yes, but not entirely wrong. We were fierce back then. If we could find that fire again, there's no way we can't make this work," he said, determination lacing his voice.

The conviction in his words stirred something deep within me. Maybe the embers of our past still held the potential to ignite a flame. Perhaps we could reclaim our story, weaving our experiences together into a tapestry of resilience and love. As we sat beneath the oak tree, fingers entwined, I took a deep breath, grounding myself in the moment.

This time, we wouldn't run. Together, we would face whatever lay ahead, building a future from the ashes of our past.

The night stretched on, a shroud of darkness enveloping us as we sat beneath the sprawling oak tree, our hands intertwined like fragile threads of hope. The stars above blinked like distant sentinels, silently observing our struggle as we navigated the tumultuous waters of our emotions. I could feel the pulse of our town echoing in the background, the faint sounds of laughter and music barely audible, yet they felt worlds away from our private reckoning.

"Do you ever wonder if we're trying too hard to fit a mold that doesn't exist?" I asked, my voice barely a whisper, weighed down by the gravity of our conversation. "Sometimes it feels like we're dancing around the same issues, trapped in a waltz of unspoken fears."

Evan's gaze bore into me, and I could see the wheels turning in his mind. "I think that's part of it," he replied, his tone thoughtful. "But what if that mold is just us trying to define what we want, instead of accepting the messiness that comes with being human?"

His words hung in the air, a lifeline thrown into the turbulent sea of our doubts. Perhaps it was time to embrace the chaos, to acknowledge that love wasn't about fitting neatly into a box but about navigating the storms together. "Maybe we need to redefine our love," I mused, the idea taking root in my mind. "What if we stripped away the expectations and just focused on us?"

A smile broke through the shadows on Evan's face, lighting up the night like a sudden burst of fireworks. "Now that's a plan I can get behind," he said, his laughter a soothing balm that eased the tension still lingering between us. "No more pretending. Just us, raw and real."

The notion felt liberating, as if the weight of the world had been lifted from my shoulders. I leaned in closer, encouraged by the warmth radiating from him, and whispered, "What does that look like for us?"

His expression turned serious again, and I could see the flicker of vulnerability in his eyes. "It means we communicate—really communicate. Not just words thrown at each other, but understanding the feelings behind them."

I nodded, absorbing the truth in his words. For so long, we had let our insecurities dictate our actions, allowing misunderstandings to fester in the dark corners of our minds. The shadows that had threatened to pull us apart were born from our fears, not the love we shared. "And if we mess up?" I asked, my heart racing at the thought of potential heartbreak.

"Then we fix it," Evan replied, his confidence unwavering. "We've done it before. We can do it again. Love isn't perfect, Cassie. It's messy and complicated, but it's also beautiful in its imperfections."

The promise of resilience washed over me like a warm wave, pulling me closer to him. "So, we take it day by day? No pressure?"

"Exactly," he affirmed, his thumb stroking the back of my hand, sending tingles up my arm. "We build our own path, one that honors where we've been while looking forward to where we're going."

I felt a surge of determination, the fire of hope igniting in my chest. "Then let's do it. Let's build something real, something that can withstand the storms."

The words hung between us, thick with potential, and in that moment, the world outside faded away. The bustling town, the twinkling lights, the laughter—all of it became a distant hum, overshadowed by the connection blossoming between us. I could see the future unfolding in Evan's eyes, a tapestry woven with threads of resilience, love, and shared dreams.

"Let's promise to always come back to this," he said, leaning closer, his voice low and sincere. "No matter how hard it gets, we don't run. We talk, we listen, we fight for what we have."

"I promise," I breathed, feeling the weight of my words settle in the space between us. As I looked into his eyes, the storm within me calmed, replaced by a steady current of hope.

We shared a moment of silence, the air charged with unspoken vows and unyielding commitment. Then, as if the universe had conspired to bless us, a shooting star streaked across the sky, a brilliant flash of light that seemed to echo our shared resolve. I closed my eyes, making a silent wish that this moment would last forever, a beacon guiding us through the darkness.

The cool breeze ruffled my hair as we sat together, laughter and warmth mingling in the crisp night air. I couldn't remember the last time I had felt so at peace, so connected. "You know," I said, breaking the comfortable silence, "I think we should plan a trip. Just the two of us. Somewhere far away, where we can really figure this out."

Evan's eyes sparkled at the idea. "Where would you want to go?"

"Somewhere with beaches and sunsets. Maybe the coast? I've always wanted to walk along the shoreline, the ocean stretching out endlessly before us."

"Sounds perfect," he replied, a grin lighting up his face. "We'll make it happen. Just us, no distractions."

As we talked, the night felt alive with possibility, our laughter mingling with the distant sounds of the festival. I imagined us exploring the shoreline, collecting seashells, and savoring the salty breeze. With each passing moment, the shadows that had threatened to pull us apart began to dissipate, replaced by the warm glow of connection and trust.

"Can we promise to keep finding ways to grow, even when it's uncomfortable?" I asked, feeling the weight of my question.

"Absolutely," he said, his voice steady. "We owe it to ourselves to keep evolving, to embrace the messiness of life together. And if we stumble, we'll pick each other up."

With those words, I felt the final vestiges of fear slip away, replaced by a fierce determination. The journey ahead would be anything but easy, but I was ready to face it with Evan by my side.

As we stood up from the bench, hand in hand, I took one last look at the oak tree, its branches stretching skyward like a guardian watching over us. The world around us buzzed with life, and for the first time in what felt like forever, I felt free—free to love, free to be myself, and free to forge a path into the future, together.

With each step we took away from the festival, I knew we were heading toward something beautiful, a future we would shape with our own hands. The whispers of the past would no longer dictate our present. Together, we would create a legacy of love, resilience, and unyielding hope, ready to embrace whatever adventures awaited us.

Milton Keynes UK
Ingram Content Group UK Ltd.
UKHW040257181024
449757UK00001B/90